GHARAIN SAID NOTHING. HE SIMPLY REACHED OUT A tanned finger to touch the first feather very lightly. It shifted slightly on the rock and for a brief moment caught the gleam of dawn.

"You are Lark." Finally, as he spoke, he turned and looked straight at me.

Into me.

I think Wilh and Brahnt stepped back. Or maybe they just disappeared in that expanded moment. And I think I whispered, "I am," but I don't clearly remember. What I remember is the color of his eyes. Gharain pulled my gaze with him as he stood up tall above me. I could not tear my eyes away from his—their depth of sage green, glints of golden brown flecked within.

The light was rising, and with it a fresh breeze bringing the smell of the pine and eucalyptus. It caught Gharain's chestnut curls and tossed them lightly.

"Lark," he repeated, looking down at me. And he smiled.

My first dream.

# GUARDIANS OF TARNEC

*Lark Rising*

*Silver Eve*

GUARDIANS OF TARNEC BOOK I

# LARK RISING

SANDRA WAUGH

EMBER

Text copyright © 2014 by Sandra Waugh
Cover art copyright © 2014 by Marcela Bolivar
Map copyright © 2014 by Rhys Davies

All rights reserved. Published in the United States by Ember, an imprint of Random House Children's Books, a division of Penguin Random House LLC, New York. Originally published in hardcover in the United States by Random House Children's Books, New York, in 2014.

Ember and the E colophon are registered trademarks of Penguin Random House LLC.

Visit us on the Web! randomhouseteens.com
Educators and librarians, for a variety of teaching tools,
visit us at RHTeachersLibrarians.com

The Library of Congress has cataloged the hardcover edition of this work as follows:
Lark Rising / Sandra Waugh — 1st ed.
p. cm. — (Guardians of Tarnec ; book 1)
Summary: Sixteen-year-old Lark sets out on a journey to help her village fight off monsters called Troths and learns she is the Guardian of Light, fated to recover a powerful amulet from the Breeders of Chaos.
ISBN 978-0-449-81748-3 (trade) — ISBN 978-0-449-81749-0 (lib. bdg.) —
ISBN 978-0-449-81750-6 (ebook)
[1. Fantasy.] I. Title.
PZ7.W351Lar 2014 [Fic]—dc23 2012040107

ISBN 978-0-449-81751-3 (tr. pbk.)

Printed in the United States of America

10 9 8 7 6 5 4 3 2 1

First Ember Edition 2015

*for Jonathan,*

*my husband, my love, my everyday hero*

*Circle of Balance, chosen of White;*
*Power of hand renders dark into light.*
*Sun in earth proves her worth,*
*And rises the Lark, set free by Sight.*

# 1

MIDSUMMER

THE HAWK BROUGHT the first of the signs.

I would not have paid attention to him, as creatures of leg and wing often follow me. But this young male lit upon the fence as I pulled at the roots of a ghisane. Ghisane and hawk are unwilling neighbors. If it dares, a dormouse can find protection beneath its branches, as a hawk will not come near. And yet this hawk flew to the fence, nearly brushing the leaves of the hated bush, and sat watching me. I had to pause in my work and regard him sternly, saying, "If you stay too long, young harrier, I will not finish my task." And so he stayed but a moment before taking flight, yet not without leaving me the message he carried. As he left the fence, a small thing fell from his grip and fluttered into my lap. I picked it up: the feather from a lark.

"Lark!"

My grandmother's voice was loud enough to carry across the field. Turning, I could see her standing by the herb shed, another bundle of something or other weighting her arms. "Come, Lark. Leave that!"

And so I left the ugly ghisane half ripped, and crossed the shorn grass. Rileg, the sheep hound, heaved up on his three legs to follow.

"Grandmama, I should not leave the bush undone. It will reach its roots farther and double by the evening," I warned as I neared.

"Then be quick with this meadsweet. The buds must be pulled immediately upon cutting." She gave over the enormous bundle into my arms. "Put the leaves in the green pot and any flowers in the blue, but bring the buds in your apron to the press. We must squeeze them before that cloud passes the sun." She pointed to the single white dab in the bright sky. "Hurry, then. What's that in your hand?"

I opened my fist to show her the feather. I did not tell her how it came to me. She looked at it for a moment, and then at me. "A third one?" she asked.

I shrugged a little hard.

Grandmama gave her half smile, the knowing one. "Hurry, then," she repeated, and stumped away on stiff limbs.

"Three is not so many," I said to Rileg as he joined me to sit in the shade of the herb shed. My hands made light work of the meadsweet. Poor Grandmama. Her gnarled fingers would no longer work the small tasks; Evie and I were required for those.

Yet she had no less energy, and so put her leftover stamina into creating more oils, balms, and medicines from the variety of herbs we grew. No one could enter the village of Merith's marketplace without a stop at our booth. It smelled sweet and warm and healing all in one breath. Even Krem Poss had ceased selling his herbs at market and let us pay to harvest his lavender for our own concoctions. "More profit thisaway," he'd said with a shake of his bald head. "You've powerful magic, you ladies."

Magic it was not, though a little might do no harm. Hard work was the way of getting things done, and, Grandmama would scoff, Master Poss had little enthusiasm for *that*. But magic is always the easy interpretation for things. And besides, since I had the Sight, and my grandmother and cousin were Healers, it was a natural expectation that our abilities included making spells.

*Three is not so many.* One feather I'd found under a stone the morning before when I was weeding through the mugwort. I happily showed it to Grandmama, for it is a blessing to find one's namesake. The second was threaded into a lilac, brown against the green. Grandmama saw me working it out of the branches that afternoon. This third one I'd not willingly discuss, though. Grandmama would rightly see it as portentous, for things that came in threes were always of note. But that this feather was brought by the hawk meant something more:

It was a sign.

Our village of Merith enjoyed all whims of Nature, whether as harbingers of news or insignificant pranks. But things messengered or distinguished by animal were a more serious matter, for they were signs, and if three signs were bestowed on a person, it meant that person was summoned, bound to a task, whatever the task might be.

Now a hawk had brought this—a sign made of my own namesake, even, as if he'd shaken his wing at me and said, "You, young Lark, may not ignore this."

My first sign. But would I be summoned? And if so, summoned to what? Anxiety nipped at the edges of these thoughts, but I pushed them aside; I *would* ignore this. Grandmama might hold her suspicions, but not I—not on this beautiful day, not here within our peaceful, beloved cottage and grounds. A bound summons was rare anyway; the last one I could recall involved our neighbor Gaben Rawl, who was summoned to divine the placement of a new common well in Crene. Villagers chuckled that the sheep shearer was the one chosen to find water, but in truth Gaben had masterfully selected the spot to dig where no others thought to try.

If I were summoned, what would I, the shy granddaughter of Hume Carew, be asked to do? I was good only at working in our gardens. Maybe I'd have to find one of Gaben's sheep.

The thought made me grin. And within this safe moment of a pristine afternoon, I took the lark feather from my pocket and held it up. "If this be the first sign, is there another?" I called out, giving a challenging stare over our land. "Am I summoned?" But the sky held no birds; the fields showed no creatures. I looked over to Rileg, who sprawled at my side.

"Well?" I asked him with a laugh. "Have *you* anything to give me?"

Rileg lifted his head, panted a wet grin, and licked my hand.

Grandmama had her meadsweet buds before the cloud nudged the sun. I returned to the fence to find the ghisane sprouting two new bush roots. I let Rileg worry at one of them while I tore at the other. Usually, I feel sorrow for weeds as I pull them, but never for the ghisane. Black-leaved and thorny, it is an evil little thing, like a spy from Dark Wood, ready to infiltrate and consume all beauty. Any bush roots must be pulled on sight and burned, and it is no easy task to get all of the bits from the earth.

Hard work did not bother me, nor any of my small family. We each had our talents—instinct-driven perhaps—and used them for good. In return, the earth was generous, creatures were fair, and we drew respect in our village. I liked the repetition of this quiet earthwork, the simplicity and comfort of the familiar. This day, like most summer days, the sun beamed down warm and encouraging, the breeze was soft against leaf and skin, and my fingers dug deep into the moist dirt. I was happiest at these outdoor chores, which kept me close to home and family, kept me far from crowds and strangers.

"Come, Rileg," I said. It was late when I had finished. The original ghisane was at last uprooted; so were its volunteers, as well as four other bush roots I'd found. I'd lit the fire to burn them, done my silly superstitious dance to ward against more invasions—leaping with Rileg while he barked at my laughter—and scooped the ash to toss over the fence, back into Dark Wood.

That is when the second sign arrived.

The hush before something powerful occurs makes the hair prick on the back of my neck. My hair is heavy and long; the pricking runs like a cold breath across each strand. It was so as I stood there, ash in hand. The cold blew over my neck, and I looked unwillingly to the far edge of the field, at the fence bordering on the other side of the surrounding Dark Wood. A fox was there, his height not quite reaching the lowest railing. Rileg tensed beside me, quiet.

"Stay," I whispered. Rileg sat like a stone.

I threw the ash, for it is not something with which to greet a visitor, and walked toward the end of the field. The fox came under the fence a few lengths and paused. There was something in his jaw. He met me halfway, dropped the wretched thing, and backing up two steps, waited for my response.

Had I been Grandmama or Evie, I could have looked at that thing in the grass without horror. But I am not of their Healer stoicism. It took a moment before I could speak.

"This is not your fault," I whispered, a little hoarsely now. "I thank you."

The fox inclined his head and turned, letting his beautiful tail spiral as he ran off.

With fingers that trembled, I undid the sash to my apron and took it off, using it to collect the object. I called to Rileg and he loped across the grass, elegant in spite of his missing limb. Together we left the field as the sun was setting.

"All right. It is time."

The hour was late, and only now would we inspect the thing I'd brought home. Grandmama insisted when she saw my awful expression that the bundled apron remain outside, and that we continue with our evening meal and chores as usual.

"All will be well, Lark," she'd said simply, and told me to set the table.

We ate our cress soup and oat bread, though I had little appetite; we listened to Evie's tales from market, washed our dishes, swept the floor, and made all the necessary account-ings in the ledger of the day's profits and expenses as if nothing were different from any other evening. But then Grandmama took out the special bottle of honeyed mead and poured three thimblefuls—a swallow is all that is needed for fortification. And she said, "Get the apron, Lark."

I retrieved it from the porch. Dark stuff had already seeped through the fabric. I liked that apron; I wondered if anything would take out the stain, or if I could even bear to wear it again. I laid the bundle on the kitchen table, atop an oiled canvas that Evie had spread.

"There, now, let us see what this is about." Grandmama undid the wrapping, taking responsibility for whatever bad thing could enter our home. I winced as she spread open the cloth. Evie and Grandmama did not.

"The fox did not do this," I whispered.

"One of our townspeople?" Evie mused, regarding the sev-ered hand. "But why such a presentation?"

"I believe it's more of a warning than a presentation," Grandmama answered. "Look there: no ring on the finger." Every male villager upon his twelfth year weaves his own unique strand of leather to wear on his left third finger. This hand belonged to someone who could have worn one for more than sixty years.

"Perhaps he was not from our town." I still whispered. "A traveler, then?"

"Nay." Grandmama answered to that too. "Look at the mark—the change of color on his finger, like a band. He wore a ring once."

"But those bits of leather hold no value for anyone but the owner," reasoned Evie. "Why would someone remove it?"

"Someone, or something. As I said: a warning."

I looked to Grandmama, saw her face draw ever so slightly into an expression of concern. I looked over to Evie, my beloved cousin, who, rather than concern, held an open look of curiosity—the mind of a scholar. Like Grandmama, Evie could help most anyone in need. And if she could not, then it was not to be; the Earth was reclaiming her children and Evie was not pained. It was so with this hand. Gruesome as it was, Evie simply wanted to know what had happened.

"This hand was severed on purpose," continued Grandmama. "No battle would yield so ragged a cut."

Evie nodded. "Yes, but look—the fingers have scrapes and tears, and a nail missing. There was a fight."

"Or at least he resisted." Grandmama's voice had dropped a bit, losing some of its musical quality. I took a shaky breath at that, for there was foreboding now in her tone. "Let's turn this over, shall we?" And on saying so, she took a corner of the apron and placed the orphaned hand palm down. The fingers curled under.

Grandmama's intake of breath was awful in its depth. She stepped back, her gnarled fingers grabbing for the chair nearby. Evie and I immediately put our arms out to support her, but already she was upright and solid once more. I looked to the table, to the hand buckled upon it. It had been burned, the back of it—some sort of brand seared right into the flesh. For a moment I stayed still, letting the thimble of drink I'd swallowed work its soothing effects, drawing the last pleasure from the heat that ran up and down my throat. Then I made myself join Evie, who was bent over, inspecting the marking. Our hair fell straight, pooling together at the edge of the table in similar fashion—mine the bright brown of an acorn, hers the silvery color of the moon. We were like that: odd complements of each other. Cousins, born on the same day, in the same hour; single daughters of twin sisters. We had the same birthmark too, just above our left shoulder blades, an outline of a circle. I thought it was what made Grandmama gasp so, for a circle was crudely branded on this hand—but within this circle was a *z,* slashed through diagonally to connect the loose ends. Roughly done, and brutal.

I held my breath while I studied it. "It's an angry mark," I murmured finally. "The edges are still raw. And black. What makes it so?"

Evie said promptly, "The hand was branded with a hukon twig. 'Twill pitch both blood and skin a midnight black."

"Aye, hukon," confirmed Grandmama quietly. "It poisons from within. But hukon cannot be found here. Troths have done this."

I flinched. We both looked at Grandmama. *Troth* was a name we'd heard few times in our near seventeen years, but it was enough. They were the feared horde of legend in our village, savage beasts of barely human form and mind. Two times past they had destroyed our town, killed our men and women. The last time our parents were among the victims.

"A warning indeed," murmured Evie. She too drew back, and then looked at me. "Yet the fox brought it. I did not think Troths could pull favors from the woods' creatures."

I was shaking my head no, but it was Grandmama who said aloud, "I think the fox risked life to bring us this. This is his warning, to give us a chance to prepare." Then, more softly: "Unlike the last time."

Evie and I looked at her. Grandmama's voice could give away much that her strong, stout body would not. She had survived the last massacre, as had we. But we were barely three years aged at the time; we held no memory. Grandmama had witnessed, had lived with the horror full on. She'd survived; she'd rebuilt; she'd raised us—as the other elder villagers had done with home and grandchild. Still, it was not something that could be truly forgotten or worn away with time.

"We must call a Gathering," said Evie. "I will carry the news through market tomorrow."

A Gathering. I hoped it was not necessary, for then the entire village would collect in the town square. Kind and friendly as

Merith villagers are, a Gathering holds too many people for me, too many energies whirling in one place.

But Grandmama agreed. "I think we must." She paused then, as if to consider something, but maybe she simply hesitated for my sake. "First, we should learn more from this." She gestured at the hand. "We must know for certain who this is."

Grandmama looked over at me now, and Evie, understanding her, did as well. Grandmama said carefully, "Will you do this for us, Lark?"

Rileg whimpered from his bed by the fireplace. I nodded, but too slowly, and Evie reached out to grip my elbow. My touch will draw energy. Hers bestows it; she was giving me strength. Grandmama simply waited. She knew, perhaps better than I, what my reaction would be. She would help me when it was over.

Taking a breath, I put my hand to the severed one, whose story could only prove ugly as I reached to learn it. I did not need to place my palm close, nor even to concentrate; anger and hatred were already rising from the burn, coming in waves, turning the air black before my eyes. The comfort of the kitchen disappeared, and for the first time I saw Troths.

I could not help a cry of horror. They hunched like goblins, but were larger, with gray mottled skin—as a charred piece of wood made wet. Lank strands of hair covered their heads; two filmy circles were the eyes, something like gashes for nostrils, and a snarling grin over fiercely jagged teeth. The creatures were loping . . . no, *chasing;* a lone man as prey was tearing through Dark Wood, desperation and dread wrenched from his pores.

But there was no match here. The man was old; he had no hope of escape from those shadowed, grotesque forms, and so at last he did what all our villagers do when death claims life: offered his body in noble silence. Yet these hunters wanted none of that; they wanted the chase. Thrusting the old man forward, then dragging him down, abusing his body until his heart gave up for him and there was nothing left to do but rip up the flesh and scatter it into Dark Wood as an offering, the hand saved for last so it would bear the mark of the victor. And yet, what victory? What challenge? I was crying, I knew; I could feel the tears on my cheeks, but nothing more. Somewhere, Grandmama's voice was saying out loud, "Closer, Lark. You must know the man." And then there were more tears, gushing now because I hated to touch the dead fingers—it was too powerful, the fear and hate and violence . . . and somewhere I sensed a grinning smile yawning open, so malevolent that it made a thread of cold arch right down my spine. *Closer, Lark* were Grandmama's words, commanding: the understanding that it must be done. And so my fingers touched the hand, and knew it belonged to Ruber Minwl. The old man would twice a year venture into Dark Wood to collect the skins of dead animals, those unwittingly trapped by the growing things that held them fast and starved them slowly. Ruber Minwl, the kind tailor who wanted such a loss of creatures not to be a waste—to use their skins for warmth and protection gave those useless deaths at least some purpose. And pulling back, I saw something else, something new: the glimmer of daylight, and more Troths. This time their hideous eyes were turned to Merith.

And then I was on the chair, hunched and sobbing and sick, and Grandmama's hands were at my temples, pulling the horror from my mind. The waves that had rushed in were now receding, seeping into her bay-dusted palms, the pressure great against my head until the black subsided and I'd stopped retching.

This was always the aftermath—the miserable leftovers of a talent that separated me from others and kept me hesitant and shy. This was the dreaded consequence of having the Sight, the unique and, for me, unwanted ability to read energies—worse, to see, to *feel* histories and intent. Drawing knowledge from surrounding energy was the Sight—a rare gift, indeed. Only it was others who perceived this as my gift. I did not; it was my burden.

The cold sweat would last awhile longer, so I curled on the chair while Evie put a shawl and her arms around me, whispering in sympathy, "I wish I could do what Grandmama can do for you. I wish I could take away this pain." But she could not; she was too close to me for that. She hugged me instead while Grandmama went outside on the porch and clapped the powder from her hands smartly until the bad thoughts were shaken into the breeze and whisked away from our cottage. Grandmama washed her hands with fresh water from the well and returned inside.

"Bravely done, Lark," she said simply. "Bravely done."

"It's too awful." My teeth were chattering.

"Yes. But at least now we have time to prepare." They'd learned the story as I saw it. I have no memory of my voice when I am with the Sight, but I know that I speak what I see as it plays in my own mind. As for whatever decisions would be made about the threat of Troths, they would be discussed at the Gathering. *Thank you, fox.* I shivered. At least now we'd been warned.

"Poor man," said Grandmama. "Ruber Minwl did not deserve such an end."

"Raif's grandfather," Evie mouthed softly. Raif was a friend, a young man who I believed was in love with Evie. I could find a reason to touch Raif, to gain proof of his feelings, but I was too close to Evie to know if her feelings matched his; I could not read her as I did others.

Thinking such thoughts eased the cold somewhat. I sat up a little straighter. Rileg saw his opportunity and weaseled his way between cousin and grandmother to lick my hand. I smiled at him, and his tail madly swatted the two women. He made us all laugh.

Evie turned her attention to making a sleeping tea while Grandmama removed the hand. It was done. I would never see where she put it, but I knew that was the end of my apron. Favorite or not, I was glad both it and the dark thing were gone from the cottage, and the simple habits of bedtime rituals and kind good-nights were completed and bestowed untainted.

Evie and I climbed the stairs to our attic rooms. Each night before retiring we sat on the bench on the landing, braiding our hair and gossiping, as any girls might, about the daily doings of the boys and girls of our age. Since I did not venture out of our property every day as Evie did, she held court with her information and I loved to listen. Evie's voice is musical and sweet; her words slipped through and over me, little details added to her supper tales—enough to keep me smiling, picturing a happy and pleasant market day of bustling business and amusing folk.

"Tell me more of Cath," I asked her. "Did she find a way to put the daisy in Quin's pocket?"

Evie grinned. "Has Cath ever worked a spell properly the first time? Rather, we'll soon see Quin's infant cousin making moon-eyes at her."

I said with affected concern, "Then she will be disappointed. I do not think little Nalen will take his thumb from his mouth to steal a kiss."

Evie smirked, then shook her head. "'Tis well that Cath does not know Quin is sweet on Nance. What hex might she try instead?"

"*Poor* Quin," I mocked. "Serves him right for all his teasing." Though truly, I'd want to spare my good friend from Cath's suffocating attention. "Well, if she asks you for any hexes, Evie, tell her she must put walnuts in her shoes."

"Walnuts"—Evie looked as if she were seriously considering—"are an excellent cure for rheumatism." And we giggled, a little more foolishly than we would on other nights.

And then, maybe because Raif most likely would not have entered the conversation, or maybe because I was wondering what Evie had felt when she learned the hand was from Ruber Minwl, wondering if she herself would bring Raif the sad news,

I blurted, "Are you sweet on someone? Would you sneak a daisy into a pocket?"

"Lark!" Evie feigned her blush, I was sure, for she never blushed. "You ask for secrets."

"Nay, I only ask what you'd share with me. You would share this, Evie, wouldn't you?"

"Always. No daisies. There, I've told you. I've no wish to catch a heart by spell."

"Captivated instead by the pure magic of your presence," I teased. "There would be many suitors to choose from, then."

Evie did not respond with humor as I'd expected. "Many? Nay, there should be just one."

"Then who *should* it be?"

She was quiet, regarding me, her blue eyes taking a somber gaze. "Choose for me," she said suddenly.

I did not like this change of mood and so laughed at her gravity and how silly that seemed. "Me? Why so?"

I'd teased too much, or touched a subject she did not like, for she was silent for a longer moment. But then, like a lamp lit to break the dark, Evie grinned and tugged my brown braid. "Because you have the Sight, dearest Lark. You will know. You choose the one I will love. I trust you—you'll choose well."

I would always marvel at my cousin: how she could be so frank with her thoughts, yet betray none of her feelings. She'd spoken honestly, but if she was asking me to choose Raif, she'd given nothing away. I'd prove my suspicion anyway—I could learn Raif's feelings, at least, and know for certain if he loved her. So, holding a hand to my heart with great formality and trying to sound very serious, I announced, "Then 'twill be so, Mistress Eveline. It nears our birthday, so for your gift I promise this: I shall use all the wisdom of the Sight to choose your love. A *very* grand choice he will be."

"Just let it not be Nalen," she said.

We laughed; we'd not dwell on bad thoughts. The Gathering would not be for a day and one more; Evie was patient to wait, and I was relieved I'd have time to prepare to be in a crowd. Tonight we were content to chatter on these little bits of nothing. The sleeping tea had its effect; I was soon yawning.

No magic in this house, just generous knowledge of herb and kin. We hugged good night.

Sometimes dreams are portents, glimpses from the Sight of moments yet to come. Their impressions linger long after waking, coloring thoughts and feelings with anticipation. Such were my dreams that night.

The young man stood tall, filling my gaze as I sat staring up at him, openmouthed, I was certain, for I'd never been so overwhelmed by someone's beauty. He was perhaps two or three years my senior, strong and lean, with hair the color of chestnuts and skin burnished by sun and wind to a warm gold. He spoke my name, and I felt my breath catch when he smiled at me—a release, a joy, and something more. The way the lips curved against his white teeth plunged a longing so sharp through my belly that I gasped in my sleep, and I woke up.

It was near morning; the sky was pale through the window of my room. I lay for a while blinking into the gray light, trying to hold on to what I'd seen—yet it was elusive, the face already slipping into that fate of dreams where details dissolve. The sage-green eyes glinted with flecks of golden brown and then faded; the chestnut curls were tossed by the breeze and then scattered. . . . Finally I hugged my pillow into my chest, to hold hard this new longing, to keep it close against my heart and not let it dissipate.

We'd spoken of love last night—it must be why I was so enchanted with this fading image. And so I yearned, I imagined, and I drifted to sleep once more. A half sleep, I think, because I was able a moment—an eternity—later to pull from the next dream like an arrow released from a bow. I was across my room suddenly, huddling in the corner with Rileg snuffing at my cheek. I could not pet him, for my arms were wrapped tightly around my body, clutching now in instinctive protection. For in that half sleep I'd seen the young man again. And this time, with drawn sword, he slew me.

No sign, this. This was simple truth.

2

"ALL COME! ALL come!" It was Semel Lewen who rang the village bell for the Gathering.

Our village is not large in number, but we filled the market square well enough, making a colorful group. Colors are like names here, and the colors we love become our signatures. Semel Lewen was the village dyer. He artfully blended ingredients from all the earth's bounty—vegetables, leaves, nuts, and berries became the richest and most vivid hues in his pots, and the recipes for our particular favorites were recorded and labeled with our names. Then his wife, Carr, and her sister, Beren, would weave exquisite cloths with the threads steeped in his special concoctions. They were as enticing in market as Grandmama's balms or Rula Narben's sweets.

Reluctant as I was to be in a crowd, focusing on the colored cloth was a way to keep from catching the gaze of too many eyes, friendly though they might be. A gaze is powerful, as is touch; I pull energy too quickly through those senses. So I watched the colors move and blend across the cobbled square. The flitting girl in the buttercup apron was the pretty, silly Cath. Tall and gaunt Kerrick Swan strode by in purposeful fashion in a pale gray tunic that was much like a dawn sky, whereas Raif, who stood tall in the center of the market square, wore the deeper blue-gray color of dusk.

I could see Evie's turquoise frock not far from Raif, and then her silver-blond plait. She was greeting people by the well, and I moved to stand close to her, smiling a little as I passed neighbors and friends.

"Ahh, Lark! How good to see you!" This was Dame Keren Whim, one of the oldest members of the village. Like Grandmama, she was arthritic with age, but her eyes were still bright and her hearing was keen. I made my bow, as we do for those respected, and murmured my greeting. And then it was Thom Maker and Daen Hurn in brown and red, and others in varied colors all joining in for greetings. I backed up a bit before murmuring my hellos, until Benna Jovin laughed at me and pinched my moss-green sleeve, saying, "Lark is still our shy one. We can barely hear your sweet voice, my dear!"

I laughed a little too, for she was right, but Evie, always at ease in crowds, brushed my hair from my shoulder and replied, "Powerful oaks from acorns grow. Lark must stay soft or she might burn us with her brilliance."

I blushed, but Dame Keren cast her bright stare at me and said, "Very true, Evie. Very true. Come, now, let us begin." She and the two other oldest members of our village, both men, moved to climb the few steps to the wooden platform that was only brought out for a Gathering. We could see them clearly now above the heads of the villagers, even as they took seats on the three chairs. The rest of us settled to listen, some sitting, some standing, as they wished. I perched on the edge of the wide well, where I would have open space at my back. Evie stayed with me.

It began as always, first with a small bow, hand to heart, to the eldest on the platform, then a gentle nodding once more to our neighbors. The eldest three might lead a Gathering, but it was understood that each and all were important. No voice would go unheard here.

Grandmama then stepped up onto the platform to recount the tale of the hand. I did not wish to dwell on that memory, so my mind went elsewhere, thinking again on what Evie had just said. Loving as her words were intended, they were laughingly false. My hair was the color of acorns, but I was not the oak of proverb. And I certainly could not burn others with brilliance, though 'twas true that I took care to stay *soft,* Evie's kind word for my reserve. Energies flowed through me like music. While a plant or animal's energy was usually soothing to absorb, a person held so many conflicting emotions, tempers, and changing histories that I was quickly overwhelmed by their discordant and jarring pitches if I stood too close. To touch someone might bring up visions of things unbearable. I needed time to grow accustomed to an individual's energy so that it would wane in potency—time that crowds and strangers could not give. Any market day, pretty as it was with its gaily colored flags and white tents done up with ribbons, was a challenge of endurance that I could but tiptoe through with hope that no one would engage, surround, or even jostle me. I'd learned not to go to market, not to greet strangers. And, as kind-spirited as the people were in Merith, too much of even good feelings was likewise dizzying and made me sick. The villagers accepted my distance, though they could not truly understand why I preferred—nay, *needed*—my solitude in the fields and gardens, where almost all things hummed sweetly low, and in harmony.

I looked up over the thatched roofs that surrounded the square, taking a deeper, calming breath from the wide sky. I heard Grandmama's voice rising and falling with her story, and the airy, whispered reactions like wind chimes floating up and away.

The dream pushed into my mind then, unwelcome. I'd not slept again that first night, nor hardly the next one, lying awake instead, seeing nothing but the contorted face of the young man. And while I could not hold the first dream, the second one would not go away. Both nights it worked its way into my head and taunted me with the image that I was to die with such violence at the hands of someone hardly more than a boy.

This second dream was heavy with terror. The face swam up before me, powerfully handsome, but there was no beauty in this. He was high over me, as though I lay in the dirt, his features ferocious—anger, and a deeper horror that I could not fathom. He was shouting—I could not discern his words—and then he raised his sword high. It was meant to come down on me, I knew it; I knew I was dead. A flash of white then wiped him out, and I was in the corner of my room, shivering and sick.

Signs. Dreams. I did not know what to do with my feelings.

"Lark!" A short whisper at my side.

I looked around and grinned briefly with relief to see Quin. His cheerful nature usually steadied me, his energy as simple and pleasing as any of Earth's wild creatures. Quin was like a brother: both great comfort and merciless tease. But today there was no teasing. He plunked down on the well beside me, his reed flute dangling between his fingers. It was never far from his grasp.

"Lark." He lightly touched the returning frown on my brow and whispered, "I'm sorry it was you who found Ruber Minwl's hand."

Not to Quin, not to anyone, could I admit I was thinking of those dreams of desire and death. I nodded back, unfortunately glad that there was a grim tale to cover my private distress, and Quin slung a comforting arm around my shoulder. We both turned to pay attention to the Gathering.

Murmurs of concern were running through the crowd. Heads turned to search for Raif, to offer sympathy. Raif stood tall off to the side, taller than most of our young men. He kept a tight rein on his feelings, staying quiet under the attention, though his jaw was clenched. I glanced at Evie, but her face gave nothing away.

"Mistress Hume, we thank you," Dame Keren said to my grandmother as she left the platform. "This is a dark tale indeed—one that reopens old wounds, and suggests new worry. I think we are in agreement that we must take seriously the fox's bringing of the hand." She looked around the open square. "That the creature did indeed want to warn us?"

General rumbles of "Aye" skittered through the Gathering. I watched various faces. No one doubted my recounting through the Sight; each was now struggling with the idea of the Troths returning. The younger villagers held expressions of hesitant curiosity.

One of the youngest asked aloud her query: Quin's sister, Minnow, in her marigold apron, whom we cheerfully called Min, to rhyme with her older brother. She stepped to the base of the platform to be better heard and used her most grown-up words. "Are we to be certain that these Troths mean us harm? Perhaps . . . perhaps poor Master Minwl stumbled upon the Troths during their hunt?"

Dame Keren looked kindly down at the fourteen-year'd girl. I thought if anyone were to ask such an ignorant question, then it was good it was Min. Her fresh, freckled face with its rosy cheeks was endearing in its simplicity. And Dame Keren's interest was sincere—all the elders took Min seriously.

Jarett Doun, another of the eldest, took the opportunity to speak. "My dear Minnow," he said, easing his frail bones forward in the chair, "look about this Gathering. What do you see?"

Most eyes were on Min as she looked around, her cheeks even rosier under such attention. "I—I see my neighbors, Master and Mistress Wilhock; my friends, Cath and Druen; my grandmother is over there; and my brother, Quin, is there on the well with Lark Carew—"

"Ah. Look again, young Min. *What* do you see?"

Many could answer for her, but she needed to search this out, to understand this for herself. The answer held a cruel truth; I felt a wave of sadness rush through the group, as if it was a pity the brutal memory was to be brought forth. Min stared and stared about, her lips moving as she attempted to solve what was clearly a puzzle. "I see the pretty faces of the young," she said at last, "and the beautiful faces of the old. Is this right?" she asked brightly.

"Nearly, Min. Well done." Now Sir Jarett stood, an auspicious gesture. "Here, indeed, are the pretty faces of our young villagers and the beautiful ones of our elders," he called out. "But, I ask, do you not also see what is *missing*? Do you see any village members in their prime? No, you do not, for there are none. They were culled from our group by the Troths thirteen years ago. Not one remaining villager of childbearing years was left alive. Only those too old, and the young we had chance to hide, were . . . *spared*." The word was apologetic; not one of us felt spared by this loss. Sir Jarett paused and cleared his throat. "Or so we thought. In retrospect, I understand what has been done. They slew our children—your parents—and now look about: there is now a new age of parents upon us. The Troths may well believe the time has come to take those."

There were loud gasps. Thom Maker marched to the front of the crowd, the little thatch of white hair on his crown bobbing above his short stature. "Wait, Sir Jarett! There is error in your reasoning! The eldest of our grandchildren have barely begun siring families. This is too soon!"

Some nodded in horrified agreement, but then Kerrick Swan strode forward, his furrowed brow more deeply creased. "Thom, did they not take your parents some five decades back, as they took mine? We survived, but then they took our children! Fifty years, thirteen—there is no pattern to carnage. Troths are more beast than human; they hold no plan, they simply wish to kill. We are their blood sport. They want to watch us run."

These were ugly thoughts coming from our villagers. Words of violence were awkward on our tongues, and to be forced to confront something we'd hoped to forget, something so appalling to our natures, made their very sounds shocking. Sadness blurred to a palpable unease, with worried murmurs rippling through the crowd; my own breath heaved a little faster. The sky seemed to darken.

"But we don't run."

A silence fell over the square. The oldest villager of all had risen from his chair. Farrin Rawl—the shepherd, the sage. The one who rarely spoke. "We don't run from death. It is not in our nature."

That pleased us. "Aye, Sir Farrin! Let them come," said Kerrick. "If they look for sport, they will find none here!"

"My friend—" But the eldest man's voice was temporarily drowned out by concurring shouts. A wonderful idea: the Troths would leave us alone because we would give them no game. What should be feared? Relief washed through the group. This was a plan of action that involved no act at all.

*But they made Ruber Minwl run,* I thought. *They made him run until he broke.*

"Lark?"

I looked up and realized that Quin's arm was off my shoulder, that the entire Gathering was hushed, looking at me.

That was not my thought—that was my voice, quite loud.

"Lark?" Dame Keren repeated. "What did you see?"

I hesitated, looking down to avoid their eyes, but they waited. "I saw that the Troths inspired terror," I said after a moment, knowing my voice was now most likely too soft to be heard. "Their brutality awoke such fear that he could do naught but run."

Silence, still. Now I forced myself to look up at the villagers watching me, to search out Raif and plead an apology with my gaze. He did not need to know that part of his grandfather's fate.

"Lark, are they near us now?" asked Sir Jarett quietly.

"Not yet." I needed to clear my throat. "I think not yet." I looked at Grandmama, who nodded; she'd left it for me to tell. And so I turned to Sir Jarett, eyes wide, a tiny detail from my Troth vision now looming enormous. "I saw the crescent moon at the sunrise."

"Ah." He nodded solemnly. "The old moon. And we are near full. . . ."

Anxious whispers, calculations. Ten days it was, between a

full moon and waning crescent. I could sense this added tension, the building worry, the feeble desire that I be wrong, but I was not wrong. I blurted, half apologizing, "It was quick what I saw, to be sure. But the Troths looked to Merith, and beyond, the sky was dawning and—"

Dame Keren said, very kindly, "We believe you, Lark. You would not recall this, my dear, but that terrible night thirteen years back, you sobbed uncontrollably the entire day before the attack. You—who had smiled your way through life before! We did not know then that you had the Sight, that you felt their presence as they neared. You, Lark, tried to warn us once, as you have again."

But of what help was that? I feared what everyone feared: warned or not, we could not protect ourselves either way.

"My friends." It was Sir Farrin. "I am misinterpreted."

We all looked to him.

"We of Merith do not run. But I do not likewise imply that we should face the Troths, simply hoping we will"—he nearly smiled—"*bore* them into leaving us alone. I mean to say that we will not run, but rather stand and defend ourselves, and each other."

If the villagers of Merith did not run, neither did they fight. There was a shocked pause, until someone called out, "With what, Sir Farrin?" It was Rula Narben, who made sweets for market. "I have but wooden spoons to stir the treacle."

"Axes might do well," muttered Perdy Ginnis. "Though I have just one."

And already the crowd was looking to our blacksmith,

Mirk Jovin, as if he could promptly supply us all with necessary, wicked armament. As if we would be capable of using any. Mirk scratched his bald pate and shrugged his indigo-clad shoulders.

"Nay, we have few weapons. But—" Sir Farrin spoke a little louder, enough to make the crowd silent again. "But we have friends."

Friends. I looked about at all my friends—really, at the entire village. I could not bear to think of Rula Narben, or Kerrick, or little wizened Perdy attempting to defend themselves with their nobly useless tools. My heart quickened, imagination running wild. They would be slaughtered, all of them. My dearest friends—how could I bear to see Quin facedown in his own blood? Or Evie's silver-blond hair running red, and Grandmama—

"Lark! *Lark!*" Quin was hissing at me, his arm once again a comfort around my shoulder. "Your face! Your beautiful face! Do you sense something?"

I shook my head no, but too violently. Were we all feeling this helpless? I leaned into Quin, drawing from some of his warmth. People around us were murmuring, thinking aloud: which friends would come to our aid? Other towns and villages traded well with us, sipped ale with us, but would they fight for us? We had never been asked to fight on another's behalf—we were a peaceable village; no one bothered to request our support. Would anyone come for us?

The town of Crene was mentioned, as was our neighboring village, Dann. I think Benna Jovin brought up the option of Tyre, a city, fifty times as big as Merith. They would have soldiers.

The hum and buzz of ideas crisscrossed the Gathering. There was excitement now, the possibility of victory and an end to the lingering dread of Troths. . . . And then, one by one, like little bubbles bursting, the ideas fizzed out. Dann was as ill-prepared as we; Tyre was unfamiliar to us, and at least a fortnight's journey away. What could we do in ten days?

Sir Farrin alone looked the least grave, calmly waiting for the murmurs to die. When it was finally silent, and perhaps when we felt most anxious, he spoke four words:

"There are the Riders."

The Riders.

The energy from Quin's arm changed. A little tremor of excitement passed through him and into me. I did not understand it, though. I had not heard of the Riders, nor, judging by the expressions in the crowd, had most of the younger folk. But the oldest villagers seemed to know. It was their pause that created the sudden weight to the atmosphere. An apprehension, almost, hovered wordlessly above our group.

Dame Keren was nodding slowly. I looked to find Grandmama's face in the crowd. She was grave. Evie too had a thoughtful expression.

"Quin," I murmured, "who are the Riders?"

He leaned close to my ear. "They are the twelve who might save us."

That was of no help, but he did not offer more. Sir Jarett was speaking. "They would come," the elder was agreeing, almost to himself, but we hung on his words. "They would come."

Min was going to ask about the Riders; I could see her heading toward the platform again, newly boldened by the attention given her first question. But her grandfather pulled her back, hushing her with a touch to her shoulder. I was sorry for that. I wanted to know as well about the Riders, yet the answer was lost in the sudden and tacit agreement that these dozen should be contacted apace. A quick, almost frenzied discussion ensued among the three eldest—which was the formal way of contact, where would it be done. Memories needed to be jogged as to the proper way of approach.

I watched it all, a little confused, a little disembodied, with Quin's arm the only thing that seemed to keep me attached to the stone edge of the well. My mind was swirling back to my dream, miserably so. The young man's face filled my view again, his horrified, furious expression distorting a once beautiful smile, and then the sword was flashing up, pointing to strike down, straight through my heart. I could not feel the stab, but before the flash of white mercifully wiped the vision, I could see the sword in great detail: the straight gleam of silvery metal, the intricately tooled handle with inlays of gold. It too was beautiful. It was huge.

"Lark," Quin murmured. I looked up.

The Gathering was parting in the center, drawing back to create a circle. Milo Swan, Kerrick's oldest grandchild, was walking into the middle, weighted under a wooden tub. He had the stones. I'd missed the conversation, the agreements, the decisions, and we were suddenly at the stones.

It was time to choose who would carry the request to the Riders.

Milo placed the tub on the quickly provided stool. We would file past, reach in, and draw one of the smoothly polished gray stones—one for each member of the village over the age of fifteen. One of these stones had a small circle chiseled from it; the person who drew it would be the volunteer. One only would journey for help from the Riders, for in their world, it was remembered, one makes a friend. Two or more make a challenge.

It had been a very long time since our village had used the stones. They were brought forth for only the most serious of tasks; I'd never before been of age to be included. A rustle of anticipation passed over the group as we began to sort away the few youngest villagers and to form the line, each wondering: if chosen, would he meet the Riders or the same fate as Ruber Minwl?

And yet, there was no opportunity to choose. Raif Minwl strode to the front of the line and said commandingly, "Let me go. Let me bear the request."

Surprised murmurs rose from the crowd now. I saw Evie watching from where she stood farther ahead in the line. Kerrick Swan said gently, "That is not how we do it, Raif."

"I know," he replied. "But let me go."

And while the rustle and mutterings flickered through the Gathering, and all eyes focused on Raif, no one noted the black speck hurtling across the sky. Even I was delayed in looking up; but then the hair on my neck pricked.

A raven, huge and glossy, streaked straight to us. It was only when he reached the square that people gasped and pulled back. He paid no attention to the villagers, diving instead for the tub of stones. It took but a moment, a flash of folded wing and strike of beak, and then the bird had selected its object and was back in the air. His wings flapped twice to bring him to where I stood; I had my hand out already, for I knew what was coming. The raven dropped the stone into my palm, whirled, and arced away, back toward Dark Wood.

There was no need to say aloud that I held the marked stone.

## 3

"NO, LARK!" I think both Evie and Quin cried it out at the same time.

"This—this is very odd!" Kerrick Swan sputtered in shock.

The eldest were all standing now, and somehow I'd become the center of the village circle. No one ever expected me to be the messenger; they knew my reluctance to leave home, my avoidance of strangers. This was a mistake, certainly. The barrage of comments and concerns was washing over me, through me—a telltale vibration of energy that would soon make me ill. I forced my focus to the stone, warm in my hand, my thumb filling its little hole in the center. Only when I heard Grandmama's voice did I look up at the surrounding faces and realize I was shaking.

"We should consider whether we must abide by the raven's

intention," she called out. "Perhaps such a sign is merely a solicitation, not a requirement."

"I'll go instead!" shouted Quin. "I am quick and strong."

*If only you could.* A sign. Grandmama herself had named it.

Quin took a breath to continue, but Raif interrupted, facing him. "Nay, Quin, this is my task. It was my grandfather; the warning is mine."

Then other members of the village, men and women alike, put forth their reasons why they should go in my place. Bravery from all of them while I stood in their midst, trembling, gripping the stone. I do not think they even saw me anymore, but they filled my senses. It was like market day now, all the noise and bustle of bartering for this task. The voices grew in fervor; my head swam. My hands went to my ears, hardly blocking the sensations, the little stone still crushed in my fist and pushing against my temple. The smell of the square intensified, the warmth of bodies exuding fragrances of sweat, of earth, of plant and mineral; the smell of the water from the well rose up and over me; the very cobbles of the square reeked of their dusty weight. I would be sick.

"Stop," I gasped. "Stop! *Stop!*"

And then it was quiet. The villagers widened their circle around me. I could draw a breath again. I sank to my knees, uncertain of my balance.

"Lark." It was Sir Farrin. "We care for your well-being."

"I know it." I'd not stopped shaking; my hands shivered against the pale cobblestones, and the stone rolled from my grasp.

Someone cried, "We motion to ignore the raven's intent. Any number of us will go in Lark's stead."

"Go home, Lark," Grandmama called out. "Your participation is not needed further."

I forced my hands to be still. "No."

"Lark, I will do this. Let me do this."

It was Quin; it was Raif. I was not hearing them, but working too hard to look calm, to push out my words evenly, when I was everything but. "This is to be my journey."

"Lark—"

"No, Raif!" I shouted, overly loud, shoving back from the young man who had stepped too close to me. "*Believe* me."

He meant to understand; he pulled back a bit to make more space before saying gently, "Lark, you don't have to go."

"I wish that were true." *I wish.* I clutched the marked stone again, gripping it as if it could anchor my body, keep me from splitting into a thousand shrieks of *no*. And I spoke as clearly as I could to all, raising my arm and holding the stone high over my head: "This, from the raven, is my *third* sign. And this—" I slipped my other hand into my bodice and drew out one of the three lark feathers I'd tucked there, holding it high. "This was the first. I am summoned. I am *bound* to seek the Riders." My arms sank back to my sides and I looked at my grandmother, knowing she was remembering my dismissal of the third feather. It was hard to plead this truth; her face was so awful, reflecting my own fear. "It was meant to be so. You knew it before I did."

An exhale of breath ran simultaneously through the crowd. There could be no more disagreement.

I took my own deep breath, then looked up with the bravest face I had. "Please tell me who the Riders are?" Then—and with, unfortunately, less certainty—I added, "And how I shall find them?"

The villagers turned to the platform. Dame Keren stayed standing, though the eldest men sat down again.

"There is little information, my dear," she said. "A dozen men are they, rarely seen. The Troths are their enemy; that much we do know. They came to our aid those fifty years back, and saved us from complete devastation. But the last time we were . . . we had no chance." This she finished softly. Pain never completely dissolves. I wondered back to her explanation about my tears those thirteen years ago, how she must wish she'd understood my cries. Dame Keren, the one villager whose color of choice was a lifeless charcoal, lost her six daughters to the Troths. One of them was with child.

"But fifty years!" I asked instead. "How can we know that the Riders still exist after all this time?"

"Oh, they exist," she answered. "Once in a while we hear of things, little things that keep their legend alive."

"Like what?" This was Min. She was as curious as I, as the rest of us.

"Stories sometimes filter between towns—the sound of hooves far in the distance, or the discovery of a hoofprint on a trail."

"Ponies . . . ," I muttered, thinking how this could possibly hold importance.

"Horses," Dame Keren corrected.

I had never seen a horse. I did not think any of the villagers of Merith had seen a horse. Ponies are not uncommon, but horses are the stuff of bedtime tales and children's make-believes. A moment was needed for all of us to consider such an image.

And then darling Min spoke once again what we each were thinking. "And they would help us, these riders of *horses*?"

And, after fifty years, *old*. I kept this to myself. These old riders of horses.

"Yes, Min." Dame Keren smiled. "I believe they will." Then to me she said, though speaking out clearly as if to inform each of us, "Lark, it is you who must bring the flag to Bren Clearing. It lies a day's walk past the northern edge of Dark Wood, between the Cullan foothills and the hills of Tarnec. You will know this clearing by the single rowan tree that stands in its center." She paused before saying, "The journey there should take you all of two days.

"Once there you must scale the rowan and tie the flag to as high a branch as you can. Let it fly free. Wait there, then, by the rowan tree. It should be naught but two or three days more before you will be approached and can make your request. The Riders will remember Merith, and if not, they will still hasten to destroy a Troth."

"This seems no great task," I said with forced lightness. "If I am quick about it, I can perhaps save half a day."

I could not fool Grandmama. I sensed her behind me.

"Dame Keren, please," my grandmother entreated, her voice unbearably deep. "Lark should not go alone."

Dame Keren answered with gentle authority. "Hume, it would be more dangerous should she be accompanied. It is their rule. You know this."

"I know my granddaughter," Grandmama answered back. "She is inexperienced in any journey. She can be easily over-whelmed with the Sight."

But I shifted around to her and said as evenly as I could, "Grandmama, it will be all right. These are lightly traveled paths; I should meet no strangers." I had no idea whether that was true, but I conjured a laugh, for she was shaking her head, and offered, "I can climb a tree far more nimbly than Quin." As if agility could prove more convincing than a bound summons. As if I could prove to myself I could do this.

"Lark Carew." Sir Farrin had risen once more, and he moved to look down at where I kneeled on the cobbles. I rose to my feet slowly. "Lark Carew, beware these things: Stay on the path. Light no fires. And, most importantly, do not venture into the hills of Tarnec. Past Bren Clearing is not of our dominion."

"Then whose?" asked a voice from the crowd.

"The hills of Tarnec belong to the Riders, and they protect their secrets. A trespasser will be killed outright. Beyond those hills are the Myr Mountains. Troth territory." He coughed abruptly. "No one, however, would make it past the hills."

I watched him. We all watched him, wondering what this oldest man of our village had witnessed in his lifetime. The shepherd's charge, the powerful bond to grass, to rain, to sun . . . Nature holds many secrets, but she will willingly give them up to those who are patient, to those who watch and listen.

I wondered if Sir Farrin had ever seen the Riders.

"Heed those three rules and your journey should be safe, young Lark." Then, his voice rising with strength I did not know he possessed, the oldest man said, "Let us give Lark our wishes for a good and quick journey, that her venture be the first step in protecting our beloved Merith."

Every villager turned and made a bow to me, hand to heart, chin to chest. My gaze flew over the small sea of faces, breath catching in my throat as I saw Grandmama and Evie making the same acknowledgment as the others, this gesture suddenly separating them from me. Raif, Quin, Minnow, all of them giving me the tribute saved for our most respected. In this single moment, I felt a wave of kindness wash over me, surround me, and then let go.

The words came out hesitant and foolish. "Do I—do I go now?"

Dame Keren gave an encouraging smile. "The sun is but midway through the day. The sooner begun, the sooner ended, my dear." Then, with less of a smile, she asked, "Are you ready?"

I tucked the lark feather back into my bodice and said more firmly, however false my conviction, " 'Tis a beautiful day for a walk."

Evie packed food for the journey in the small, thickly stitched satchel, which Grandmama had taught me to sew on: bread and cheese, a handful of hazelnuts, and dried apples. Grandmama poured a tiny bottle of the honeyed mead. "Just in case," she said. My cloak was shaken and brushed and folded; it would do well as a sleeping blanket. I added a small knife and a water flask to the pack, and changed into my light walking sandals. Then Kerrick Swan arrived at our cottage, bearing the flag that I was to raise for the Riders, a long, trailing banner Carr's great-grandmother had spun in a radiant hue of deep rose. "I imagine that it can be seen even at night," I said, focusing on detail rather than departure.

"All the best berries and fruit skins would have been brewed for so brilliant a color," Kerrick replied more gravely than usual, and brushed his long, age-worn fingers once over the cloth.

Too quickly, it was time to go. I kneeled down and buried my head in Rileg's soft fur. "Be good," I whispered to him. "Take care of Grandmama and Evie." Rileg whined. He wished to follow me; I wished I could let him.

I looked up at Evie; both of us were pretending not to be worried. "Watch for the ghisane, will you?" I asked. "They're sneaky little things."

She nodded. Then she held out what she had in her hands for me to take. "Carr whipped this up with her needle. I know you hated losing your other one."

It was an apron. Like my ruined favorite, it was of finely spun cotton and dyed the softest color of moss green.

"I was going to give it to you on your . . . on *our* birthday," she said. "But . . ."

But on our seventeenth birthday, I wouldn't be here.

I pulled the new apron over my head and tied the ribbons at the sides. It covered my frock, a slightly darker shade of moss. "There, now." I grinned. "I'll be most presentable to these elderly Riders."

"I'm thinking that your favorite color can at least hide you among the trees or what, if you—" She took a breath. "If you ever have need to hide."

"Then it is lucky that you were not summoned." I pointed at her brilliant turquoise dress.

We both laughed honestly at that, and Grandmama came to surround us with her Healer arms. "Fewer than seven sunrises and we'll have you back, Lark, and Merith will be safe from harm."

Then she pulled away to look me deep in the eyes. "Trust that you can do this, Lark. No doubt you were summoned for good reason."

Good reason. To that I had no answer. I hugged her goodbye.

As paths go, this was a pretty ribbon of trodden dirt, kept smooth and open with communal help from Merith and neighboring Dann. Bordered by Dark Wood, it ran the short distance between our villages, along the pastureland, and then farther on and into the Niler marshes. After that, I did not know, but the road at hand was open and untraveled, and I could skip upon it, which I did to make the length go quickly. I had companions. Song sparrows were always ready to serenade from the outstretched limbs of the Wood—those boughs that still reached for light—and in the growing fields were the villagers who'd returned to work after the Gathering. They waved at me, a long sweep of arm over their wide-brimmed hats.

But I did not expect the two figures that I spied in the distance resting in the grass. My breath caught, anticipating a too-soon encounter with strangers, then released in a relieved sigh as I heard the faint trill of Quin's flute. The figures rose to greet me when I neared—one short, one tall—and I laughed before reproving: "You should not be here. I journey alone, remember?"

"Who implies we accompany you?" asked Raif serenely as they fell into step. "Do you, Quin?"

"Nay. Raif has remembered an errand in Dann, and needed my assistance." Quin grinned his sunny grin. "It just so happens we've met you on the way. No one will think it wrong that we had to share the path."

"But now you'll miss an afternoon sighing at Nance's window." I laughed back, adding to Raif, "Evie put you to this." They'd not admit it, but I was sure it was true.

And then Raif was grave. "We can only go so far as Dann. It cannot be farther."

It was easier to pretend I was not scared now that I had company. I squared my shoulders to look taller. "Well, Dann has people and the path does not, and encountering people is the worst of it. 'Twould be silly if I could not accomplish the rest on my own. They'd hardly choose to bind a ninny to a summons."

Quin said with all seriousness, "Oh, I don't know. I've heard ninnies are in great demand." And then he jumped out of the way before I could punch his arm.

The path went quickly—too quickly—with these friends. Despite Quin's humor, we were not quite jovial; Raif's reserve was heightened by his grandfather's death, a sadness palpable even to Quin. But we walked comfortably side by side, and I was glad to be with them.

Dark Wood tracked our route—it followed the path to the very end of the Niler marshes, the sun-splashed fields to the right sobered by the dense mass on the left. Nothing was harmonious about Dark Wood; it was Nature's tantrum. Stepping beyond the boundary was to be lost in a choking, furious tangle of growth, swallowed in a cloying mist that crept into one's chest and under one's skin. Villagers did not exactly fear it—Merith had Dark Wood at its doorstep; grew up with it in sight, in mind, and in legend—but accepted that it was best left untouched. Only one path ventured into Dark Wood from our village, only one from Dann, and I could name the two men and one woman of our time who chose to travel within the chaos—one being Ruber Minwl.

I caught Raif staring at the Wood, as if he could peer through the impossible, snarled mess. "Did you ever go in there with your grandfather?"

He shook his head. "I did not follow his trade. I prefer work in the orchards to the labor of a tailor, and he understood that."

There was wistfulness in Raif's tone, which made me sorry I'd asked, but Quin broke any awkwardness. "Lark tried her hand in Dark Wood once. She didn't fare well. She'll call in the soldiers from Tyre to accompany her next time."

Raif actually laughed, while I scowled at Quin's returning grin. When we were quite young, Quin had dared me to run ten paces into Dark Wood, and of course I dared. It took four men from the village to find me an hour later, pulling me from inside a hollowed tree where I'd taken refuge. I had not stepped much beyond the ten paces, but I'd frozen from the maddening sensations that bombarded my mind, my soul. Whatever turmoil others might feel in the Wood was a hundredfold greater with the Sight. Grandmama spent much of that night pulling the frenzy from my mind with the bay dust, and I never dared anything after that.

"Next time go in yourself!" I challenged lamely. Quin threw his arm around my shoulders and whistled a small teasing note through his flute.

Dann was a happy little village, somewhat larger than Merith, known for the riotous colors of the border roses that enclosed the town square, and for the Danns' mastery in ale brewing. The Troths had never attacked them—a good thing, since they, like Merith dwellers, abhorred violence and had no experience in battle. The people of Merith wondered at the Troths' choice, why we should reap their ire and not another. We planted rosebushes, thinking they were perhaps a natural defense. But our roses grew in hues of cream and honey and apple blossom—we could not draw out the vibrancy of Dann's petals—and the Troths came. If color, then, was the proper deterrent, we flew brilliant flags of cherry, and pink, and poppy in the market and on our rooftops. It did not matter. The Troths were making their way again to our town.

It was best not to upset the Danns with portentous tales, we three had decided. They would learn of this soon enough at market. A pause only for a drink and to fill my flask from their well in the square. Their water was sweet, from the same river as ours, and I might not find as good a source later on.

"Ho, what's this?" Raif murmured as we turned into the square. A small crowd was gathered by the well. Even from this distance their energies buzzed along my skin, excited and anxious; little goose bumps shivered down my arms in response. Quin tugged my sleeve to keep me back—but I'd not have allowed myself to be surrounded.

"Maybe they've already learned of the Troths," he said, sobering.

But that was not what drew the crowd. As we skirted the group to reach the well, a shift of bodies showed us a piteously ugly little man in their midst claiming their full attention. That he was a journeyman was obvious—his grizzled beard was untrimmed; his clothes were worn and grimed from travel. I'd seen such in Merith. But he wore an odd-pointed, sky-blue cap on his head, which I'd never seen.

Raif had. "He was in Crene a fortnight back. He's called Harker. Someone said he was banished from his home, forced to wander. Rather a seer of some sort, I think. He was telling fortunes."

"And that cap is their distinction?" I asked.

Quin murmured to that, "Distinction? It makes him look more like a dunce."

"Nothing to worry; they spread tales of wonder for money," said Raif. "People like to come and hear such fantasies, but seers only pretend trances and their stories are made up. Hold here, Lark, fill your flask."

I did, and my two friends formed a barrier before me, though the villagers had paid no interest to our arrival. The visitor had riveted the crowd; they called to him: "Harker, tell me!" "Good sir, what is my . . . ?" *Will I marry? Will my gout ease? Will my son grow strong? Will the crop yield early?* All the *will*s that could be crowded into this circle, so eager was the desire to know the future. And the ugly little Harker hopped about the crowd, pointing and obligingly spouting bits of fate like gossip: "Your tankard runs dry too quickly." "Your hair falls out by first snow." He made them laugh or shriek, and they dropped coins in the funny cap he held out.

But the crowd went expectantly silent as the cap fell to the stones and the seer froze in the center of the circle. Then, shriveled and awkward as he was, his voice rang out rich, and deep, and foreign-toned: "Beware! Earth weeps! She groans in agony—great rifts and yawning caverns upturning whole villages! Mark me: Crene splits, and there! Haver sinks beneath the sea!"

"Now comes an end-of-the-world vision," Raif scoffed under his breath.

The voice was building in volume: "Watch the water;

beware the skies. Night takes day, and terror moves with sudden force! Ruin! Ruin! You will march into doom; you will cry for mercy!"

"Troths couldn't improve on this," Quin murmured, straight-faced.

"They like to be scared." I could feel the crowd's delighted horror well enough, like a drone of bees tickling inside my skin.

Raif added softly, "And better to be scared by things unreal."

I stuffed the water-heavy flask in my pack and drew close behind Raif and Quin to watch. Harker was a rigid pole now, with face upturned as if he pulled his story from the sky. "Woe to those who do not believe. Beware them that come! We will drown in madness!" He reached his hands above his head and clasped them, confessing, "My blame! My blame!" And then, reversing the piteous cries, he spit at us with furious insistence, "I share this to *save you*!"

His hands fell hard and his feet began to move: one step, then another, stumbling in a lopsided circle like a string puppet. I swallowed, anxious. Above the crowd's warm excitement, I could sense this stranger, his energy hollow and lonely and bitter. I did not wish him to come close.

"What?" Harker gulped in a convulsive jerk as he neared our side of the crowd. "What?" And then his eyes rolled up a little to show the whites, and he screamed so that we all jumped: "Lady—she is here. Power and hand . . . Where? Where?" His own hand reached long from his tattered sleeve a finger, pointed up to the sky, and then dragged a circle with it as if he would pick one of the crowd. A tremor ran through his body, narrowed, and shot down his arm straight through that finger. My breath caught.

"Step back, Lark," Quin said.

I did, and Quin and Raif closed ranks as we withdrew. There was a titter from the crowd; the old seer must have pointed to someone, and he was crying out, fainter now, "Those of the circle cannot hide. Those who *are* cannot run! Come forth! Help us!" And then, with cringing sobs, he screamed, "Do not force me away! I am sorry, I am sorry, I am sorry. . . ."

"He makes no sense." We'd taken the north lane away from the town's center. My laugh was loud and nervous in the sudden quiet.

"It is a pretense of visions," Raif said. "The more wild his tales and reactions, the heavier the coin tossed to him."

"Still," said Quin, "better he not choose you for his stunt." He flashed a grin and tugged a strand of my hair. "*Lady*," he mimicked.

I grinned back and nudged him with my shoulder, but he wasn't fooled. He sobered. "The old man didn't upset you, Lark, did he?"

"No."

Raif studied me for a moment. "Troths are at hand, but he told of earth rifts. He's more a fool than a seer."

It was suddenly over. We were at the end of the lane, the end of the little village. Raif and Quin could accompany me no farther, and I could not dawdle. We looked at one another silently.

"Good luck to you," Raif said at last, giving me a tiny and

unnecessary bow. We'd not touch; he would pass too much pain.

"Here," said Quin, handing me a sprig of fern, a little crumpled from being in his pocket. "The protection of friendship."

I could hug Quin, which I did. "I hope I don't need it."

He nodded. "You'll get to Bren Clearing quickly and signal the Riders."

"And be quickly back to fend off any Troths," I finished for him. I would. I had to.

But Raif said, "I wouldn't mind a little battle with the Troths." To our surprised stares he answered lightly, "One of them scavenged my grandfather's ring. I want it back."

4

I MET NO one; I walked freely on the path, and quickly. When the sun had left the sky, I'd reached the far pastures, a good advance in my journey. With that as reward for what I considered a brave beginning, I scouted farther on for a place to sleep, choosing, at length, a wide, flat boulder that bordered the path. I spread my cloak on it, making certain an edge of it still touched the path. Sir Farrin's warnings were not to be taken lightly.

I'd shared heartily in the midday meal; I'd not waste my provisions. I broke off some nearby spears of wintergreen and chewed them instead, enjoying the soft settling of dusk. Finally I lay back, luxuriating in the heat releasing from the boulder. There were the last, floating notes from the birds as they turned to sleep, and the little humming of the stone at my back—simple songs of harmony. Then the night sky grew enormous, bountiful with light—shooting stars so close that I felt they brushed my cheeks as they whizzed by. A tiny shrew crept up onto the stone, and then two more, and they snuggled into my sides, pleased at my opportune presence—they could sleep safely in the open and enjoy with me the grand spectacle. The moon rose high, nearly at her full mark. The stars bowed and dimmed at her summit, and our little world was bathed in silver, the color of Evie's hair. I realized, suddenly, that I'd forgotten to learn of Raif's feelings for my cousin.

A pang of homesickness, a sigh. The little shrews snored softly, and then I too was asleep.

The journeyman Harker was there in my dream, standing in the cobbled square, laughing out fortunes. I was cross at his ill-placed humor, that he'd taken me from my chores, and I looked to the others to see if they enjoyed his performance. The audience was small this time, four of us only. Four girls who encircled him, watching his deformed body writhe in glee as he gasped for breath and claimed we were doomed. "You suffocate!" he giggled to the ragged-thin girl with the moon-pale dirty face. "You beg for life far from home!" to the taller one in sturdy trousers with hair that shone red-gold. "You drown in sorrow," he cried out to Evie.

*Evie!* I called to my cousin, but no words came out, and the girls faded from sight. Harker sneered and wagged his finger at me as if that were my fault. "If you warn, you lose!" He turned and limped across the square. I stamped my foot at him. "You did not tell my fortune, old man! Do not go!" And he shook with laughter at my vexation. "You need no fortune; you already see!" Then he hopped up and down and pointed at me, calling out like a tattletale, "One is here! One is here!" And in response the cobblestones beneath him cracked wide open in a violent shudder. The seer lunged back then and cowered in awe by the gaping hole, shrieking, "She comes!"

From deep within the crevasse, up to the broken stone rose a woman. She was tall, and cloaked, and beautiful, with ebony hair lushly tumbling over her shoulders and dark, dark eyes that searched around as if she couldn't see. Light radiated from her breast, silhouetting something she held out in front of her, a heavy-looking sack. She might have stayed staring like that, but Harker suddenly leaped up, crying, "Mine! Mine!" and jumped for what she held in her hands.

He missed. With a terrible shriek, he was gone. "Harker!" I cried, and ran to the edge to watch him fall. He must have brushed the edge of the sack, for it tumbled after, spilling its contents: books, with bindings open and pages fluttering like birds, followed the man into darkness.

Unobstructed now, the light from the woman pierced the gloom and poured over me. I looked up and gasped: her eyes had fixed on mine. Eyes black, and empty.

"There you are." She smiled. It ruined her beauty. "There you are." And then her smile yawned open and more open until, terrible and grotesque, it widened larger than the crevasse and just as brutally deep. And I was dragged up from the earth and sucked into this frenzy of nothingness.

∞

It was still dark. There was still time before dawn. I was on the boulder by the path, shivering and sweating both at once. Slowly I pushed myself up from the stone, bringing one of the sleeping shrews with me. She let me rest my cheek against her soft fur, and I sat there for a time, hugging my knees into my chest, laying my head on my folded arms with the little shrew tucked in between. Her tiny heart was purring rapidly, mirroring my own panicked beat.

That smile. I'd seen it before, when I touched Ruber Minwl's severed hand. That horrible gash of mouth opening from malevolent sneer to ghastly void, swallowing me whole. What had old Harker said before? *Drown in madness.* . . . If dreams were foretelling my destiny, which end would it be? Slain by sword or pulled into oblivion?

I could not dwell on such thoughts or I'd be trapped by them. I gently moved the little shrew from my chest, picked up my pack and cloak, and began to walk.

Hours went by in a blur. The path wound along the side of the far pastures; grass for a half league or two, across a rolling landscape. Dawn came, bringing the sun over the grass, coaxing forth its sweet scent. My feet tripped across the dirt, swiftness without joy—but at least I was quick. It was buoyant and beautiful to the east and south; Dark Wood hung heavy along the west. North was the unknown. I concentrated on the sunshine polishing my right cheek, and the path dividing the green and the blackness.

Well before the noon hour, I reached the Niler marshes. It

was the end of my knowledge of the route, but I plowed right through the trail of muck and scythed reeds, fiercely determined. I would finish this task. I would finish it and not care beyond anything except returning home.

Somewhere I knew I was being silly. Troths were more real, more threat, and yet I was scared of dreams. A young man to kill me. A lady who would swallow me whole. Or even what the seer said: *You will cry for mercy.*

"I am a ninny, Quin," I muttered aloud as if he were still there. And yet . . .

The thing that gnawed through rational thought was what I had not admitted to Raif, to Quin, not even to myself: I'd read old Harker's energy. He'd not told a false tale.

Like some grim joke at that acknowledgment, I was suddenly thrown to my knees—a shock from the earth shaking beneath me. There, in the middle of the Niler marshes, with its already weak ground and soggy hillocks, the earth was rocking and bumping, heaving me up and tossing me back— bounced like a child on a blanket. I screamed out loud, thinking of Harker falling into the darkness, fearing the mud would tear open and drop me too, or the dark lady would reach from beneath and swallow me down. And so I wrenched myself up from the squelching muck and ran. Even as I stumbled, fell, and regained my footing, even as the earth calmed and straightened and behaved as if I'd merely imagined its shudder, I ran, not stopping. Never mind the Troths. I was like those gaping villagers of Dann, spooked by things that might not be real.

I broke through the end of the marshes in a rush, thudded across the harder ground, and stopped, gasping for breath. Before me spread the broad scape of the Cullan foothills and the northern border of Dark Wood, with the sun's rays glinting on its frayed edge. Quiet, wide-open, and simple, and showing me as the fool chased by her own shadow. I staggered a few lengths on, to hunker down by a boulder that jutted like a tooth from the earth, gathering into the stone as if it were a mother's embrace and letting the coolness of its surface seep into my body while I reclaimed my breath and raged at the cruel joke played by sending me on this task.

The wrong person had been summoned. Raif had scoffed at Harker's display, Quin had made us laugh; neither would need to grovel at the foot of this stone for support. Not any from Merith would behave as I—even Cath could have gathered her scattered wits for this journey. But instead, here I was, the chosen, a scared and silly girl. Had I been born as anyone else, not plagued by the Sight, not afraid of my own thoughts and senses; had I been born a stoic Healer, even . . . I put hands to my temples, wondering if I too could drag out the awful feelings in the way Grandmama could with her bay dust. But it simply made my head thrum, and I dropped them listlessly and lay gazing at the pale sky.

I would lose time. I had to move on. With little desire to leave the solidity of the rock, I forced myself up and then promptly sat back down, dizzy—I'd forgotten to eat. I fumbled open my pack and spread the parcels of food, washed my muddy hands with the water from my flask. It was a feast without pleasure; my body was ravenous, but I had no appetite. A portion was gone quickly, remains of bread, cheese, and nuts scattered for the birds and little creatures, the flask of water emptied. I stood up and surveyed this new territory. The Cullan foothills were the smallest offspring of the Myr Mountains: ripples of gray stone pushing up between short grasses, with few trees or shrubs to offer protection or catch the wind. I'd hurry. I wanted this over and done.

The path was rough from here on, harder to follow. Dirt and trodden grass wound its way between expanses of green stubble and tumbles of boulder. I trudged on, the small hills growing steeper, a monotony of green and gray with few birds and even fewer animals. At each gap, I paused, looking into the little valleys and wondering if any of these held the single rowan tree. The sun fell west; my shadow changed sides. I was scrabbling by then over wide swaths of cracked rock and moss, utterly alone on these hilltops, pushing ahead, thinking the next hill will be the last . . . then the next.

Sometimes gorse had grabbed hold in boulders' crevices and spurted tufts of yellow buds, brilliant on the gray. In one place I spied the sweet purple blossoms of minion. Grandmama would dearly love to have a rooting of these to start in the garden. "The most healing of herbs," she would say. I hoped I'd remember where I saw them when I returned.

I had a funny image, then, of these elderly Riders escorting me on horseback to Merith. Their long, white beards would flow back along the horses—horses, in my imagination, had fanciful tails and manes that streamed back as well. I would hardly be able to see forward for all the hair.

That made me laugh, a welcome relief.

On and up, on and up. One more hill, and then only one more again, I kept promising. They were big enough to close in my view; I hadn't yet glimpsed the hills of Tarnec, let alone the Myr Mountains. I stopped once more to take some bread from my pack and refilled my flask from a trickle of stream etching a rock. I took a swig of the honeyed mead. I was aching but I was closer, I knew it, and felt the thrill of accomplishment surge through and carry me forward.

The air had cooled and a breeze picked up. My shadow was now twice my size. I paused near the top of a hill, for I heard a piercing shriek from far away, and turned back to look—an eagle soared high above in the distance. I watched him drawing nearer. Then, with one stroke of his powerful wings, he swept over me and away, as I, in turn, spun around and began to run up the last of the rise. Eagles nest in the hills of Tarnec; I knew I must be near. If I could crest this slope, perhaps—

And then I was at the top, mouth open with the awe of what lay stretched out before me. The ground sloped down and away, offering the expanse of distance: the hills of Tarnec shot up from the earth, matted in the deep green of fir and eucalyptus; beyond and behind them were the ashen, sheared crags of the Myr Mountains. The tips were tinted in gold and pink—I think it was the snow catching the dying sun. They took my breath, those mountains. They began far beyond the hills, yet they loomed over all, forbidding one to cross. I remember someone once said to me—was it Daen Hurn?—that you did not climb over the Myr Mountains, you went through them.

I dragged my gaze from the gray and looked downward. A little valley was created between the slopes—these last of the Cullan foothills—greenest of green carpeting, with three streams pooling around a scattering of boulders into a smallish, icy-clear, oblong pond. Snowdrops dotted the hills like sprinkles of faerie dust. They were blooming late, for certain; perhaps the sun shone a bit differently here. Perhaps there was magic at work in this sweet valley.

Perhaps there was. Bren Clearing. The rowan tree stood stark in the center like a beacon, immensely tall, young leaves of green gently sweeping the sky in the breeze. The path led straight to its roots.

In a moment's breath, exhaustion was gone and I was flying down the hill. My hair tugged loose from its braid, but I did not pause to set it right; it felt glorious sailing free. My feet hardly touched the trail; the rocks I think I leaped over, gleefully. The scent was young clover and fresh-cut hay and spring rain all at once. There were songbirds too, nesting in the rowan tree, which spread its canopy wide for all.

And then, in a radiant welcome, the sun sank below the top of the rowan and beamed out through its leaves like golden arms reaching to embrace me. I laughed and opened my arms wide in turn.

The boulder hid him, but I was too enraptured to have paid attention anyway. The hair did not even tremble on my neck—or if it did, I did not feel it. I raced down the path with face to the sun, so that when I rounded the great rock that curved the trail, my eyes were too dazzled to even rightly see. But then I stumbled in shock as a smell seared through my nostrils.

Death. Rancid, rotting death.

A Troth.

# 5

HE CROUCHED AGAINST the green background, chewing at something—mouth smeared red, and glazed eyes turning to look. I gasped, jerked backward, stumbled. He pulled back too, but only for the tiniest instant. Then he sprang at me with a violent gnash of those hideous teeth, snapping at the air where I'd been poised a moment before. But I fell and the Troth leaped at nothing, landing in a hard tumble on his side. Breathless, I scrambled back on the grass, horribly aware that I held no weapon, had no cover, nothing to prevent the next assault. The beast grunted, righted himself, and made to spring; I threw up my arms in futile defense.

There was no attack. In a rush of brown snarls, two foxes were on the Troth, teeth and claws and guttural, nasty yelps forcing him to spin away from me. But the beast was powerful; the foxes were no match.

"No!" I shrieked at them. "No, don't!" I would have thrown myself into the frenzy, but one of the foxes turned and looked at me so fiercely that I paused in midmotion, stunned. I understood him exactly:

*Go. Run. Head north.*

Words could not have been spoken more clearly. I hesitated, but the fox stayed turned to me, teeth bared, blocking me from the fight. *Go now!* Then he lunged for the Troth—who had the other fox by the throat—with such ferocity that the beast fell back.

I burst into tears at their sacrifice but did as I was bidden, tearing down to the bottom of the clearing and curving to head north. Across the pretty green, crushing the white snowdrops, up another crest that cupped the edge of the valley, and then I was into the hills of Tarnec. My task was abandoned—I'd left the path that Sir Farrin warned me to stay on, breached the territory he warned me against, and was running blindly up the hills. Moments later the Troth crashed into the forest behind me.

There was no tangle of brush here as in Dark Wood. It was open beneath the evergreen canopy, easy to run through despite the deepening dusk. The fir and eucalyptus were a pungent mix, tickling my nose and clearing my sobs. But I think the scent distressed the Troth; for a time I could hear rapid snorts through those slits of nostrils until they faded in the trees. And then I knew why the fox had said north. If the powerful scent hampered the Troth, I had half a chance to outrun it.

I clambered up and slid down the great hill, then crossed

a short space to confront another towering rise, scrabbling with both hands and feet up that next pitch, until night swallowed the remaining light and I was stumbling blind. The trees hummed low and soft, but there were too many to single out, energy too diffuse to give me fair warning. Starlight, moonlight, lamplight—there were none of these. I bumped hard into many trunks before using them to pull myself forward.

I'd nearly crested the second hill when the Troth shrieked hideously close by. My knees went soft. Of course: *his eyes.* Never mind stilted breath; if Troths lived within the Myr Mountains, they would easily see in the dark . . . easily find me. Those filmy disks were made for night.

· My little knife was somewhere in my pack, but it was a choice I never had. Three chilling snorts I heard, each one nearer than the first, and then the beast was behind me. I lunged forward as he scraped at my cloak, but was tugged right back to those gruesome claws.

I cried out, hands flinging wide blindly. My palm hit the Troth's arm as it came slashing down, and I felt the skin, moist and spongy like a slug, and the iron rod of bone beneath. The blow took my breath, as did the awful knowledge that I had no defense against such force. But it was the Troth who shrieked and leaped away, yelping and squealing like a bow pig, slithering back the way he came until the labored squeals grew fainter.

I didn't stop to think what had happened. I rolled over and scrambled upward, crashing into trees, falling, but ever upward. That the Troth could have easily killed me was clear. I could only imagine that it was too easy; what was wanted was the chase and torture that had killed Ruber Minwl. The Troth had gone to round up its mates, came the horrific realization. The blood sport had just begun.

I bit back fear. There was no time for panic. I should return to Bren Clearing, now, before they banded together. I had to at least try. With any luck, maybe I could get to the rowan tree and spread the banner before the slaughter.

And even as I made up my mind to go back, I reached the top of the hill and stopped dead still.

The trees ended. As abruptly as they'd begun, they ended. The sky was visible there, beyond the last boughs, and I stepped gingerly onto a split of rock that jutted over a valley and into the light of infinite stars. Silent, achingly clear, almost cold. The hills of Tarnec continued beyond, dark-sketched, daunted only by the massive shadows of the Myr Mountains. Below me, the valley was bare of trees, gleaming instead with slashes of silvery gray rock—huge boulders and ridges, nooks and crevices and promontories all punctuating the hill's slope. Grass lay like blankets over the tops and spaces between, and the whole of the valley floor was carpeted in green.

The moon was rising full, an enormous sphere of silver already paling the sky and sweeping back the shadows. I watched the light spread and took a relieved breath of the cool air. I could find a hiding place in these rocks. Troths might not see so well under the moon's bright beams; this close to the trees they might not smell me. At dawn, when my eyes would be as sharp as theirs and I still had the advantage of the forest's scent, I'd begin my trek back to Bren Clearing and to the rowan.

"Thank you, foxes," I whispered. A faint breeze bore the grateful words away.

I walked a little farther, keeping close to the trees, and climbed to a grassy ridge that dropped in a dizzyingly straight fall. There was a lip of rock near its edge I could use for cover as I waited for the sun. Troths were no more than the size of a man, but neither would fit easily there. I dropped to hands and knees and crawled to the hollow, then stopped—hair hanging over the edge and gaze riveted to the valley floor—at the sound of a distant rumble.

Ponies. The wild gallopers came streaking out of the valley shadows into the brilliance of moonlight. I was high, and the silver light played tricks; they seemed long of leg and spine. I squinted to see better, wriggling belly-flat to hang farther over the edge, then froze once more, prone and vulnerable, for I heard a new sound.

Something was moving up the ridge, something large. A ringing step against stone, a thudding upon the grass, and the little gusts of air through nostrils. I went to spring for the over-hang, then froze again, too late, for he was up over the ridge already. I clenched for the strike, barely breathing. . . . But nothing. My head turned stiffly to look.

"Oh!" was all that came out.

The stuff of make-believe was glowing there against the night sky, with the sparkle of stars like little bursts of celebration surrounding him. A horse. A white horse.

My gaze whipped back to the valley. Not ponies. Horses. All of them. I, who had never seen a horse, was suspended now above a hundred or more—was confronted by this singular, stunning one. I turned back slowly, blinking, to see if this horse would disappear like some apparition, but he stood solidly before me, watching as I pushed to my knees, mouth still open, and choked out inanely, "Oh, but you're beautiful!"

He did not reply, of course, but I thought he shook his head for my benefit. A tiny shake, just to fluff the forelock from his eyes. The light of his coat flashed. I had to crane my neck to meet his stare; his eye was solemn, deep and dark, utterly passive and yet totally alive. He waited. I stood up slowly, transfixed, coming barely to the top of his shoulder, tentatively offered my hand just beneath his velvet nose. He blustered into my palm. I stepped closer, brushed my fingers along his powerful neck and smooth swath of cheek, and he turned and brought his soft muzzle to touch my own cheek, just at the edge of my jaw. Then my arms went around his neck and I leaned into him, breathing the wonderful smell of hide and mane, feeling his calming energy run through me—feeling, for a blessed time, safe.

The horse let me stand there for I don't know how long. We both faced the valley, witnessed the herd running freely, all colors of hide and hair made silver-dark under the moon. A toss of mane, a whisk of tail to catch the light; a prance, a buck, a gallop across the open grass. Muscle and bone melted into a singular grace of motion. I was utterly still, hardly breathing, drinking my fill of beauty. An enchanted place. No wonder the Riders protected these hills.

Finally and almost ruefully, I lifted my face and released my arms.

I suppose that I expected him to turn away then, and leave as he had come. But the white horse touched his muzzle to my cheek again and blew through his nostrils right against my hair. Then he turned, exquisitely graceful despite his size, and started down the ridge.

A signal to move if I'd ever understood one.

He nimbly picked his way among the rocks and I scrambled behind, but when we turned to what was a sliver of path precariously winding down toward the valley, I stopped, disappointed.

"I cannot follow you." I had to return to Bren Clearing. Back through the forest. Back to the Troths.

The horse's ears twitched.

I reached once more to touch his bristled coat. "Go on, then." I was speaking softly; even so, my voice vibrated against the rock surrounding us. "Thank you for this. I won't forget." The horse shook his mane and watched me with those deep eyes.

"Rune," I said suddenly with a grin. "I would call you Rune."

The horse shook his head again as if he accepted, and then he stepped away, leaving my hand open against nothing.

I watched Rune disappear through a tight crevice, a last gleam of his milk-white coat under the moon. No dark fears from the past days could have any hold in this place. I turned my face up and smiled at the sky, and then climbed awkwardly back up the rock.

The hair on my neck pricked.

Two things happened at once. I heard the harsh snort of the

Troth somewhere above my head, higher up on the ridge, and then I heard a step that was much closer—a soft, leather-shod step that I was not meant to hear, as if the foot was versed in creeping quietly to the attack. I felt my shoulders hunch protectively in surprise, and as I started to turn toward the noise, a voice roared in fury so loud that it echoed through the whole valley.

"Trespasser!"

I knew who it was. I knew it was my final breath. Even so, I could not help that my body pulled back, and my head whipped around in shock and fright, so that I caught his eyes with my own. And there was the timeless moment of my dream hanging suspended between us, eyes locked. Half a breath was all it was, yet it lasted an eternity. His beautiful, beautiful face was contorted by rage melting into some sort of frigid horror. My own expression, I know, was the shock of recognition. I was unbalanced. I fell hard back onto the ground, and over me he seemed impossibly huge.

"Trespasser!" The voice was hoarse this time, and I saw him close his eyes.

Yet he lifted his enormous sword in a graceful arc, and there was no hesitation as it struck down.

# 6

I WAS NOT dead. I could not be dead. I heard my struggle to take a gasping breath and my heart thudding wildly against my ribs. I heard roaring in my ears and the strangest sensation that I was underwater, or at the very least under a tremendous weight pressing me heavily into the earth.

And, I felt pain.

Yet all of that was insignificant against the shock that it was not over. My mind ran frenzied: the dream was not wrong— the sword had come down; my mind dissolved into that blissful white—but I was not dead.

He was swearing, I think. Harsh, sharp words were falling from above as the roar in my ears resolved into sound. "She is to die! She is supposed to die!" he shouted into the clear sky. And he cursed for this, I supposed, error.

Time is fickle. Moments we wish to hold are gone in an

eyeblink; things to be agonizingly endured seem to last forever. And sometimes, the space between breaths yawns open into a cavern—a great suspense of nothingness and everything at once. There is clarity in the tiniest detail. Mine was in my hearing. My ears were so attuned in that space, I swear I heard the stars burning. The curses falling from those beautiful lips, the echoing clang of sword against rock, the soft brush of the leathered step and creasing of woven tunic and braided belt. Then powerful snorting surrounded me, above, behind. They merged, split. Rune was whickering; beyond that was the Troth's harsh slurp of air. I heard a grunt from the dream man as he sprang from the ridge and ran lightly across the boulder, a sharp squeal from the Troth, a thud. . . . And all I could think was how could the Troth die before I did?

Then my hearing softened and was funneled from a place far away, and thoughts swirled to another distance so that nothing seemed to matter anymore. My vision floated away too, and suddenly I was looking down at my body sprawled on the grassy ridge like a cloth doll, hair and cloak tossed every which way. And I saw that the pressure pinning me was Rune. He lay over me, his great forelegs pawing at the dirt as he worked to keep himself from crushing me, to bring himself upright. His great haunches flexed and pulled, and then he was up, standing over my limp body, with his muzzle against my cheek, nudging at me. And the dream man was striding back down to the ridge, sheathing the sword he'd just wiped against the grass, glaring at Rune and coming to pause by my head, staring hard down at my face for a moment with an unfathomable expression.

Abruptly, he reached an arm back in a wide sweep and sent his palm slamming down hard into my shoulder.

I gave a great gasp of breath, felt my lungs fill with cool air, and I was suddenly looking up into his painfully beautiful face.

My shoulder ached.

"Your breath was knocked from you," he said, as a curt and by no means apologetic explanation for his action.

I didn't speak, disoriented and dumbfounded. Three moments ago he'd stabbed his sword down on me. Now he'd brought my breath back.

And for no purpose. There was no attempt to include me in conversation. He was turned, staring at Rune now with incredulity. He opened his mouth as if to ask the horse a question, and then shut it, lips clamped tightly over whatever thought he'd had.

"Get up." He ordered that of me without looking.

I stayed motionless, and he swore again angrily: beautiful voice, beautiful face, beautiful smile—hostility piercing all, like little stabs from his sword. How old—nineteen years or twenty, perhaps? His anger aged him.

"Get up!" he demanded again, still without looking at me. He was busy with something tucked into his belt. A cloth.

I did not wait for a third command. I sat up and pushed into the grass to rise, then groaned as pain seared through my ankle. "I cannot—"

"Don't say a word!" He whirled on me, exclaiming with fury, "I will kill you if you do."

My eyes were wide, waiting for him to take his sword. He

turned back, the anger now making him clumsy. He fumbled, not for the sword but for the cloth, finally pulling it free with another oath. He turned back in my direction. "I said to get up!"

But I was frozen in place, unblinking. To my right I heard Rune pawing at the sod.

The dream man caught, then fought my gaze. Whipping his head away, he muttered something under his breath. Then he reached down and, taking the cloth, wrapped the thing around my eyes and knotted it at the back of my head. The moonlight disappeared. Rune snorted. A leather braid was lashed around my wrists next. It was not his belt, I noted with odd detail. It was too thin, too cutting.

Not gently, he pulled my arm to drag me up, and I yelped at the warm shock of his touch, dangling there in his strong grip, caught by the force of it. Maybe my ankle was broken and the dark and the unbalance made me dizzy, but his touch was what truly stunned—an energy both delicious to my senses and fraught with a terrible pain.

"What—?" The man was ready to shake me into standing straight; his hand trembled with the impending force of it. But suddenly he stopped. He must have looked at my foot, for I sensed him stoop over. Then he straightened. In a heartbeat, I was off the ground and tossed over his shoulder like a sack of barley. My hood fell over my head. The pack I wore slipped and banged against his back, but he didn't flinch. The young man merely brushed my cloak away from his face, gathering it along in his grip, and started to walk.

I wish that I could say I struggled. Or that I argued. I wish, even, that I could say it was my Merith upbringing that inspired some sort of silent dignity in the face of trauma. But there was nothing noble in my action; I merely lost consciousness. I remember sensing from his grip a piercing anguish, and a fleeting glimpse of a cup of spilled wine—remnants of some terrible story. Then exhaustion, pain, hunger, fear, and the simple act of hanging upside down brought blood rushing to my head too fast. It seemed to boil in my ears, and then there was nothing.

It was very quick. I should have told him he'd no need for the blindfold.

Jarred awake, laid back down on solid earth, something soft between me and a wedge of rock—a blanket, or my cloak. I remembered the cloth being knotted around my eyes and the man from my dream, but little else. I could not feel sun on my face. My mouth was dry; taste was nothing. I could smell moss and stone and good, dark earth. I smelled a fire burning low. Yet that described every place I could think of. I could as well be in Merith.

But were I in Merith, I would not be blindfolded and bound, nor would I hear so rapid and heated a conversation as the one that fired just above my head.

The dream man had companions—angry companions. This was no Merith.

I was scared. Nay, panicked. The desire to be home, for this to be unreal, burned with sudden, terrible fierceness. I clenched my teeth hard against it, against any groan, any movement, and pretended unconsciousness to be invisible.

"We take no prisoners, Gharain!"

"I know."

The dream man's name: Gharain. He—the one in terrible pain.

"You should have put her to death already," the deeper voice filled in with a horrifying pronouncement. "Dragging her with you has only prolonged her misery. And yours, it seems."

Gharain was sharp. "What mean you by that?"

"Look at you!"

He snorted. "I cannot."

"I'll look for you, then." This was a different voice, mild and amused, and younger, like Gharain's. There were three men here. "Your eyes stare hard and wild. You breathe heavily—"

"I carried her, Wilh."

The first man laughed. "As if you could be winded by that!"

True. He'd lifted me as if I had no weight.

"—and you pace like a wolf!" Wilh continued, but seemed to lose his smile. "On all accounts, Gharain, this has shaken you. Why bring this on? It should have been over immediately. With no look back."

"Then let's be done and quickly." The first voice was brusque and emotionless. "This brings no pleasure."

"Aye," said Wilh. "Gharain, it was your charge. You must do the task."

"I cannot."

I closed my eyes behind the blindfold, grateful for those

words, but relief was sinkingly brief. Wilh ignored his refusal. "Our law, Gharain. Trespassers must be killed."

"I know that well," Gharain returned fiercely. "And I—I cannot."

The first voice broke in, angry now. "Gharain, for you to do this again—"

Gharain swore at that. "I will *not* repeat my error, Brahnt, and do not think I do this for myself! Look! Look there, beyond the circle of firelight. Law or no, look at what stopped me!"

There was a pause, a rustling, the turning of heads and bodies to witness something. Two sharp intakes of breath, then Wilh and Brahnt stumbled over one another's words in surprise.

"The white one—!"

"Is it he? How?"

"He prevented me, Wilh. He leaped between my sword and her body. I swear, had I not jumped back, he would have struck me dead with his hooves or I'd have killed him in her place."

"What?" Brahnt scoffed, unwilling to believe. "He leaped from nowhere?"

"'Twas no accident," Gharain said flatly. "'Twas protection—he protected her. He's still protecting her; he's followed me here." A pause, and then a sigh almost. "As if he's . . . *chosen*. I could not ignore this."

The other men were considering this. I was too. The flash of white in my dream had not been the moment of death. It had been Rune saving me.

"*Chosen of white*," Wilh seemed to quote. "This makes for a unique dilemma. We should hold Council—"

"Wilh!" Brahnt interrupted. "Do you not smell Troth on him?" He must have turned to Gharain. "You found Troths?" he demanded.

"Yes. One. He was quickly dead."

"She brought the beast, then. White stallion, or no, the girl has trespassed; she must be done away with here. Now." Brahnt was adamant. "If you will not do this, Gharain, then I will in your place. The horse will not be harmed. I will not miss."

I had no time to react. There was shuffling of footsteps, nearer to me suddenly, and the rasp of metal sliding from leather. And just as suddenly Rune neighed harshly. A clatter of hooves sounded by my head.

Wilh said, "Put your sword away, Brahnt!"

"What is this?" Brahnt swore under his breath. "The elusive one—guarding like a dog!" I did not hear him resheathe his weapon. I dared not breathe, biting the inside of my lip to hold steady.

"Like it or no, Brahnt, there is reason in this," answered Wilh. "If the steed has indeed chosen her."

"*Chosen* is but a word. Our *laws* are to safeguard these horses," Brahnt stressed. "And leave no trespassers to tell tales."

Gharain made a hard sound, but Wilh exclaimed with frustration, "But it is the *white* steed. And this but a single girl!"

There was a terrible pause at that, as if a single girl could do much harm. Wilh offered instead, "If we are uncertain, let's unleash her wrists and leave her pointed toward Tyre."

"And if she brings the dark city dwellers back?" Brahnt demanded. "If she shows them the way? Or what if the horse follows her? Would you have him appear in Tyre? Never mind his fate there; consider the poachers who would soon invade our hills to steal them all."

The voices stopped. My blood went to ice. It took no special gift to know what they were thinking: put out her eyes, and she cannot find her way back.

"Then there are only ugly choices." Wilh's words sank like stone.

Silence followed until Gharain said hollowly, "I should have done the deed. I have brought distress upon us again." His voice was turned to me. "I am sorry." Kind words that were cold.

But it was Brahnt who swore again and walked away. "No. We are done. I have no stomach for this anymore. I understand you, Gharain. The horse, a girl. It makes us no better than Troths."

"So? Cut her loose and, what, blind her? You have stomach for that?" Reprieves were fleeting. I swallowed back a whimper, held my breath—

"Nay, Wilh, that is neither my aim. She cannot leave."

Not leave! But I had to leave; being spared was not enough. Even now there was a new scent in the air; my head shifted ever so slightly, breathing it in. Dawn was fast approaching, bringing worry of time wasted. One night was already lost. I needed to find my way back to Bren Clearing quickly, and to break free was daunting at best. The binds alone would take hours to sever, and they had horses, and swords—

"She is awake," Wilh said suddenly.

In a flurry of sounds, hands reached and grasped my shoulders, my waist. I was pulled to sit upright, my back pushed against hard granite, surrounded by the men, who leaned close.

"You!" Brahnt's voice was purposefully harsh. "What have you listened to? What have you witnessed?"

"Nothing!" I gasped, spitting back a piece of hood that fell against my mouth. "I—"

Gharain interrupted from farther back. "You were spied on the peak, watching."

Fingers tightened on my shoulders. Wilh and Brahnt were closer to me now, leaning in. I smelled horse and leather and the scent of the Earth's riches borne on the wind. I felt their energies, pulsing through fingertips, through breath. It was strong energy, two at once, yet unlike the shock I was used to from strangers. But I sensed a history that did shock, a violent conflict. My breathing quickened.

"Tell us what you saw," Brahnt demanded.

"I did not see you!" I cried out, tensing. Images from their touch were in my head now: a flock of ravens shrieking across a stark sky, smoke filtering through trees and a sudden rush of bodies pounding by, innocent people caught in a horrific battle. Their faces crammed against my own, eye to eye, haunting looks of terror—

Gharain shouted, "Not us! *Them!*"

"What 'them'?" I was crying the words without thinking. "Please! You are too close!" The gnashing of a Troth's sharp teeth sliced across my gaze, and I jumped. There were shouts now, the people screaming as they ran. Swords and blood and hooves and the roar of fire; men on horseback, Riders, arcing their weapons. Troths like gray moths, smothering bodies, leaping for throats—animal or man, it did not matter which. The air stank of blood. "Too much!" I sobbed. And then I don't know what I was saying, for the words were for the images and the images were too brutal to hold.

At some point, the hands released me. The men shifted back and let me fall over on my side. I rubbed the cloak away from my cheek so the hard rock beneath could grate my skin and take me somehow out of that darkness.

"Is this sorcery?" demanded Brahnt. "Is she possessed?"

"No." Awe slowed Wilh's words. "This is not possession; 'tis the *Sight*. She saw our battle—seven days have passed, yet she recounted it as if it happened now. What—not willing to believe it was our touch? Then let us know. . . ." I felt Wilh's hand brush my cheek, shimmering new images. I heard Gharain swearing as I screamed.

The hand was wrenched hard away from my face. "*Stop!*" Gharain tore from the group, footsteps fading.

Wilh made a move to follow, but Brahnt hissed, "Let him be."

"The *white* horse *chooses* the girl; now she shows something of the *Sight*—"

"You might use those words, Wilh, but it can be simple coincidence. Do not be so quick to suppose anything good in this."

Hands reached for me again, but more gently this time. They turned my face from the rock and brushed strands of hair from my mouth. "Hold still," Wilh demanded. "You won't be harmed." But I struggled anyway, fearing him, fearing visions, until he pushed my hood back, pulled the blindfold off, and let go. "There, that's all," Wilh said more gently. He sat back, regarding me.

Brahnt made a low sound, like a whistle. "Maybe this is what stopped Gharain."

But Gharain was already storming back, lashing out at that fiercely: "Only *once* will I be deceived by beauty." Then he was before me, defiant and harsh, to prove so. "Speak! Why are you here?"

My eyes blinked hard against the early light, sick from the Sight, the three men swimming before me. Wilh and Brahnt kneeled close, studying; Gharain stood tall, eyes averted. Wilh was fair-haired and Brahnt was not; Brahnt was older than Wilh and Gharain together, and all in their own way handsome— though it was the one who demanded my confession who took my breath.

"You—you are Riders," I said as no answer, hardly believing. I closed my eyes against the careening sky, insisting faintly, "It is not possible. You are too young."

Wilh's friendly laugh was unexpected. "This is from someone who looks barely old enough to be in a forest on her own." Then, to Brahnt's warning hiss, he answered calmly, "Just because I am not suspicious does not mean I am fooled."

There was a long silence in which I could hear only my shallow breathing. The raw pain I'd sensed in Gharain now hung between all the Riders.

*Riders.* I forced my eyes open. "I came to find you." I couldn't remember what I'd planned to say; tree branches and faces whirled above me. "My village needs help. . . . There are Troths."

"Troths! At your village?" Brahnt snorted. "That is not possible. We beat their scavengers not seven nights back. They cannot regroup so quickly."

"Not yet!" I was going to be sick. "But they will come."

Wilh was curious. "Why would a village ask one so young to venture on such a journey?"

"They did not ask." Then I added absurdly, for Gharain's sake, "And I am not so young."

That was ignored. "Not ask? A volunteer, then?"

"Are you alone? Were you appointed?"

These were not questions but interrogation—nothing that I was used to, nor could I answer anyway. My head reeled. I lay back down on the rock so that I could feel the cold of it, hearing Gharain swear again with impatience. How could they stomach the fight? How could they wield weapons as ferociously as Troths?

"She needs help." This was Brahnt. I saw him through the fog squinting down at me. "Her hands—we don't need to keep them tied. And wrap her cape more tightly; she looks cold. I'll get her the drink."

Pain, death, fear. The fear was the worst of it.

"Here." It was Wilh, exchanging places with Brahnt. "Let me help you up."

I flinched as he gripped my shoulders once more.

"Your—your battle." The words stuttered out as he eased me upright. "It was very awful. . . ."

"They usually are," Wilh answered calmly. He went to work at the knot in my binds. "Your horse," he said with a nod thrown in Rune's direction, "is concerned. Do you hear how he paws restlessly at the dirt?"

"He's not mine," I panted.

"He most certainly is," murmured Wilh. "A horse claims his rider. Though this is . . . unexpected. There, now. Undone. I'm sorry for this." He put a finger on one wrist. "A salve will make this better—"

I didn't care. I pulled away and pressed my temples. My teeth chattered until my whole body shook. I lay back down. "My head. I cannot clear it."

"Brahnt!" Wilh called. "Gharain!"

"Here." It was Gharain's voice close by. I tried to open my eyes again, wondering if he would look at me. He was wrapping something around my shoulders, something light and soft and comforting. His cloak. "She's had a shock." Gharain was turned to Wilh, who leaned next to him. "She needs warmth."

His hand touched the back of my neck as he tucked in the cloak. I gasped at the jolt and his fingers jumped back. Still, he did not meet my eyes.

"This will help." Brahnt had returned as well. He helped to prop me up against the rock and then held a cup steadily against my trembling lips, urging me to drink. I cannot say that I was graceful, but I managed to swallow.

I had never tasted anything like it before. The drink was

like warmed milk, rich and soothing, but there was a spice in it that I did not recognize—something slightly sweet, and likewise pungent, making it deliciously fragrant. I pulled the cup from Brahnt, ravenous for this medicine. It slid through my bones, slowing their shaking, and then cleared away the fog and eased my rapid breath. I finished it all.

Wilh and Gharain had shifted back, watching me. At least Wilh was. He leaned to touch a fold of the cloak to my mouth to wipe what I'd spilled. "Better now?" He smiled, his voice soothing.

I nodded. I gave him, even, a hint of a smile back, and looked to each of the men crouching there, cautiously hospitable to this trespasser. Calm now, the battle history done, I could feel only the energy they radiated. And it was good energy. Each with his burdens and prizes, perhaps, but it was good. It surprised me that I was not disturbed by them. A weathered seriousness was in Brahnt, something immensely sweet in Wilh, and something—however masked with anger—something terribly sad in Gharain.

He moved impatiently when Wilh leaned to me, snorting, "If she's healed, then, might we *politely* ask why she's trespassed?"

Aid was over. I relinquished the cup and cleared my throat. "I came seeking your help." And then, remembering, "I have the sign—"

"The sign?" they asked in one voice. There was a heightened focus; the Riders drew close, waiting.

"In my pack. Here." This must be the needed proof. I

shrugged the thing from off my shoulder and under my cloak. I began to open it, but Brahnt took my wrist and pulled my hand away gently and undid the loop and lifted the flap in my stead, withdrawing the deep-rose flag from underneath the remaining food packets and spreading out its length. There was an equal pause of breath between the three of them. They were disappointed.

"That," said Gharain, not kindly, "is something that should be flying from the rowan tree in Bren Clearing. You are forbidden to come this far. You know it."

"It was not my intention to trespass," I answered carefully. "The Troth surprised me." I told them as briefly as I could of the encounter and fight in Bren Clearing.

"The foxes bade you run to the hills?" Brahnt sounded disbelieving.

"You forget who is speaking," Wilh answered for me, softly.

"*Maybe,*" cautioned Brahnt. He studied the flag. "You are from Merith. You volunteered to make this journey?"

"No. I—I was summoned. I was bound to it."

The Riders all turned to me. For a moment we faced off, three sets of eyes staring into a single, uncertain pair. And then I understood, murmured, "*My* sign . . ." I turned slightly, reached into the bodice of my dress, and pulled out the three feathers that I'd left tucked there. I laid the one the hawk brought me on the stone for their inspection, then added the other two as some heightened proof of it—my journey.

In the young light, the feathers were hardly special, hardly something for presentation—simple brownish objects, a little weathered by the heat of my body. Yet the Riders did not laugh. Instead, there was a new hush in the already silent camp.

At length came, "Summoned, indeed."

"The lark rises."

Murmured portent from Brahnt and Wilh. Gharain said nothing. He simply reached out a tanned finger to touch the first feather very lightly. It shifted slightly on the rock and for a brief moment caught the gleam of dawn.

"You are Lark." Finally, as he spoke, he turned and looked straight at me.

Into me.

I think Wilh and Brahnt stepped back. Or maybe they just disappeared in that expanded moment. And I think I whispered, "I am," but I don't clearly remember. What I remember is the color of his eyes. Gharain pulled my gaze with him as he stood up tall above me. I could not tear my eyes from his— their depth of sage green, glints of golden brown flecked within.

The light was rising, and with it a fresh breeze bringing the smell of the pine and eucalyptus. It caught Gharain's chestnut curls and tossed them lightly.

"Lark," he repeated, looking down at me. And he smiled.

My first dream.

# 7

BY MIDMORNING WE'D already passed two more of the great hills of Tarnec. We made easy speed on the horses. My frock did not allow me to sit over the horse as they did, so I hung my legs on one side and leaned back into Wilh's chest—grinning madly half with terror, half with delight at this first ride—my hands gripping the pommel of his saddle. Brahnt followed behind us. Gharain rode ahead.

We were heading to Council—a Gathering, I was told. I expected I would be tried for trespassing, guilty as I was of it, and I didn't resist. I needed their help and would beg my case there. The Riders were decisive, but there was nothing I sensed that made me fear them any longer. More importantly, they had sworn to me they would not let Troths destroy Merith. Whatever my punishment, I would believe that as truth.

This was not my intended way, bouncing lopsidedly into

the unknown, but I had completed my task. I'd found the Riders. I was no longer bound to a summons.

We cantered in single file, cloaks—rather than beards; I smiled—sweeping out behind us. I knew Rune followed last. Whatever Wilh had claimed about the horse choosing its rider must have been so, for since the previous night Rune had not been out of my sight. I wondered at the brown steed that Wilh rode, or Brahnt's striking black mount, that these horses had chosen them. Certainly, Wilh sat, as did they all, like a part of the horse, with ease and assuredness. A few spoken words were enough to have the horses heading at swift speed toward their home.

When I asked what made it so, Wilh said, "Choosing is the horses' right and their instinct, and so the camaraderie is pure. Riders protect the hills from poachers who would breed horses for sale, for such would distort the natural bond." And then he said, "Rune, is it? You've named him well."

Gharain's stallion was the dappled color of smoke.

The dream man's attention had been brief. He'd summarily handed me, pushed me almost, to ride with Wilh, and now I watched him leading us. I could not help but stare. A strong back, a long and straight spine. Gharain leaned forward into the stride, his head low, the curls blown back. Once or twice he turned to glance to his side and the slant of cheek stirred something inside of me. I could not help it. I could not shake the power of his smile. Gharain's mouth was tense again, but I'd seen it differently—his face had lit as he spoke my name, as if he'd made some great discovery or some burden was lifted.

That light was gone now, shut and masked by something far more agonizing. Having acknowledged me, he'd turned his back—allowing no glimpse into his thoughts, allowing no smile. I was left to stare, haunted.

We stopped briefly before the sun reached full strength. A small stream careened between the trees, down from a height we'd not yet reached. Wilh took me from his horse and carried me to the water's edge, setting me down so that I might drink and shake off the ride while the Riders guided the horses farther up the bank for their own rest. Rune stayed with me. I cupped handfuls of the clear water and Rune followed, air bubbling silver around his white muzzle. Then he took his head from the stream and snorted, blowing the cold droplets across my neck and making me laugh. Gharain was visible beyond Rune's sturdy neck, purposefully turned away.

Brahnt came to offer me a helping of their food: cold meat and oatcake. I thanked him but refused, so he returned with what remained of my own supply—the slices of cheese and bread that had been carefully packed by Evie. As I ate, I looked down at my moss-green apron, brushed the crumbs from the beautifully colored weave. I thought of Evie saying such color could hide me if ever needed. It wasn't needed now.

"It's not much farther." Wilh had come over. "We'll arrive well before nightfall."

I nodded.

"You did not share our meal. Was it not to your liking?"

"You did not expect a fourth in your group. I'd not take your portions."

"Ah. Well, soon you'll be able to rest comfortably. Your ankle will be tended."

"Thank you."

He was assessing me. "And your wrists."

"Thank you."

Wilh grinned and cocked his head. "Hmm. Considerate, extremely polite, a bit timid."

This was nothing new, but I blushed anyway.

"And yet, not *timid*. You've courage enough to have made it this far from Merith." He watched me, my cheeks turning scarlet. "Wary of us, then, I guess, and why not? We've frightened you with all of this."

"And what is *all* of this?" I could be direct as well, he'd neglected to say.

But Wilh had turned, the smile leaving his face. He looked up the ridge to his horse, who was rearing abruptly with a harsh whinny. The other horses were pulling back too, white-eyed. And I turned to the stream with a gasp, for I understood suddenly what had brought their fear.

The little stream was expanding.

It started abruptly as a spurt of water, ripples coming to splash heavily at the edges of the bank, slivers of light leaping across the stream's spreading surface. Wilh was rising to his feet, reaching his hand. Then the hill above was lurching—no, it was no more a hill, but a torrent of water rushing toward us. I heard Gharain yell for me to stand, but I'd no chance. Even as I shifted, the stream slammed into me, Wilh, and Rune, and the bank beneath us dropped away. Wilh was quick. He caught my sleeve, and for a moment he had me, but then the sleeve tore and I was gone, caught up in the tumble, swallowing great mouthfuls of icy water. I do not swim as well as Evie, but even she could not have mastered this raging swirl—pummeled and tossed until which way was up was lost in froth. I could not even think to wonder where the others were flung.

It was a tree that saved me. I hit it hard, stomach to trunk. The impact expelled the water from my lungs in a great cough, and the branches snagged my apron, my frock, and held me until my arms could clasp around it—hooking elbow over bough, clinging hard to what was the only solid thing left to hold.

And then the flood was suddenly over. Like a splash, a slap of palm to water, the wave exploded and was done. It happened all in the space of three breaths.

I slid to the ground, stunned, in a sopping heap of clothes and hair, looking back to Gharain and Brahnt . . . to where the water had not reached. They were poised to strike: swords pulled, blades pointing out shoulder high, as if they could tame water with a slash of steel. But there was nothing to fight. Around us the quiet had returned save for the dripping trees and my ragged coughing. A few pebbles and clods of earth dropped into the gouged scar that was now four times the size of the original streambed, the water a docile trickle in its center. The Riders looked at one another, looked at me, looked at my sprawled state, my hands dug into the dirt to hold the firm ground. I stared up at them, speechless.

"Wilh!" Brahnt shouted into the silence.

"Here!" was the returning shout from some distance away. "I've got Rune."

Gharain sheathed his sword by slamming it into his belt. He, with Brahnt following, slid down the new ridge, eased me up on my one good ankle, and lifted me to stand supported by Wilh's horse. They did it matter-of-factly, as if nothing had occurred, despite a sheen of sweat at their temples and Gharain's paled complexion. His hand was warm on my arm before he let go.

I found my voice. "H-how did that happen?"

Brahnt took charge with quickly adopted cheer. "There." He gave an awkward pat to my shoulder. "Just wet. You're all right."

But I wasn't. "It's as Harker said."

As quickly, his cheerfulness was gone. "What?"

"From last morning, the village of Dann. An old man was traveling through." My teeth were starting to chatter, maybe from the cold. "A seer. He said the world is in agony, upheavals—"

"A seer spreads tales of this?" Gharain interrupted, grim. He passed me his cloak.

"Not tales! He spoke true enough. He warned of Nature's turmoil. Was this flood not such? And yesterday the ground shook when I was inside the Niler marshes." *Only yesterday?* It felt a lifetime.

"Far away, then. What else?"

I did not tell him of the dream, of the books or the girls, or Harker's anguish. I shook my head and dried my face on

Gharain's cloak before wrapping it close. It held his scent, faint with juniper. There was a noise and we looked to see Wilh clambering up the ridge with Rune, one hand clutching the horse's mane, one holding his side. "That boulder was none too kind to my ribs," he said to us with a half grin as he neared. "There's a long scratch down Rune's flank, but it's not deep. 'Twill not hamper his speed."

Rune came close, nudging at my hair and sleeve to judge my sopping state. I looped one arm around his neck and ran my fingers along his wound. Thankfully, Wilh was right: it was not deep.

Brahnt was muttering to the other Riders, "They toy with us."

"Toying is what they'll do," said Gharain, his voice bitter. "For now at least."

Wilh moved to close ranks with the Riders. "But more than toying, I think," he murmured, with a glance to where I stood. "They're looking."

"*Who* is looking?" I shivered, picturing Troths, and leaned into Rune's warm side.

Brahnt ignored me, saying low and with some severity, "You assume, Wilh. We don't know."

Wilh raised a brow. "And yet, maybe *they* do." They walked off to argue away from me. Their hands stayed on their sword hilts.

I was left with Gharain, who finally returned my stare. "Who are *they*? Troths?" I asked.

"It is nothing."

As if I should be content with so ridiculous an answer. "*That* was not nothing."

He held himself rigidly. "You are perfectly safe with us."

"I expect I am. But it's not what I asked." I was as rude as he, for his eyes were so coldly disconcerting and his demeanor so stiff that I couldn't remember manners or timidity or even the fear from moments ago—only the urge to somehow bring back that smile, or at least effect something more than disdain. Finally I dragged his cloak off my shoulders and pushed it back at him.

Gharain hesitated for the briefest moment, but gave a little jut to his chin as acknowledgment, took the cloak, and walked away.

As the sun was just past the midpoint, the horses came to the edge of a wide plateau, pausing above a grass-carpeted, granite-rimmed valley.

"Home," announced Wilh.

I looked down from the height of our shared saddle. "Home?" What could bring the note of pleasure to his voice? The emerald expanse was pretty, but there were no cottages, no tents, no shepherds' huts, even. I wondered that they might live in caves.

"Little Lark," Wilh laughed gently. "Not down. Look there." And he raised his arm to point west across the dale.

Sir Farrin said the Riders protected secrets. I was wrong to think it was only the horses.

Stone battlements rose from a precipice that jutted out and

split the valley nearly in half. A forest of turrets spired up from the sheer face, grown, it seemed, directly from the hard earth. Surrounding them, and sweeping back from a wide terrace that ringed the back of the castle, was the green of grass, and trees, and woods, even. Woods—not of fir and eucalyptus, but most likely oak and chestnut and birch. The pines took over only farther up the wide slope that spread out like a cape. There was space enough for cottages to scatter across the green swath. Even from this distance I was certain I could make out sheep and other livestock dotting the green next to rows of what must be farmed offerings. And beyond I saw the even spacing of orchard trees. Only the Myr Mountains stretching north dominated Tarnec's height, and they could not cast the land in shadow.

Wilh grinned at my expression. "Quite the view. This is Tarnec."

"I've never seen anything so grand," I said with true awe, watching the banners waving atop the spires. A kingdom. An entire kingdom crowding to the edges of the jutting cliff, at once huge and contained.

There was a small spiral of energy whirling in the pit of my stomach—not the usual dread of unfamiliar people and places, but rather anticipation. I looked over at the other two Riders. Something too in their pleasured expressions made me want to climb that precipice, enter the realm. Even Gharain's face had relaxed.

"Come!" Brahnt set off, calling out to the others, "We're not there yet!"

It was impossible to reach Tarnec along the plateau, so we traveled down in tight single file on the only path carved into the cliff, spreading out for a final gallop when we reached the valley floor. Gharain took the length at a wild speed, quickly outdistancing us; Wilh and Brahnt let the horses run open at their own pleasure while I held on, breathless.

We'd been spotted by lookouts. As we neared the halfway point, I saw three men on horseback filing down the last path from the castle lands to meet us. Wilh yelled to me over the sound of hooves, "Three of our brethren. Now you have half our group to lead you home."

I frowned. Kind, but odd words. This was not my home.

Nor was the greeting entirely hospitable. The three new Riders had pulled their horses up, blocking the path.

"Ho! Wilh! What have you brought?" came the cry as we neared.

"Nay, it is all right!" Brahnt shouted back, and I tensed again at that. He'd said as much to me after the flood, and neither time did he erase the gravity of the mood.

Gharain reached the three first, gripping forearms with each in salutation. I heard him mutter as we approached, "Careful. Don't crowd her."

Stern and serious looks from the Riders—eyes to me, to Rune, to Gharain, then back to me, with suspicious curiosity. Hardly surprising; I was both trespasser and frightful mix of mud and pine needles and wind-dried clothes. I heard one murmur, "Again?" before it was lost as Brahnt called out, "Lark, I offer you Taran, Dartegn, and Cargh. At your service."

The Riders stayed where they were but bowed their heads to me briefly. From this distance I took none of their history, only their energy: a sensation of something both earth-rooted and pliant, the way wheat fields ripple in a breeze. They were strong-built, of differing ages, though all far younger than I'd first pictured. Cargh was blond; the others were dark-haired. Blue-eyed, brown, hazel—they had pleasing looks. None had Gharain's chestnut curls and sage eyes.

"How?" asked Taran, his eyes on me.

Gharain was quiet. Brahnt grunted, "Later. Bring us home."

There was a pause, a hesitation that swelled as the Riders waited. A flush spread along Gharain's cheek. Gazes flicked back and forth in silence. Then Brahnt said roughly, "It is well. I believe it is well. I will account for this."

"So be it, then. After you, my lady," Dartegn announced with a sweep of arm, gesturing Wilh to move ahead.

Taran fronted the way up the path, and Wilh followed. The others filed behind, talking—of me, I assumed, but I did not hear their words. I was rigid and wide-eyed at the straight drop but an arm's length away. Up and up we progressed. The castle was lost for a time behind the height of the cliff walls. And then it reappeared, much more huge and imposing. Windows, battlements, massive blocks of stone, all hanging, suspended, as if it would at any moment tip over on us. I caught my breath.

Wilh sensed my reaction. He laid a gloved hand over my hands gripping his saddle.

"Welcome to Tarnec," he said.

# 8

WELCOME WAS NOT enough of a word to describe our arrival. Many came running as we entered the courtyard through the towering oak gates—guards, groomsmen, men and women of varied rank and uniform. I held very still as the crowd gathered, waiting for the onslaught of sensations. But there were none, other than the pleasant buzz of conversation and motion. Wilh helped me gently down to the waiting arms of two servants, arms that passed no unpleasant visions. I'm not certain if I was more stunned at the ease I felt with the residents of the castle, or at the impressive structure itself; all of it was unreal. I turned to look back at the Riders—Wilh, Brahnt, and Gharain. They were dismounting, laughing, leaving their horses with affectionate slaps to the capable hands of grooms. And though he had no lead, Rune docilely followed the others through murmurs and exclamations at his appearance. The white horse, it seemed, was already known.

If murmurs trailed me as well, I could not tell. I was whisked inside Castle Tarnec in the opposite direction that Gharain headed.

I wished it had not mattered.

I suppose the mere size of a castle implies that most things will be done on a grand scale, but I'd never seen anything so huge. The entryway alone was more than twice our cottage. The ceiling rose until it was lost in shadow; timeworn floors of stone stretched through arched doorways leading to places of mystery. I was carried—neck craning, trying not to miss any feature—through winding, tapestry-lined halls and into an airy room where I was at last set down.

It was simple and sparsely furnished, and lovely. A candelabra set with fat tapers hung from the soaring ceiling; slate floors were scattered with thickly woven rugs of blues and greens. Opposite the huge fireplace was an equally wide down-stuffed bed, and a looking glass stood by the door. An armchair and footstool were bathed in sunlight pouring through the leaded casements and small doorway that filled one wall. They opened to a cloister and interior garden where ivy climbed around the stonework, and flowers scented the air with heady sweetness.

I took my first deep breath then, drawing in the hush and peace of the room—but for a moment only, since behind us crowded a lively force of helpers. Information, it seemed, had traveled as quickly through the castle as I. "Haste now! She is here!" echoed in the corridors, and in came servants bearing a hip bath, buckets, clothing, food, and an assortment of soaps and brushes and towels. A cup of sweet tea was given to me to swallow, then the pine needles were shaken from my hair, salve dabbed on my wrist burns, and my clothes unlaced and bundled away. Two girls casting curious glances hurried through the cloister door and began drawing water from the pool that graced the center of the garden. It was done so quickly that I could only blink at the busy figures and wonder why I was not overwhelmed.

It was too beautiful; they were too attentive. None of it appropriate to my status. I said aloud to anyone who might stop long enough to listen, "This is a mistake. I am the trespasser the Riders brought from the hills." I grimaced a little at my own honesty, expecting I'd just asked for some dank dungeon to replace these pleasures.

A stout, motherly, apple-cheeked woman came over to pull the last burrs out of my tangles. She smiled at me. "We welcome all who reach the castle."

So, if not killed outright, as Sir Farrin warned of trespassers, then welcomed? I stared at her. I would have sensed a lie through her hands even if her smile held. But she spoke truth.

"But what of the Council? I was brought here for that."

"Council will be tonight," the woman said. "You shall rest and heal first."

Nayla was her name. She announced herself my attendant, and with brisk efficiency directed my arrival. Trays placed here, towels stacked there—she helped me limp to the bath, shushed a young girl who was pointing to my shoulder, and asked brightly, "Found on the hills, were you?" I'd barely nodded before buckets of freshwater poured over my head, *warm* freshwater.

"A spring-fed pool, my lady, but our kitchen fires burn directly below it," Nayla explained, then turned a stern eye to my filthy hair. I gave over to the luxury of assistance. Not even at market day had I been so close to so many people at once, and yet here their touch showed nothing disturbing, simply the soft hum of tranquil energy as they scrubbed me clean with soaps and oils, unfamiliar but enticingly perfumed.

"Colraigh and elspen," said Nayla with a nod when I murmured something about it. "They take to water. In it their scent expands. Some are growing just outside." She tsked, "Pine sap," and scoured my elbows.

I looked out at the girls drawing the water, running along a footpath leading to the wide pool. The garden was enormous; one wing of the castle must have been built to surround it. The deep-green lawn was bordered by white flowers—not quite the shape of roses—jumbling up the stone pillars spaced evenly along the cloister. Ivy and boxwood draped and bordered as well—a tease to conceal stone and space. This was not what I'd imagined. The directions to Bren Clearing had not included this.

At last, cleaned of three days' travel, I was dried with a sheet of linen warmed by the sun and helped from the tub. The other assistants withdrew with their buckets and bath while Nayla lifted a gown from the bed. "For sleep," she said just as I yawned, and exchanged the linen sheet for this. "Now come sit by the window and eat something while I attend to your ankle."

There was stew, hard cheese, and bread. There was fruit, and some sort of cake with a sugared icing. I sat back with a handful of blackberries, not quite relaxed but lulled anyway into the afternoon, breathing in the scent of those pretty flowers, feeling the shifting sun glint here and there across my face while Nayla unwound neat folds of linen strips into a brass bowl that she'd warmed in the fireplace. She poured in two tinctures, and I watched their clear colors turn deep violet as they mixed. A rich scent wafted up from the shallow depth. Pungent herb and dark flower—I thought, almost, that I knew it, but then the memory was gone.

"Minion, stonecrop, and thyme," Nayla said, catching my faint frown. "Heat releases their power."

"Heat releases the healing properties of these herbs," I mused sleepily. "And water releases the scents of colraigh and elspen. What else?"

The maidservant laughed, pointed at the pretty flowers climbing in the cloister pillars. "The scent of the bell roses. They soothe and heal as well."

Piece by piece, Nayla wrung out the linen and wrapped my ankle. There was a pleasant heat, and then I felt a tingle swirling my ankle, reaching deep. I nearly jumped.

Nayla nodded. "The healing begins." Then she nodded again with approval at my yawn. "And that is the tea having its effect. Come take your rest."

Cloud-soft, I told Nayla, sinking into the bed. Sunlight streamed through the green leaves in the cloister, making dappled patterns of shadow over the white comforter; a light breeze stirred the shadows and ushered in the sweet smells of the garden—

"Wait!" I said, rousing as I heard her collecting her things. "Water, fire, and air you have told me. But what growing things are enhanced by the earth?"

"My lady, it does not work the same for Earth," Nayla responded, though she was now by the door. "With Earth, it is what *we* do that enhances its bounty."

"I don't understand."

"But you, my lady? Do you not? 'Tis a cycle: plants harvested from the earth heal us. And it is we who, in turn, affect the earth. What we give to Earth encourages her ability to provide for us."

"What—provide what?" I murmured. I was nearly out. "What do we give?"

It was so sweetly said, my lashes flicked down. "Love."

I dreamed of home. I dreamed of things I loved: the smell of cut grass, lilacs blooming, the nudge of Rileg's cold nose. I dreamed of the comfort of Grandmama's plump and sturdy embrace, Quin's laugh, and Evie's fair gaze. I dreamed of Gharain's smile.

But then another, terrifying smile consumed all, yawning huge and black and greedy, whispering, *"There you are. . . ."* I woke with a gasping jolt.

Shadows had deepened across the room, but the rich scent of the bell roses lingered still, a reminder of how distinctly my life had changed in a single day. The sweet dream was gone.

Home was gone. I sat up slowly, hugged my arms around my knees to clasp what was familiar.

As if she'd waited to hear me stir, Nayla bustled in, arms laden with a splendid-looking gown. "A pleasant sleep I trust, Mistress Lark?"

Maybe enchantment could be broken if confronted. I fixed her with a severe glare. "Tell me: Am I magicked? Is this a spell?"

Nayla laughed at me. "Now that would be a most difficult task: to weave all of this into a spell." She nodded at the room, the garden beyond, and, I assumed, the entire realm. "Too exhausting" was her pronouncement. She draped the gown on the chair and proceeded to light the candles. I scrutinized each motion with suspicion, but the tasks were too ordinary to be working enchantments. Finished, Nayla turned, hands on hips, wondering that I waited. "Time to rise, my lady; the king waits to meet you."

*King.* My mouth fell open. "But there was to be a Council! Of the Riders."

"And so there is. A Council and a king. Here, now, I'll take the wrapping from your ankle." Since I'd not moved, Nayla came and drew my foot from beneath the tangle of bedclothes. "It's dried quite nicely," she murmured, inspecting the linen strips. She pulled a tiny blade from her pocket to cut them away.

"But *king*!" I'd imagined a simple circle of the dozen Riders, out of doors . . . a bonfire, maybe. "There is no need, surely! I've asked only for help, for a village too insignificant in size to merit the attention of a *king*." Even as a trespasser, I too was insignificant; this could not be necessary. I wondered how enormous the king would be, how opulent his throne. Someone so powerful would overwhelm the Sight. What terrible history would he pass?

"Do not fret so, or I might nick your skin." Nayla sawed at the stiffened cloth patiently until it split up my ankle and came away as one piece. Then she looked up at me. "All will be well, Mistress Lark. There, now. Try out your foot."

*All will be well.* Grandmama's words. I wiggled my ankle back and forth. Healed, no pain—nothing that could help to postpone or protest. I should have thanked her, but I did not.

"Very good," she pronounced. "Now, then. Let us have you dressed." She walked over to the chair and waited for me to obligingly follow. Off with one gown, on with another—she was leaving me little time to hesitate, to think on what was coming.

"A good color, I think. Come, my lady, take your look and say that you approve." Nayla had turned me so that I faced the looking glass while she did up the buttons. A rare, full-length view. I stood tallish and slight-framed in the candlelight, a reflection too beautifully tinged by the flickering gold to be believable. Hip-length hair, serious brow, and skin, already tanned from the sun, now glowed. Even my brown eyes were dusted with golden light. I blushed and focused on the exquisite gown. Moss green: a bodice of braided ribbons stitched together with gold and copper threads, skirt and sleeves in richly soft velvet. Nayla's nimble fingers made quick work of the tiny loops at the back.

I was suspicious too that this would fit so well, be of my favorite color. But the maidservant shrugged as she stood behind me, busy. "We have clothes to spare for our guests. I chose well, did I not? You look quite lovely."

"Very opportune, these spares."

Nayla finished the top button. I could feel her smile all the way through her fingers. "No spell, my lady," she said with a little pat to my shoulder. " 'Tis exactly as you see it. Come, now. Let us get you to the hall."

The passages glowed with torches ensconced in iron fastenings hung high above the tapestries. I counted them as we walked, abandoning the task after thirty, for there was much to look at, to wonder at. The stones held spatters of onyx and mica; I brushed my fingers against the hewn blocks, over the rough or smooth breaks. Then my hands crossed the tapestry borders, silk and woolen threads adding layers of lush texture. I drew in warmth; I drew in a richness of time. There was history here, ancient, deep, and powerful.

I do not know how long we walked or how many turns; it seemed, at least, a complex distance. But suddenly we were before a set of enormous doors of oiled oak, carved in intricate pictures—spirals of vines, leaves, fruits, richly darkened with age and what must have been countless years of polish. Pulled by guards who stood within, they opened wide before us.

I gasped.

A golden glow from what seemed a thousand candles flooded the enormous room with brilliant warmth. More tapestries—these as wide and tall as our cottage—hung from the walls, gleaming in the flickering light. Stories played out on these weavings, green and gold tales of fantastical creatures, enchanted groves, and exquisitely blue magical lakes. Bits of vermilion stitching shone so radiant in the candlelight the color alone seemed to heat the room.

Along one length of wall stood a line of carved wooden seats, six of them, all unique, all empty. Other than that, the room was bare of furnishings, and of people. Or so I thought, until my gaze traveled to the far end, where two great fireplaces burned brightly, between which stood a grouping of men— the Riders, I imagined; there were twelve together—and four women. Gharain stood with them, I knew immediately. And there was one more: a tall, slight, white-haired figure seated in an oak chair centered on a slight platform, his hands resting on something he held in his lap. Not as opulently presented as I'd anticipated, but I did not doubt this was the king. One of the Riders shifted his stance, and I saw there was a second chair. This, like the rest, was empty.

"Go on," said Nayla, turning to me with a smile. She stepped to the side so I was exposed.

The group faced me, and my heart shrank. More strangers to meet, more histories of violent battles—the bombardment on my senses would begin even before I had to admit my trespass and beg for help before this king. My fingers gripped the edges of my velvet sleeves.

"Go on," repeated Nayla. "Your Council."

She left then. The great doors shut.

## 9

*GO ON.*

They watched me. The king, Gharain, the other Riders—all eyes on me as I hesitated. Even from this distance I sensed the strength present here. A good strength, but so powerful I had to catch my breath. *Do not let it overwhelm,* I charged silently. And then just as silently, I reminded, *Ninny.* I took a deeper breath and walked forward, eyes to the ground, trying not to see how small I was in the enormous room.

Gharain stiffened. I felt him brace just as I braced, knew that he looked away while the others watched me approach. His rejection stung, but then the whir of the group's energies overtook—the inevitable charge and spiral, surrounding and singing into my body. I faltered again, not from any discord but because I was *not* being made dizzy by their hum. Unusual and unreal in its ease, I'd stumbled because there was nothing to ward against.

"Come forward." The king's voice carried across the hall, propelled me center before the platform. I kept my gaze down, bowed as I assumed I must.

He did not demand, but neither was it a request: "May I see you." I gathered courage, raised my eyes to the withered man in the chair.

A smile hinted at the king's mouth. Lines were etched there, finely drawn, intricately webbed lines that spread out along his paper-thin cheeks. He was old—no, he was ancient. His hair was brilliantly white, with only a strand or two of gray that matched his velvet robe—a sweet gray, like a rabbit's fur. My gaze strayed. The borders of his robe were trimmed with silvery threads, which sparkled a bit when he breathed. His hands rested on a book in his lap, a handsome, smallish, leather-bound thing tooled with inlay on the cover—a circle threaded with filigree—as ancient-looking as the fingers that touched it, and yet unworn . . . or unused. I thought of the fluttering books that the ugly Harker had leaped for in his panic to claim them. This one rested so still beneath the king's wrinkled hands—

"Your eyes," the king insisted gently.

I looked again to the aged face, to the clear, piercing stare under the white brows. I recognized then the connection: these eyes were Gharain's eyes, green with those flecks of golden brown, earth-colored and warm. The gaze went deep, straight into my very center. Yet it was his faint smile that was unnerving. It hinted at both sadness and, more strangely, hope, as if he recognized me as well.

"Lark Carew."

I'd not shared my full name. "Yes."

"Daughter of Meilsa, granddaughter of Hume."

"Yes." A shiver ran up my spine. How did he know?

"You will be seventeen years on the seventeenth day after the midsummer mark."

"Yes . . ."

"And you carry the sign."

The sign. I shook my head, gulping. "No, I am sorry. I do not remember what happened to the feathers. I must have left them back in the forest. The Riders saw them—Wilh and Brahnt, and Gha—"

"That is not the sign I speak of. You carry a mark on your body. The mark of Balance."

At those words the entire room seemed to hold its breath. I looked back in surprise.

"The mark on my shoulder—" I swallowed then, to say more clearly, "The mark on my shoulder blade?"

"The mark of Balance," the king repeated.

"'Tis only a small circle. An outline. It is not unusual. My cousin has the same mark—"

"But you bear the Sight. You hold connection with Earth's creatures."

I protested, "And she is a Healer. She is far—"

"The sign. We must see it, Lark Carew." There was no pause to wonder if I would agree to this. "Ilone, if you would."

A young woman broke from the group where she'd stood partnered with the Rider I recognized as Dartegn, and crossed the distance to me with a light step. Her dark brown hair fell almost as long as my own, rich against the ruby color of her gown. She took my hand with an encouraging smile—passing no frenzy of sensation—and drew me up onto the platform before the king. I was meek in her hands: letting her push me to kneel and turn me just so, letting her pull my hair from my shoulder and expose my back to the scrutiny of the king—to all, for all eyes were fixed on this mark. My mark.

"Just one," Ilone murmured, undoing a single button, and the sleeve was slipped down.

It is not that a mark on one's skin should be considered insignificant. Many carry a brand of some sort, birth-given, directing their paths—for good or bad. Evie and I liked that we shared a similar mark, but we'd paid little attention to these small things we could not see.

*Ruber Minwl bore a mark too, when he died,* came a sudden, vicious memory. We do not always wish for the brands we are given.

"Lark . . . ," Ilone said, nodding toward the Riders.

Gharain had stepped forward from the group, some acknowledgment having passed between himself and the king. For whatever reason he was singled out, it was an unwelcome designation. And, quiet and stiff as he was, the young Rider's voice held true desperation. "Must I?"

The king said nothing. Gharain closed his eyes. Some agony flickered across his brow, so heartbreaking that I caught my breath to see it. Then his eyes opened, focused on some far-off detail, and he slowly walked to where I kneeled. I watched him not look at me, watched him move with deliberate purpose, with an expression of pained resignation—a dutiful servant ready to perform a loathed task.

I had the horrible thought that he was going to draw his sword.

My eyes flicked back to Ilone. She shook her head. "It is just for a moment."

And then Gharain was there and Ilone bent my shoulder to him. My head went down, but I turned my face so that I could see out of the corner of my eye his right hand reach out. He had a mark too, on the back of his third finger just above the knuckle. It was a tiny scar, whiter than the rest of his skin—a cross of two even lines. And he was placing his mark against mine. I felt the light touch, the warmth of his skin—

A shock of brilliance burst through me. I screamed. My back arched, throwing my face into the light of the thousand candles. Their glow exploded through my vision, and something gripped me—a power beyond all I'd ever seen or felt before. A homesickness, a pain of the deepest level, ripped into my heart, simultaneously washed smooth by an ultimate, exquisite burst of joy. It was need, and it was need fulfilled.

I tipped from the small platform onto hands and knees, gasping for breath. The move broke Gharain's touch, and almost immediately the color, the heat, and the explosion inside were dimmed. I tried to rise but my arms were jelly.

"Is she strong enough for this?" Ilone asked the king.

"She is," he replied.

It was a terse exchange. I quit any attempt to stand and stayed crumpled on the stone, looking at the company in the room. They all stood straight, nearly severe in their attention and surprise. I looked at Gharain, caught his stare. He was as shocked as I. His face was lit with the heat of the touch, radiating a power and beauty so extraordinary. It was the release I'd seen before when he'd smiled my name.

I was hoarse. "What is this? What—what has happened?"

"You are awakened, Lark," answered the king. "You are proved."

My entire body was tingling, charged as if by lightning. I looked up at him. "What is proved?"

"That you are who we hoped." His hand brushed across the book he held—striking because it was the first time, I think, that he'd moved. But then, to my utter shock, his hand went to his heart and he bowed—the traditional Merith acknowledgment of respect. Every member of the attending group followed his gesture. "We welcome you home."

"This—this is not home." The tingling was expanding. "I am from the village of Merith, sent to request that your Riders protect us from approaching Troths."

"We know of your village. We know you seek our help, but it is we who have need of yours."

"*My* help?" What meant any of this? The group stood, calm and silent, while waves of something huge seeped through body and mind, building in force—not painful, but powerful and uncontrollable. "I've nothing to offer."

The king simply looked at me, waiting the way the Riders did up on the ridge, as if I had something of importance to say, to impart. I stood, trying not to tremble.

"You wish to go," he said. He read what was in my mind.

"Yes! I wish to go home!" Home. I saw our cottage. I saw Grandmama and Evie and Rileg. The waves of energy heightened, and a rush of sound raced in that I pushed against. I saw myself weeding in the garden, fingers deep in the rich earth—

"You do not lose these precious things. Look deeper, Lark. Trust yourself. What else do you see?"

"How do you know?" I cried, gasping at this strange force. "How do you know what I see? How do you know me?" And yet I *was* looking deeper: before my eyes my garden expanded, opened, flashing rapidly the changing seasons, my hands in the dirt dug deep and gripped stone, and the stone became the walls of Castle Tarnec—

"Lark," the king called out above the roar in my ears. I clamped my hands over them to shut out the vibrancy of all of it, closed my eyes. "You have lived your life with the Sight as a burden. Too sensitive, you shy from people to avoid absorbing their energies, good or bad, shy away from yourself even, to hide from what might expose your own energy, your own power. And yet now you stand where you belong, believing you should be frightened of Tarnec, bracing against what does not hurt you, confused that you suffer no discord, that here the people do not jar your senses, that *this* is the place where you are in tune."

He paused then, before claiming, "I hear you, Lark. I know you. For it is you we summoned. And you are home."

"Summoned! It was for the Troths!" I cried. "I don't know what to do with this! I don't know what this is!"

"Listen," commanded the king. His aged fingers smoothed over the book he held, then pulled open its front cover, so very, very carefully. He brought it up close to his eyes; Ilone drew one of the standing candles near so he could see. And then he read, with a lilt that was ancient and not his own:

> *Circle of Balance, chosen of White;*
> *Power of hand renders dark into light.*
> *Sun in earth proves her worth,*
> *And rises the Lark, set free by Sight.*

It echoed through the silent hall.

"These words are the beginning," the king finished. "But it is enough. We have found you." He added softly, "You have the mark of Balance, and the Sight, and the white horse chose you." He closed the book gently, pressing on the cover as if to seal it for good. "We have been waiting for you, Guardian."

There was absolute silence in the room. Every eye watched me, watched for some reaction.

I turned and ran.

# 10

GHARAIN WAS THERE. I never even saw him move. He was simply there, his hand closing on my arm to stop me, with all its power and warmth and glorious energy shooting straight through my body, grounding me to the spot.

"Stay," he said. "Stay."

Fierce regret, terrible need. They warred in Gharain's expression before he looked away, refusing my gaze. The doors, with a creak of hinge and clanging of iron latch, were opening for me. I could go if I wanted. I drew a great breath. Relief? Surrender? I wasn't certain.

Gharain released my arm; I'd stopped tugging. I turned around, taking those few steps back to the others, not even sure why—except, maybe, to please the young man who'd done nothing but hate me from the start. And maybe to apologize; I certainly couldn't help them.

But the king was not upset. He smiled at me. "You run when you have no need, Lark. Do not fear your own power. These energies are your guide—the Sight is your understanding."

I straightened. "You called me Guardian. You say I am proved, that those words claim me as the one you summon, who will help you, as if that"—I pointed at the book—"holds your answer. And yet you ask me to trust myself. So believe this: I trust myself enough to know I cannot be what or who you look for. I am no Guardian." It was a noble enough denial.

Still, he ignored it. "We know it to be so. What was written is our clue, you might say, a clue shared with us so that we could find you. And you are proved, through your mark."

"And I say that my mark is not special, and that is a book from which you have read but a single verse. What is the rest? May I see?"

The king's hands quivered slightly, splayed as they were on the book, but he shook his head. "It is unnecessary, for you already see," he said.

The seer had said something like that in my dream; I felt my cheeks grow hot at the echoed refusal. How reasonable the king was with this outrageous claim of guardianship! But then, truthfully, I could not reject it outright. I said, a little hoarsely, "I cannot change my mark, but at least tell me how you came by this . . . *clue*?"

"Call it payment, perhaps." The king's eyes left mine, only briefly, flickering to the young man standing so rigidly at my side. I turned.

Gharain said abruptly, "May I go?" It was hardly a request.

There must have been some slight nod from the king, for Gharain turned on his heel and strode from the room. He would have broken through the doors if the guards had not still held them open. It's what I had wanted to do. He told me to stay and yet he'd left.

I looked to the king. He was watching Gharain's departure, his face a mixture of something like sadness and patience.

"He needs time," he said to all without apology. Then, with a completely different tone, he called for some refreshment to be brought and smiled again.

"Lark, I may not show you the book, but I will show you something else that explains your purpose among us. Come close."

I did so, kneeling once more at the feet of this aged king. The remaining company turned to better hear him. They must have known their history, but seemed to wish to hear it once more.

And yet I was wrong. It was not words they waited for. The king shifted, tipping the book a little so the gold filigree caught the candlelight. He reached for my right hand, taking my index finger to guide it along the thin circle etched in the book's cover. Three times he had me trace it, then placed my finger in the center of my left palm and had me retrace the circle three more times. The king cupped my upturned palm, lifted it so all could see. I gasped. A spark of light jumped in its center and steadied, a little glowing flame that held no heat.

The king said to me, "Life, Death, Dark, Light. What are they to you?"

Maybe it was a challenge. I felt suddenly like Min, when she stood before the Gathering wondering what meaning to put to our faces. I knew enough about life and death from Grandmama's and Evie's healings; I knew enough from my own daily chores in the gardens. Still . . . I looked at him, looked again at the little flame of light, and answered carefully, "Life and Death are a cycle for Nature's creatures. And Dark and Light are a cycle as well—the way night follows day follows night. 'Tis like a cycle within a cycle. It is the working of Nature."

"It is what *sustains* Nature." The king took the flame in my palm between his thumb and forefinger and drew with it a circle. It stood vertical in my hand, a glowing loop. "The cycle of Life and Death," he said. Then he pulled the flame horizontally, threading another circle, saying, "The cycle of Dark and Light." It hovered in my palm for a moment, this outline of a sphere, then the king cupped both hands around mine.

"Life, Death, Dark, and Light," he said, "are the four primal forces. They are what bind Nature to the Earth. Linked as they are, these forces create essential cycles in Nature, cycles that must be equally balanced so that Nature—all of the Earth— may thrive. Balance, you see, is the root of what supports our existence." He looked down then and smiled at me.

"We of Tarnec are the Keepers of Balance. Ages ago amulets were placed in our care for this purpose—four amulets signifying the primal forces: a shell for Death, a stone to represent Dark, a blade of gold for Light. . . ." He paused. "And this."

The king released my hand, and there in my palm danced a whole sphere—crystal, with blue, gold, and green threads weaving through it. It was an apparition only, but I felt from it a tiny pulse, a tug of energy. I grinned up at him. It was beautiful.

"The orb," he said. "The amulet of Life."

"These—the primal forces are in your care?" I asked.

He smiled again. "*Balance* is in our care. We cannot hold Life, Death, Dark, or Light any more than you can lift a mountain or gather the sea. But we hold these amulets safe in our possession, deep within our castle walls, so that the four forces remain equally charged, and equally neutral." There his smile faded, and he said gravely, "It is the Keepers' birthright and eternal duty to protect this Balance. Because, my dear, if Balance is ruptured, then the cycles are broken, distorted. In other words: devastation."

The king closed my fingers over my palm, and the sphere was snuffed. I was stunned at how empty my hand now felt. "But an *entire* kingdom," I blurted, disappointed, "pledged to the safekeeping of an orb, a shell, a stone, and a blade? Why, then, do you look to me?"

There was a shifting of weight in some of the Riders. I saw the king's eyes unconsciously flick to the empty chair beside him.

"We are not infallible, young Lark. Size may well belie power." His voice saddened. "A simple-seeming arrangement, true, but understand this: while we protect, there are those who seek to destroy—who wish to manipulate Balance and bring full destruction to our world."

The Troths.

The king said softly, "No, my dear, Troths are merely foot soldiers of a greater power."

I stared in shock, looked away to the others. Wine had been brought after the king's request, was being served. The Rider with the tawny eyes and molten bronze hair passed my cup to me; the king accepted his from Dartegn. Neither of us drank. "What can be greater than the Troths' ferocity?" I finally asked.

"Ferocity is not the truest threat; the threat is the intent behind the ferocity," the king murmured. "A *choice* of malice—that is the greater power." And then with a resigned sigh, as if loosing a tremendous weight into the Great Hall, he said, "That, my dear, defines the Breeders."

"What—what are the Breeders?" Even the name thrust a dark chill into the room.

"Our nemesis, Lark, our greatest threat. Chaos is the opposing force of Balance, and the Breeders of Chaos work to spread such force just as the Keepers of Balance seek to hold against it. As it is our task to preserve, theirs is to destroy: take what we have, rend the Balance, and watch us die or distort into something unrecognizable. A cunning, malevolent power they are, akin to us in form, opposed to us in purpose. Beyond the Myr Mountains—beyond what is known—lies the Waste, realm of the Breeders. It is doom and madness; it is what they intend for our world—to consume us with. They match us in strength; they never rest in their effort to foment Chaos within and around us. We are locked in endless struggle. . . ."

The words trailed away and the king's eyes drifted from my

face. At length, he took a sip from his goblet for fortification, and I saw for what seemed the first time how extremely fragile he was, watching his thin hand trembling with its weight.

The king recognized his feebleness. He sat up straighter and cleared his throat. "While Tarnec holds the amulets, the world is safe. But Tarnec was breached and the amulets stolen, Lark, ripped most cruelly from us by a single Breeder. Now we all stand to suffer, unless they can be brought back. They *must* be brought back."

My own goblet was trembling; I set it down. "And I am a part of this?"

"More than any Keeper." The king looked down at me again with his sad smile. "Lark, do you understand why the Troths attack Merith?"

I could answer this. "Because we are near Dark Wood, because we have no weapons and are far from—"

"That is not the reason."

"And, we have not yet learned the correct defense. There is something about color—"

"That is neither the reason. The Troths attack Merith because they are *told* to attack Merith, Lark. They look for you."

"No." I stood quickly. "No."

"Lark."

"*No.*" It was petulant; I was like Min again, I knew, like a child. "*Please.* I accepted my summons—that I was bound to venture forth for help. But you cannot also place in my hands the burden of the Troths' cruelty! Please do not do so!"

"Lark." It was a command. I had to stop, to sit once more.

I waited furiously for him to speak, my breath making impatient little snorts while the king took time choosing his words.

"We are entrusted with Balance, and yet we are but *Keepers*, Lark. While we can protect Tarnec, protect what houses the amulets, we cannot protect the amulets themselves. Yet"—he leaned a little closer—"there are four who can. Four descendants of Tarnec, to whom the amulets 'speak'—four who alone may find the amulets should they be lost, who alone may carry them, hold them in their grasp, and who alone can return them to their rightful place in Tarnec."

The king paused a moment before adding solemnly, "They are the Guardians of Tarnec, awakened only when such crisis demands."

Then, with that hint of sadness, he repeated it: "One Guardian connected with one amulet . . . *Only* when crisis demands." He looked over at the empty chairs along the wall. "We have not needed the Guardians in a very long time."

I watched, dreading how his eyes moved from the chairs to me, dreading that he sat up a little taller, a little more commanding. I whispered, "And now you say I am needed."

"Yes, I say it. You might have lived your life peacefully unaware of this calling, but crisis demands. You, young Lark, are one of these four Guardians; you are the first of these four. You are our Guardian of Life."

Guardian. The Guardian of Life. I could only stare as he spoke the words.

"I will not say we knew it would be you, for on purpose we scattered our people, left little trace of lineage and of destiny, trusting that the Guardians will rise when needed." His eyes crinkled a bit. "You wonder why we did not keep everyone here, that Tarnec is strong. But even Balance must be balanced, for concentrating power in one place only weakens the whole. So, through village, through town, Keepers were spread as allies to Tarnec, as were those in whose line is destined a Guardian."

"My mother was a Guardian? My grandmother?" How could it be—how could I not know this?

He shook his head. "The line that I speak of is the extraordinary connection that links a Guardian to her amulet, her primal force. You know this, Lark, you've felt this connection all your life. The Earth speaks to you; creatures speak to you. But, no, it is not a direct bloodline, for then it would be too easy for the Breeders to track you."

"And they cannot track the bloodline of the Guardians, so instead kill indiscriminately," I whispered. How many villagers had Merith alone lost?

His gaze did not falter. "Our task, Lark, is to protect the amulets. To this end, of our people and creatures we may ask for sacrifice." And then he said harshly, "Understand this, Lark: innocents will be killed. Allies of Tarnec, all living things, are at risk as they offer us help. We know this; we allow this. *Regardless* of the sacrifice," he repeated, "the amulets must be protected, returned, *balanced*, or our world will be destroyed."

We sat for a while in silence. The fires roared, rippling their dancing light across the tapestries, across the stage, making the wine sparkle. I could have been alone, hushed as it was. I wondered at their fortitude, in the face of this horrible news, these men and women standing so simply, so quietly, for so long a time. Perhaps it was a strength of these Riders of Tarnec and their loved ones—a strength of all Keepers of Balance—this acceptance of sacrifice. I did not possess it.

The king was weary, troubled, maybe, as I was. He said, "The Breeders would not unwittingly kill the Guardians, Lark, for they need them as we do. Instead, they spy, stir up fear. They manipulate, and weaken, and erase the Keepers and their allies as they can, looking to *find* the Guardians and separate them, not obliterate them. They need the amulets destroyed in order to unleash permanent Chaos on the rest of the world. Only the Guardians can do that."

"We can destroy what we are born to protect? Why?"

The king's eyes only flickered, but I found myself looking again at the empty chair beside him. He said it slowly: "We are all at the mercies of our own frailties. Choices are not always made with clear mind and heart."

There was a change then; the king made to rally. "Lark, truths reveal themselves in time. It is enough to know that the Breeders found their opportunity to steal the amulets. With Balance undone, Breeders' powers are no longer in check. They will toy with us now. . . ."

*Toy.* Brahnt had used that same word, as if we were there for Breeders' whimsical pleasure.

"It will begin with small rifts of Nature, or the vicious attacks," he was saying, "as you've already witnessed. Uncontrollable things, things to frighten and instill unease in an innocent population. It will lead to worse—as fear and anxiety grow, so too will anger, and then violence among ourselves. Breeders can plant such seeds and cultivate the madness. But . . . for Chaos to triumph, the amulets must be destroyed. They need the Guardians for that, just as we need the Guardians to bring the amulets home."

He looked at me then. "Lark, you are the first of the Guardians to be sought, for the Life amulet was the first forged, the necessary foundation for the other primal forces. You were awakened for this."

The king paused, then said formally, "Lark, Guardian of Life, will you reclaim your amulet?"

My eyes were wide. "I have no experience in battle."

"No? You fight for Balance every day. It is your chosen daily task to root out the ghisane and its insistent efforts to claim your land."

I flushed, admitting, "I weed the gardens, pick the herbs, and yes, dig up the ghisane. That is my strength."

"The Earth is indeed a strength, but you underestimate yourself," he said. "You are here, are you not? Your courage in the face of uncertainty still brought you to us." A bit of humor crept in as I met his gaze. "Neither, I would add, do you fear challenging a king."

"Am I bound to this?"

There was a slight pause before the king answered very clearly, "No. A Guardian cannot be bound to protect her amulet. To protect or destroy: it is a choice she must be free to make." Then more softly came, "*Always* Balance."

And I looked—hard—at my reluctance.

Ruber Minwl had not expected the Troths' attack, nor that his hand would be my second sign, but he'd stood still and accepted death. Raif, Quin, Evie . . . not one of the villagers in Merith would have pushed me forward could they have given their life in place of mine. And the foxes: what of their sacrifice, or even the Riders who protect with their lives this secret kingdom of Tarnec and its precious burdens? Who was I, then, to wish my burden away, off of me?

Even if I did not believe I was worthy of it, I'd been given this task. What sacrifice would I make? I hung my head under the weight of such choice. "I will seek the Life amulet. I will return it to Tarnec." My voice was low, but at least it was clear.

There was a collective breath—one of relief—from everyone, before the king said, "We Keepers thank you."

I looked up at him. "Do I journey to the Waste?"

He shook his head. "Lark, the Sight is your extraordinary connection to all things belonging to the Earth. Embrace this power; *use* it. The orb will reveal its whereabouts. But remember too that the Breeders want you. They will know you are awakened. They will find you, and they will lure you, using the people and things that mean most to you. They will attempt to trick you into destroying your amulet."

"Then I have to go home. Merith is too vulnerable—" I stopped, counted the days I'd been gone—three. "The Troths attack six days from the morrow."

The king said, "Lark, the Riders will go. There is time. They will help Merith."

"I have to go with them. I *must* return—if even for a short while. I have to know that Merith stays safe, to let my family know that I am safe. . . ." I swallowed. "Or at least to make farewells."

The king was so very tired. His eyes watered slightly; his smile was not as full. But he said as loudly as he could, "You make a choice. I cannot refuse it, young Lark, though once you leave Tarnec, you will be exposed to grave danger. I would you remained here first to better prepare for the great challenge you face. Do you still insist?"

I nodded.

He made a little sigh. "Then take with you this knowledge: three items—three small tokens—I will give you to help you in your task; wait for them. Do not choose your way from impulse or fear, Lark; listen and look for signs of your path. Trust that you *will* know what to do."

The Merith elders had similarly charged me with warnings those few days past. Now it seemed a lifetime ago.

"Ask for help, Lark, for you are not alone." The king paused then to draw breath before calling out to each of the men who stood so calm and strong beside him, "Laurent. Dartegn. Sevrin. Ian. Arnon. Cargh. Marc. Taran. Wilh. Evaen. Brahnt. And, our absent Gharain. Lady Lark, meet your Riders."

I found myself rising as the eleven turned to me to pay homage to their Guardian of Tarnec, and the king repeated, as if he commanded it to be so, "You are not alone."

It was late when I returned to my chamber. Sleep forsaken, I sat by the fire cupping a mug of tea between my hands, glad for its warmth though I was not chilled.

The king's strength had failed after he'd presented the Riders. With something like a sigh, he simply stopped. Wilh, Evaen, and Laurent moved quickly to support him from the hall, Ilone carefully taking the book from his grasp and following them. We'd watched their exit somberly, yet the remaining Riders were not distressed; they seemed to expect this. It bothered me, though, his grave departure. I'd left too many questions unasked and knew that I had not long to learn from this man.

But now I sat with my tea, not thinking on the king, or the book he'd held in his hands, or how the amulets were stolen, or on the empty seat beside the king. I was not thinking on this crystal orb—small enough to cup in my hands—this symbol of Life. And I was not thinking that it needed to be found, needed to be placed back in the embrace of Tarnec, was not thinking even that the beautiful Earth and all people would suffer without the balance of the primal forces, the reclaiming of amulets. I suppose all of those thoughts hovered above, waiting to be introduced for brooding, but that time was not yet.

I was thinking of the burst of light I'd felt inside when Gharain had pressed his mark against mine.

The charge in my body remained, like a flare of light in a dark room. After all the experiences in these past days, this touch was an insignificant moment of time, and yet in its aftermath the light remained. And it still burned.

I set down my tea finally, having to stand—no, to move under this sensation, which propelled me nowhere and everywhere at once. I paced to each corner and back again, but the room was not large enough for this. And maybe I would have gone without prompting, but a sudden waft of air carried in the scent of the bell roses; I turned in my tracks and went out into the garden.

Enchanted, this heightened space of midnight. A hush first—a lull—then the crackling of the hearth fire disappeared, replaced by singing night things. Perfumed air slipped along my arms and neck, and I breathed it in, deeply. Dark overwhelmed the garden; the moon had passed the heights of the castle walls, leaving only gleaming bits of silver between long shadows. The windows behind the cloisters glowed with candles, some of them, but not bright enough to pass more than feebly between the leaves of ivy. I did not mind. This dark was beautiful; the garden was beautiful. I was barefoot, the grass wet with dew . . . and I ran. The energy buoyed me up, let me dance and leap and gulp in the lovely fragrances of night. I wished Rileg had been there to leap with me, the way we did at the burning of ghisane.

I collapsed at length to the ground, palms deep into the grass, laughing with exuberance. *Awakened*—I whispered it into the dark, rolled onto my back, hugging my arms close like I'd spilled some secret. I smelled the bell roses so sweet, felt the wetness of the dew seep into my skirts, and tasted the dark, almost, on my tongue.

And then I heard the splash from the pool—the sound made when an object is plunged in water. I rolled over with a gasp, watched the body rise behind the pool's edge, tall and dripping, gleaming in the night air.

Gharain pushed his hair back from his face with both hands, watching me.

I spoke, barely. "You? How are you here?"

He still watched me—I think it was the longest amount of time that his eyes had ever lingered. Finally he answered, "Usually I am the one to make use of the garden at night."

It was simple clarification or outright hostility. Yet a tiny glimmer of humor laced his voice, and why not? I'd looked the fool leaping about the garden. I started to rise from my clumsy sprawl, but that made me taller than he standing naked and waist deep in the sunken pool, so I abruptly sat on my heels. I was glad that the darkness covered the fire in my cheeks.

"All that happened," I said, a bit in defense, a bit in truth. "It's racing through my bones. I needed to release it somehow."

I waited, hoping for a response, anything that might show understanding or at least recognition of this feeling, but there was none; his eyes went elsewhere. I finished awkwardly, "Anyway, 'tis beautiful here."

Gharain wiped his brow with a careless strength of hand. "You are staying, then."

Stay. He'd already asked that of me. Or, not asked; he'd simply told me to do so, the way he told me now—as something already determined. I almost liked that I could refuse. "No. I return to Merith—"

"Merith!" I'd surprised him. Then, flatly, "It is not safe."

"Nowhere is safe," I said, likewise abrupt. That left us silent.

130

At length and without looking back, Gharain murmured, "How is the king?"

"Not well. Not . . ." I stopped. I was only repeating myself to fill the emptiness in this conversation. Somewhere a night thing rasped its wings in brittle song. I should want to get up; the dew had soaked cold through my gown. I shook my head. "I expect you already know."

He stiffened immediately. "Why do you say so?"

"Because you were there. Even if you were gone when he faltered, you must know he is ill."

"He *is* ill. He has little time left." There was a deeper silence, and a slight release to Gharain's shoulders—only slight. "I call him Grandfather. But he is greater, far older than my father's father."

Old indeed. "I saw," I said carefully, "the eyes. Are you alone related to him?"

"Ilone is my sister."

*Sister.* How silly to be relieved by that answer. I'd already assumed she was paired with Dartegn, and what did it matter anyway? This Rider could barely look at me. I nodded to no one—Gharain's focus was entirely on the boxwood at the far corner.

He moved a little then, his fingers brushing through the water. The ripple shuddered in sound, like musical notes piling together, and the little circle on my shoulder blade tingled. It had never done that before. The flame inside of me flared very bright.

And so I said on impulse, "What is our connection, Gharain? What happened when you touched my mark?"

It was direct, terse, and I'd used his name, but I did not anticipate the sudden rage that flashed in his gesture. He turned sharply, gaze piercing through like a blade. "Why ask? You've been awakened, Guardian. Why do you need to know more than that?"

This was all wrong, but I blundered on, "Because I was awakened by you. Why you?"

He was harsh. "As if that should matter more than your purpose, more than what the king has confirmed, or that the queen—"

"The queen!" The empty chair? "Where is she in all of this?"

"The queen is dead."

Such a rigid, final announcement—not a good death, it was clear. The intent of malice, I remembered with a shiver, the Breeders. "I—"

Gharain cut over me again furiously, as if he'd heard my thoughts. "No, it was *not* a good death. It was violent, and brutal, and meant to inflict pain on all who loved her. We *all* loved her—"

"I'm sorry!" I cringed under his vehemence.

"—and yet you ask of our connection, as if that were of importance!" He'd ignored the condolence, his voice still harsh, challenging where I'd placed my interest. "You already know one exists. You saw, you felt, the charge of marks when they touched—that it should *matter* to you!"

I stared at him. "That it matters to me makes you bitter?" And then I could not help my own challenge, my own snipe of bitterness, because I was humiliated that I'd cringed before him again, and that he saw through my need and rejected it so coldly. "You despised that touch."

He bristled. "You know little."

"I know *you*. I've seen your beauty and your rage in my dreams, Gharain. I did not understand that in between there is simply hostility."

"Dreams! Dreams of what?" His laugh was raw. "You do not understand—"

"Understand?" I was angry now. "Of course I don't understand! All of this came to me unbidden. *You* came to me unbidden!"

Now there was pure silence in the garden. Not even the night things dared sing. We stared at each other—I in defiance, he in shock. Whether it was shock that I'd scolded him or shock that I admitted he'd been in my dreams, I did not know. At first, a flicker of alarm crossed his gaze. And then there came a moment that I felt too intensely—a moment where, though he hadn't moved, I sensed him reach out across the distance, brush my heavy hair back from my temple, and cup my face in his hands.

I felt his breath on my cheek, and I felt my eyes close.

"Don't," Gharain said sharply, painfully, from across the lawn.

I took a shaking breath, forced open my eyes. "What—?"

"Don't do it," he interrupted roughly. "*You* must be strong."

"Strong for what? I don't know what this is!" It was the second time I'd said that, and I said it loudly, but was ignored.

Gharain had already turned his back and pushed through the water up the far steps of the pool. It did not seem to matter to him that he was wearing nothing, or that I made a small, awed gasp at this. He strode a few feet into the dimness, reached for the linen sheet that lay tossed on a stone bench, and threw it around him.

"You will need to learn how to ride," he said fiercely, inconsequential as it was in that moment. "Marc or Evaen can teach you. You will have to keep up."

He was walking now, away into the night, starlight and shadow streaking over him, the bell roses closing their scent around his path.

And, ridiculously, I could not let him go like that. I called out before he disappeared, "I did not yet thank you, Gharain."

That made him stop. He hung midstep; I could see his shoulders clench, and the harshness was shaken from his voice. "Thank me? For what?"

"For saving me. Last night. From the Troth."

He turned slowly, looking at me fully for a moment, though we were now far apart and little could be seen. Then his voice came quiet and clear from across the way. "Save you? I meant to kill you."

And he turned and walked away.

## 11

DESPITE LITTLE SLEEP, no appetite, and three previous falls, I still stood fairly bravely before my horse.

Marc was cupping his hands, bowing over—waiting for me to place my foot in his palms again and somehow throw myself onto Rune.

"It's easy, little Lark." He was laughing now; I'd been delighting him all morning with my ignorance of horses. "Step in; grab his mane for balance. There, now . . ."

I stood on tiptoe once more to catch Rune's mane and put my weight into Marc's hands. There was the sway and release of ground, and then finally I was high, scrabbling my legs over the horse's side and sprawling full length on the broad back. Rune stood solidly in place with only a twitch of his tail as I worked my way up to a sitting position, spitting my hair from my mouth.

"There you are, Lark," Marc called up. "Does it not feel better to be there than two-footed on the ground?"

"I—I'm not sure. I like the ground well enough."

Marc laughed at me again. He had an easy way with laughter, a gentle way of teasing me into challenge. I remembered him well from the night before—he with the unkempt brown hair, standing at one end of the grouped Riders close to his pretty, soft-eyed wife. He'd smiled at me then, a little welcome grin when he—like everyone—returned my bow. For all the seriousness of what must be a Rider's life of risk and danger, Marc seemed to let such slide off his shoulders, finding humor in the details. I'm certain, though, that teaching me to ride a horse would have been a laugh for anyone.

I yelped as Rune gave a little shake of his head, grabbing fistfuls of his mane. "I'm not steady! What do I hold? How do I stop him?"

"Find your seat, little Lark. Let him walk you a bit; you will discover how fluid it can be." He made a little clicking noise and Rune started forward.

I swear I shrieked again. It is one thing to be awed by the beauty of a creature that one has only dreamed of; it is another to claim it, to climb on its back and to share its power.

"Trust, Lark. Trust." Marc called this to me as Rune walked away along the edge of the clearing. Castle Tarnec hung out enormous over its cliff in the near distance, meadows and gardens and orchards spread around me, the forests beyond. It was beautiful—magnificent, like Rune.

"He's waiting for you to give in!" Marc shouted across the lawn.

I heard him, but resisted, staying intent on my whirl of thoughts, cramming in all the things Marc had taught me since early this morning, all the things I'd tried to pay attention to. They flickered through my mind—the stalls of beautiful horses; the fresh, sharp smell of hay; the intricately woven leather reins and the rich gleam of dark saddles. I'd already forgotten how to strap them on, but Marc had said no matter, for what was important was the trust forged between rider and horse; accessories were merely accessories (or for maneuvering in battle, I interpreted). He explained that not all horses take a rider, but once a horse had chosen, there was no reason to break in the animal. "They wait," he'd said, "until they know. No need to force a steed's will to anyone else—such would destroy a most powerful bond with these treasures."

Treasure—an apt image for Tarnec's ruthless protection of its hills, I'd noted. Marc replied that Tarnec closely guarded its territory against Breeders, of course, and to stay free of any outside influence so that Balance would remain undisturbed. And, he'd added, looking at me for the first time with a serious expression, they could not let the extraordinary horses be discovered, pilfered, or used for ugly purpose.

"Imagine the dwellers of Tyre finding the source of horses. Desire to own them would lead to avarice, and as well to jealousy. They would be harnessed, collected, corralled; the creatures would not be able to choose their riders, and the bond would be destroyed, diluted to a meaningless relationship of owner and chattel."

"You determine rather harshly that people are greedy," I'd said to him.

He'd laughed. "You are from Merith! Tyre is an unpleasant city of desperate and needy sorts, long a stronghold of the Breeders. I do not assume that greed controls us, but I do understand that the Breeders feed on people's desires—and they work to brew the things in each of us that can lead us to ruin."

I wondered if the Breeders would feed on my desires.

"Lark!" Marc was shouting loudly now, shaking me from my stupor. "Let go of your thoughts! Feel your horse; move with your horse."

I took a breath and focused back on the present. Rune had walked me nearly in a full circle and I'd not noticed, other than gripping wildly with hands and legs. Taking another breath, I released the handfuls of mane that I was pulling at and wiped my palms on my buckskin leggings—another gift from Nayla's store of clothing—surprised, then, that I did not fall. I patted Rune tentatively. He blustered and shook his head, inviting me to place my hands there, on the length of his neck. I slid them down slowly, and felt the warmth and strength and solidity of this horse—

And I did not fall.

His energy shot through me, strong and breathtaking. A memory flashed—of leaning my head against his shoulder that first night—and I felt suddenly safe. Reaching down, I wrapped both arms around his neck as I'd done the first time, laid my cheek against his soft mane, and breathed. Rune began to move.

How we went, how fast we ran, I would never know the details. I think I heard Marc say, "Yes, Lark!" but then again that could have been my own voice, for I too was feeling *Yes!* My legs unclenched and simply held against the wide back. At some point, I lifted my head and unwound my arms so that I could hold his mane, gently this time, merely as connection, and so that I could see. But I did not need to see, for now I trusted he would see for me.

We passed once more by the grinning face of Marc, standing singly in that green field, and I shouted to him, "It's glorious!" Then we were gone, streaming beneath limbs of trees, taking a stone wall in unbroken stride, and I laughed, swept away with the speed and thrill of motion. We left the clearing, the orchards, and climbed into the forest. Oaks and chestnuts swept over us, but we pushed higher, ascending the hill like a ladder into the pungent-needled pines. Up we climbed. I did not know, nor care, which way Rune chose; I let the power of momentum charge through me, and abandoned thought for pure exhilaration. Farther and farther up, Rune began to snort his breath in powerful bursts, pulling hard until at last we came to level ground.

He stopped then, ears flicking, and I sat back, glad for the pause, but not before throwing my arms around his neck.

"Thank you!" I was breathless with delight. I released him, flinging my arms wide, breathing deep, exhilarated and *alive.* Rocks, trees, creatures . . . "I feel you!" I shouted to what surrounded me. And then I yelled it as loud as I could: "Guardian of Life!" and laughed. Even alone on this hilltop I blushed to voice what I'd accepted so quietly in my life: the energy of everything humming through my body. But there it was, done, aloud and owned, and maybe that was what being proved meant. And for the moment there was no burden, no dark quest, but only the brilliance of this sharing. "I am awakened!" I yelled, and leaned to hug Rune again.

Rune stood alert and poised, the way Rileg would at the scent of a badger, his neck strained and still with my hands resting there. He shifted once, I remember, changing his balance as if to charge forward. There was a call of a bird too—one sharp, alien caw that stood out from the muffled sounds of the forest. I sat up tall, alert now as well. I was not afraid, yet something was here, it seemed, and Rune was waiting.

"Rune—"

He turned suddenly, moving north some lengths, and stepped out onto a ledge laid bare to the sun. And then I gasped, seeing why we'd come this way, why he was cautious. The Myr Mountains exploded into view, imposing on all the senses. Ash-gray crags were etched in hard detail; I could see the brush of snow whitewashing the peaks, feel its cold breath on my face, taste, even, the icy sweetness. It seemed almost that I could reach out my hand and touch the slabs of stone that jutted from the earth, so heavy and so huge. My fingers tingled and the mountains pushed at me.

Tombs of rock. Desolate. Crushing. They swelled dark despite the daylight, and I heard nothing now but a small whistle of wind. For a long while I sat motionless, listening to that hollow sound whisk over stone and bury itself in the trees.

And then, from somewhere in that weight of cold stone, I sensed a pulse, a little throb of light. The same small heartlike pulse I'd felt from the image of the orb glowing in my palm last night. Energy. Life. I knew what it was.

"That," I whispered to Rune, "is where I have to go."

At my voice, the horse turned his head, catching my gaze with his solemn eye. I looked back out, sighing, I suppose, wondering if the sky was indeed less blue at this height, or if the gray cast a pall over all. The Myr Mountains. I watched them, watched how the sun seemed to slam into the solid facets and lose strength, watched how everything was absorbed into this bleak surface, unreadable and forbidding. And as I stared long, the lifeless stone began to burn its gray into me. The wind whipped bits of the snow off the peaks and spiraled it wildly; the shadows lengthened and sharpened the blade edges of the mountains. There was an eerie whirring from far off. *Far off*, I repeated aloud slowly, feeling the hair on the back of my neck prick. Beyond those crags lay the doom of the Waste.

I dragged a breath in and out, and the Earth seemed to respond, answer my sigh with one of its own. There seemed some tremendous weight pulling me, toward and into the ground, drawing away my strength. And the sigh resolved into a whispering borne on the wind:

*There you are. There you are. There you are. . . .*

Rune reared, turned, and with one leap plunged back into the pine. The sharp scent of eucalyptus exploded in my nose and dissolved the trance. I put my head down once more on Rune's neck and closed my eyes. He raced, back through the trees, back toward the clearing. It was quickly over. He would take me home.

*Home.* I shook awake, regathered my thoughts, disturbed by what I'd felt, at that strange whorl that seemed to drain energy from my body. I wondered at that. There had been no pain either. There had been nothing.

I rubbed my cheek a little into Rune's sweating hide. The eucalyptus and pine were fading now, the rich smells of decaying leaves replacing them. We would soon be home—

I shook myself again at that word; how could it be so soon that such a sense had seeped into my bones?

Still, I was glad to see Castle Tarnec reappear in the distance. Marc was not in the clearing where I'd left him, but Rune knew that. We flew across the lawn, slowing only as we reached the main path to the stables. And there was Marc, leaning against a stone pillar of the stable entrance, speaking to one of the stable hands, a water flask in his hand. His surprise was not for our return, but I think what might have been my expression—that, and Rune's sweating, panting sides. He took one look at me and threw the flask to the ground. In two strides he'd met the horse and, reaching up, let me fall right into his arms.

"Lark," he said, not gently. "Lark, look at me."

I looked up, disoriented, since only a moment before I'd been looking down. Mark helped stand me on my own feet, keeping a hand on my arm, asking, "What happened?" I sensed the energy from his hand; he was ready to spring to his own horse.

"The—" But I stopped. Clearly Marc had not felt what I had; he was only concerned at my behavior. "Nothing," I said then, in all honesty. Perhaps it was enough.

Perhaps it was. There *was* nothing wrong. Marc looked over at Rune as if to judge my answer true. The stable boy had claimed the horse, was giving his wet sides a swipe of sleeve before nudging him toward the stable. Rune's ears twitched away a fly.

Marc relaxed. He shook my arm, looking back at me, changing the mood. "And here I thought you'd come back exhilarated, putting a blush into your pretty cheeks. You left shouting with the most beautiful joy." He smiled at me, cajoling my humor to return.

I pushed away the strangeness. "I am; I was. I don't know. It was exhilarating, Marc, it was—I was . . . I was riding! Marc, I was riding! It was magic—!"

"She went up through the forest?"

Gharain was striding out of the stables, his hand fisted around a length of bridle and rein that dragged in the dirt, glaring at the two of us. His face showed white beneath the bronze of his skin. "She should not have been up there alone." Gharain looked accusingly at his friend. "You know that."

But Marc was not perturbed. "Reprimand her horse." He shrugged with a nod at Rune's retreating backside. "Lark was within the castle boundaries. In my opinion, she was well guarded."

"Marc, it is dangerous for her to be alone!"

"Easy, man." Marc's calm voice held the subtlest note of

warning. "All is well. Rune brought Lark safely back. You have no need to race after her."

I looked at the reins in Gharain's hand, almost at the same time he did. He didn't seem to remember he still held them.

"All the same," Gharain said stiffly, embarrassed now, "it would be well if she were accompanied always—by a Rider. With weapon at hand."

"Understood," replied Marc softly, though Gharain had turned and was already striding back the way he'd come.

Absurdly, I ran after him.

"Gharain!" I called to his rigid back. He walked very quickly and his legs were long. "Gharain!"

I followed him through the stable and into the separate room where he'd stopped to rehang his tack. "You are back," he stated flatly at my quick footsteps. "Nothing more needs to be said."

"That was unjust," I panted. "It was not Marc's fault that I left the grounds."

"It is not safe. He knows better, even if . . ."

He did not finish, so I offered it for him. "You mean to say, 'Even if he didn't feel what happened.' You felt it too, didn't you? That pull of Earth—you felt it when the others did not."

Gharain stared at me, brief as it was, then looked away to busy himself with straightening the reins.

"Gharain!"

"I heard you."

"Have you nothing to say?"

And he turned. "What would you like me to say? That, yes, I felt that pull? That it compelled me to come find you? Are you sorry that I was hard with Marc? Would you have preferred my anger to be with you?"

I flushed, but squared my shoulders. "If you must be harsh, then, yes, be harsh with me."

"Very well. *Never* leave the near grounds without accompaniment. Is that understood?"

Not even Grandmama had been so fierce with me. He barely raised his voice, but his tone was like iron. I looked down, feeling like some naughty child under this young man's remonstrance. My cheeks were hot.

"Lark."

His voice had softened, but I didn't raise my eyes, for I thought I might rage at him, and hostility would only lead to more hostility.

"Lark." Gharain gripped my arm. His touch shot through my body, at once warm and powerful; he shook me, briefly, to force my gaze to his, and we looked at one another, guarded. Suddenly, and not gently, his hand slid from my elbow to grip my wrist. He turned my palm up, studying the underside of my wrist, holding it exposed and vulnerable for a moment, simply looking. My hand was shaking in his grasp, and there was warmth to his sun-bronzed cheek. I felt, suddenly, the terrible agony I'd first sensed in him pierce sharply through me. And yet, there was something more: hope or need or promise; I couldn't quite tell, for his emotions ran like quicksilver, and the charge that I felt at his touch overwhelmed it all anyway. Gharain turned my palm over, and his hand slid once more to catch mine, but his touch had changed—no longer a grip but a caress. He bent over our clasped fingers the way a nobleman might pay homage to a lady, lingering, but then he released my hand quickly, as if he could no longer bear to feel what I felt, whatever it was that traveled between us.

"If—" He muttered what else under his breath, to himself or to me I didn't know, but then his voice was earnest. "Lark, they can make you feel things, and then they can find you. Claim you."

They. The Breeders. "Rune knew what to do—"

"You've barely learned to ride. Rune is powerful, but what if you couldn't stay on his back?" He paused and made a bitter noise. "Or do you imagine he'd protect you as well if you were standing—the way he protected you from me?"

It was enough. "I don't know why I came after you," I whispered, still shaking from the touch. "I suppose to ask you to apologize to Marc. But if you need to stay angry, then I will apologize instead. I am sorry I left the park."

He nodded; if he meant to say anything, it was too late. I'd turned and gone back out of the stable.

Marc chuckled at me, at my red cheeks, and the way I stalked out of the wide doors. "Thank you for defending me, brave little Lark."

"You do not take him seriously?" I asked, a little astonished. I'd been severely chastised; the same brushed off of Marc.

Marc shrugged. "I take him seriously, just not his ranting. He's young, his passions dominate, but Gharain is also one of the most giving and loyal souls I know. He's only being protective of you."

I swallowed wrong and choked into a small coughing fit. "He's been nothing but furious since I met him," I managed to gasp out. I looked at Marc shaking his head. "Protective or not, he hates me," I muttered. That was silly, I knew, but it was spoken before I realized.

Marc looked down at me, his head shaking still. "No. He's in anguish—anguish over our queen."

The poor queen again. "That she died," I acknowledged with a more solemn nod.

He corrected. "That his error caused her death."

I froze in surprise, waited for the reason. But Marc looked back at me and gently shook his head. He would not tell tales on another Rider.

Slowly I closed my gaping mouth, closed over the questions that piled up, that I wished answered. If Marc knew my desire, he ignored it and laughed at me, a hand going to tousle the top of my head. "Come, there must be a meal for us inside. I'll guard your way back into the castle. Gharain will thank me for that."

And he took my arm while curiosity burned its little path inside me. Burned, until I remembered that I had a maidservant who might be willing enough to share knowledge.

❧

"A Viewing?"

"Of the queen's last moments," Nayla said to the old woman who sat grinding joma seeds in a mortar. "Of Gharain's place in it. I told Mistress Lark 'twas no story for young maids. But she asked."

More truthfully, I'd begged. Three times. Nayla provided the barest of information, busying herself with my dinner, my snarled hair, the buttons of my nightdress, anything she could to avoid discussion. I'd learned only a perfunctory "One moon ago we lost her," and a sighing "What lovely light shone in her smile . . . !" But I persisted until Nayla took my hand and marched me down long steps, past the kitchens to the fragrant herbary, and presented me to this ancient herbswoman, Trethe. A *Viewing,* she requested.

Trethe pursed her lips, her mouth nearly disappearing into the surrounding wrinkles. "We would need something to connect."

"I remember," Nayla said promptly. "Happenstance, I brushed this from the sleeve of Mistress Lark's tunic." It was a strand of chestnut-brown hair she held. Gharain's. "This should do very well for such purpose."

"What is a Viewing?" I asked, looking around. Something, obviously, that required this room full of drying plants hanging from the rafters, jars of salts and spices and seeds lined on the shelves, and trays of stones and glittering pebbles. It smelled of licorice and savory.

Trethe put the mortar to one side of the table she sat at and wiped her hands on her apron. "A Viewing creates a picture of a past event." She studied me for a moment. "I am glad to see your ankle healed so well, my lady. My own recipe, those tinctures. Now, then, you wish a Viewing." She sighed. "That you desire to know requires it be shown. 'Twill bring you no pleasure, but I suppose 'tis better to see for yourself than have the evil recounted as gossip."

Trethe gestured me to sit by her. There was plenty of room on the bench to share; her body was rail-thin, skin wrinkled around her bones like a withered plum. She smelled of the room, of the fire burning nearby. She lifted a milk-white shallow stone bowl from her table and gave it to me to hold, adjusting my grip with cool, strong fingers. "The elements will open truth in a Guardian's hands. We will blend the four, beginning with Earth." Trethe touched the bowl. "Stone for Earth. Hold it firmly, please, mistress. Good. Now to Earth I will add the element of Water." She took up a flask and poured enough water into the bowl to cover the bottom, then switched flask for a jar at the end of the table—a small one, filled with tiny clear beads. She tipped several into her palm and added them to the bowl, explaining, "These gases represent Air. They will stir Water and allow the element of Fire to ignite."

Already the beads were bursting in the water, throwing up little sprays of color, like tiny rainbows dancing. "Keep it steady, Mistress Lark," Nayla whispered, her weathered blue eyes sparkling with the light.

Trethe shuffled away to collect things and returned to show me her tiny handful. "Dried minion flower, and simple rock salt . . . and Master Gharain's hair. Vegetable, mineral, and animal—the properties of Earth." She rubbed them between her palms and sprinkled the mix over the fizzing water. "A hair of yours, Mistress Lark."

Nayla tugged a strand and gave it to Trethe, who added it to the mixture. "Like so. Now for Fire." Taking up her flint, Trethe struck a spark against the bowl and red flame shot up, then died back to a short lick of color glowing in its center. It began to smoke—creating a whitish cloud over the circumference.

Nayla whispered, "Watch the smoke." It was unnecessary; my eyes were fixed hard on the bowl.

"To look on this now," Trethe murmured, "we see how even within these solid walls of Castle Tarnec we too can be made vulnerable. All that is needed sometimes is to sow a little seed—of doubt, of impatience." She paused. "Of desire . . ."

Within the cloud appeared images, wavering into clarity. Gharain was there, saddling his horse with haste and galloping out of the Tarnec stables. There was energy in his posture, an expression of happy anticipation so unlike the hard-jawed responses I'd drawn from him.

"A message came for Gharain, originating with a trader from the sea," said Trethe. "Our merchants carried the words home to him: *'She waits on the ledge,'* the trader had told them. *'Tell Gharain she waits on the ledge.'*" Trethe made a faint sigh. "Poor Gharain is of that age: restless, his yearning to love acute, just *aching* in his heart."

Images resolved again. Time had passed, for Gharain was there, dustier, disheveled, dismounting to stare in awe, at which the three of us squinted to gain better view. An apparition was before him, standing on a wedge of rock, someone in a hooded cape of dusky, swirling colors. Gharain was stepping nearer, and so too were we. The hood fell back, revealing the stunning lady with the brilliant smile, lush dark hair.

"The lady of my dream," I whispered.

"Erema," Nayla whispered back. "No lady, that thing! A *Breeder*. She read his desire, *used* his want as the way to gain passage into Tarnec."

It fell quiet at that, as we watched Gharain sink to his knees before this beauty. Her hand was outstretched; a mark of something was on its soft underneath. I shuddered, understanding then why Gharain had grabbed my wrist to study. I saw his eyes close and his head fall back. And then the images began tumbling one upon the other: Gharain reaching for the dark lady, a caress at which I had to look away. She, sitting before him on his horse, racing back to the castle, which shimmered into view—there, the courtyard, the entranceway, Gharain shouting something to all who gathered. . . . I felt Nayla's flush as she reminded me, "We welcome all who reach the castle."

The smoke revealed a grand feast in the hall, where I'd met the king—a table longer than I imagined possible laden with bountiful trays of exquisite foods. Gharain was standing, lifting his goblet, toasting the lovely Erema opposite him. And there at the head sat the king and queen. The queen was indeed full of lovely light as Nayla had said, and the king was not frail as when I met him, but strong and lively within his aged frame. He looked at his queen with utter devotion.

I sensed the room shift; Nayla and Trethe braced themselves.

The queen was taking her goblet in response to Gharain, lifting it to her lips with a somewhat sad smile, swallowing her wine—and then the goblet was falling, falling as the queen fell and a great cry roared out. Gharain's own wine spilled to the table, his face contorted. The guests rose in terrible unison, surging toward the queen, while Gharain stood frozen, staring in horror at his evil guest, and Erema smiled. The smile, once so exquisite, turned hideous and gaping, and then Erema took a step back out of the candlelight and simply melted from view.

Trethe blew out the flame.

Nayla spoke first. "Now you have seen it: the queen poisoned at the hands of an impostor who presumed to be our guest, who preyed on the heart and hopes of poor Gharain."

I was confused. "But the queen was smiling, as if she knew. As if she understood what she was about to do."

"If the queen understood the deception, then she chose to accept it," answered Trethe. "You shake your head, Lady Lark, but sacrifices come in all ways."

"Perhaps it was the only way to expose the evil," Nayla agreed. "A Breeder's lure is strong. Woe to Tarnec if Gharain had remained under her spell. A worse outcome could have been."

I did not see it. But Nayla insisted, "A worse outcome. Look, now you are here, young and beautiful and capable. And you have claimed Gharain's attention—"

"Mayhap Tarnec had become too complacent. Mayhap it was time and the queen knew it," Trethe interrupted flatly. She brushed her hands clean. "Destiny advances darkly, sometimes."

"It advances," Nayla echoed, "whichever the reason. And

while the castle was in uproar, our attention diverted, Erema stole away with the amulets."

"But if no one can hold the amulets except the Guardians, how—?"

"Breeders can ensnare them," answered Trethe, "if they use something made of hukon."

"Hukon!" Evie had said it about the severed hand. "It brands—it is the mark of the Troth."

"It is the mark of *them*," Nayla whispered. "They use it for dark deeds. Poison, webs—"

"The Breeders' greatest weapon," interrupted Trethe. "The black willow."

We all stopped—no talk nor movement. There was a little tingling across my chest; I should not have asked for this, opened this wound. At length, Trethe took the bowl from my hands, breaking the silence gently. "Do not be frightened. The Breeder has long gone."

But I was not shivering at the story; I was thinking of Gharain. To have found me on the ledge after he'd found Erema . . . "What he must have felt at such betrayal," I murmured.

"The betrayal is done. It is rather what he feels now," said Trethe solemnly.

"*Revenge*," mouthed Nayla.

Trethe halted her. "Best not to mention such a word." She turned to me and said shortly, "Guilty is what he feels—guilty and alone in his agony." She began arranging things on her table. She was weary of this dark talk.

"Gharain is not alone," Nayla said quietly as she walked me back to my room. "But he blames himself too deeply. He wants to make right his error."

Revenge. I knew she thought it. We were silent down the long halls. It was my doing, this shadow that had come over us. "It's a wonder that you could welcome me at all," I murmured at last.

And a wonder that Gharain had not killed me outright.

I sat by the window, watching the darkness, waiting. Around me the castle settled for the night, but my own sleep was elusive. I waited to hear Gharain's path to the pool and the small splashes that proved his nightly swim.

Unfulfilled need makes a painful companion—an unwelcome follower, waiting for the moment it is allowed in, allowed to pierce through and fester inside, until such yearning becomes rage, and then—

And then Chaos.

I sighed and laid my head on my folded arms. The bell roses were achingly sweet this night, so scented as to be sugar on the tongue, and the splash of water accompanied with crystal notes. Sense of smell, and sound, and taste were stirred . . . and sight? I had seen Gharain rise from the water, naked, and gleaming wet. His touch—

*You must be strong,* Gharain had said. This could not be; I could not bear this ache so deep.

I forced myself off the chair, forced myself to the bed. Yet it was too deliciously soft. I dragged a pillow and one of the comforters from their nest and threw them down by the fireplace, curling there to wait for sleep, which of course would not come. I was wary of all my feelings now, intent as they were on usurping any sane thoughts. This was how the Breeders worked. Desire, impatience, doubt . . . little seeds sown to bring down a castle, bring down a Guardian. They throbbed inside, pulling every which way as I forced myself to lie like a stone on the hearth, forced myself to stare at the red embers of the fire, noting how they could not ever remain the same. Each breath of the fire changed it; each glowing pulse subtracted something from its place. Giving and taking—a breath of air, a wisp of smoke, a flake of wood; heat into chill. Nothing was ever the same, and yet nothing could change.

Nothing.

## 12

YET—

Something was happening. It was the air, so dry and dead-smelling. It brought me awake with sudden force.

I lay blinking into the darkness, not remembering that I'd fallen asleep, trying to take a breath in this deadness. Heavy-headed, I looked to the fireplace, knowing already that the embers were suffocated. There was no light from the fire; there was no light anywhere.

The little whirring in my ears started, that strange sound from the hill yesterday. The weight, the drag into earth, was repeating too. I could not breathe—there was nothing to breathe—and the hair on the back of my neck pricked like needles. Panting, I forced back the comforter; worked to my knees against invisible hands that pushed me down, then to my feet, but swayed there, a lodestone riveted to its place. Finally I leaned into the mantel, sweat breaking on my forehead, unable to propel myself somewhere, anywhere.

I heard the horses then, a hideous sounding from the stables. They neighed as one voice, one body, raising alarm in a swelling force of sound. Dogs too were barking somewhere. They sensed what I did, this fearful drag of energy, this suffocation, this utter darkness; the animals and I were frightened and calling the warning to all.

No, I was not calling. I'd opened my mouth to yell, scream, shriek, but my voice fell away, evaporating before it could sound, the dead air sucking life from each breath. The cold of the mantel stone was seeping into my palms, taking away warmth and strength; I was fast losing the will to move. I turned my head, tried to pull it once more from the mantel, but then I simply stared, suspended in an endless moment. The dark overwhelmed and began to absorb, to drink the room slowly in. The chair, the bed, and I was next—

"Lark!" Gharain's voice came from the garden door, harshly urgent above the shriek of animals. "Lark! Are you there?"

"Gharain!" Immobile, no air, the word died a whisper. I screamed his name again and again until I was hoarse. Each time his name was swallowed by the dark.

"Lark?"

He would not hear me. He would pass by the door—

But suddenly his presence filled the room. I heard him swear at the shock of force that hit him. Then, gloriously, he shouted out of the doorway, "I have her!" and pushed into the room. In two strides he had his hands around my arms, then my waist. Breath burst into the space, like the gasp of lungs, and Gharain was pulling me from the mantel and propelling me outside, where the dark faded under a night sky rich with stars. He stopped us in the cloister, holding me close, listening, senses alert, while I gulped in the newly sweet air.

"What was that? What was that?" I panted, still clutching his sleeves. The animals had ceased their alarm, and my voice was suddenly loud.

"They took it. The air," he muttered against my hair. "They play to frighten us."

They. *Breeders.* Small rifts of Nature to frighten, the king had said. A cold flick of terror sliced down my spine. "They're here?" I whispered. The only warmth was Gharain.

He was shaking his head, his gaze somewhere else, searching out the night. "They can't be here—they don't need to be here. They have the amulets."

"That was but *play*? Tarnec suffocates? Gharain, I swear the dark would have swallowed me!" I tugged his sleeve, pulling his focus back.

"You saw their emptiness." Gharain turned and looked down at me. He was so very close, his arms a strong brace. "They mean to frighten, but they cannot destroy Tarnec unless the amulets are destroyed. Look about you. There is no damage. Fires and candles can be relit."

"You say that as if there was something worse."

There was. Gharain said it in a low murmur: "As a Guardian senses, so can the Breeders sense a Guardian. You sense things more keenly, hear things, see things, feel things more deeply than others. That sensitivity helps the Breeders to track a Guardian." He brushed a strand of hair back from my face. "They've found you."

Never mind sensitivity, I'd shouted my name to the world on the hilltop. And the Breeders had whispered back, *There you are. . . .* I looked up at him: his slice of jaw etched against the midnight blue of the sky, and how the air still seemed to shimmer in upheaval around it. "I brought them here. From my ride yesterday."

"I told you it was not safe." Gharain seemed to suddenly remember he should assist the others. He released his embrace, pulling me over to the cloister wall. "Stay there," he ordered, and disappeared into the garden. I could hear him speaking a moment later to others across the lawn—Brahnt, I think, and Laurent. The words were unclear, but the tone was urgent and I imagined the meaning well enough: I was found and now everyone was at risk. The king had said the Breeders would use the people and things I cared about.

I pulled my knees up to my chest and hugged them close, holding in the awful thought. Around me the rooms glowed again with candlelight. I smelled a fire rekindled on a hearth—

As if concern inspired some terrible prophecy, flames suddenly leaped across my gaze, harsh in bright sun. There were screams and pounding feet across a cobbled square. I was cold, even as the flames burned around me. They danced and shifted, then parted to show me a well in the center of the square. I knew that well; I knew it, though its familiar stones were blackened by smoke. Merith—

The vision was extinguished abruptly as Gharain squeezed my shoulder signaling his return. I looked up at him, stunned at the sudden evaporation of those wild flames. His beautiful eyes were dark.

"Are you all right? You were—" He released my shoulder to gesture, and I gasped as a second vision flooded in.

Damp cold and terrible pain seeped through my bones. It was blacker than night; there was but a single light far ahead. I crawled toward it in slow agony until at last I saw that the glow was a sphere, luminous and isolated, suspended in some swirling dark cloth. Closer still, and the sphere revealed tiny gold, blue, and green threads spiraling along its surface. The Life amulet, the crystal orb. My hand lifted to take it. Suddenly, a pitch-black streak broke its light in half, and then another and another dark streak slashed at its surface, crossing and recrossing in that hourglass brand of the Troths, the Breeders, ensnaring it in a web of darkness. And it was dimming, losing strength, and my body hurt so and I could not breathe—

"Lark!" Gharain's hands once more were gripping my arms, holding me upright as I slid from the cloister ledge. My eyes opened and I looked up at him stupidly.

"Where were you?" he exclaimed, half shaking me. "You called it by name! The orb!"

"You stopped them." I dragged in a ragged breath. "How did you stop them?"

"Stop what?" He was impatient.

"You! You affected the visions!" I cried, sick from the Sight. Gharain's eyes widened and their sage color flared light. He

160

stared at me for a moment, then at his hands, which encircled my arms.

"I affect *you*," he said very softly. And he let me go.

I slumped against the stone ledge. Gharain's hands dropped to his sides, though his fists stayed clenched. He said, very carefully, "You said you saw the orb. You said they are trying to destroy it."

I dragged in a breath. "Streaks of black slashed across it; it dimmed—"

"Hukon," he interrupted.

I nodded, which only made me dizzy.

"Where was it? Where was the orb?" Gharain was brusque, unable to contain his eagerness at this supposed clue.

I shrugged, disoriented and irritable from the swell of nausea. "How am I supposed to—?"

"What did you see?"

"I don't know! It was black, and cold. A cloth. The light was dimming—"

"What else?" He was desperate. "Lark, think! What else did—?"

"I did not see her!" I put my hand out to brace against a pillar. "If that's what you want to know, I did not see Erema." The ivy was spiraling around me. "I feel sick."

Hard-jawed, Gharain took my arm again, hustled me out of the cloister right to the pool. "Sit down," he said without ceremony, and I did, heavily, on the stone rim. He took the cloth that he'd used as my blindfold, dipped it in the water, picked up my hand, turned it over, and pressed the wet thing against the inside of my wrist at my pulse. "Hold it here for a moment, and then do the same to the other hand." He turned and stalked over to one of the borders and returned, crumbling fistfuls of plucked bell roses.

"Breathe this," he said, opening his hands right beneath my nose.

"Let me help, Gharain." Ilone, walking with Dartegn, appeared from out of the dark. If I'd paid attention, I would have realized that the cloisters were bustling with activity. There were people everywhere.

Gharain deposited the flowers in her palms and stepped away, murmuring something about my vision. Ilone's pretty face filled my gaze, and she said kindly, "Close your eyes, Lark." I did, and her hands came to my temples, like Grandmama's. And just as with Grandmama, the sickness seeped out from my head and into her rose-filled hands. In a moment, she'd released my head and brushed her hands free of the tainted things.

I looked up, grateful. "You are a Healer," I whispered. It should not have surprised me as it did. "Thank you." I felt better, though the whirring noise was still there, a tiny humming boring through my temple like a pinprick. It must have been what Ilone was reacting to, for her hand moved inadvertently to cover her ear before she forced it down and placed it on my head.

Gently, she smoothed my hair back and asked Gharain, "They know she is here?"

Gharain nodded, and Dartegn, in his deep voice, said, "There is not much time."

"Then we go." Gharain looked down at me. "Not you, Lark. The Riders."

Ilone gave me a little smile. Her eyes were sweet, but there was tension in her face, as if she were holding against some pain. Dartegn touched her shoulder, saying to both of them, "We'll ride south from the western route. Maybe we can draw their attention." He turned as someone shouted his name and strode away.

I looked at his disappearing figure. The Riders were leaving. "You are going to Merith after. I know it. I am coming with you."

"You will not," Gharain said immediately. "It is not safe."

How irritating these oft-repeated words! But Ilone broke in before I could respond, saying tightly, "He is right, Lark. Better you stay here. The Breeders are attuned—" She took a sharp breath.

I looked quickly at her and then at Gharain. He was watching his sister, standing tensely ready, like a coiled spring. "The king said he could not refuse my request," I countered.

Gharain did not take his eyes from Ilone. "But I can. It is safer to stay in Tarnec."

I stood up, angered by Gharain's refusal and that terrible, insistent whirring. "Nay, I was promised!"

Ilone murmured, "Think with a clear mind, Lark."

I whirled to her, anxious, nearly shouting over the noise.

"If I stay, Merith is sure to be attacked! The Breeders will harm those I love to draw me out! Let me be out, then! Let them come for *me!*" I spun to Gharain. "Please!"

"Lark—"

Turning back to Ilone, I begged, *"Please."* But Ilone had forgotten me. Her hands were over her ears, her face ashen, staggering as the buzzing became a roaring shriek of sound. I looked up.

Hundreds of darting black shapes were streaking toward us—shapes that others recognized. There was a collective gasp of shock.

"Get down!" Gharain shouted.

I was on the ground before I realized that Gharain had grabbed my arm, and his sister's, and thrown us both to the earth. The shapes dived toward us, coming but a breath away from collision. These were not birds, I saw, as they swooped close, but something horrible. Twice the size of a heron, grizzled black-feathered things, with the beak of an eagle and the eyes of something human. The buzzing noise was piercing in intensity—a cacophony of low-pitched shrills that swarmed through my head. My hands could not block it out. I turned my head to Gharain and Ilone—Ilone was in terrible pain.

I screamed, "What are they?"

Gharain looked over from where he was shielding his sister. "Swifts!" he cried. "Stay close to the earth, for they cannot touch it!"

The bombardment was over, momentarily. They had

skimmed the ground and were sweeping back up toward the sky. Gharain seized the opportunity.

"Now! Run!" And he dragged Ilone up and half carried her through the cloister and into a room, with me right behind him.

All of those in the garden had run for the castle. We crammed into the first room we found and spilled into the hallway. The buzzing of the swifts increased in strength as they turned and dove once more for the earth. The stones rang with their noise. There was a sudden explosion—a swift had brushed the wall and burst into flame.

Gharain shouted over the sound as he clasped Ilone's contorted body, "They explode at the first touch with anything earthbound. We are safe inside. But they are persistent; they will pin us to a spot where other enemies can attack, and if we run, we can be badly burned or killed."

"Gharain!" It was Dartegn, pushing through the others. Gharain gave Ilone over to him, and Dartegn pulled her toward the fireplace, sinking to the hearth to hold her close.

"Healers have little resistance to the swifts," Gharain said to me, though I had not asked.

"Will she be all right?"

"The noise does something terrible to their minds—the longer it lasts, then—" He snapped at another crash of sound and light: "The creatures are relentless!"

I looked about the crowded room—faces determined to remain calm despite the piercing shrilling, the sudden explosions, the smell of the swifts' burned flesh. But there too was Ilone convulsed and white in Dartegn's arms, his own face drawn and hard. This was what Tarnec would face should I stay. Merith, Ruber Minwl, the foxes, Ilone—everywhere I went something suffered in order to protect me, to help me on my way. *Regardless of the sacrifice ...*

So the king had said.

Without a word, I turned and pushed my way out of the room and ran down the corridor. The swifts had pulled up, preparing for another dive. There was a momentary lull in which I ran to my room and threw off my nightdress, then tugged on the leggings and tunic that were folded neatly by the bed.

"Lark!" Gharain had entered the room a moment after me. He turned away abruptly as I finished pulling on my shirt.

"I'm going," I said quickly, and ran to the door. But he stepped in front of it.

"You're reacting impulsively to the swifts. That is what they want."

"Not *they*—I'm doing what *I* need to do."

I feinted to the right, but he stood firm. "You will not go!" he ordered. "This is the safest place for you."

"But not for anyone else! I hurt people by being here!"

And we both flinched as the third wave of attack swooped over the castle. A swift exploded at my window, and far away I heard Ilone scream out in pain.

And since Gharain had blocked the door, I turned and ran the other way, to the garden.

"Lark, don't!"

But I was gone, ducking under the final sweep of creatures as they arced up in preparation for another assault. I had but moments. I tore through the garden and into another entry, down a hall, down many halls, until I found what I was looking for: a door to the outside.

It was a sprint to the stables. I hit the ground once before I reached them, covering my head with my hands. The swifts were so close, the wind from their wings ruffled my hair. How many times could they do this? How many times before this would destroy Ilone?

Then they were gone, flinging skyward once more. I picked myself up and ran the last stretch to the stables, tearing open the heavy doors.

The animals were restless, snorting—the straw, the stall doors, crunching and slamming as they shifted. No lanterns had been relit in the stable, so I felt my way down the length of the corridor between stalls, counting, smelling, sensing.

And there was Rune. He snuffled into my outstretched hand, glad, it seemed, that I'd arrived.

"Come," I said to him. "Quickly."

There was no sense in looking for a saddle; I'd not learned to ride with one. I simply led him to the stable doors and waited for the shrieking swifts to rise. Then, out of the stable, taking care to shut the doors tightly once more, drawing Rune toward the stone gates. I climbed on one of those to mount him.

Had it been only this morning that I'd first sat upon my horse? He felt like a part of my body.

"Run to it, Rune! The forest!"

It seemed he already knew. We were off, racing toward the shelter of the trees. I held my breath and dropped lower on his neck. The swifts had reached their peak and were plunging toward the earth.

"Run!" I urged.

The black wings were pointed back, streaming toward us like arrows. Surely they would destroy themselves in order to burn us. Surely they could not stop.

The trees were ahead; the blackness thickened.

*Run, Rune, run.*

One would hit us. I heard the whistle of air through its feathers. And before I could stop myself, I looked up at the thing diving straight at me—the fierce beak and those human eyes, so light against the dark of its body. My gasp would not have the chance to reach my lips.

And then, just above me, the swift burst into flame, casting the earth in appalling light, sparks of falling wing singeing my cheek and Rune's flank.

*How—?* In the ghastly flare, I could see Gharain flying toward us on his horse. He'd hit the swift with a stone.

Gharain. He'd only make me turn around, and that was something I'd not do. I faced forward and shouted to Rune, "Go!"

And in three strides we were in the forest.

# 13

RUNE SLOWED HIS gait as the forest gathered black around us. I hugged the horse, dragging in breaths to steady myself, shuddering a little to hear the screams of the swifts—so thwarted and angry, for they could not reach me in here.

Gharain would be likewise thwarted and angry. "Never mind, Rune," I whispered, as if those had been his thoughts.

Slowly I sat up and looked into the pitch-dark space between the soaring oaks and chestnuts. I'd drawn the enemy from Tarnec. Now where? I was torn between the impulses to race to Merith, or head straight north to reclaim the crystal orb for Tarnec. Love for Merith made me yearn to return, to do something—anything—to help my village. But what if I brought the swifts to them? And besides, the task I'd promised lay in the opposite direction.

Gritting teeth, I nudged Rune with my knees, saying, "We go the way you took me yesterday. To the Myr Mountains."

Rune pushed forward into the thick of the woods. Strange to be once again in a forest at night—but such a difference to be with so sturdy a companion. We moved with a slow but steady pace, working through the trees. I had to close my eyes to sense and avoid the nearness of boughs and scraping branches. It made me lose track of our route—we'd not headed up the steep slopes as we'd done yesterday. Instead, we were moving across the vertical rise—southwest, I thought. The moon was no help to my sense of direction—she'd not yet risen.

"The mountains, Rune," I instructed again with the tacit assumption he understood my words, surprised that he'd not taken yesterday's path. But then, this darkness was a challenge for any creature.

The buzzing was no more, I realized suddenly. The swifts had quit their attack. I sighed, glad for what I hoped was not temporary respite, thinking of Ilone, if her pain had eased. I could not help but think as well, embarking on this solitary journey, of Dartegn's arms tightly about her in so protective an embrace. One's love, there for comfort, for aid . . .

I'd lost track again of our direction. "Rune!" I said severely. He'd paid no mind and was continuing southward on his sideways route. I tugged his mane now, trying to steer him differently. "We must go north! The Myr Mountains, Rune, to the Myr Mountains!"

"He will not take you there."

I shrieked at the voice, whipped my head around to stare

into the dark. How had Gharain come up behind us without my sensing it? He was but an arm's length away, and I could barely make him out.

He said, "You would simply leave Tarnec? Run?"

It was a question, not a reprimand, yet my back stiffened in defense. "I brought the swifts to Tarnec. . . ." But then it seemed more important to contradict him: "I am *not* running."

"My pardon, you have a plan: *The mountains, Rune.*" I could hear him grin. "The range is rather vast. Did you have a specific peak in mind? Did you think Rune would simply take you blindly into Troth territory? To the Breeders?"

"I thought," I said fiercely, "that he would take me to the amulet!"

Gharain sat back a little on his steed, relieved, I supposed, to have found me. His breath, like a short sigh, eased out of his chest. I felt its heat.

He asked, "So the orb is in the Myr Mountains? This was what you saw?"

"This is what I *know*. And now that I am no longer reacting impulsively to the swifts, as you so brashly accused, may I go?"

He paused for a moment, and then said, "Still, Rune will not take you there. You are not ready."

"Ready! When have I been ready for *any* of this?"

"What of the king? What of his appeal that you prepare for your quest? What of the tokens he warned you to wait for?"

"What of Ilone?" I challenged. Gharain fell silent at that, but I stayed fierce. "I *will* find the amulet and I'll return it, somehow, but I *won't* be responsible for anyone else's pain!"

"You look at it wrongly," Gharain retorted. "We mean to keep you safe so that you might save us *all*. We are charged to help you; we do it freely."

"No!" I thought again of the sacrifice of the foxes and felt my throat close up. In another moment I would be near tears, and I'd shed too many of those in front of Gharain already.

"Lark," Gharain said softly.

"Just let me go. . . . Let me do this *alone*."

There was a sound he made that was almost laughter, but laced with something too dark. "I pushed my destiny before its time and did much damage. Do not repeat my mistake."

"I promise I will not repeat *your* mistake. Go on," I ordered Rune.

Rune made no move. I prodded him with my knees, my heels, tugged his mane, but he stood firm while I looked the fool for thinking I had any dominance over the beautiful creature.

Finally I said gruffly, "What do you suggest?"

That I'd been harsh held no lasting effect, for Gharain answered readily enough. "Come with me. We'll meet up with the other Riders tomorrow evening in Bren Clearing." That grin was in his voice again. "You wanted to go to Merith, no? I concede. Now is your chance."

Bren Clearing. Should I laugh? If I thought about it, this would be the time the Merith elders had imagined I would meet the Riders there. It was strange how fate turned on itself. I sighed. It was only a tiny surrender, but I immediately sensed Gharain's smile widen in the dark.

I was severe. "Do *not* think I choose your way. I follow my horse." I hoped Gharain was right and that Rune would follow him, though I'd hardly admit how much I preferred the prospect of Merith to the imposing mountains.

Gharain's smile stayed, but his voice was more hushed. "I wonder at you, Lark," he said. "Your manner was first so quiet, submissive even. Yet in these short days . . ."

"What have you seen of me?" I was afraid he knew my deeper feelings.

He shook his head. "Treat your passions with care. They can be your downfall."

And then I knew Gharain spoke of himself. But he was right. He was so right.

We traveled side by side through the night. Neither horse led the way. They simply walked together, stepping assuredly in the dark, first through the oak forest, back across the castle grounds, and ultimately in single file down the narrow trail that led away from Tarnec. Gharain paused once, to show me where to hold Rune for the steep descent. "Give him a little more lead," he called, and then slid from his own horse to show me, his hand taking mine and shifting my grasp. Our fingers entwined briefly in the silk of Rune's mane. "You blush," he murmured before he turned away. I think he was smiling.

It was blessedly quiet. The swifts were gone. Gharain said they would not attack again this night, even exposed as we were in the open valley. And so the stars were left to litter our way with light, a touch of mica sparkling in the gray cliff faces. We climbed back up to the other side of that great chasm, to the edge of eucalyptus and pine, where the moon passed overhead and was lost behind the trees. Only then did Gharain suggest we rest.

"There's a small pool of water just beyond those boulders," he said. And there was. A slab of rock behind the tumble was hollowed enough to hold the remains of a long-ago rain. The horses drank their fill, and I gulped handfuls of the clear water and washed the ride from my hands and face, glad for this stone bath, of being outdoors again.

I returned to find Gharain spreading a blanket, his mood likewise lightened. A water flask and sachet of hardbread were in his pack nearby—things he'd brought while I'd given no thought to food or protection. He was right: impulse had pulled me and I was unprepared.

"Our packs are always at the ready," Gharain said, taking in my look. "I stayed but a moment after you to saddle my horse." Then he added almost insignificantly, "And we are never without our swords." He laid his to the side of the blanket.

*Except when you swim,* I thought, at the sudden memory of Gharain gleaming wet in the garden pool. Then I told myself I was ridiculous and focused on the sharp gleam of his blade.

Gharain sat down, brushing his hair from his forehead, and pulled his pack over. "Sit," he suggested, looking up after a moment with a shrug to the sword. "I have no intention of using it." Seeing my eyes still wide and fixed on the weapon, he said with that hint of humor, " 'Twas only a jest." And then, more softly, "Lark, I will do you no harm."

It was not the sword that made me uncomfortable. I kneeled carefully, at the edge of the blanket, and hoped the dark masked my returning blush.

"Hungry?" he asked.

I was. I reached for the hardbread Gharain held out like a peace offering. But he did not release his end, and so we paused at this tiny challenge, his eyes fixed to mine, waiting.

Gharain spoke first. "This is not jest, Lark: I behaved harshly. It is not how I wished it."

"Wished?" He would feel my fingers trembling. "What did you wish?"

"That we did not begin as we did."

He said it low, soft and earnestly, and my cheeks flamed. I made a false laugh, which came out as a hiccup. "You meant to kill me, but you did not. We can be glad enough for that—"

"That's not all of it, Lark." Gharain hesitated, and then, "Do you forgive?"

A flutter, a thrill, a skipped heartbeat—things I could not help. I'm sure he knew, for he tugged a little on the bread, knowing he'd won, willing me to smile. "We are friends, then."

Friends. It was a silly sting of disappointment, but I did smile. "Well, for this night anyway; I do not know your humor for the morrow."

"Jest or truth?" he asked me with a brow raised. But he let the bread go and turned to his own fare, stretching long on the blanket to chew and study the sky. His body relaxed, eased into the earth he'd made his bed.

He'd not said a word of the touch that sparked my

awakening. He'd said nothing of the connection he'd so bitterly acknowledged that night in the garden. He was not awkward and blushing, so it seemed necessary to ignore it as he did. I busied myself with my portion—nutty and sweet, and richly filling after the long ride. But it was soon finished, and I was still acutely self-conscious.

"Great nourishment before battle, this," Gharain was saying. "It travels well." There was a long silence while I kneeled on my corner of the blanket and he lay stretched, an arm pillowing his head. I heard my own heart beating. Gharain's horse made a little clinking noise with his bridle.

Gharain looked over at me. "It is safer that we stay together." After another moment he added, "It is also easier to sleep lying down. You might try."

I nodded, shifting to lie on my back as he did. Side by side, a hand's width of separation. I took a breath, willing myself calm, and wondered if this pretense of ease would suffice an entire night.

Gharain chuckled. "You'll find no rest tangled as you are." He reached to draw my hair out from where it had bunched at my shoulders. His fingers brushed the side of my neck, an accidental touch, and we both flinched. I caught Gharain's look.

"You blush easily," he murmured.

"Perhaps," I whispered back, half-truthful, "I am not used to your friendship."

"Friendship?" he asked, as if he'd not chosen the word.

Gharain pulled away, but left his arm stretched out above my head, and we let the silence fall heavy around us. He forced his attention to Tarnec, I could tell, while I watched the stars, savoring his nearness, his warmth like some heady drink.

"Ilone," I said, sensing his thoughts, and asked, "Your sister will be all right, won't she?"

"She is strong." Gharain sighed. "I suppose I must thank you for drawing the swifts away when you did, foolish as it was."

I smiled a bit at that, then shuddered. "That terrible whine—"

"You heard them, then? From far away?" Gharain was quiet for a time after I nodded. "We cannot. But something beyond hearing—some vibration of the creatures' pitch, maybe, or how their wings beat the air—can drive a Healer mad. The closer they are, the longer it lasts. . . ."

"I wish I'd understood. I didn't know what it was. I thought the mountains hummed or . . . I don't know." I rubbed a hand over my face. "I was stupid. I could have warned Ilone, warned all of you. I learn by mistake."

I thought he'd agree, but Gharain turned on his side suddenly to face me, curious, eager. "Do you see it differently as a Guardian, this Nature around us? How is it that you can see people's histories, or know that an attack by Breeders is nigh? What is this Sight?"

I stared, taken aback by the barrage of questions. "I—I'm not sure if it is different as a Guardian. But . . . if you ask me what *I* know, then I will say that it isn't only having visions, or reading people's energies. The Sight means *seeing*, through all my senses. It—it means I see, as in I am aware."

"Then, Lark, what do *you* see?"

Gharain was truly curious, asking what others had simply allowed. His gaze held mine, strong enough that I could not look away. I hesitated—how could I describe what was so personal, so intangible? Finally I said softly, "You ask about the things I consider the dark parts of the Sight. Yes, I can read a person, especially upon first meeting, and it is frightening because emotions are wildly unpredictable and stories sometimes brutal. I know little of violence, but when something powerful is imminent, an ugly sensation invades my surroundings, pricks at my hair, or runs through my body. . . ." I stopped. "There are dreams and visions too, which are warnings." I thought of the visions of Merith under attack and the Life amulet being suffocated by hukon—things that were yet to be.

Gharain's gaze was boring into me. "You suffer all this?"

Maybe it was the pleasure of sharing this night with him that made *suffer* seem too harsh a word, for once. "It is not all dark, Gharain. There is another part of the Sight that is . . . wondrous." I turned to look up into the starlight. "To see this dance of stars across the sky, to feel the stone beneath us vibrate with its tiny hum, and taste night on the air. To hear the trees breathe and the sky shimmer with each exhale, to smell the Earth growing, changing. It's all I've known, this awareness. Earth fills me—all the things that surround us pulse with life, and they . . . they pour into me like music." I was quiet for a moment. "The king said that the amulets speak to their Guardians, but I think they sing. Life sings to me."

I'd said more than I ever had about the Sight, more than I should have. I waited for a response. Gharain faced me, watched me, but said nothing while the night surrounded and hung poised on a collective breath of anticipation. I felt a stirring in my chest, and in his, as if a flame burned bright between us. And then it was necessary to change the subject, for the silence was too great and his gaze too deep. "And the Riders?" I asked in return to break the spell. "What do they sense?"

"Danger," he answered simply after a moment, and rolled onto his back. "We are keen to the imbalance of things."

I couldn't help it; I grinned, remembering. "When I first heard of the Riders, I thought you to be very old."

Gharain snorted. "Very old would hardly do. We are the strongest of Keepers, and the best horsemen. Many volunteer, but only twelve are selected."

"And you are Riders forever?"

He laughed first: "Until we are very old." Then sobered: "Or . . ." There was a brief, grim silence. Then he said proudly, "We protect Tarnec. It is a sacrifice we gladly make."

*Sacrifice.* That cursed word again. Maybe Gharain sensed my unease, for he added, "Not to worry. We're a tough lot."

"I wonder why you chose so dangerous a path when you are in line to be king."

He said very firmly, ending the subject: "I am not the right one to lead."

We were quiet then. Gharain would have fallen asleep. I was tired too, though I watched for a time the stars wheeling high above, listened to Gharain's steady breathing, and thought about his beautiful smile. I wished it were enough, this closeness in sleep.

Just before I drifted off, I heard him say very softly, "Lark?"

I closed my eyes. And dreamed.

Daylight was filling the window of my attic room in our cottage. The sheets were tucked into my bed tightly enough so that I had to struggle to push them back. I rose in slow motion, feet hardly touching the floor, and fought my way through aching lethargy to the window, looking out at green grass and brilliant sun. A lark shot up from the earth like a spray of bronzed water and swept across the sky above the field. I smiled and looked down then, to the little stone path that led from our cottage through the cutting gardens. Evie was there, attended by Gharain. They walked along the path away from the house, their backs to me. So close they were to one another—I'd never even seen her stand so close to Raif—their arms brushed from time to time as they moved. I remember how the sunlight caught her fair hair as she paused and turned to him. She was speaking; he was listening. I heard no sound, but even from my distance I understood the look on his face, and how she leaned slightly toward him. Gharain's expression turned from earnest to joyful as he took in her words, his thrill visible in his posture. And then he reached out and pulled her into his arms. Evie's arms went around him; she looked up, smiling so beautifully, and he bent his face to hers—

I dropped to the floor of my chamber.

It was before dawn, the first fingers of light attempting to pierce the veil of dark. I lay hovering half in, half out of my body, aware of myself as one of two figures on the blanket. I was rolled into Gharain's chest with his arm draped over my waist. We'd lain like that for a long time, it seemed—with his breath close enough to ruffle my hair, his warmth deeply comforting. The silence was softened by the faint hum of the earth; the rock we lay upon cradled us. And if I looked up, his mouth would be near enough to touch mine—

I shut my eyes against the need. Cruel taunt! Even in this brief moment between sleep and wakefulness, I could not pretend I didn't know what my dream meant: that touch was not mine to have. *Choose for me, Lark,* she'd said. *Choose the one I will love. You have the Sight. . . . You will know.* And I'd promised her I would.

I'd promised.

Brutal, honest Sight. It had made its choice—or not even a choice, simply an answer. *You will know.* Her words came back to me, and bitter tears smarted suddenly behind my eyelids. Unfair—this hateful awareness that I'd only just described to Gharain as *wondrous.* Wondrous! I wanted to spit the word now. This dream, this new, unhappy knowledge, burned at me from inside. Unfair: Life Guardian, bearer of the Sight— kinship with all of Earth and her creatures but the one I wanted most. I lay completely still for a time, wishing I could undo my sleep, my dream, my life.

But it was done. I could not change what I'd seen. Worse,

I could not change that I'd promised. I meant to be happy for Evie; I wanted to be happy for her. Instead, I buried my face in Gharain's shoulder one last time and breathed in his delicious scent, swallowing the terrible pang of envy that I could not help but feel for my cousin, my closest friend.

*I'm sorry, Evie,* I was whispering. *I'm sorry. . . .*

And Gharain said, "Who is Evie?"

His question startled me; I didn't know I'd spoken aloud. I pulled away and sat up abruptly so that his arm fell back. "Evie is my sister—my cousin, really. You will meet her when we reach Merith." I said that fiercely, brushing away sleep. "I was dreaming," I added for protection, and looked down at him. His eyes watched mine; he'd made no move to draw from his place, too close, still, to me.

"So was I," he said. And then he said a little more softly, "I've seen many emotions haunt your face, but not this one. You look sad."

We watched each other, and I was unable to tell if he knew what I'd dreamed, or maybe even shared it. Then Gharain's eyes flicked away.

Unfair. Unfair.

But Gharain spoke first. "We should go."

## 14

IT WAS A long day returning to Bren Clearing. The hills of Tarnec marched a downward course in an endless display of rock edges, soaring pine, and eucalyptus. The horses' hooves mashed the bed of pine needles in a dulled progression of steps. I wondered how Gharain knew his horse was going true. It appeared the same—the straight, tall trunks, the sharply mingled smells, and the brown carpet.

The monotony did not matter. We were making progress; we'd catch up with the Riders and be on our way to Merith. And . . . I was with Gharain. Guiltily, that was all I thought of. I watched him with both need and resistance so acute that Rune felt the tension in my body and every so often would shake his head as if to stir me awake and have me focus on descent.

That I was not alone in this tension did not help—it hummed between us, and I sensed Gharain's gaze forced away more than once. I wrestled with my conscience, shamed myself for my desire. *He's meant for Evie; he's meant for Evie,* I repeated over and over in my head. If only I'd not dreamed.

If only I'd not promised.

I was aware as well that Gharain's sword stayed snug in its hilt. "Do you not worry for Troths?" I asked him.

"Not here," he replied, pulling up a little on his reins as his horse stepped over a hillock. "The smells are too potent here for them, and daytime too harsh."

"But you said the hills of Tarnec have been breached."

"They have. With the amulets in their grasp, the Breeders are bold. The Troths are sent—to divert our attention, maybe keep our focus from seeking or," with a nod at me, "protecting the Guardians. Still, this forest is an almost lethal venture for those creatures. They would not stay here long. Most are likely too far away to sense us now."

Troths, worming their way into other territories, compelled to kill at the beckon of Chaos . . . I thought then of the swifts. "Are there many creatures conjured or dominated by the Breeders?" I asked. "More than what I've seen?"

Gharain's expression darkened. He dismounted then, having paused on an outcropping of rock at cliff's edge where some grass grew. As the horses set to graze, I wandered a bit, letting my face drink in the sunshine, and watched the two steeds moving together in a slow motion, the dappled gray and the white.

"What is the name of your horse?" I asked to change the subject.

"Petral." It was muttered inconsequentially. Gharain was busy with something by the edge, so I walked to where he stood.

"What is that?" I asked.

He looked up from his belt, where he was unfastening something. It was the leather braid that he'd used to bind my hands, though neither of us acknowledged it. "Do you see?" He stretched an arm out, pointing down toward something between the craggy rocks.

I squinted. "The small hare there?"

"Yes." Now Gharain was digging a stone from the hard ground. I watched as he wrapped the stone in one end of the braid, in quick, practiced fashion. His elbow was up and he was swinging the braid over his head before I realized what he intended.

"Don't!" I said. My hand shot out and closed over his forearm, a move I immediately regretted. Energy surged through cloth, through skin.

Gharain started at my touch. The braid dropped sharply, and the stone ran off the end of the leather and rolled away on the ground. He looked down at me. "That is a share of the meal tonight when we meet the others." Then, "Lark . . ." His hand was reaching up to cover mine.

I jerked back. "Just—just don't," I said. "Please." I turned away, then rounded back with a grin to cover my reaction. "Guardian of Life, Gharain. You can't think I would eat another."

It was why I'd never chosen to eat meat, I thought absently, tucking in the hand he'd just grasped. Answers for things I'd never questioned. Then I was off, skittering away from him down the steep slope toward the animal, who was far less upset by her close call than I was by that simple touch. She waited as I neared, nose quivering and eyes steady. And when I sat down close by and held out my hand, she made a hop toward me and let me scratch her between her ears. One connection erasing the other.

*I shall never touch him again,* I promised myself.

Gharain made a small sound. I knew he watched, but I was afraid to look up and relieved when he walked away. I was left with the hare, soft and warm beneath my fingers. Her eyes were wide and dark-deep. Darkly deep.

Nature will give up her secrets . . . if you know how to listen.

*Listen for the signs,* the king had said.

"What do you know?" I whispered, only half-serious. "What secrets would you tell?"

And right through my fingertips came the words: *Dark entry to the world . . . the last stand on the windswept face. Go left—stay true.*

My hands flinched around her fur, and the hare jerked back. I let her go.

*Stay true,* the words echoed. *Stay true.* From her mind, from mine, I didn't know.

"Lark?" Gharain was back, watching us from above. "We should leave."

I stood and reached to wipe my hands against my leggings, but not before I breathed in the scent of the animal's fur, sun-drenched and musky. *Thank you,* I mouthed. I turned, and then madly stumbled as the ground shuddered beneath my feet.

"Lark!" came Gharain's shout.

"I'm all right!" But another rumble took my legs from under me, and a terrible cracking sound dropped me crouched and gasping in the dirt.

"Lark! Come, quickly before the ledge breaks! Can you?"

I looked up at Gharain lying flat, hand outstretched, farther away than I wished. I think I nodded. I lurched for the incline, scrabbling my way up the solid face even as it heaved, reaching for fingerholds that pulled away in my hand.

"Lark!" Another rumble of earth, and my own cry, and I slid back as far as I'd come, scraping my belly on the grit that sprinkled down and over the small fissures that seamed the dirt around me. *Small rifts of Nature,* the king had said.

"Breeders?" I yelled up at Gharain. "Is this—?"

"Stay there!" he was shouting. "I'll come to you." Then came a sharp "Watch yourself!"

A large stone barreled downhill; I ducked my head under my arms. It tore past me and I regrouped, slamming my hands into the earth to push myself forward. I could not let Gharain come down; we'd both be trapped under this ledge of loose rock. I yelled, "Wait!" and gathered breath, cursing at these Breeders. Slithering, wriggling up the short length, palms smeared on the stone—

The earth stopped moving abruptly. I slid down once more

in its surprising last gasp of violence, and then all was still. I lay breathing heavily, hearing, oddly, the soft feet of the hare hopping out from a protecting crevice.

"Lark!"

"Here." I could stand. I dusted off my clothes, loosed my tangled braid, and stumbled my way back up the slope. "You tell me not to worry about Troths," I gasped, reaching for Gharain's hand, letting him help drag me up the last length; he pulled me right into him. "Now you'll tell me the Breeders only *play* with the amulets."

Gharain too was breathing hard, but managed calmly enough, "You are all right?" He eased his embrace as I nodded, stepping back a little. Hadn't I vowed not to touch him?

Yet, one of his hands still held mine tightly and he reached the other up, his thumb rubbing a smear of dirt from my cheek—a steady, gentle sweep despite the heat that sparked from his touch. Then he answered me: "This is only play."

Bren Clearing had not changed. Almost. There was the rowan tree in the center, huge and strong. There was the path that I'd run down so wildly happy. After the pine and eucalyptus, the air was sweetly fresh. The snowdrops, though, had died. They lay brown and shriveled, dotting the green grass like tiny sores.

The Troth's presence had done that. And I shuddered for the foxes. I hoped I would not see any violent reminder of their defense, their sacrifice, and thankfully or not, there were no remains.

"Look," said Gharain, pointing, diverting the ugly thoughts.

The other Riders had arrived before us and were setting up camp south of the rowan where they were hidden by the tree.

It was Dartegn who first signaled our approach with a wave. Gharain shouted to him, "What news of my sister?"

"Ilone rests, Gharain. No lasting harm," Dartegn called back. He made a little nodding bow to me.

As we drew up, Arnon and Sevrin walked forward to greet us, similarly tall and sturdy with their shocks of dark hair and brows. "You took your time!" they scolded in jest.

"So you could do the hard work!" returned Gharain.

"Nay, we left it for you!" came their retort, and Gharain laughed.

I looked over at him. There was such pleasure in his face at the news of Ilone and joining with his friends.

Arnon took Rune's mane while I slipped from his back, and Marc came toward us, saying, with a wink at Gharain, "Now we have not one hotspur but two. Surely, Lark, you did not need to prove to us your fleet horsemanship a second time."

I flushed a bit. "I did not intend to be followed," I said, uncertain if he joked.

"Nay, Lark," he said, reaching us. "There's safety within a group." And then something more like a reprimand: "I did not teach you to ride so that you could run away."

"Don't tease her, Marc. She's here now."

"Lucky for you, Gharain, that you sit so well on a horse. I imagine she gave you quite the chase."

"That she did," Gharain replied. He grinned at me, and

with the pleasure of being accepted into this camaraderie, I could not help but grin back.

"Come, little Lark," Marc said, and threw a friendly arm over my shoulder.

We ate as the sun settled between the Cullan foothills and the hills of Tarnec, sitting in a large circle around the fire, where Sevrin had concocted a stew from root vegetables. The dark came up from the east, and then firelight alone was left to color us gold and orange. I looked around our circle. Taran, Evaen, Cargh, Marc, Arnon, Sevrin, Dartegn, Wilh, Laurent, Brahnt, Ian, and Gharain—the twelve Riders, whose strength, horsemanship, and courage heralded them above all Keepers. Odd that I sat so easily with these men, dwarfed as I was by such ability. Most of them were still strange to me, yet I casually shared their meal and talk—I, who rarely left home and dined only with my grandmother and cousin. There were village festivals sometimes that I was obliged to attend, or I'd shared a picnic with Quin, but he usually had to coax me from our fields for that.

Quin. A tremor flicked through me. Was he all right? Involuntarily, my hand touched my chest, thinking of the fern he'd given me, but of course it was not there. It had gotten tossed into my pack long ago and probably lay withered somewhere in the hills of Tarnec. I felt bad for that, that I'd not protected it the way he'd offered it to protect me.

And then I felt something as insubstantial as a shadow brush my cheek, and I looked up to see Gharain watching me from across the bonfire.

"A day and some to Merith." The dark-curled, blue-eyed Laurent was speaking.

"A leisurely pace?" asked Evaen with mild curiosity. I remembered him as the one who, with his wife, Mara, had left the Council to arrange for refreshment.

Laurent made a small nod in my direction. "A necessity, not a waste," he answered.

"The swifts are up," said Brahnt. "They will hunt for us."

"Or not," Sevrin interjected. "They may be sent to where we are, or where we go."

"So the swifts could attack Merith too?"

The men paused at my question. "We cannot anticipate the Breeders' intentions," answered Laurent, who seemed to be the accepted leader of the Riders. I accepted it too, for he had a soothing, deep voice and demeanor of calm strength. "But I would not fear the swifts. The villagers can take shelter. Remember, the swifts cannot touch things of earth."

"But they explode. The damage—"

"There are other things more deadly to hold our concern."

Gharain made a small noise in his throat, but Laurent looked over at him, saying pointedly, "We should not hold back any truth from the lady. It does not help her."

Then Wilh, sitting next to me, added with a wink, "I doubt we could keep much from her anyway. Little Lark seems very capable of having her way."

There was a low chuckle all around the circle.

I ignored the lightheartedness and looked to Laurent. "My cousin is a Healer. A swift could destroy her, then, without touch, and yet you speak of things more deadly than swifts. What more?"

Ian spoke up. "Lark, do not worry on things left to imagination, for that inspires the fear so welcome to the Breeders."

I looked back at Ian—the most handsome of these striking twelve, his face and hair glowing gold in the firelight. "I *saw* flames consuming my village square. That inspires fear just as well."

Ian shook his head and smiled a wickedly endearing smile. "Maybe it should not. Trust what you know, what you *feel*. What do you feel?"

I said, "I feel I want a sword."

Brahnt laughed out loud. So did Marc.

"Merith has no idea how to defend with force," I retorted. "But I will not stand calmly unarmed to face Troths, or anything else that can be sent to destroy my family and neighbors. I want to learn how to use a sword so that I can help when we reach the village."

Ian said, "Lark—"

"No! Please, hear me: Ruber Minwl had no defense. What if he'd had a sword? What if there was but one Troth who attacked him? What if he could have defended himself?"

I told them of the poor tailor; the Riders accepted my disconnected argument, but not the way I imagined. "And if you give Ruber Minwl a sword," asked Evaen, "and another man a sword, and another, where does defense begin and end? When does defense become offense?"

Marc added, "It is something like the horses, Lark. Those

who are armed with weapons should not use them lightly. Too many weapons cheapens power—cheapens life as well."

The fire was dancing little flames of green. "He had to sacrifice himself," I said obstinately. "He died alone. In Dark Wood."

"You saw this?" Laurent asked this over the sputter and hiss of burning wood, and I nodded, thinking how immensely lonely it would be to die far from those I loved, to—

"Lark." Gharain was there across the fire, his eyes a deeper green from those flames. "It is not your fault, Ruber Minwl's death."

"He died alone," I repeated. In this company of friends, it seemed a terrible end.

There was a long pause before Laurent asked, "But was he afraid?"

"Yes!" My voice had risen, and the twelve men looked at me patiently. I quieted. "Well, maybe no. He made a valiant attempt to survive. . . ." The memories of his desperation were filling my thoughts now; my hand shook around the borrowed cup. "Dread," I whispered. "There was terrible dread. But not at the end. At the end he stopped and waited with dignity."

Taran spoke for the first time, a silvery voice to match his gray eyes. "There is no fear in dignity. Fear is a reaction to a threat, when you do not think you know how to respond. Dignity is quite the opposite."

"But he could have fought with dignity as well, could he not?" I argued. "As you all do. A sword would have given him a chance, not a dishonor."

Once again there was the heightened pause—the silence between words and voices that meant more than could be spoken.

"Did you ask Ruber Minwl what he wanted?" Laurent asked.

"No." And beneath this quiet, logical query, I felt suddenly silly.

"Perhaps," said Evaen, "you want Ruber Minwl not to be the victim in a sign meant for you. You do not allow our sacrifice."

Arnon said, "There will be others. It is a part of what we do. But you are a young Guardian. It is difficult to accept this at first."

"I am not too young," I protested. It was true: my birthday and Evie's was fast approaching. "I still want a sword. Then let the Breeders come find *me* with steel in my grasp."

Wilh chuckled and said, "Gharain, this must be your influence. Hardly the considerate creature we captured but three days ago, is she? There could be no harm in letting her pretend it helps."

"I agree," said Marc with a grin.

That deflated my desire somewhat, for in their humor the sword became a little toy. I looked to Gharain, wondering whom he would agree with, but he seemed wrapped in his own thoughts.

Laurent said, "Lark, your power lies with no weapon. If you believe protection is through some object, then how do you learn to trust yourself?"

"Am I to simply *trust* myself? As if that will be enough against these Breeders of Chaos?"

"Yes." Maybe just one spoke, or maybe they all said it. The answer was not what I'd wanted.

There was a lull around the circle then. We'd finished our meal; we'd finished our talk. The fire crackled. We watched the flames jerk and tumble, the little green ones spitting beneath the orange glow; watched them with a resignation that this calm, however peaceful, was only temporary and that battle lay ahead. And perhaps in this lull we would not have learned that we'd been spied on and watched, or how great the extent of the Breeders' powers, but that Arnon made the simple movement of reaching to adjust the fire. As he prodded at the burning pile, there came a horrid squeal, and one green flame snaked out suddenly like a whip and snared his arm, tugging him toward the blaze.

With a shout, Taran threw Arnon back from the lash. And Dartegn cried out, "Gharain, *move!*"

The green flames shot straight up from the ground with a loud hiss and crack. High and aggressive, they leaped sideways, streaking toward Gharain, reaching now to engulf him with fiery arms. But Riders were quick, pushing Gharain from his spot even as he somersaulted back. The flames did not touch him—as if on a leash, they could only fling so far before snapping back.

I was far slower, screaming out only then, "Gharain!" and, "What is this?"

They paid no attention to me. Laurent was shouting to all, "The ring! Make the ring!"

And the men sprang up, circling the fire, this time with swords drawn, holding them tall before their faces, blades flat, so that the fire was reflected upon itself. Wilh, I think, had pushed me back and out of the circle, and so I stood watching them, breathless at the speed at which this was happening. The green flames were caught by their reflection—their own force being thrown back at them, becoming a boundary the fire could not cross.

But it could not stay like this. Even at bay, the flames were intense; blocked by the swords, they spiraled together and locked—and, as if they held their breath and pushed, the heat from the fire became overwhelming. I felt the grass withering beneath my feet.

Laurent called out to me, "Water, Lark! Get water!"

Water. Of course, water. I turned immediately, running into the dark. Then I stopped, appalled. "I haven't a pail! I've nothing to collect—"

"Your cup!" one of them shouted. "Just one cup!"

I turned back and grabbed it from where it had dropped. Then another—Cargh, I think—yelled, "Not the pond, Lark! Take water from the stream only!"

And I ran, trying to remember in the dark which direction to find the nearest of the three streams—or any of the three. I was blind in this darkness; the brilliance of the flames had seared my vision. I ran wildly for a moment, and then stopped and closed my stinging eyes, forcing myself to remember that I could use the Sight. At first, the surprise and fright and haste of everything whirled chaotically inside. The need to be quick had made me frantic. Frantic—what the Breeders would hope for. I exhaled as slowly as possible, letting go of the wild thoughts, and taking in another deep, steady breath.

And I could smell it. I turned left, took some ten paces, kneeled at the bank of the little stream, and dipped my cup into the bubbling water.

The Riders were drawing from every strength they had to keep the fire at bay, faces fierce and turned away from the ghastly brilliance, but holding their swords true, pushing hard against the force of heat. I ran to them, one hand over the mouth of the cup to keep the contents from spilling, and when I neared, Gharain shouted, "Lark, now!" And I threw the tiny splash of water into the roar of flames.

It was enough. In one explosive pop, the fire went out.

The men let down their swords, breathing heavily. We all waited in silence while our eyes once again adjusted to the night.

It was Laurent who spoke first. He was grave. "We should have anticipated—I should have anticipated this."

"What was *this*?" My own voice sounded hoarse and dry.

Taran answered: "They reached through our campfire. They thought to eavesdrop, to learn of our actions. They sensed you, Lark; they know you are with us."

Someone muttered, "And Gharain."

But I only heard Taran. Horrified, I shouted, "I've brought this upon us again!"

"No, Lark, don't think that." This was Dartegn coming toward me. "They would not have used force if Arnon had not touched the fire. He made a connection; they reacted and were exposed, and so they made an attempt to destroy us here."

"They can do that?" A twinge of hysteria squeezed my voice.

"They have the amulets."

How I hated that simple, all-answering refrain! "Troths, swifts, earth rifts," I choked, "Flame, flood, suffocation—what more will they do? What should it be next time: an attack by some beast running from the woods, or perhaps from that pond? Through a storm or wildfire—or will we just kill one another out of fear?"

"Maybe all of those things," Sevrin said darkly.

"Balance may be adrift." Dartegn tried to soften. "But remember that the Breeders cannot destroy the amulets by themselves. And attacks can still be defended."

Brahnt muttered under his breath, "Unless they are lucky."

"But they know where we are! What's to stop them?"

"Lark," Laurent said evenly, "we are not without our own strengths."

"Strengths that they are trying to exhaust," I muttered, more to myself. And then I looked to Dartegn, to ask something that frightened me more. "Why did you yell for Gharain? Why did the flames reach to him first?"

But it was Wilh, behind me, who leaned down to whisper in my ear, "Maybe for the same reason you thought to ask this."

❧

It was not a typical burn that circled Arnon's wrist. Sevrin and Dartegn brought him down to the stream by the light of torches we'd staked at intervals in the ground—for Laurent said that the Breeders could not work through such small bits of flame. Arnon's wrist and arm were soaked in the running water over and over, and though the snake of flame had barely time to snare him, the skin above the joint was already swollen and puffy.

It was his sword arm.

Brahnt said as much to Laurent as they stood there watching Arnon. I stopped in my path to the water to listen.

"They've hobbled one. Who's to say that they won't strike at each?"

"They will," muttered Laurent. His jaw was hard and his nostrils flared, angered with concern and regret. "This was my fault. I should have known better."

"We let down our guard," said Brahnt. "With swifts attacking last night, we did not imagine they could gather strength again so quickly."

"They've the amulets; why would I think the Breeders' power not strong enough for this? Take us down, one at a time. They'll need no respite—"

"None of us knows what their powers can do," Brahnt returned firmly. "For they've not had the amulets in our lifetime. *Nothing* can be anticipated—nothing but that Lark is both greatest threat to the Breeders and greatest necessity. They want her."

Laurent nodded. "And so eliminate us. And Gharain? He

made the bond, but is she vulnerable, or ineffective without him?"

"Perhaps," said Brahnt, who held a streak of cynicism, "Erema is a jealous lover."

So I was not wrong in my fears. Uneasy, I made my way to the stream, where Riders directed me to remove my boots and step in as they did.

"It helps cleanse any remains of the attack," said Taran, who splashed at his feet next to me.

"Then why don't we wash in the pond? This is but a trickle." I could not help sounding cross. Anger made a good distraction.

"A small cupful extinguished that fire," Taran reminded me with a wry grin. "But, truly, still water can be manipulated, whereas flowing water is free of any distortion. It is pure power, neither good nor bad, and will erase the properties of certain spells, wash away magic—some anyway. You would do well to remember that."

I wished it would wash away emotion. "Is it erasing Arnon's wound?" I muttered.

He shrugged with another grin, but it was not an easy smile. And he left me to wash alone.

# 15

EREMA STOOD BEFORE me, extraordinarily beautiful in blue-tinged light, a pungent odor of Troth and cold earth surrounding her. Her cape billowed in the darkness while her cavernous smile gaped with triumph and exultation.

"Look what I have," she was saying to me. "Look, Lark Carew, look what I have!"

And she opened the cape she held close to reveal the Life amulet, the crystal orb, trapped in black webbing against her breast, where it reflected not the blue light but its own warm, though weak, glow.

I lifted my hand to take the amulet but had no chance. Time was spinning and I spiraled with it, writhing in sudden agony. I could not turn my head; I could barely breathe. The Breeder of Chaos was laughing at my helplessness, saying, "It is mine!"

Pain smashed through my body, roared through my ears as she called out in her exquisite voice, "Rider!" And then I watched in horror as, birthed from the rock on which she stood, emerged Gharain, rising from her feet as I'd seen him rising from the pool at Tarnec. He stood tall, facing me, his sage-green eyes gleaming blankly. And liltingly Erema sang, "Now, Gharain, finish what you began. Finish what you meant to do." And with silent, final words, Gharain reached his arms over his head and brought down his sword against my brow. I called something to him, but the blade cleaved straight through anyway, clanging to its completion against the rock floor. There was no flash of white this time. The dark consumed me.

"Lark."

"No!" I shouted, coming too sharply out of sleep.

"Softly, Lark." It was Cargh, very quiet, above me. "We should not wake the others; they've had their turns holding watch and must take rest. Come, Lark. We need your help."

I jerked upright, panting, rubbing my eyes and my sweat-damp face, sick inside at what he'd ripped me from: another dream, another death.

There was a pause while Cargh watched me struggle. He pushed his blond hair back from his brow and said a little curiously, "I suppose I should not be sorry to wake you—but, please, will you come quickly?"

I nodded and scrambled up, followed him, shivering, back to the stream, dismayed to see that Gharain waited there with

Arnon. He smiled, but I did not return it. I looked instead to the patient.

Arnon suffered. He sat hunched and rocking from the pain, saying politely enough through clenched jaw, "They thought you might have knowledge that we do not. I'm sorry that your sleep was disturbed."

"It was not sleep." I moved past Cargh and sat down next to Arnon. He gave me a brief nod and then closed his eyes to concentrate on steadying breath. It was a wonder he did not scream—his arm extended straight out from his body as if he dared not let it touch anything. Swollen and discolored, throbbing hideously in the flickering light—this was my doing.

I held my fingers just above the steaming, sickened flesh. Even so, Arnon flinched in pain. Poison reeked from his pores, pushing madness and fury through my open hand—the excruciating torture the Rider so stoically endured now licked along my bones. Arnon flinched again and I pulled back, stomach clenched in revulsion and dismay. He bore the wrath of the Breeders for me, and I could not help him.

"I'm not a Healer," I murmured, defeated.

"But your cousin is," said Gharain. "Might you have learned something from her?"

I could not look at Gharain; I still heard his dream sword crashing through me until it rang against the stone beneath my feet; I saw his arms around Evie. I was sick from all this anguish. "You are Ilone's brother; you know it is not study that makes one a Healer." Then I said more loudly, "This is poison, not a burn. This—this is the Breeders' *play,* as you call it, their spreading of evil. Those flames were green—" *Finish what you meant to do,* Erema had said. Gharain's voice so clear in the garden: *I meant to kill you.* . . . Arnon saying, *There will be others.* . . . Did he expect it to be himself? Miserable, useless, I looked to Arnon, pleading apology. He nodded and closed his eyes once more.

Cargh said gently, "Lark, you are not without gifts. Even if you lack a Healer's hands, as Life Guardian you might have some knowledge, some ability that could help."

It was true enough. There should be, *must* be, something I could do to help. It was selfish to dwell on my own misery. I pushed away the ugliness and took a breath, trying to release worry, remembering how quick was the search for the stream that evening when I'd relaxed and allowed the Sight to open my senses. All the while the Riders remained patient and still.

*Trust,* the king had said. *Trust that you will know what to do.*

Slowly the scents of water and the green grass and rowan tree drew in and calmed me, and I breathed and the men waited silently—

"The snowdrops," I said abruptly. "Those tiny white flowers sprinkled through the grass."

The three turned their heads to stare at me through the dark. "Do you mean wicks?" Gharain asked.

"Wicks, then. They pulled bad things from the Troth when he attacked me here. Maybe they'll do that for Arnon."

"I have not seen wicks," said Cargh.

"Because they were shriveled by the Troth. But there might be more, somewhere that the beast did not spoil. We can spread out and search—"

"Do you remember where?" asked Gharain. "The clearing is large."

"We'll look! We can take torches—"

But Arnon cut over me, insisting, "You must not spread out. Lark would be vulnerable."

Cargh turned to him. "We are all vulnerable now."

"We can wait for morning," Arnon hissed through a sharp breath.

"No," I returned vehemently, "we cannot." Arnon had little time. How long had the queen lasted?

We grasped for ideas in anxious silence. The night hovered, hushed and poised, in the way it seems when things wait just behind the dark. I'd spoken of the Troth; now I felt its filmy eyes on me. I felt it on my fingers—its sluglike, spongy texture. And the reeking filth as well, which I'd felt consuming Arnon's arm . . . I wanted to go back to the stream and wash the taint away.

And, surprised, I said, "The stream!"

"That was already tried—"

"I know, Gharain, but if moving water cleanses, then let me gather snowdrops—wicks—the dead ones. I'll wash them— they might be refreshed."

Cargh hesitated. "It is possible—"

"I'll go with Lark." Gharain jumped to his feet.

And the two of us took a torch and bent our heads over the

grass, plucking up the brown and shriveled flowers, roots and all, as many as we could. I found my hands shaking, pulled between desire and fear, and the desperation in all this.

"Will this do?" Gharain asked, showing me his handful under the torchlight.

"I don't know, I don't know," I fretted, holding out my own pitiful, crumbled bits. "I'm making a guess at all this. I don't know if this will work."

"Simply having an idea helps Arnon. 'Twill keep him alert, hopeful."

"Hope is not a cure," I hissed, frustrated. All of this was blind—I didn't know what I was doing.

"Right now it is all we have," Gharain said grimly, and bent his head to study the ground.

A few minutes more and we both held sizable enough handfuls. I ran behind him to the stream, taking care to be quiet for the Riders' sakes. I dropped my small bundle of wicks on the ground with Gharain's and kicked off my boots to step into the stream. Gharain kneeled on the bank and held the torch, silently handing me the clump of dead flowers. I plunged them into the little trail of running water, remembering how Grandmama would wash clover or blueberry blossoms—a gentle swish in the cold water and then lifting them up to let drip between opened fingers.

Gharain leaned the torch forward so we could see.

"Nothing," I sighed. The wicks remained brown and lifeless.

"Try again," he suggested. "Hold them there a moment longer."

And I dunked my hands again into the shallow stream and let the fresh water run between my fingertips. The night was cool, the water cooler still, but it felt good. Some of the anxiety dissipated, washed downstream. I thought of Nayla saying we offered love to the Earth and in return it was bountiful. I thought of the pleasure of digging my hands into earth to plant, to weed, and what it offered back—

"Lark?" Gharain said gently.

I lifted out my hands, shook the water away.

Gharain tipped the torch again. The wicks were not as brown, nor as shriveled as they were before—the water did seem to have drained the Troth's presence out of them—but they were still limp, lifeless.

"Oh," I murmured, disappointed.

"It was a good try." Gharain touched a hand under mine cupping the wilted flowers.

I gasped. The energy ran between hands, and the wicks suddenly sprang to life—the leaves and flowers plumping and greening before our eyes, even as they fell from our shocked grasp.

We laughed aloud, quickly clamping hands over our mouths lest we wake anyone. And then our eyes met—equal gazes of thrilled surprise.

He affected me, he'd said. The strike of lightning, the extinguishing of visions, and now the power to burst life into something that seemed dead, all from his touch—

I had to look away. I had to remember. If not love for Evie, Gharain was still the one who would kill me.

Gharain cleared his throat. "Arnon." We rose quickly.

To our dismay, we'd not found a cure. It was impossible to make a paste, a poultice, or anything else from the wicks. They'd sprung back; now they would not crush or be ground smooth, and they popped out from any wrappings we tied onto the silently agonizing Arnon. We tried laying the individual stems along his arm, but though he claimed he could feel a healing chill at their touch, they rolled off his skin immediately. It would have been comical if Arnon's pain had not been so deep.

"Some magic," growled Cargh. It was the first time I'd seen him out of sorts.

"There must be something else to this," Gharain said, exasperated after so many attempts. "If we could but stick them to his skin."

Cargh snorted, but I said quickly, "Sap will work. From the rowan."

"No," the three men decreed simultaneously. "The rowan is sacred," continued Cargh. "No branch may be stripped from it."

"Then I'll ask for one." And I was away, running to the rowan. They let me go alone.

Within the wide boundary of its branches, I paused. *Wait*, I told myself. *Wait*. Time was scarce, but I could not make a request of the tree with the jumble of emotions tearing through me. I put my hands against my mouth, breathed hard into them, and flung my hands away, again and over again until I panted, sweating and empty. Only then did I wipe my palms on my leggings and step forward to place them on the smooth, gray bark, listening to the ancient music few could hear. I thought of Arnon, and the ugly hukon that had killed the queen, trapped the amulets, and threatened the fragile balance that brought life to this Earth.

And then I whispered, "Please help." I looked up into its dark canopy. "An offering?"

Silence. The rowan's song—like distant bells—whispered through the leaves. My fingertips pressed against the horizontal etching of lines running up the trunk, feeling its hum running into my fingers—

A wave of energy spilled through—a power from eons of seasons, of standing watch over this magical clearing. I was not the first to ask of the rowan, for I felt the presence of many others who'd stood beneath this tree entreating help long before my time. Voices of anguish, fear, and even, sometimes, greed. The roots ran deep; the leaves branched high—connecting earth and sky to this place where a small being could stand and make a request.

And the tree spoke to me.

*Bring light into dark.*

There was a rustle in the branches high above, and through the leaves dropped a twig at my feet.

Smiling, I pressed hand over heart and bowed to the rowan, picked up the gift, and ran back to the others.

The twig was fresh, covered in young, fine hairs and rich with oil. Neither Cargh nor Gharain spoke, but Arnon gave me a grateful look.

"I don't know if this will do anything," I warned him quietly.

"But you tried, and I thank you." His voice was very tight.

The sap was smeared as lightly as possible, and the wicks we laid in rows up his arm—and they held. Arnon took a deep breath and said it was not so bad anymore. I didn't expect that any of us believed him, but after a few moments his tightly clenched eyes relaxed and his head tipped to one side in some sort of rest.

It was all we could do for now. Cargh claimed he'd take the watch and told us to go back to sleep for the last hour or so; I went to the stream to wash my hands.

And I washed and washed, and tried to erase everything I'd seen from Arnon and dreamed about Gharain—of death and pain and heartbreak, of the Breeders of Chaos wreaking destruction over all. Somehow, finding the Life amulet would help make this stop, but now I didn't even know if I would live long enough to recapture it.

Gharain had followed me. He bent and rinsed his hands—we both worked silently. Even from his distance I could feel him like a shock, warm and vital. Despite everything I'd foreseen, my desire still burned.

I had to end this terrible, futile need.

I sat back on my heels and faced him. "Laurent said no truth should be withheld," I began, then gritted my teeth, meaning to be bolder. "This connection between us pulls me strongly. But . . ."

My voice fell away; Gharain had met my gaze in the dark.

For a moment we were frozen in place, eyes locked. The air stilled, and the water at our feet was the last remaining sound jingling over the stones.

And then Gharain stood up, took two steps toward me, and pulled me to my feet, his touch charging through my arms.

I think time stopped. He would kiss me; his mouth dipped to mine. And all the rumors I'd ever heard of first kisses—a sweet press of lips, shy glances, and a stolen touch—this would be none of these. This would be fierce and full and all-consuming. And this would shatter me—a million pieces of desire, and despair. I could not have that kiss. I had to look Evie fair in the eye someday.

I shoved him back, stumbling from my own force. He reached out to catch my arm, to right me, but I found my footing and jerked my arm away.

"Lark!"

"Why? Why would you do that? You said yourself we must be strong!" My hands went to my cheeks; they were fiercely hot. "I promised myself not to let you—you *burn* in me so deeply. And then you do *that,* and it ruins every resolve!"

"And so you push me away?"

"Yes!"

That surprised him. "Yet you speak of our connection—"

"Not through a kiss! You cannot kiss me!" I clenched my fists again.

He said roughly, "A kiss is the most powerful of touches. Of *connections.*"

"You cannot want this—*me.*"

"And why can't I? Deny that you want me."

I ignored that. "For two profound reasons, Gharain!"

"All of two?" He was mocking in his defense. "And those being . . . ?"

"That you are meant for another. And, that you will kill me."

He disregarded the first reason. "Kill you? How?"

"By sword."

He laughed. "I already tried that. Fate thankfully intervened—"

"Rune intervened," I interrupted to correct. "But fate will ultimately have her way. It is what I have foreseen."

His breath exhaled harshly. "No. That cannot be. Our destinies entwine—*merge*, not destroy. You know this as well as I."

Destinies entwined. It hurt to hear that, and it was likewise thrilling. I didn't want to remember that he was destined rather to fall in love with Evie, kill me. Still, if I focused on those agonizing truths, I might find strength enough to keep away. "You don't want me."

His smile was devastating. "You're wrong. It's all that I've wanted. I've fought myself from the beginning. I didn't want to believe I deserved—"

"No! Don't say it!" I was fierce. "There is no beginning— it's too late! It's always been too late." There was a tiny, miserable pause. "I have the Sight, Gharain. It does not lie."

"But maybe it can be misinterpreted." He growled this; I'd hurt him. Gharain turned and stormed off, kicking over a torch as he passed it. The flame went out.

Misinterpreted? If only I had. For just a moment I clung to that possibility—that I'd erred. But no flash of white had protected me from this sword strike; it had sliced straight through. And I'd promised Evie, and Gharain had held her so close. . . .

"Maybe," I whispered after him. "But not if you'd seen what I've seen." And not if you'd promised.

It was good that he was going to kill me. At least all this pain would be short-lived.

# 16

A RUSTLE, A thump, a shout, and a shriek of absolute terror woke us in the early dawn.

"Arnon!" I gasped, eyes flying open.

But it was not Arnon. In a flash, the Riders were up with swords raised, all pointing to where I lay stunned and blinking sleep from my eyes. It occurred to me that I was about to be cleaved in half by eleven warriors at once, but I suppose my new dream of death left me less than concerned at the swords raised over my head. This was not the way I was going to die.

The same calm, however, did not hold for the little, shrieking thing that dove under the blanket I slept in. Like a mole, it flew beneath the wool and shot across my legs and then curled in one lump between my shoulder and head. Yet it was much larger than a mole, possessing potent strength for its size. Its abrupt movement had shoved my head to one side.

Evaen shouted, "Draw away, Lark!"

"Watch her throat!" Gharain yelled at his friend.

"Hold!" commanded Laurent to all before any of the Riders made a further move.

And I cried out, "Wait! Wait!" and scrambled to sit up. The thing by my neck attempted to come with me. I threw off the blanket and reached up and pulled the clinging creature from my shoulder. It writhed and squirmed and shouted in a voice double its size.

"What," asked Brahnt, "is that?"

I had to hold it in both hands to still its fierce struggle. "Stop it!" I hissed at the thing. "Stop! You will not be hurt!"

"You say it! Does not mean it!" it shouted back.

"Lark!" Laurent commanded.

I looked up at him, at all of them. "It's a gnome," I said, and set the thing on its feet. It was still wriggling and so promptly fell over on its back, only to struggle to stand upright, at which point all eleven swords closed the gap and froze it in place.

Gnomes are small. This one, tall for his race, barely reached halfway to my knee. And beneath the hard stares and serious height of the Riders, he was absolutely puny. His age appeared advanced—his beard was white, long, and double-knotted to keep from touching the ground. His clothes and shoes and waistpack were of boiled wool in the browns and greens of nuts and leaves, though I did see a sparkle in one of his buttonholes, something as glistening red as a drop of blood.

"Lark, move aside," said Laurent.

I looked up at the Rider in surprise, exclaiming, "You're not going to kill him?"

"The gnome invaded our camp; he was in Taran's pack. And, he bit Gharain. He's spying, or stealing. A Breeders' lackey."

"That is untrue!" The gnome turned to Laurent, a contained little ball of fury. "I am none of those! I made my way to warmth is all! And you"—he spun to face Gharain—"you squashed my foot!"

"Never mind warmth," growled Brahnt. "What brings you here? To us?"

The gnome looked around at the circle of suspicious and intimidating men, and then pointed at me. "I came for her."

Marc laughed. I would have too had I not felt a bit sorry for the little man. None of us quite believed him, but he took much pride in his offense at being threatened, and I had not the heart to accuse him of any sort of treachery, though I was not certain he spoke any truth. I had little experience with gnomes, other than seeing them once in a while rooting around our gardens. Whether honest or wily, thieves or friends, I held no knowledge.

But the gnome dug his heels into my tossed blanket and drew himself up as tall as he could. "For her I came!" he repeated with his finger still pointing at me. "She called for me!"

"I did not!"

"You did!" he insisted.

Gharain muttered, "Belligerent thing."

But Laurent demanded, "Explain yourself."

None of the Riders had relaxed his sword grip. The gnome eyed the sharp points and remained obstinate. "The lady summoned me last night. Here I am."

The Riders looked at me; I looked at the gnome. "I did not," I repeated.

But the gnome, now insulted, said with absurd formality, "I take great umbrage at your denial, my lady. But I am forgiving, and so I will repeat myself by requesting of your memory: did you or did you not say 'Please help' last night beneath the rowan tree?"

"Well, yes, but—"

"There you are, Riders. Remove now your swords."

We all stared at him. I said, "But I asked help from the tree for sap, and she gave me the twig. I did not ask for you."

"By asking help, you asked for me. A tree cannot leave its roots. I can."

I was repeating myself. "All I asked was sap for Arnon."

"No. What you asked for was *help* and then an offering. The tree was more than generous last night, giving you the sap— but do you know how to use it? Ah, I thought not. If the rowan has allowed me to help you, I shall begin by improving upon what must be woeful attempts to use its offering properly."

Woeful was right. "Riders?" I looked up at them in their tight surround. "We might trust him."

Laurent dropped his sword tip to the earth. "Let him show us what he can do for Arnon."

The gnome made a stiff little bow, but Gharain scoffed, "You don't imagine that he's a Healer, do you? Look at him."

"It has already been determined," the gnome said point-edly, "that you, sir, have impulsively poor judgment. I will not pay attention to you." He turned to me. "You, my lady, may direct me."

We were all looking at him with surprise—except for Gharain, who stalked away a distance, flushing. But what the gnome said was true.

I thought to defuse some of the tension. "*Are* you a Healer?"

The gnome shook his head gravely. "Not as you people interpret. But we gnomes are Earth creatures and so know many of its secrets—some of which will help heal an injury."

"Then you can start with my finger!" Gharain grumbled from his farther spot.

"The finger, sir, simply needs a bit of your spit," the gnome replied coldly. "The wound to your pride, however, I cannot determine."

"Gnome." I jumped in. "Our friend was poisoned through a lash of green fire—a Breeders' attack."

"And what have you done for him?"

I explained, leaping up to head to where Arnon slept by the stream. The Riders parted and let us pass, then followed curi-ously, and protectively.

"Wait! Wait!" The little man toddled as fast as he could across the grass in my wake. "You cannot move so quickly!"

I stopped and he reached my foot and climbed onto my boot, gripping my leggings for balance. "Now," he said.

I took two steps. "This is too awkward, with you hanging from my leg. Let me carry you."

The gnome looked pained, but he suffered my suggestion and let me pick him up and tuck him in the crook of my arm. He smelled like the forest and like dirt, dark and rich. In my hands there hummed the low energy I preferred from things of Nature. He *was* of Earth; at least on this he spoke the truth.

I set him down when we reached Arnon, and the Riders gathered around so that we all regarded the man who slept an uneasy sleep on the bank of the stream. Cargh, who'd sat last watch, reached down and gently shook his good shoulder.

The Rider woke immediately, and—despite pain—fully ready. He took us in as he sat up, using his good hand to push himself right, saying with grim humor, "It is that bad?"

Laurent forced a chuckle, "We've not lost you yet, my friend."

I kneeled down and put the gnome on the ground. He trundled over to the Rider, who regarded him with mild surprise.

"The gnome offers his knowledge of healing," I said by way of introduction.

Arnon raised a brow. "I am open to all efforts."

"Nothing we did last night helped?" My heart sank. The wicks had sprung to life—I'd so hoped we'd found a cure.

"Nay, it helped. I think, at least, staunched the poison's spread." Arnon stiffly lifted his arm, and we leaned nearer. I swallowed. Arnon's humor covered a far worse condition. The arm was ridiculously grotesque—slicked with sap, the little wicks laid out in rows up his swollen and discolored skin. The wicks were no longer white, but a sickly yellow.

The gnome waddled up and down by the Rider's arm, his head cocked to one side. He nodded; he tsked. He stopped and peered close. "Not bad, not bad," he said at last. "I am pleasantly surprised." He looked at me. "This was your idea, my lady?"

"I had help." I nodded in Gharain's direction, and the gnome sniffed. Apparently, it would take much to make a gnome forget what offended him.

"The wicks and sap were your suggestion. This is not bad for one who is no Healer and ignorant of her own strengths."

Compliment and critique well blended—I blushed at both.

"You trusted your choices—that shows some talent. You were near right," he added. "But you neglected an ingredient. You need the barren stone."

"Barren stone?" We all looked at him blankly.

The gnome sighed. "Easy enough to find one in the stream. Look for it. It's round and smooth, a silvery gray." And he waddled to the water's edge, then began walking down the length of the bank peering into the clear run.

I joined him, as did Taran and Wilh. There were many stones—shapes, sizes, and colors. I probed the bottom, fingers digging among the rubble. Mottled whites and blacks and browns were plentiful. I finally pulled one up that fit the description: a smooth, round, gray pebble. The gnome was appalled that I held it out to him.

"That? That's a cinder stone! That would start a fire, not quench one!"

Meekly, I put it back.

Wilh held out another stone from a distance. The gnome,

with his keen eyes, exclaimed, "Yes! Bring it here." He himself fished a white stone from the stream and went back to Arnon. Standing over the Rider's poisoned arm, the gnome chafed the white stone against the silver-gray.

"A mal stone is the best choice for grinding," he explained of the white stone as he walked up and down the length of the arm briskly rubbing the two pebbles together. "It is neutral; its residue will not change the properties of any potion." Tiny grains were filtering onto the sap-smeared arm as he moved busily back and forth, and he made small mutterings of approval at his own efforts. Then, suddenly, he finished. "There! 'Tis enough."

I, who, like all the Riders, skeptically watched this odd little service, asked, "But what have you done?"

The gnome's pride in his task was only slightly deflated at my ignorance. "The barren stone draws fire and poison," he said, shaking the pebble at me. Then, with an enormous sigh of exasperation, he exclaimed, "For a Guardian, you are woefully unlearned!"

I bridled. "If I am one, then it is something I've only known for three days."

"Hmph. Most likely you refused to know it. Are you not seventeen?"

"Not yet. Soon."

"Well, then. That explains your immaturity. Though his stupidity"—and the gnome tossed his head toward Gharain— "is inexcusable."

We heard Gharain's remark at the insult, but the gnome

ignored this and simply called out to him, "You, sir, are capable of much. But you have let your passions guide your spirit. If you do not have control of them, you will do more harm than the good you were meant for."

"How would you know anything about me?" snapped Gharain.

"It is ignorant to assume that because you do not know me, then I should not know you," the gnome snapped back. Tiny or not, the gnome held no fear of Gharain's outbursts.

But then the gnome turned to me, catching my small smile. "And you, Lady Lark, you would do as well to watch your emotions. They will confuse you sorely. If they don't save you, they will be your end."

Laurent intervened after a speechless moment. "What about Arnon?"

"Watch his arm, and you will see," replied the gnome, and released my shocked gaze.

He explained to us the properties of the wicks and the sap and the stone grindings, none of which I fully heard, but, as we watched, we indeed saw the sap begin to mottle and bubble—lifting the red from Arnon's skin.

"Now," said the gnome, "a tourniquet!"

Ian was closest. He handed the gnome the cloth from his belt, and the gnome draped it over the top of Arnon's arm, by his shoulder.

"Here, my lady, fashion a knot for me. As tightly as you can."

I did so, and the gnome nodded in approval. "No finger space between the cloth and skin. There. Now, are you ready?"

I nodded, already a little sick from the poison steaming from the arm. He said, "Now tug with me! Pull the material straight down to his elbow."

We tugged the cloth down the arm, scraping up the sap. Arnon gritted his teeth against the pain, his face paling while the skin we slowly exposed returned to its normal color.

"Stop!" the gnome commanded when we reached Arnon's elbow. "Retie the knot here at the forearm. The cloth must stay tight." I retied, shakily, and Arnon caught his breath.

"Ready?" the gnome asked. I swallowed back the bile, gripped the cloth.

But Gharain stepped in, ignoring the gnome's little sniff. "Let me," he said quietly. "Let me." He took over, his hand brushing mine as I pulled back.

"Hurry," barked the gnome. "We must scrape those bubbles from his arm."

And they dragged the fabric down, stopping once more to tie it tighter just above his wrist. And finally, at the base of his palm, the gnome called a halt. Gharain unknotted the cloth. The gnome told Ian to wash it in the stream.

"'Tis ruined, is it not?" Ian asked, catching the filthy cloth that Gharain tossed to him.

"Running water will not hold poison. The sap will rinse away, as will the stone dust. The wicks you can toss back on the earth. They will regrow."

"Look at his arm," said Evaen.

We looked to Arnon, who flexed his arm gingerly. Blessedly, it looked quite normal—no longer bloated red and reeking.

"Was it hukon?" I whispered, still hoarse.

The gnome shook his head. "If they'd used hukon, he'd be dead." He leaned toward Arnon. "'Twill feel like jelly for a day or so, but you were lucky."

Arnon shook his limb. "Useless for now," he said. "But I thank you."

"You should not work it much until the strength returns—in particular, do not take up your sword. In its weakened state, your arm might draw the bad energy your sword defends against."

Laurent stepped forward, saying, "You have our thanks, little man." And he bowed, head to chest, hand to breast. All of us followed suit.

The gnome nodded, and stayed standing stiffly poised. We looked at him. He looked at all of us. I wondered if he expected some sort of payment.

"Your task is complete," said Laurent gently. "You may go at your leisure."

"Complete? Leisure? What nonsense do you speak?" the gnome asked, drawing up as tall as he could.

"We would not keep you longer from your business," Laurent said.

The little man turned to me. "You are my business."

I looked at him blankly. "But you've helped Arnon! That is what I asked."

The gnome sighed. "It is not my concern that you so poorly stated your request. You would do well to be more specific next time."

"But I don't know what else you can do to help!"

The little man stamped both feet at me. "How is it a Guardian may be so dense? Tell me: Are you simply on your way home? Are you returning to *your* business?"

"We go to defend my village, the village of Merith—"

"Then you go wrong. That is not your battle," the gnome interrupted.

I stared at him. "What do you mean?"

"Exactly as I said. That is not your battle."

"But the Troths attack!"

"And that is not your battle, Lady Lark. This is your fight, but *that* is not your battle. The Riders will protect Merith."

"I don't understand." I was purposely contrary. I didn't like that he implied I was not meant to fight for Merith. It was the same as being told I could not use a sword.

"Yes, you do," the gnome returned bluntly. Then he sighed again, as if he would have to remember to be very patient with me, and announced to all, "I ride with Lark." He turned back to me and asked, "Have you something that I can be supported in, on your back? For I will *not* be carried in your arm again like an infant."

I shook my head. But then Gharain said, "Wait," and went to retrieve something from his horse. "Here," he said, returning and holding out a familiar, small crumple of sturdy cloth. "This remained with my things."

Silly, but there was great comfort in seeing my pack again. I shook it open, knowing it was empty, but stuck my hand in anyway. And I brought up Quin's fern sprig, which had wedged itself somewhere in the seam. It was dried but intact, and I was happy and strangely relieved to find it. I looked up to thank Gharain and blushed to find him grinning at the pleasure he'd brought me.

"That is an excellent travel container," the gnome announced. "Just right." He walked over to where I still sat on the ground and took the fern from my fingers, sniffing it. "This is a good friend," he announced, and tucked it inside his own waistpack. "For safekeeping." Then he climbed into the center of my pack and pulled it up around him. "I am ready," he announced, as if we were waiting on him.

The Riders and I exchanged glances. I looked down at the gnome. "When do I say my farewells?"

"We will know when we know," the gnome answered. "For now we ride with the Riders."

"We should start," said Laurent. "The morning is full on."

There was a flurry of motion as the Riders made ready, but it was done quickly; they were expert at departing at a moment's notice. I slung the pack on my back carefully, and Marc, being closest, lifted me onto Rune. But it was Gharain who trotted his horse near to give me some of the Tarnec hardbread. I'd included him when I called the Riders my friends. And we behaved now as friends might, not speaking of last night. If Gharain was upset, he did not show it, nor would he have seen I was sadly grateful that he bore no grudge at my rejection.

Gharain held out some hardbread then for the gnome, but the gnome turned up his nose at the offer.

"I have my own sustenance," the little man said to Gharain, who glared in equal disdain.

"Gnome!" I said loudly to prevent further quarrel. "We do not know your name."

"That," he answered, "is because I have not told it to you."

"Well, then?" asked Gharain.

"Nay." The gnome shook his head. "You would not understand it, for it is not of your language."

"Try us," Gharain said dryly.

The gnome eyed him for a brief moment. And then, with a little gleam in his eye, he opened his mouth and emitted a series of terrible, rasping, unintelligible shrieks.

"That," I interrupted, wincing, "is rather long!"

"Yes, well, we add to our names as we age. And I have reached a *substantial* age," he said proudly. Then he shrugged. "But you may choose a name to suit your weaker ears."

"We should call you Runt," Gharain muttered.

"Twig." I intervened quickly. "We'll call you Twig."

I felt the gnome shrug again behind me. "A true name matters only if one has earned it," he said. "But this alias makes some sense and is easy for you, and so I do not mind."

Gharain spurred his horse and moved ahead. I patted Rune, who'd accepted the odd little passenger with only mild curiosity, and followed the Riders out of the clearing.

"You are to stay with me?" I asked Twig again. "You'll go with me to find the crystal orb?"

His jaw was level to my shoulder, and he said in my ear, "I am your help. You were wise to ask for it."

"But how long—?"

He answered as I should have expected: "We will know when we know."

## 17

RIDERS TRAVEL IN single file. I'd seen this earlier; I suppose it is habit from traversing the hills of Tarnec with their narrow and treacherous paths. We were strung along the Cullan foothills like beads adorning a garment, a green garment that stretched on in all directions. Sitting higher now than when I first walked this route, I was even more aware of the vast expanse of rolling land punctuated here and there with the bits of jutting boulders and stone slabs.

It was still as bleak.

Twig had been quizzing me incessantly since we began our ride. He'd asked of Merith, of my family, of my friends. He'd asked about the village elders and the fox and Ruber Minwl's hand. He'd insisted on knowing the herbs Grandmama grew and how many ghisane I'd ripped in the early days of summer; when I'd sewn the pack he sat in, what we ate for supper, and whether I combed my hair with wood or shell. All these things in no particular order, all in annoying, exhausting, and overly specific detail; Twig ate up the information as if it were food and he were starved. His questions grated, since it seemed he already knew the answers and yet could not be more curious at how I would respond.

And then there were questions on the Sight and my recent visions and what did I see and how did I feel and what did I learn. . . .

Finally I'd said, "Enough." He'd given me a headache. With a not-so-discreet sniff, Twig fell silent and I could at last try to turn my mind to pleasanter things.

Yet I couldn't think of anything pleasant. Whether from the burden of questions, the lack of sleep, the threat of Breeders and Troths and vulnerable Merith, or all of it, I was short-tempered and impatient. The sky itself lowered with a similar mood, darkening with the hint of rain—unusual, for it had barely rained this midsummer. I watched Gharain's back. I stared at the landscape; I stroked my fingers through Rune's mane and felt, overall, melancholy at the prospect of being home so soon.

It was the imminent introduction of Gharain to Evie that upset me. We'd shared the past days. Now the inevitable was soon upon us, and it made me ache that this short time together would be forever gone.

*E'en so quick may one fall.* . . . A phrase of song rolled around and around in my head. Gharain had fallen quickly for Erema; he'd briefly thought to fall for me. With Evie it would be even more rapid—with her temperament and beauty, how could it not? And Evie's feelings? That too was something I could not criticize, for with the very first dream of Gharain I'd lost my heart.

I felt sorry for Raif.

A hawk was circling in the distance ahead. We were nearing the edges of Dark Wood and the Niler marshes. I saw the stone where I'd stopped, exhausted and scared—how small it stood against the landscape! Insignificant now, when once it provided a place of support.

I sighed. Nothing changing and yet nothing the same.

The hawk drew a lazy arc in the sky, gray against gray. Twig had fallen asleep, or was sulking. We plodded, one horse behind the other, the Riders always upright and alert, while I sagged into Rune with unpleasant lethargy.

And then Twig said suddenly in my ear, "Have care, Lady Lark!"

I think I answered, "What?" But then the hair on the back of my neck pricked, and I gasped. I saw a wall of flames shoot up before me, was raw to the blistering heat and acrid smell. I heard shouts, and then—

And then I was seated on Rune, panting for air, looking around wildly even as the Riders had halted and Ian was calling and Gharain was turning Petral to reach me.

"It's—I—" Then I went rigid, for the hair on the back of my neck jumped, and I was no longer on Rune but watching Troths running, scrabbling, and slithering out of Dark Wood toward Merith. Through Krem Poss's field they streamed, through the lavender, and straight through the cottage belonging to Daen Hurn. The village bell was clanging wildly, discordantly, and I heard voices screaming, but they were not human voices. I could see no villager—only the Troths. They were headed toward the village square.

I tried to yell for the Riders, to call out to Evie and Grandmama, but I had no voice—I was not there. I could only follow madly as if I too were charging through Merith, as if I were a Troth. And then the earth was shuddering from the violence of battle. I saw a chimney topple—I thought it was Thom Maker's cottage, but I no longer recognized what I saw. Thatch was flying in the hot wind that sprang up. There was the smell of stone dust and stinging bits of grit in the air; I turned a corner and saw in the market square that wall of flame. The screaming wouldn't stop—frantic, vicious, and terrifying. From out of the fire a sword came arcing down, and then another, and then shadows were running in the haze of smoke and heat—the Riders swooping in with savage fury, answering shrieks of sheer horror. My eyes were unfocused; I was tumbling, rolling over the ground between wall and stone and leg. The smoke was less dense near the ground, but the dust choked and clung, and I could smell the stench of the Troths all around me. I smelled blood.

And then, as I righted, I saw through the fire the tall shape of Rune, wheeling, rearing, mane flying as he turned and pawed the air. His hooves slashed down, and his beautiful white forelegs were red with blood.

I was not on his back.

And I screamed and screamed and could not stop screaming, even as Gharain's hands closed around my arms, cutting off the awful images.

"No, don't! Stop!" I struggled to break his grip. "Let me be!" I had to finish witnessing this horror, had to know what would become of my beautiful horse. "Rune!" I screamed once more, "Rune!"

But I was here, by the marshes, and the returning whinny came, not from the vision but from the horse, standing now above me, looking down at my ungainly sprawl beneath him in the grass. I opened my eyes to see his pristine coat, and the leg that pawed gently at the ground near my head, and I burst into tears.

"Lark!" The Riders must have all said it at once. The noise in my ears was unbearable; sobs convulsed my whole body.

"Do something!" It was Gharain, frantic. "Do something, gnome!"

And Twig's smaller but deep voice was replying, "This I cannot fix."

Gharain swore, whether at Twig or his own helplessness, I didn't know, didn't care. Rune . . .

I rolled over to one side, retching up an empty stomach, as if it could spill out the gruesome images. I wrenched from the ground, clawing at my hair, my tunic, anything to wipe away the brutality. I caught Gharain's side hard with my wrist, felt his sword. And I dragged it from him even as I shrieked at its burning cold, unbearable weight. If he'd not twisted it from my grasp, I would have sliced it across my belly to tear out the vision.

"Lark! Lark! Stop!"

"Get it out! Get it out!" I sobbed, trying to grab back the sword. "Get it out!"

"Lark! It's all right! It will be all right!"

"Merith! They are taking Merith!" Hands held me down, forced me back on the ground. And then, "Rune! Rune!"

The horse was there, leaning down to nudge me with his soft nose, blowing grass-scented breath over my cheek.

"Let him breathe on you, Lady Lark!" Twig's voice was harsh. "Draw it in!"

"The Troths! They are running from Dark Wood! Hurry!"

"Hush, Lark. Breathe."

I gasped and choked and writhed out the horror until I had nothing left to expel and lay spent on the hard ground, feeling my own tears thin, then dry. Everyone was quiet; only Twig paced back and forth—his little steps sending tiny vibrations against my cheek.

My voice was ragged. "They're coming—"

"Lark." It was Taran. "How many Troths? What else?"

"Too many." I rolled, my head coming against something firm—Gharain's leg. He knelt at my side.

"Not good, not good." Twig was near, still pacing. His voice came close and retreated. "Too soon this comes. Too soon!"

"Hush, old man!" Brahnt exclaimed. "Let Lark calm!"

"No!" I gasped. "He speaks truth! They come too soon; I saw it!"

"No, no, no, no . . . ," Twig muttered. "No."

"Lark, this warning: *How* soon? How much time?" asked Laurent.

"There was fire." I wasn't making sense. I wanted Grandmama desperately. I pushed my forehead against Gharain's thigh. "Please, we need to go."

He murmured, his hand on my hair, "We will go, Lark, but rest a moment."

There was no option but to obey. I could not stand. Evaen brought me his blanket to wrap against the shock, but even Gharain's nearness did not calm my trembling. I felt sick and filthy from the violence, while around me a buzz of concerned voices discussed speed and enemy and ugly tactics.

"We're heating the balm," Wilh called back from somewhere. "It helped her before."

"No fires!" I cried out, but was hushed by Gharain, who moved a strand of hair back from my face. The gesture made me weep again.

"How do we stop this?" Gharain gritted, hand tensing against my cheek. And since no one answered him, he snapped loudly, "Can you not hurry?"

"Gharain, take yourself in charge, man!" Marc was pointedly forceful. "You do no help by letting your emotions run away!"

"Too soon it comes. What to do, what to do . . ." This was Twig, still in his pacing, muttering anxious things.

"You too, little man," growled Marc in ill humor. "Your worry helps no one."

Twig glared and moved off a distance.

Quiet then sank over our group as they waited for me, save for a harness toss or the firm steps of a Rider. This was not camp, and the Riders were restless. The air vibrated with barely contained urgency; they needed to move to task. There were lower murmurs between men, and then at last a clink of metal—of a cup hitting stone—and I was propped up, the drink put in my hands, and I gratefully swallowed the fragrant balm and let it heal me.

A moment later I pushed off the blanket. "We go," I said abruptly. Too much time was already wasted. Gharain stood quickly and reached to help me up, but I shook my head. I'd not let them think I remained weak. He dropped his hand and went to get Rune.

The others looked at Laurent, who, after giving me a long, assessing stare, nodded. They turned to their horses, to the marshes.

"Lady Lark," Twig called loudly.

The gnome was standing some paces away, facing west. I strode to him quickly, anxious to get started. "The pack," I said, pulling it from my back and offering it for him to climb into. "I hope I did not crush you when I fell."

"I am quite resilient," he answered. And then, "Cargh should not have lit the fire."

He was too slow; I was impatient. "Yes, but it was very little fire. Cargh has already put it out. Let us hurry."

But Twig was staring into the tangle of Dark Wood. "It comes too soon," he said softly. "I hope you are ready."

He walked a few steps forward. I followed with the pack. "Twig! We have to go."

He turned to me and said, "I know." He looked sorry.

A thunderous roar, and then all of us were knocked to our knees as the earth gave a great leap. There was a tearing screech, and like a bubble bursting open, the rock and grass exploded.

I scrambled to my feet, the earth still trembling beneath us, and cried out. The ground was split, a long crack parting Twig and me from all the Riders.

"Lark! Make haste! Jump to us!" Brahnt and Gharain were at the edge on the other side, joined by Laurent and Wilh and Ian, and then the others. "We'll catch you."

I reached, but then the ground heaved wider with an enormous groan and we all fell back. "Quickly!" they shouted, leaping once again to their feet.

On knees and elbows, I wriggled to the edge, gasping. It was not so far, maybe only the length of my body. I had no doubt they would all pull me up safely should I fall short. But then, as I gauged it, the gap doubled in width and I was flat on my belly looking for something to hold. *Don't let it take me,* I begged silently. I would disappear like old Harker into that blackness, into the yawning emptiness of Erema's smile—

"Lark!"

I gritted my teeth, pushing against my fears, and stumbled into a crouch, ready to spring. But then I hesitated, stunned. I heard the Riders' shouts, watched the gap widen further. The grass crumbled away, little pebbles dropping into the nothing-ness that opened below.

"Lark! You can do this!" Gharain was there across from me, thinking I was too terrified to jump. "I will catch you!"

Twig had lurched his way next to me, and I turned to him, saying in disbelief, "You knew this would happen, didn't you? You called me over to you—you meant to divide us."

He said, "Lady Lark, I am here to help you."

"Help!" I hissed. "How does it help to separate me from the Riders?"

"I remind you, my lady, that is not your battle."

The earth rumbled; we all struggled to catch our balance.

"Lark!" This was Laurent. His voice was commanding.

"I should be there! I should be over there!"

"My lady," Twig said, barely above the noise of the heaving ground, "that way madness lies."

"Madness!" The roar of the earth was very loud. Now I shouted at him, "*Madness*, in the company of the Riders?" I looked to them, to him; I said frantically, "What am I to do?"

Twig closed his eyes and looked away. "I point the path. You make your choice."

I glared at him. The little man stood at my feet, eyes shut, betraying nothing that would tell me his purpose. Twig—the gift of help, at my request. I looked back over the gap, at the Riders standing poised on the edge and Rune, who shifted ner-vously by them.

And then I remembered: I'd not been on Rune's back in my vision of Merith.

I wanted to go home. I wanted to help my village. And I wanted to be with the Riders; I wanted their safety, strength, and companionship. And, despite a promise, and death, I wanted Gharain. But I looked at Laurent and slowly shook my head.

"Lark!" Gharain cried.

"My journey lies another way!" I shouted over an ominous rumbling, across the widening crevasse. "Take care of my horse."

"Lark, don't!"

The earth buckled, tipping all of us again. I smashed my hands against the ground to gain some sort of hold, feeling it shudder and deflate then under my weight, and come to a sighing rest. I dragged myself up, still feeling the last tremors in my palms, gasping relief as we all did at the sudden calm.

Twig spoke from where he'd tumbled. "We must go."

Rune reared, grounded, and broke into a canter running along the length of the gap and then back again.

"Stay with the Riders!" I yelled. Then I had to turn away.

Gharain shouted my name once more, but I held my arm up in a final wave without turning back, and looked down at Twig instead. "I hope you speak truth, little man."

"Are you afraid?" he asked me.

I snapped at him, "Yes!"

"Fear belongs to the Breeders. They will use it to prey on your sanity."

"Well, thanks for that," I muttered.

"Lady Lark," Twig said, "fear is only when you believe you

don't know how to respond. You've done well thus far. Trust yourself."

I'd heard all that before.

"And your *truth*," he continued, "will be your greatest aid."

"We'd better go." I began to walk back the way we'd come.

But Twig said, "Not that way, Lady Lark."

Before I could ask what he meant, there was a shout from the other side. We wheeled around and I screamed out, "Gharain!"

He was leaping the gap. He'd run, and jumped, and as I screamed, he was suspended in the space between the two edges, caught in midair. And then in a tumble he was down, hard, on our side, but only just—half of him was hanging over the edge, with feet scrabbling for a hold, swearing and digging his fingers into the stubby grass even as he slid backward, the earth crumbling beneath his body.

I was before him, dropping to my knees, grabbing his arms. "Hold on!" I yelled. It was a ridiculous display of effort. He was too heavy for me; I had nothing with which to brace myself.

"Lark," Gharain gritted out, "my fault—I misjudged. Let me go. I'll not pull you down with me!"

"No!" I shouted at him above the others. "No!" I gasped against the weight. "Twig! What do I do?"

"Lark, you are connected with Earth; you know what to do!" Twig shouted at the other Riders, "Stay back! Do not cross!"

I screamed at Twig, "I don't know what—Gharain, don't let go!" I couldn't tell anymore if Gharain was trying to clamber up the edge or push me away.

"Trust yourself, Lark. Trust!" Twig called.

I had no idea what Twig was saying to me; I could only feel my fingers slipping on Gharain's sleeves, his beautiful, warming, needful energy sliding from my grip. I cried out.

Gharain looked up at me. There were beads of sweat on his brow, but he managed to say, "This was my doing. My error. Let me go, Lark."

With a groan, I locked my gaze with Gharain's, dug my toes into the ground, gritted my teeth, and pulled. Pulled with a desire and desperation that was beyond anything I'd needed before. It burned fiercely through my body, igniting into something I didn't recognize. My toes rooted into the earth, my hands wrapped like vines around his arms, and I wrenched him back the way a birch springs a child who swings from it. "I . . . will . . . not . . . let . . . you . . . go!" came from somewhere inside me, but it didn't matter, because we were up and out of the chasm, flung far back on the grass, tumbled together, panting and sweating and disbelieving what I'd just done.

Gharain had landed hard on top of me, smashed flat to my chest before he tipped to one side and rolled back to stare up at the sky, gasping for breath. "What was that?" he forced out after a moment, and turned his head to me.

I could not answer him. I could not believe the strength I'd drawn. I simply stared back.

"That," said Twig, who waddled over to us, "is making use of power. And did I not tell you, Rider, that your passions might do you harm?"

"Gharain! Lark!" The other Riders were calling from across the divide. Eleven men on horseback and two unseated horses stood on the other side, poised to leap or leave us behind.

Twig spoke. "Go, Riders. The Guardian takes her own journey hereon." He bowed to them hand to heart. And when the Riders looked to me, I could only nod that it was so.

They understood. A return bow from all of them, then they wheeled their horses and cantered away into the Niler marshes. Rune and Petral each gave a final whinny, and with a toss of mane dove into the wet behind them.

And it was only a moment later that the reeds stopped rustling and the silence of the place closed round once more.

"They're gone," I said softly. The Riders were fulfilling the task I'd set out to request of them. How utterly different it was from my original expectation.

I looked over at Gharain. He'd dropped onto his back once more and was staring up at the clouds, still breathing hard.

"Why did you do that?" I asked.

His head turned and curls fell over his brow. "I'm not leaving you."

"Some at Tarnec think that you are consumed with guilt for your mistake with Erema. I rather thought you were hoping I'd let you go."

One side of his mouth curved. "I rather hoped you wouldn't."

Twig came to my side. "Do not choose your rest here," he said with annoyance. "This is not the time. Your journey is long, and this is only its beginning."

"I wish I'd not stopped Rune from leaping the gap." I said this to Twig while Gharain had walked away to find the end of the earth rift.

"Dark Wood is no place for a horse," he replied with one eye on the sky and one on Gharain's retreating figure.

"Dark Wood!" I stared down at him. "We do not go in there."

Twig said, "By foot is best."

"Twig!" I said more firmly. "The amulet I seek is in the Myr Mountains, to the north!"

He snorted. "North is north and east is east, but direction does not necessarily determine route."

"I do *not* understand you, gnome."

"How will you go north from here? Would you attempt to jump that rift?" Twig shook his head. "What is that young man doing? He'll find no way across. The split is wide and long."

"No way across?" I was startled. "Then how do we get to the mountains?"

He pointed. "That way, of course. 'Twill have to be."

My breath went out. I sat down. "No. I cannot."

"You merely think you cannot. Remember, fear is only when you—"

"Stop! I know what you've said. I—I just cannot; I will not go into Dark Wood. There is wild energy in there; it brews inside—"

"It is Breeder energy. Chaos," Twig acknowledged with a

little nod. "Harder for you, I am sure. Nonetheless, I am with you, and your Rider is with you. We will watch your path."

One thing, at least, I could refuse. I said flatly, "The Rider is *not* mine."

Twig raised a brow. "Of course he is yours, Lady Lark. He was made your Complement. As said, you are not alone." Twig turned and walked from my stunned expression, back to where we'd left our packs. He could move faster than he'd shown before.

I picked myself up and ran after him. "Complement? What do you mean, made my *Complement*?"

The gnome shook his head at me and opened Gharain's pack. "Do they teach the Guardians *nothing* these days?" He stuck his head inside, rummaging.

"Twig, stop for a moment and speak plainly. What is a Complement?"

There was a sigh, and he pulled his head from the pack. "You did the bond seeking, did you not?" At my silence, he fumed. "How is it they send *fledglings* to face the most difficult of challenges?"

"Twig . . . !"

He tsked at me, and reached now for my empty pack, turning it inside out to inspect the seams. While he scrutinized the rough stitching, he said, "The bond seeking is the awakening of a Guardian, and the purest proof in determining she is a true Guardian. As well, it has secured your connection with the Keepers, for the one who awakens the Guardian becomes the Complement." He looked up at me, still squinting. "Balance, of course. Pairs are good."

I kneeled next to him. "The touch of marks."

He nodded. "The *first* touch of marks. That is a bond seeking. It does not have to be a formal ritual; a seeking can happen sometimes by accident. But the connection is made."

"Are there only four who can be Complements, the way there are only four Guardians?"

"One for one?" He snorted. "That would hardly offer choice, would it? Nay, many Keepers bear special marks. So do"—Twig's voice dropped for this—"many Breeders." He brightened. "Good thing the Riders found you first! Though the king's choice is an interesting one."

"That he made Gharain do the bond seeking, be my Complement?" Forced him, rather. I remembered the terrible resignation on Gharain's face. The *king's* choice; what choice was that? I looked at the gnome. "Does Gharain know this? Does a Complement *want* to be a Complement?"

"No more than a Guardian necessarily wants to be a Guardian. And yes, Lark, your Rider knows what he is. Do not look so distraught. Perhaps the king was wise to choose this, fates being intertwined and all that."

"What do you mean fates intertwined?" Gharain had said that too.

"Oh, a complex business it is, how one person's twist of fate can send so many others' into wholly different directions. Everyone's story is changed."

"Twig!" I stamped my foot. "Speak plainly."

"The Breeder, Erema, read Gharain's fate. She looked into his future, adapted herself to fit his yearnings, and so stole the amulets. Now look where we are! And, no, Lady Lark, she will not read your future; your book is safely held at Tarnec."

"What *book*?"

"The one of your fate. You saw it in the king's hands. The verse the king read, the one used to find you—that is the opening of your tale. What, did you not know that the story of one's destiny is held between the covers of a book? You are woefully ignorant! We all have tales told of us; each of us has a book—a fate. The Guardians' books are held at Tarnec now. So, not to fear, they are safe from any meddling."

"My fate is held in Tarnec? This is what the king would not show me?" I spluttered in surprise and impatience—not that such a book existed, but rather that it languished in Tarnec's possession. "Why do we stand here, then, ready to plunge blindly into Dark Wood? Why did we not read this *book*, find out where the orb lies and how to retrieve it?"

Twig looked at me as if I'd stabbed him. "If you turn so quickly to learn the ending, what happens to choice along the way? I shall tell you: 'twould be manipulated, changed, the way Gharain's fate was changed by the Breeder and so all of ours as well. No, you must not tamper with books of fate!"

"But the *king* is allowed to hold my book? Why?"

"It does not belong to the king! Loaned, only! Oh, the *ignorance*!" Twig stamped around a bit to control his temper. Then he came back to me and said more calmly, "That is old Harker's tale to tell, not mine. What is important is that the Guardians' fates are safe in Tarnec now. It is one small relief in this grave business of retrieving amulets."

Harker and his books—I remembered my dream. But Twig had effectively ended this argument. The odd little seer was long gone; I could hardly ask him anything. Still, I muttered, unwilling to concede, "I don't see what possible relief it is if the answers lie within a book we cannot use!"

And at that Twig smiled happily as if I'd handed him a better answer. I think it was a smile anyway; it was hard to see it beneath his impressive beard. "Oh, Lady Lark! You have the Sight; you know already how to find the orb. *Trust* yourself."

I was silent, furious. How many more would tell me I should simply trust myself? Twig, unperturbed, took out a little white-handled knife from his waistpack. From the selvage of the pack's bottom seam, where Grandmama's hands had so carefully guided mine, he began cutting a little strip of fabric, removing a rectangular piece and placing it and his knife back into his waistpack. He shook my pack right side out and put it next to Gharain's with a little pat, announcing, "Yours is a good family. Strong in your bond."

Then he looked at me. "You remain distressed, Lady Lark. The Breeders will enjoy that. Ah, the young man is returning, and high time it is."

Gharain was approaching—my *Complement* was approaching—calling out to us, "The rift goes on. It splits Dark Wood from the marshes and the Cullan foothills as far as I can see—"

"We waste the hour, Rider," Twig interrupted.

Gharain glared at him, but Twig glared back and said,

"Have you not looked at the sky? A storm approaches from the east. That is never a good sign."

I broke in, also glaring at Gharain. "And neither is it a good sign that a Complement does not introduce himself to his Guardian."

Gharain turned slowly to me, a flush appearing along his cheek. "Would it have changed your rejection?"

"Why? You were loath to make the connection."

"Rider, Lady—" Twig attempted, but we ignored him.

"Loath?" Gharain snorted. "I share my feelings, you reject them, and *I* am loath? Does a *title* change anything?"

"It would have helped me understand *my* feelings!" Frustrated, I waved him away. "Oh, there is no point in this! You do not understand!"

"I suppose, then, you've an *official* reason now to be connected!"

Twig shouted something in gnome language so wretchedly screeching that Gharain and I clapped hands to our ears, cringing. "Now!" he commanded as we went silent. "Are we done with silly arguments? Dark Wood is a treacherous enough place to breach. Let us not do it as enemies."

"Hardly enemies" was Gharain's responding mutter. He gave me a stern look and sighed. "Dark Wood is it, then?"

I swallowed and nodded, and Gharain made a low whistle as he surveyed the barrier of tangled growth. "Is it not better to attempt crossing the rift? If the Breeders wanted Lark separated—"

Twig interrupted, emphatic. "The Breeders wanted Lark with the Riders."

But Gharain turned again to me. "Are you sure?"

I said a little crossly, "At least we'll find no swifts in Dark Wood."

"At *least*." But I suppose Gharain was satisfied, for he added, "So be it."

"So be it," I echoed. *Complement.* The word, the idea, would not stop rolling around my head. Complement: bound, but not by choice. And the king himself had chosen wrong; it was Evie Gharain should complement. What did my book say about this?

Together we reached for our packs. Twig walked ahead, announcing, "I will find an entry."

I sighed. "Don't you mean to be in the pack?"

He was insulted. "I should think not, my lady. *I* am a forest gnome." Then he added, peering into Dark Wood, "But you two will have to take hands."

How funny that sounded! I giggled, suddenly shy again, but Gharain reached his hand out and took mine willingly enough. The charge thrilled up my arm and through my body.

Twig moved on, calling back to us, "You would do well to remember to stay within touch of each other."

And Gharain murmured, "It's only my hand, Lark."

Only.

# 18

"YOU GO TOO fast!" Gharain shouted to Twig, who sprang over the gnarled hurls of roots and stems while we staggered our way behind him.

Twig's returning shout was faint: "You do not wish to be exposed to this storm! We must hurry."

"Hurry to where?" Gharain muttered.

I said nothing, intent on staying upright, on hanging on to Gharain's hand. We'd been traveling for what seemed hours in Dark Wood, though no clue could be drawn from the sky of our whereabouts. It was all simply dark.

Twig had found an opening in the matted boundary of the Wood some lengths from where we'd begun. It was a very narrow gap; Gharain had to use the flat of his sword to push it wider so he could slip through. And it seemed that once we stepped in, the vines simply closed behind us. I think the last thing I said aloud was, "Where do we go from here?" And maybe Gharain said it too; we were both in awe.

A knotted tangle of growth confronted us. Trees, vines, bushes, weeds, distorted to what seemed enormous proportions. Even if there had been no storm brewing, I do not think the sunlight would have penetrated through the thick veil of leaves that blotted out the sky. It was densely moist within, and the air smelled of rotting wood. I spotted a ghisane bush immediately, growing wildly huge, wrapping itself around several trees together—not to choke them, but to use them like a ladder, to climb up and watch things from high above. The trees I could not identify—they were old and gnarled beyond any recognition.

Gharain held my hand firmly, and I was glad of that. The energies in the Wood crept toward me, hovered around me, but could not seem to enter me; I felt the strength to repel this turmoil. He pulled me behind him gently enough, his sword in his other hand outstretched, but Twig had warned him not to slice anything; he was only to use it to widen a passage.

And we needed it. We ducked, we clambered over, we snaked between—an incessant winding of motion that made me dizzy. The earth squished beneath us with no sense of solidity—too many centuries of fallen leaves; who knew how deep the ground cover? We sank to our ankles before we pulled for another step. Gharain shouted to Twig again to slow down, but he called back to be quick, that time was short.

At last, Gharain's sword tip poked through a curtain of twining and we stepped onto firmer ground so suddenly that we both tumbled onto the dirt, landing before Twig, who'd finally stopped.

"Now we may pause," the little man said.

We got to our knees to brush away the decay and reclaim our breath. Gharain said the obvious: "A path."

Twig nodded. "Now 'twill be easier. Safer."

"This is what you were looking for?" I panted.

"'Tis the beginning," the gnome responded. "You cannot traverse Dark Wood without a path."

"That is clear," muttered Gharain, rising to his feet. I stayed on my knees, but Gharain did not stray from my side.

"'Twas rough for you, I know it," Twig acknowledged. "Stay on the path from here on. It is protection. Without it, none would last very long."

"Protection?" I managed to ask, courage sinking. If he spoke of safety, this could not be it.

Twig continued without answering me. "Still, we cannot linger. The storm breaks; we need true cover for this."

In reply, a tremendous crack of thunder roared through the Wood. We all jumped in shock, but I swear that the surrounding undergrowth actually danced a little to the noise.

Twig followed my gaze. "You will soon see things you will wish you hadn't, my lady."

"Then let us go." I said this rising quickly. My skin was already crawling.

"Keep your eyes to the path," warned Twig.

I looked at the length of bare dirt disappearing into the

darkness and swallowed hard. Was it on this path that Ruber Minwl met his fate?

Twig shook his head. "Many paths cross Dark Wood. It was not here, Lady Lark. It was not here."

I stared at him. "How do you know what I am thinking?"

Twig shrugged with a little grin. "You are easy to hear."

"Easy?"

Twig did not answer. He took a few steps forward and turned back. "Come now," he said.

I started, then stumbled. Foolish; I'd only moved a few steps from Gharain, but the force of the Wood hit me hard.

Gharain moved to stop my fall. "I have you," he said under his breath. Then he called to Twig, "Lark needs to sit. She's neither rested nor eaten in many hours."

The gnome shook his head. "We cannot afford a longer pause."

"I'll be fine, truly. The energy here shakes me. It—it's stopped now."

Gharain followed my gaze to his grip and then looked again at me. "We go, then."

Twig nodded and turned. "Try to keep up," he advised, and took off running down the path.

I'd never seen how fast gnomes could run in their own element, but if it was true that garden gnomes were quick as rabbits among the lettuces, here the forest gnome could nearly fly. We tore after him, hand in hand, with Gharain ever tugging me forward, barely keeping the little brown figure in sight. At least the path was flat and free of roots, for the dark was nearly all-consuming.

"Stay with me!" Gharain shouted.

Another burst of thunder shuddered through. I saw the woods shimmering from the sound again; a rustle of leaves, maybe, but I thought it was more.

"What is that?" I screamed to Gharain above the echoed rumble.

"Don't look!" he shouted back.

The thunder crashed again. The rain was falling; I could hear it pound on the leaves, but neither it, nor the lightning, nor the wind had yet reached us. And then, horribly, I knew why Twig was racing for shelter. Dark Wood was not holding back the storm, it was absorbing it, filling with it, until it could explode on us in its full power.

Gharain must have realized it as I did, for his pace quickened and I struggled to keep up.

"Twig!" Gharain shouted once more.

The thunder boomed, this time with the first flash from lightning. And I shuddered at what I saw in the garish light, tripping, then falling hard on the ground, my hand wrenching from Gharain's grip.

Dark Wood was alive. The trees and vines and bushes and the very undergrowth *were* dancing in the thunder—a wild frenzy of passion. It wasn't the wind; it was the flora itself writhing in distorted glee. The trees shaped hideous faces in their gnarled bark, and branches and vines waved unbound arms.

"Lark!" Gharain had to pull up short, nearly falling in his

own speed. He whirled around and grabbed me quickly, jerking me upright.

"The woods," I gasped, teeth chattering. "The woods! You see it, don't you?"

Twig shouted from somewhere far ahead.

"We'll lose him in a moment! Can you run?"

I panted yes, and we took off again. As we did, the canopy opened up, the wind went racing through in a triumphant shriek, and the rain came down in a torrent. A waterfall of wet—we were drenched at once. And if the dark hid Twig, then the rain made him invisible.

"Where is he? Where is he?" I screamed above the thunder.

"Just keep forward," came Gharain's breathless yell.

We were pushing through the storm as if pushing through a wall—a living wall. The rain held us, the lightning made us fall, and the wind tore at us from every direction. And at each flash of light, I could see the Wood in its horrific dance, joined now by creatures I did not recognize—wretched things belonging only to Dark Wood—leaping from the ground, dangling from the vines, clinging to tree bark. The light shut quickly, but their eyes took it in and glowed long after the lightning strikes—gleaming slits of bronze and yellow, throbbing to the thunderous roars. A wail of terror wound out of the woods like a lash, striking our ears with awful noise and sending a knife of cold fear slicing up my spine. Gharain shouted, "Banes!"

"What are they?"

"Death knells! Do not catch their eyes—keep your focus on the path, or they will lure you in!"

I was warned, but I could not help myself. I thudded behind Gharain, my gaze no longer searching for Twig but peering, morbidly fascinated, at all the things that pulsed on the path's border. Which were the hideous-voiced banes—those things of matted fur and loose limbs and bulbous-tipped fingers that held them firmly suspended, or the sharp-scaled lizard beasts that slithered up the vines? A tail, a claw, a fang, a wing: glimpses of other noxious creatures shaking the leaves. Beetles and bugs swarming on the bark, limbless things worming through the fallen matter—how many creatures throbbed in Dark Wood? The rain sluiced down dark within the tangle—it was blood gushing from a wound; it was black sap from the hukon tree. The glowing eyes danced behind slimed, dank leaves, and the smell of decay rose up from the floor of the woods in a reek of slow death. And then the wailing became song, high-pitched and sweet, the tune like a thread to snare and be pulled along. My hand stayed in Gharain's grasp—I could feel it—but my arm was lengthening, extending, disconnecting from the rest of my body until there was left but a tiny charge somewhere far away in my fingertips.

*Come.* Dark Wood pulsed in invitation. Gleaming wet now, densely rich, it was seductive, and intoxicating, and teeming with vibrant life. The song swirled in my head; the melody beckoned. *Come dance.* And the path was suddenly plain and bare while the rest of life whirled and spiraled but a step away. The wind, thunder, rain, and banes' calls were in exquisite harmony. The charge in my fingers disappeared.

I saw them: the creatures, the trees, the vines reaching

out to embrace my step into the woods. *That way madness lies* rang once more in my head, and I laughed, fear dropping off me like a cloak. Of course it was madness to be in that dry space, following that rigid file of horse and man; of course it was madness to plow the field, trim the hedgerow, scythe the grass, find the Balance, choose but one. It was madness to think I mattered. . . . More was offered here—a release of everything at once—no choice, no decision, simply everything at once, whirling before me, offering to absorb me. The path was stark and still—but here! Only a step beyond! I yearned for it, my hand reaching into the web of dark. . . . Vines, leaves, fingers, and claws, all shiny wet, reached back to help me in.

And then the air was knocked from me, hard. I landed on my stomach on the bare path, Gharain above me, breathing as heavily as if he'd shoved a horse from its way.

"What—what is in you?" he yelled out against the lovely shimmers. "Lark! What are you doing?"

"The Wood is dancing! Let me go!" I cried at him. I struggled to move; I could feel the heat of his body warming through me. I didn't want it. I didn't want it.

Gharain swore at me. He shouted my name, and then he cursed aloud to the crawling woods around us. "Leave her! Don't touch her!" He grabbed my shoulders and turned me over and rattled me so my teeth knocked and my breath was forced out of me. "Close your eyes, Lark! Close your eyes! It's a terrible beauty! It's not real! Don't allow it in!"

I laughed at him, but then I had no breath. I began to choke, and I closed my eyes to pull for air. Gharain's energy was drawing through me, coursing in, shaking the dark out of me with every cough. The powerful frenzy was dissipating, and I pounded at him, screaming to release me back to the wilds of Dark Wood so that I could exult in its dance, but Gharain grabbed my head and pulled it into his chest so that my eyes could not see. And even as I fought him, the harmony soured and clashed and became roars of horror and fury, and fear crashed in. And then I was no longer fighting Gharain but pressing into him, breathing into him, wrapping arms around him so he would not let me go. And he hugged me back, tightly, as the storm raged on.

It seemed forever before he relaxed his grip. I raised my head to look up at him—barely; the rain poured into my eyes. I coughed up water.

Relief and anger warred in Gharain's voice. "Do you understand its power now?" he gasped. "What were you choosing? You broke hands. You were trying to climb back into the chaos!"

"I—I thought . . . It was beautiful." Part of me still ached for the fever.

"It is not beauty," he said grimly. "It is manipulation. I know it well." He lifted off of me, taking care to keep hold of my shoulder. The banes wailed as he helped me to my feet, and I cringed now at their piercing anguish.

"We've lost Twig." I gulped, looking over the path. It sank away in eerie darkness. "I'm sorry."

"It's all right." Gharain helped me stand, rubbed my arms to stop the shiver. Then his hands gripped my arms and he pulled me close to make me look at him. "Lark, it will be all right. He said to stay on the path; we'll find him. Ready?"

I nodded and we pushed forward, more slowly and tightly together this time—arms entwined. The rain drenched us until our clothes and bodies could hold no more and then it ran down our lengths, leaving streams in our wake. We sloshed along the path of what was now a stew of mud, blinking the water from our eyes to see only an arm's length ahead; churned through this mess of earth, careful not to slip or break our hold. Then another flash of lightning showed something more frightening: the weight of rain was sliding debris from the woods onto the path—the rare open space was filling slowly with the matted wreckage of Dark Wood.

"This is not good," muttered Gharain, half to me, half to himself.

"Look!" I cried out. "Did you see that? It's growing—where it pours in from the woods, it starts growing! Look for it when the lightning next strikes!"

And indeed, the following flash captured shoots of snaking vines sprouting up from the path, narrowing our route. Gharain kicked at some of the tendrils and smashed them down with his foot. I yanked my boot from a twining brown thing that was wrapping itself around my ankle.

"If you don't go into Dark Wood, it will come to you," Gharain growled, and jerked me forward as another vine grabbed at my leg. "Careful."

"The path was meant to be safe!" I yelled, more to the

Wood than Gharain. They grew fast, these shoots; some of the vines had already reached the height of my waist. My heart was pounding above the noise of the rain. We would not be able to go much farther before we were trapped. I hugged both arms around Gharain as he drew his sword, ready to slice a way through.

"Do not cut the Dark Wood!"

"Twig!" we shouted together.

The gnome's voice was sharp, just ahead of us in the dark. "If you think it traps you now, cut it and it will swallow you whole in vengeance! Quickly! This way."

Twig was there up ahead, hopping out of the way of each new growth. He was fast, though; the vines could not ensnare him. "Quickly!"

And then we reached him, followed him—not his figure but his voice—ducking low and tumbling in what seemed a downward slide only a step from the edge of the path. And then we were stopped, once more on flat ground, able to stand upright. It was completely dark, but it was dry, and the noise of storm and woods suddenly felt like harmless murmurs. A calm, sturdy energy surrounded us. Sanctuary—

But I gasped, breaking the quiet. "The path! It closed on us! I thought we were to be safe on the path!"

"The path will reclaim its place afterward, but it has no strength against a storm," said Twig. "You must wait here until it subsides. We are safe beneath this footing of oak."

"Oak! In Dark Wood?" Gharain gripped me tightly still, unsure if anything here could be safe.

"Ah yes! Here and there are oak and willow and mulberry. Chaos cannot claim everything, you know—there are always objects and points of stability in the worst of it." And then Twig caught himself, as if he remembered the lost amulets, and added, "For now."

"Good that this is," Gharain said. "We need light. Is it safe, then, to make a fire?"

Twig was horrified. "A fire! Does wood not burn?" He muttered to himself, his voice moving as if he paced, "Babes they send to do warriors' work! Ignorant children!"

"My apology," Gharain said stiffly. "But Lark is cold and soaked, and it is black in here."

I stepped in, calmer now. "It's just . . . Twig, we cannot see anything."

"Maybe that is a good thing for *you*," he retorted. But then I could sense his grin in the blackness; he was proud of himself for something.

"I am aware of the wet and the dark, Rider, but you tall ones remain too attuned to your eyes. So be it, then—here is a treat for you." There was a pause, and Twig called out very politely, "May we have light?"

Overhead something flickered; Gharain and I both gasped. A starry sky was suddenly lit above us, though we were underground—a thousand pinpricks of golden starlight filled the burrow with a sweet glow.

"Glimmer moths," announced Twig.

Glimmer moths. Tiny, translucent creatures scattered on the oak roots woven across the earthen ceiling. Their wings sparkled—shimmering with each beat of gossamer. I looked up at Gharain, whose face caught the radiance of the light and reflected it back.

"Our thanks, gnome." His voice was husky, and my heart skipped at the sound. He sensed my gaze, looked down at me, and smiled.

Twig was not subtle. "You no longer have to clasp one another thus—Lark is safe under the oak."

So Gharain withdrew his arm, leaving empty space.

"Now for you both." Twig's voice broke our stare. He was holding out a bundle of something, dividing it between us, placing it in our hands: something soft and billowy, like a handful of bearded moss. "This works well to dry the skin. Now clothes and boots may go here." He pointed to some root ends that poked out like hooks from the earthen walls.

I stripped off my leggings and tunic, leaving my undershift, which would likely dry quickly enough. Gharain took off his tunic, which bared his torso, but—I was relieved—refused Twig when he motioned for his pants. We scrubbed with the mossy fluff, which drank the wet like a sponge.

This peace was glorious beyond the storm. I looked around. We were in not a cave, but a rather large, circular burrow. Its width was more than several steps across, high enough to stand straight and look up to its canopy of roots. The industrious gnome had spread armfuls of the moss at one end for bedding, and now our clothing hung at another—spare, but a homelike comfort. I went over to Twig to thank him. He was at the opening to our burrow, laying sprigs of something on the ground.

He looked up at me. "There, all better? Not quite like drowned whelps now."

I smiled at him, and Gharain called out, "All better. We thank you."

The gnome gave a little shimmy of pleasure. There was a brief moment where his body seemed to evaporate. I blinked.

"Twig, what are you doing?"

He held up a long-stemmed purplish blossom. "A little wood betony to keep out bad things." He finished bordering the entrance and stood up. "You can find it in Dark Wood if you look closely. As I said, there are things that can help you in the midst of misfortune, if you pause to look. Though"—he surveyed his work—"I cannot promise it will keep out everything."

"Banes?" The memory of their death calls sent a chill down my spine.

"Not the banes so much," said Twig in answer. "They frighten with their noise. At worst, if you see them, then their shrieks become like a siren song and draw you in. No, I worry about the Troths."

At that Gharain moved to my side—when had it become easy for him to reach for me? He looked at the little goose bumps on my arms.

"Twig, we must have something to warm us. 'Twill be a long wait underground, and Lark is chilled through."

"I am *aware*." The gnome sniffed. He shook his head and said, "If you were not descended from the king, I would not take so kindly to your tone." Then, deciding not to remain insulted, he said cheerfully enough, "Come, sit, it is high time for gift giving; we've not much longer."

Twig ushered us forward and bade us sit in the middle of the burrow, under an oak root that was crowded with glimmer moths—bathing us with light. Then the gnome sat down so that we faced each other more or less in a circle. He reached to his waistpack and fumbled with the string, mumbling, "Gifts that are requested, and gifts that are freely given—"

I asked, "What is this gift giving?"

Twig paused his movement to stare at me. "Do not say to me that you do not know."

"I'm sorry, but I have no gift for you."

"The gift giving is not for me!" Twig smacked his forehead so hard he toppled. Next to me Gharain swallowed his chuckle. "Nothing!" the gnome continued, righting himself. "I'm left to tell it all!" He tsked and muttered, "I have so little time and they leave me all of it!" Then he turned to me and stared hard. "You know nothing of the three gifts?"

"The king was to give me three tokens that would help reclaim the crystal orb. But I do not yet have them; I do not know what they are. . . ." I frowned, sanctuary forgotten. Twig would rage again at my ignorance, and why should he not? How ineffectual a Guardian I was if I'd learned nothing from this ordeal. Maybe my original fear was true, that I did not merit this task—I didn't know which way to go, how to get there, and what to do, and I certainly didn't know what gifts I needed with me on this undirected quest.

All at once, whatever pleasure I'd taken in finding safety under the oak was gone. I was simply a scared girl lost in Dark Wood, cold, tired, hungry . . . and useless.

But the gnome did not rage. He sighed and gave a little shake of his head at my thoughts. "Do not be upset. You ignore what you've accomplished, but I suppose that will change with time." He turned to his waistpack and pulled out an object bigger than his two small hands. The thing must have long weighed him down by the size of it. And now, as he held it out, he seemed to fade a little—his beard whiter and his arms and legs thinner. I was reminded of the king suddenly, and I thought miserably: *I take their energy.*

But Twig looked at me, and leaned toward the center of our circle. "Lady Lark, we are all a part of this quest, we allies and Keepers. We all share in it; we all give what we can give. The final moments will be yours to bear alone, so it is now that we can aid you, support you, so that you may stand ready for the greatest challenge. My desire remains that you trust you *will* know what to do in that final moment." He stretched out his arms. "Now, in the king's stead, here is the first gift—since it has been requested by your Complement. We may use it now for warmth."

Twig opened his hands and placed the thing between us. It was a stone, oval in shape, translucent with a bluish tinge. Its faint color was familiar.

"This is a moonstone," the little man said.

I nodded, my throat still thick with discouragement. I'd never heard of a moonstone, but then I'd never heard of the stones Twig had fished from the stream either.

Twig kept his eyes on me. "It's rather innocuous as such—a pretty stone, 'tis all—but pick it up, Lark. Warm it in your hands."

Cold fingers to warm a cold gem; I took up the moonstone.

Twig murmured, "No, truly *hold* it." And so I cupped my hands around the smoothness, pressing it between my palms.

With a little spark, I felt the energy whir inside the stone, faint at first, and then with a vibrating buzz. And suddenly there was light glowing between my fingers, and I opened my hands. The moonstone shone brighter than a candle in the moth-lit space.

"Oh!" I mouthed. I heard Gharain's sharp intake of breath.

Twig was beaming. "We know it too as the traveler's stone. 'Tis a stone for balance, for insight and rejuvenation. But *now* you understand a moonstone's power within the hands of a Guardian. It radiates her energy."

I would have sat there, awed, holding the little source of light forever, I think, but Twig said, "Draw the stone through the length of your hair, my lady. Three times should do. Rider, help her."

Gharain took the moonstone from my open palm and slid the stone slowly down my hair, threading pale blue through nut brown. The first sweep was cool against my scalp. The second, I felt the stone warm. And then by the third time it slid to my hip, the moonstone blazed hot. Gharain dropped the stone, and it rolled back to the center of our circle. We could feel a steady, surrounding heat rise from its tiny surface. It brought back my smile. Radiate energy, indeed.

Twig made a little snorting laugh. "Now you will be quite toasty."

Gharain fingered a few strands of my hair. I blushed and looked at the gnome. "Thank you for my gift, Twig."

He grinned broadly. "Gnomes are deft jewel cutters," he said proudly. "And a moonstone is one of the most intricate—the axes must align precisely or the stone does not reflect with true clarity. Highly polished it should be as well. This one I made myself, to be certain. Moonstones are great resources for Guardians. Keep it close."

For a time we all watched the light. The burrow warmed quickly, the heat like a silky caress over skin.

"Now, before the other gifts, some sustenance," Twig announced. He grinned broadly. "Tonight we feast!"

And the little man dug into his waistpack and drew out three acorns, placing one before each of us. I almost laughed; Gharain sat very still next to me, holding his tongue.

But Twig looked up at me and winked. "Do not always use your eyes to determine the value of something," he said. "These are from the white oak on the far side of the Myr Mountains. Like the rowan in Bren Clearing, the white oak is special, and a most powerful refuge in the midst of the Waste. Its acorn will sate your hunger. We may roast them over the moonstone."

We each held our single acorn over the stone's light, fingers moving so they wouldn't burn, feeling the shell grow quickly hot, then brittle. We smacked them with open palm to split the skin. The acorns revealed two seeds each—a rare thing. And we ate them, letting their burst of oil play on our tongues and trickle down our throats. Tiny as the meal was, it was utterly delicious and utterly filling.

As we ate, I watched Twig's form clearly changing. I hadn't been mistaken: he was whiter, paler, a tinge of glimmer highlighting his skin and clothes.

"Twig, what is happening to you?" I asked sharply.

He calmly finished chewing. "As I said, there is not much time left." Then he chuckled at my shocked gasp. "I am not dying, my lady. 'Tis that my help lasts but one full sweep of sun from the moment of request."

My jaw dropped. "Why did you not warn me of this?"

"And have you worry about losing me for the length of time you had me?"

That was true, but it did not make me feel better. "How can you help me if you are gone?" I asked hoarsely. Had I known him for only a day? It seemed that I should not move forward if he was not there to point my way.

But he answered my thought. "'Tis what I said before, Lady Lark. You must trust yourself."

Gharain made a little shift of movement, and the gnome added with a raised eyebrow, "And, you are not alone. So let us not waste more time on saying goodbye. Time is nearly out; we must finish the gift giving." He turned to Gharain. "You requested of me; now I request of you. Rider, would you hand me your tunic?"

Gharain stood and unhooked his shirt from the root. Twig took it with eager hands.

"Good, good," he said. He looked up at Gharain. "Do you allow me to take something from this?"

Gharain nodded solemnly. Twig spread the shirt on the floor of the burrow, fingers searching nimbly for what he wanted: the stone toggle at the neck of Gharain's tunic. He took from his waistpack the little white-handled knife, cut the threads, and returned the tunic. "All good," the gnome announced. "Now, Lark, I complete your second token."

Twig withdrew two more things from the waistpack, which he placed side by side on the hard earth: the bit of cloth he'd cut from my sack and Quin's withered fern. He moved Gharain's stone button next to them, and then rubbed his hands in satisfaction. "I craft an ally token for you, my lady. Watch. We begin here: three things of Earth, from three planes of love."

The gnome kept his eyes on me, seeing my cheeks grow hot even before he mentioned Gharain. "Look to these, Lady Lark," he said, pointing at the three items. "Plant, animal, and rock: three objects of Earth. Friend, family, and heart's desi—"

"No!" I had to interrupt, to beg, desperate. "Do not say it!" I felt the change of energy in Gharain, though he did not move.

Twig simply watched me. "Three planes of love," he whispered, insisting. "Your three planes of love. Allies to draw from."

No one said a word. My throat closed over quickened breath, humiliated that my feelings should be announced thus to Gharain. Heart's desire! He *was* so, but he could not be so.

Then Twig said very quietly, "What lies in the heart, Lady Lark, simply *is*. What you choose to do with it is your own destiny. But truth is crucial in an ally token. And this *will* be your ally, if it is your truth. Remember that." He took the three items, rearranging them in a little pile now so that the cloth lay on the bottom, the stone in the middle, and the fern on top. He looked back up at me. "Do you make this token?"

There was silence again. Burning, I understood what he meant; I suppose we all did. And the hush in the little burrow was severe in its intensity. An ally token—it had to be true or it would hold no power. I swallowed; the barest sound, admitting to truth even as I rejected it: "I make."

Gharain shifted only slightly, but his energy changed once more.

Twig was nodding. "Then we need something from you to bind these."

I knew. I slowly tugged out two strands of my hair, handed them to the gnome, and he wrapped the little bundle with my hair—winding the length down and up, covering the three gifts until they were tightly bound. Twig knotted the ends.

"There, now, this should be quite strong. Three samples of love, three symbols of Earth—one freely given, one taken, one asked for. This is your ally token—a friend to draw strength from in a time of need." Twig presented it to me, and I took it in my hands and felt each piece within the bundle—the stone warm and solid, the cloth soft and sturdy, the fern still fragrant. My hair secured them together.

"That is good." Twig reached out again to place his finger on the ally token as if he too wanted a moment to draw strength from it. His fingers shimmered now, sheer and then not. He was fading before my eyes.

"Twig—"

He shook his head at me. "All is good. The moonstone, the ally token . . . we've two tokens left. One a gift of something claimed and freely returned, and the final one to be a sacrifice—"

"But the king said only *three*. I don't wish any more sacrifices!" I said it loudly.

"But the *king* did not know that you would leave Tarnec as you did and change your path. So I will add to the gifts a sacrifice of something," he insisted. "Of something precious."

Twig reached up and ripped the tiny red jewel from the neck of his tunic and passed it to me. It fell like a teardrop in my open palm, glittering darkly under the canopy of stars. His voice was husky. "A terrible tragedy reaped this. There is no other."

Gharain spoke. "The color is very deep. A ruby, is it not?"

"In resemblance." Twig reached a finger to the jewel—a last stroke upon the minute facets. I felt bad that he'd necessarily part with two such fine-worked gems, but the gnome swallowed and shook himself. "Do not look at me sadly, Lady Lark. I am quite recovered. There are reasons for everything. That I have this means that I am meant to pass it to you. There is no value if one hoards one's treasures. They must be shared to be truly precious."

But I said, "Twig, I am sad because you are very nearly gone." Indeed, the little man had paled to a whitish transparency.

"What?" And the gnome looked down at himself and said, "My, my. How odd! Well, no mind. I am soon to be back at the task that was so abruptly interrupted when I was called to help you." He sounded pleased, but I sensed a little disappointment.

"I believe, Twig, that you might have liked to see how this journey ends," I murmured. Then I laughed a little shakily. "Perhaps you could read of it in my book."

He looked at me straight. "I do not need to read it; I have faith that you will succeed. Now you must have that faith as well."

I took a deep breath. I tried not to let my own doubt cloud the moment.

"Trust yourself, my lady." The gnome stood and adjusted his waistpack. There was nothing he could do about his collar, though. It flapped loosely, giving the neat little man a newly rakish look. I had to grin at that.

"Ah! The final token!" Twig said suddenly. "What did I say it was?"

He knew the answer, but he seemed to want me to say it. "A gift of something taken—"

"No, not you, my lady." He'd turned to Gharain. "Rider, you tell me what the final gift is."

"Something claimed and freely returned."

"Yes." The gnome stared hard at Gharain. "Claimed, and freely returned."

Gharain made no move.

"Ah," said the gnome. "Not yet ready, I think. But do not wait too long."

"Twig!" I cried out. "You are fading away!"

"Not to worry, my lady, not to worry! It is time, then. The sun has completed her cycle."

"Bid goodbye, Twig, please?"

He waddled to me. I could hear his footsteps, only barely see his form. "A true goodbye, in Tarnec fashion." Hand to heart, he bowed his head. Gharain and I both echoed the gesture, and I could see that it moved the gnome. He cleared his throat—and then it was a sound only, for we could no longer see him. A wisp of light was all that remained, like a sheer puff of smoke.

His voice stood out once more, firm and wise. "Rider, do not wait until it is too late!" Then to me, it seemed, he shouted, "Look west at the sunrise!"

"The sun rises in the east," I started to say, but already the smoke was dissipating.

"Farewell!" came his thinned voice. The smoke drifted up and was gone.

Gharain and I sat silently for a very long while.

# 19

"WHAT DO WE do now?" My question drifted like dust in the hollow space. I could have expected an answer from Twig. Now there was nothing.

Outside, the storm had not abated. Like a demon, it howled and shrieked beyond our burrow while we sat long and silent, the gnome's absence heavy between us. I couldn't look at Gharain now that we were alone. I studied the moonstone instead, which still gleamed with bright warmth, and wondered how long its helpful fire would last. And then I wondered at all the help I'd been offered along the way—wondered if it were true what Twig had said about having done well thus far. Had I been on the path to reclaiming the crystal orb, even if I hadn't known it?

"'Tis your choice, Lark, is it not?"

Gharain's response was made so quietly that I had to turn

to hear him. When he caught my eye, he gave me a small grin, warm in the gem's light. "Isn't that what Twig was asking you to do—trust yourself?"

I nodded halfheartedly and turned my gaze back to the moonstone.

And he echoed me very softly. "So? What do we do now?" I had to turn again, to see if he was jesting, but his beautiful face held no humor.

*Heart's desire*—unspoken, it filled the space. I looked away, blushing, my hand reaching unconsciously for the ally token. Gharain watched me, which made my fingers tremble. He was calm enough. "You are missing the last gift."

"From you." Now the blush crept down my chest and throat.

There was silence for a time, until I was obliged to look up. He was still watching me, something almost triumphant in those sage eyes—something deeply pained as well.

"I caused a great tragedy," Gharain murmured. "You are right to reject me. And yet . . ." He smiled a bit. "You once said that I came to you in a dream. Do you know that you came to me in one as well?"

"A dream?" I managed.

"The Guardian," he murmured, his gaze lifting as he remembered. "Calling to me, mine to awaken. I wanted—" Then his smile fell away. "It has been many lifetimes since a Guardian was awakened. I thought she was needed. I did not know I would be the one to *make* the Guardian needed."

My voice was too husky. "Fate—"

"My dream did not reveal you; I only knew you were near. When a message came, inviting me to find you, I raced to the search, and—and I found her. Erema." Gharain winced. "I was raw, so desperate to be in love and believe. . . . What you felt in Dark Wood was the same power that claimed me, only I had no one to keep me from the madness."

"She caused it. She knew your want. She changed your fate." All our fates.

"I was consumed by desire." He shuddered. "And then a horror I could not bear. I tore through our last battle with Troths with unsated fury and a feeling that I could not wait to die. But it was over too soon, and I still lived, and—"

Gharain looked at me, shaking his head in wonder. "You were there on the ledge, as if you waited for me—arms around the white horse, the two of you gleaming in the moonlight." He winced. "I watched, and waited. And I thought nothing but that I must kill you."

My voice was husky. "If not you, then someone else—"

"But it was not someone else, Lark. *I* was the one too easily persuaded—too easily manipulated." He took a breath. "Unworthy to be made your Complement."

It hurt to hear. "How can you say unworthy? You did not ask to be my Complement. You suffered the king's desire for it, didn't you?"

"Lark, I didn't have to do it. We always have a choice. Nay, I wanted to."

"But your face! You looked as if you could not bear to touch me."

"I could not *bear* that the king granted me that honor after what I did." He waited for a time. Then softly, curiously, he murmured, "You refuse me, not because of Erema but something else."

I watched him, eyes wide; I could not release his gaze. What he said was true.

A faint smile returned. "It gives me hope that I will right this wrong." Gharain shifted ever so slightly closer, quizzing me with his look, and the connection between us hummed strong. "A most terrible error I made, and yet you refuse me because of a dream."

I hesitated, then forced my head to shake, to break eyes. "I do not blame the past, but I cannot change what I have seen. You *will* fall in love with someone else, and you will kill me."

"No." He was severe. "I have caused enough wrong—"

"Gharain, you carved your sword straight through me." I was brutal, his face so awful that I added softly, "It did not hurt."

"No! I cannot, could not harm you—I could not survive that!"

But the deepest wound was already inflicted. I had to sound calm if he was not: "Two dreams, Gharain. Please understand, then, that if you could not live with the regret of one, I cannot live with the regret of the other."

He was still fierce. "I can't—I won't believe it!"

"It is what I saw, Gharain. My dreams do not lie—"

This time he reached for me. He took my arms in his powerful grip and drew me a breath away to face him. "And I told you that even if your visions do not lie, they can still be misinterpreted. Did I not misinterpret?" He leaned forward, his lips nearly touching mine. "You will not yield to truth," he murmured. "You find excuses; I think you protect your heart—"

He made me tremble. "It is not mine that I protect."

"Then whose? Certainly not mine." He whispered, "I *know* I will not harm you."

And then his mouth did touch mine, so light, warm, and my breath came out like a whimper before I pulled back.

"It is not me that you are meant to love, Gharain." I could hardly speak the words, my want for him was so intense. "It is my cousin, Evie. She is lovely and kind. When you meet her, you will—"

"I dreamed of *you*." Once more he leaned to brush my lips. "I am your Complement."

Once more I pulled back, barely, for he did not let me go. "Choice or not—you are not required to *feel* anything for . . . for me." I was breathless. He was too close. "You said yourself that you did not see me in your dream. Another Guardian it was, maybe. Evie bears a mark. . . ." And then I begged him, "*Please*. I will not be able to turn from you—I *need* to turn from you!"

"For Evie?"

I nodded because I no longer trusted my words.

Gharain sat a little straighter. "Mark or no mark," he murmured. "There is more beyond that single touch than an awakening of power. You know it, you feel it, and yet you will not yield to truth."

It was at that moment that the ground rumbled beneath us. I fell forward, my hands smashed under my chest. I screamed out at the threat this time, fearing Gharain would be torn from me here in Dark Wood, but his hands did not let go. He was solid as the earth shivered, keeping hold of my arms, keeping his gaze locked on mine.

"It won't stop!" I gasped. "This will never stop!"

"Lark—"

It would never end, these upheavals. Another lurch sent clods of dirt raining down. What defenses I'd put up crumbled under the stark fear of this endless flux, of losing him. "Don't let it take you, Gharain!" I raged at him, begged him. If he fell through as he'd done before, I'd have no strength to drag him back.

A severe jolt almost broke us, knocking us both to one side. Gharain's hands slipped to my wrists. We rolled over, struggling for a hold, for stability—struggling to clamber to our knees. There was no sanctuary, no place of safety. Even beneath the oak they'd found us.

"Lark! Listen to me! I have you! I won't let go." Gharain held on firmly even as the quaking tugged at us to part. "See? I've your hands. I have you!"

I gritted my teeth to stop their chattering. A glimmer moth fell by my knee, shaken loose by the quake, and writhed on the ground. Beneath the roar of rain and thunder and wind, and groaning earth, I watched the moth struggle, using the leverage of its wings against the earth to right itself and flick back to the safety of the oak roots.

Leverage. I looked at my hands, small within Gharain's fists. Three times, at least, my hands were on the ground when a rifting calmed. It could not be coincidence.

"Let go!" I yelled.

He shook his head, misunderstanding. "I've got you!"

"No, Gharain! Let go! Let me go!"

He released me and I reached my shaking hands to the dirt floor, feeling with sickening horror the emptiness after his strong hold and the lurching of ground beneath my cold palms. I slammed them into the dirt, grunted out a cry, and pressed. . . .

And with a hard sigh, the earth deflated beneath us and was calm.

I fell facedown, but came up laughing, spitting dirt. "I did it! It worked!"

Gharain was sitting up, sliding over to me. "It *was* you." He helped me come upright, sitting to face him, and taking my wrists again in his grasp. Immediately his bright energy flowed through. "Your hands . . ."

I was jubilant. "I pressed my palms into the earth and it calmed! The earth responded to me!"

He grinned wide. "The verse, Lark, *your* verse: *Power of hand* . . . Your hands against earth." Gharain shook my wrists gently in a loose grasp and then paused, staring down at them. In a lower voice, he said, wondering, "And yet, when we first fell and you pushed yourself up, nothing changed. It was, I think, because I was holding you."

"Your touch redirected my energy," I agreed. There was silence. And then I looked up at him, memory warming through me, beyond his grip, his words. "Your *touch*," I said very softly. "You affect me."

"I thought we shared . . . and yet we do not." There was disappointment in his voice.

But I shook my head, a light dawning. "No, we do not share. 'Tis not sharing." I sat up a little higher. "'Tis a circle. A *cycle*. Do you remember the wicks springing to life between our hands? Our touch flows energy between us—a give-and-take. Gharain, you balance me."

There was a tremor to his hold, but he laughed a bit. "So this amazing feeling is the give-and-take of Balance, that together we inspire life to thrive."

*The wicks had thrived.* I was hoarse. "Nayla said it to me: it is what we give to Earth that allows her to provide. She was speaking of me, Gharain! Of—of us . . ." My voice faded, abruptly shy.

His grip changed, warmth flowing through me, charged and strong. And he asked what I'd once asked, needing to hear my answer aloud: "What do I give? Lark, our Life Guardian, connected to the Earth and all she provides, what do I give to you? Say it. *Say* it."

My own hands were shaking. I whispered back, "Love."

His eyes searched mine. "I do love you, Lark, you already knew that."

And it was true. In this small moment in time, Gharain

did love me. Deeply. I knew it through every sense, every pore of my body. And the exquisiteness of that truth welled up and spilled into me as brilliant happiness, boundless strength.

We give love, Nayla had said, to bring forth bounty.

I took his hand and pressed it against my heart, hearing the sharp intake of breath from both of us at the touch. "Look, Gharain, at what you do."

The Rider smiled his achingly beautiful smile, which I returned, understanding. It no longer mattered past or future, broken heart or death. In this moment, Gharain loved me. And so for now there was only this: this circle of Balance completed, flowing warm and charged between us. It was brief, what I could claim, but it was pure and honest. It was my truth.

"Gharain."

"Yes, Lark?"

"I yield," I murmured, and felt his lips take mine.

Sometime later in that night, I felt the sweep of something light against my cheek and then Gharain's lips by my ear. "Lark," he whispered, "I return these to you. I'd kept them, to have something of you near always. But now I have you."

And I turned to him and sought his mouth once more, and he let the feathers brush down my skin before reaching an arm back to tuck them into my sack—these namesakes, and sign, and summons. This gift.

Mine.

The earth shook often through the night—shimmers, above and below us—powdery dirt sprinkling down and the oak roots trembling in their hold of the ground. The storm had faded; all that was left was the groan of tremors—sounds that had terrified me earlier and did no longer. Gharain's arms hugged me close anyway. "You are beautiful," he whispered warm against my neck. Dark Wood could have fallen around us and I do not think I would have minded.

The moonstone was dimming, and though the glimmer moths continued to spread their glow, our burrow was now cast in a blue-tinged hue. The ground shook beneath us once gently, once harder; Gharain's arms tightened, though he slept. I stirred at the motion and then let my head turn once more into the crook of his shoulder, smelling his bare skin against the mossy bed we lay upon.

And the ground shook. And shook again. I closed my eyes and smiled.

It was only at the soft scrabble of claws that I stirred. It was not loud, nor even frightening, just a sound that did not belong to the place. My lashes were heavy with sleep; I peered through them half-opened. And perhaps I would not have seen it in the dim light—but the smell then burned through my nostrils, rank and pungent, and I forced my eyes wide to look.

I'd fallen away from Gharain—he lay with one arm still beneath me, sprawled faceup in a luxurious and deep sleep. Our bed was warm and soft—who would not have been so innocently open beneath that starry glitter? The stench hit me again, and I froze where I lay, barely allowing my head to turn fully to the side, to look past Gharain's tanned chest gently rising and falling, past to the Troth that shuffled, then crouched at his side.

My breath sighed out of my body—the silent deflation before panic. How had the beast entered the burrow when Twig had so carefully defined a boundary? With the sparest motion, my eyes flicked to the opening, to the terrible realization that the Breeders had used the tremors to shake loose the wood betony from its impassable line—vibrations had forced the stems to roll down and away from the entrance. The passage was clear.

The Troth supposed us both asleep—a small ignorance that allowed me to watch him contemplate Gharain's prone body, as if wondering what to do with him. The thing leaned down to take in the young man's scent. My stomach churned beneath rigid limbs; I barely dared breathe. He scored Gharain up and down with his gaze, and a clawed digit sketched an imaginary line above his chest, as if choosing the exact spot where to strike. And then, for the briefest instant, I saw Erema in the creature's place, her fingers splayed above bared skin, claiming him, and then the fingers were claws once more, and gray-mottled.

Gharain's sword lay against the earthen wall to my left. I did not hesitate. The slimy arm of the Troth drew up, and I rolled toward the weapon, reaching for the hilt to pull it close and swing. At the noise, the Troth reared his head with a screech through his nostrils and his jagged teeth gnashed open.

Something was wrong. The metal of the sword was burning cold—too heavy in my grasp, twice the weight I'd imagined, resisting my efforts to clasp it. I needed two hands to drag it forward, to force it to me. And neither did that work, so I scrambled to my knees and wrenched it up, ignoring the burn to haul it toward the Troth as if the view of the sword alone would be enough to frighten away the beast.

Maybe it was. In that brief moment between shriek and sword, the Troth reared up, grunting and snorting through those gashes of nostril and then bursting forth with another screech that sent Gharain leaping to his feet before arcing back from the wild swipe of claws. The Troth bounded for the opening.

"Lark, no!" Gharain shouted as he saw me, but it was too late. I was stumbling to the burrow's entrance, into the dimmest of dawns, dragging the sword behind, fear and fury propelling me outside to challenge the terrible thing. I trampled over the useless wood betony and out into Dark Wood, which crowded, soaked and heavy, around our tiny shelter. I'd forgotten how quickly its wild energies could seize my senses. At once, the whirling fury was there, whipping straight through me. I clenched my teeth against the pulses charging up my bones.

The Troth was gone in a blink of eye—slimy skin dissolving into the wet tumble of dark matter. I spiraled once on the path to look, noting vaguely that the vine shoots that took over the path last night were gone from it now, creeping back into their own territory. But the Troth! Where was it?

"Lark!" Gharain had followed me out, and I turned to look at him.

"A Troth!" I shouted, straining against Dark Wood's insidious pressure. "Did you see it?"

"Lark, the sword! It is not for you! Let it go!"

But then the Troth was back, leaping onto the path, confronting me with gurgling snarls and snapping jaw. I cried out and tried to put the sword between us. Gharain was shouting, but so too was the Troth screeching, and I could understand neither. The Troth edged nearer; I could not lift the sword. It weighed beyond my strength—a mountain between my hands. With one sweep of its iron arm, the beast knocked the weapon from me. It held no weight for him; like a pebble it went winging away to the side of the path—no, off the path and into the undergrowth, which seemed to swallow the blade whole.

I was tossed suddenly to one side; Gharain had jerked me from the Troth even as I stared dumbfounded at the disappearing sword. His brief hold regrounded my body; I fell hard on the path, but at least I could breathe. And I found my voice, and screamed, for Gharain was diving, rolling deftly toward his weapon, snatching it away from the weeds and vines in a one-handed grip before the Troth leaped on him. I screamed again, clambering to my feet, but Gharain shouted, "Stay back!" With a will and strength I could neither imagine, the Rider contorted, forcing the Troth over him, and was up, plunging the sword into its gristly skin.

The Troth's body reacted wildly to the blade—imploding in a bloody and foul hiss. I froze and then doubled over, ill. I'd seen this before, in my vision of the Riders' battle, this grue-some carnage. How could I have ever imagined I would wield a sword to such violence? And then I shuddered, for an even more horrifying thought pervaded: I'd just nearly killed Gharain with my foolish attempt at battle. Hadn't I been warned not to use a weapon?

Chaos pounced then on my fears, tearing into my mind as I allowed in the horror of the Troth's fate—nay, the fate of every strike of fury—and my rash and near-fatal error. I shrank down, hugging my knees, the Wood's frenzy already seeping in. Gharain was not the only one whose passions could do harm—I'd been warned of that as well. I heard Gharain shout my name, but I could not raise my head. Dark Wood would take me now; my mind reeled.

"Lark," Gharain was calling out to me. "The sword is not for you. It is what Laurent said: no weapons for you. They deflect your power."

I blurted, "I'm sorry." And then, "Gharain—"

He knew at once. There were running footsteps, and he had me in his arms. Strong hold, strong aid. The gasping for breath eased; the frenzied blurring in my mind eased—Dark Wood stepped back.

I rested my head in his shoulder and let my breath shudder, then quiet. Gharain said nothing, simply held me tight, one arm wrapped in my hair, the other around my back, close and secure.

"Are you all right?" he asked, and I nodded again, trying to look up at him and mumble once more, "I'm sorry. . . ." My voice died away as Gharain's gaze moved beyond me, behind me, seeing something that caused his eyes to widen in shock.

He whispered, "Behind you, Lark. Behind you."

Gharain tensed, and his hand regripped his sword, but he stayed still. My skin crawled, anticipating a swipe of claw or slash of fang, and yet this felt wrong. Then my hair was pricking, but it was not for anticipated vision, or terrifying beasts— but something new.

Gharain murmured, "Look west at the sunrise."

For a moment I did not understand him, but then I remembered Twig's last words. I turned my head slowly, mouth open in surprise.

In the depths of Dark Wood, the wretched chaos to the west of us was dissolving in the faint glimmer of dawn—dissolving into a mist that shimmered and then slowly parted, revealing an expanse of bare brown earth. It opened, wide and empty; I let go of Gharain and stepped unconsciously toward it.

"No, wait!" Gharain's urgency stopped me in my tracks. He wiped his blade on the dirt of the path and walked to me.

"Twig's words," I repeated to him. "At dawn we look to the west. This is the way to go."

"Yes." There was uneasiness in Gharain's voice, or maybe uncertainty, but I had no such doubt. Still, Gharain reached a hand to my shoulder to stay me. "Lark, you have to be ready for this."

I looked up at him and put my hand over his. "I am ready."

There was a small chuckle from him. "Lark, our clothes— more importantly, your tokens."

I was in my undershift, Gharain bare-chested, all of my gifts in my pack in the burrow. I grinned, relieved by his humor, faint as it was. "I'll get our things."

"Be quick," Gharain murmured, and looked back at the puddle of dead Troth.

I turned and ran back to the burrow, skidding down the entry. No need any longer for such protection, I thought briefly, passing the crumpled stems of the wood betony. I tugged on my leggings, tunic, and boots, shouldered my pack, before stopping as I remembered to add the now-dark moonstone to the other tokens in my bag. I unhooked Gharain's tunic from the oak root and then made a circle in the wide room.

"Thank you," I whispered, hand on heart, to the oak, to the moths, to the spare, quiet space and drying moss. "Thank you." The glimmer moths beat their wings once, in tandem, and their light flickered out.

And then I was climbing back up the short tunnel to the dim light of Dark Wood.

"I am ready—" I began, but my words fell away.

There were three, then four Troths out from Dark Wood, enclosing Gharain, their opaque stare fixed on him as he turned slowly in their midst, his sword pointing toward each as he moved, keeping them at bay. In the surrounding tangle were the filmy eyes of so many more. So many, many more.

"Gharain . . ."

"Hush, love," he said softly, keeping his eyes fixed on the beasts. "They do not seek to kill me."

Stunned, I watched them circle him, envelop him with foul

stink and glare. *What to do?* I thought wildly. *What should I do?* And yet I could not move.

But Gharain prompted, far too calmly, "Go, Lark. Go now. You've only got this short time of dawn."

"I cannot leave you." I moaned low with the fear of it, like an animal trapped. Already Dark Wood was there, rapping at my mind—looking for an opening, a way to spring in and tear me apart.

"Yes," Gharain said very clearly, "you can."

The Troths took a step in. I cried out and one of the Troths turned. There is nothing but viciousness in a Troth's expression, but I felt too, at that moment, a glare of triumph. What was this challenge and parry? Why would Gharain not stab the thing?

"Lark, you cannot wait. Go."

I looked at the clearing. Already the mist was beginning to reclaim the open space as morning strengthened. I looked back at Gharain. Sweat was breaking on his brow.

"I can stop one, I am sure of it," I begged, nodding toward a Troth. "If you sweep the sword, if you catch two, and go for the third, I can—"

He said through clenched teeth, "'Twill not matter if I strike at one; there will be another and another to take its place. It's what the Breeders want—this distraction. Do not let it claim you. Quickly now!"

"Dark Wood will invade me! I feel it already, Gharain. Please, I cannot leave you!"

"It will be safe through the mist." And then, "Lark, go before it is too late. *Go!*" The Troths took another step to tighten their circle around the Rider.

He was right. I hated that he was right. Tears pricked my eyes. "*Please.* We were to do this together."

"Your journey, love; 'tis your journey. Trust yourself." He looked up to give a brief smile. "Trust me."

And of a sudden, he pointed his sword tip down and shouted out, "Now, Lark! Go! Turn and do not look back!"

The Troths closed on him, screeching, smothering, then dragging Gharain into Dark Wood. Their sound was horrible, and I swear I heard the banes echoing the triumph with their own terrible cries.

And then Dark Wood swallowed the group whole, even as it released me. And, for a single, bleak moment, there was no sound at all.

## 20

*IT IS NOT his time.*

I swore this to myself as I turned, fiercely shaking away the frenzy that launched itself at me again full force. *It is not his time!* I knew it to be true; I knew it. There were visions to be fulfilled; Gharain had to strike first.

He needed to be alive so that he could kill me.

I turned, struggling too to believe what Gharain had said, that it was distraction the Breeders wanted, that I should not run after him—tear into the woods with a shriek of terror and nothing else—to somehow save him. I forced myself to place one foot in front of the next; I forced my head up, to look west at the mist. It was already closing, the space. Dark Wood was shimmering through the edges of that gray light—or maybe it was not real, for there were tears in my eyes and everything glittered oddly.

But no—the Wood was reappearing, the bare brown earth

growing hazy and the veil of gray closing hard. With a moan I charged forward, pushing into the mist. For a moment it resisted, a suffocating drape of velvet, holding me back. The energies whipped, bit through me. I think, even, that a tendril of vine reached for my ankle, but I clawed at the mist, thrust it apart, and then I was through, gasping and shaking. Dark Wood faded behind, and I stood at the edge of the endless, dull expanse of brown.

How colorless was the sky! No sun, no blue, simply a sheet of gray overhead. I waited to recover, to listen, but there was nothing to listen to except my own panting breath. Complete and utter desolation. Goose bumps shivered over my skin, and the silence began to swallow me.

But then, no. The silence broke sharply. A raven's cry— severe and shrill and insistent. I looked up to see his dark form against the gray sky.

A raven . . . One had brought me the third sign, set me on the path to this very moment. However fates had transpired, intertwined, this was where I stood. There was no going back. I couldn't go back. I had to stop the tears and the moans and the whimpers. I was not the same girl who left Merith. I was a Guardian.

"Trust yourself," I said loudly, thrusting my voice into the empty air. I set my jaw; I'd shivered too much from exposure and fear and doubt, shied from too much my whole life. This was my journey, *my* task. I would find the Life amulet, the orb. I would claim it for Tarnec. I would find Gharain. I would claim him for Evie. I would trust myself.

I hoped I could hold this burst of resolve.

I took a step into the brown, and then watched the wet dirt slime over my foot and gasped. A bog.

Worse than a marsh, this was the terror of all travelers. I froze at the deadly misstep, and then gently eased my boot out of the muck and backed onto firm ground. A bog, a quicksand; frantic movements would pull a man down, and slow motions as well would sink a soul deep, make it impossible to retrieve his foot, or his footing. Movement must be steady, light, and quick. Steady, light, and quick. I kneeled down at the edge, closed my eyes, and held my hands out, sensing through them for the drier spots, the safest path to take. And I *could* smell it; I *could* feel the subtle changes against my palm. I kept my eyes closed, and stood slowly, walking right three paces before I stepped out once again into the mire. The muck bubbled and hissed but did not suck me under. I thanked Nayla for the boots she'd provided; though wet to my ankles, inside the leather stayed dry.

The squelch, the slight sinking of weight, and whining tug to pull my foot up, away, and take another step. I was deliberate, feeling my way blind, sketching what must be a jagged line across the empty landscape. I had no idea where I was going, and yet I'd come this far—something else would happen to point the way.

I walked for a long time.

It was a slow shift in sensations, beginning as a wisp of mist brushing against my cheek. Then the scent of the bog changed—a faint smell of burning wood; a fire, I thought. And suddenly my foot came upon firmer ground, and soon I was walking silently and easily across the bare dirt, following the hint of smoke. The mist swept by, still challenging any view— but I paid little attention to that kind of sight, preferring more often to close my eyes.

It is, I suppose, why the hut seemed to appear from nowhere. I stopped short.

Brown upon brown: the ragged hovel jutted out of the dirt, solitary in this middle of nowhere. A one-room, sharp-peaked, slanted little thing—precariously upright on no foundation; had there been a breath of wind, it would have toppled.

I moved to it. It had to be empty, for how could anyone live in this nothingness? Closer. The place moaned as I neared, and I stopped at the chill from that sound. Then I shook myself and walked forward. Our own cottage moaned sometimes in a harsh wind—

And then the hair on the back of my neck pricked, and I whirled around with a gasp. There had been nothing behind me—*nothing*, I knew it. And yet this thing—female or not— was simply there, an apparition from the mist but as real and brown as the dirt on which we stood. The thing's hand was out, spindly fingers scraping at my shoulder blade, jerking back at my sudden turn. Then, arms crossing chest, it inspected me with eyes sunk so deep in its bony face I could not tell their color.

"This is your birth day," it hissed. "I smell it."

And so it was. I'd forgotten.

"Birthday Girl, you walk where you do not belong." The voice was reed-thin, a whistle from a scrawny throat.

Bog Hag. Her name came to me in a sickening rush as I looked at her; was it Raif who'd described one once, said his grandfather had seen her? Maybe Ruber Minwl had reached this bog. The decaying clothes, decaying skin, decaying smell that lay heavy around her—weren't these Hags created from the dead souls of plants, animals, and persons who drowned in the bogs . . . or did they feed on them?

"You do not . . . BELONG!" The Hag shouted the last word. I flinched at her shriek, and barely held my footing.

"But I am here," I said breathlessly, for I did not know how else to respond.

"Then here you will die." She leaned toward me, toothless mouth splitting open. Oh, she smelled of dead things, and her nearness chilled through my bones. And yet . . . Troths too reeked of death, but their scent was more horrifying—of vicious, brutal death, the aftermath on a battlefield. This Hag's smell was the heavy odor of death's return to earth—after decomposition, after pain. Something about that made me less afraid. I stood a little firmer.

"I do not stay," I said. "I seek the way—"

"The way?" A cackle for a laugh. "The way?"

"Yes." I took a deep breath. "The way to the Myr Mountains."

"Hah!" Another cackle, a gloating one. "You are far, aren't you, little thing?"

I wondered why she called me little. I was no less tall than she, with her hunched back stooping no grand stature. Was this bravado? Was she also afraid? I was emboldened. "I do not think so," I answered carefully. "I think I am near." And then, even as I wondered why I made this up, I said, "You know the path. You can show me."

The Bog Hag was taken aback. She jumped as if I'd struck her. "You dare!"

I nodded, feigning certainty, and she shrieked, "The path! The path!" She turned, and I watched almost disbelieving as she ran little circles before me, tossing herself like a bundle of sticks—scrawny arms and legs flying every which way—before repeating, "The path!"

I waited, watching her leap and writhe until at length she calmed herself and returned to me in her hobbled gait. "You ask something forbidden, little thing. You invade; you ask the forbidden. My answer for you is death!"

But I said more loudly, "I ask for the path. It is the only answer I accept, for—for it is my birthday, and I have that *right*." Did I? I'd made this up as well.

She cackled again, shivering with glee. "Brash you are!" She leaned in. "But as it is your birth celebration, I will allow your question before I kill you, if you answer me this: what makes you dare seek the path?"

"I am from Tarnec. I am sworn to reclaim the Life amulet."

She flung herself back, cowering this time under my words. "Guardian!" she shrieked, as if to ward off a blow. And she leaped about me again, surveying me from all angles even as she danced out of reach. I heard her mutter about my hair, something about the sign. I also heard her curse herself. Tricked she'd been, she swore, tricked.

She lied. She knew me; she'd reached first to my shoulder—my birthmark. This display was distraction. And with a sudden dawning of horror, I looked down at my feet, realizing that the dance she was doing was scraping a pointed boundary around me in the rough dirt.

A spell. She would capture me within it. I leaped out before she could finish, shouting, "Stop!"

My voice thundered across the empty landscape, and the mist threw it back. The Hag crumpled and cowered below me, ducking under those stick arms, whining. I said sternly, "You *will* show me the way."

"Birthday Guardian," she keened, "you would threaten a helpless creature? Dark thing, dark thing—!"

"Stop it!" I yelled. "I wield no threat; I wield my right. My *right*." She cringed again, churning herself in the dirt, and I laughed, exhilarated at the power my words radiated because they were true. Guardian—it *was* my right. I was even louder. "Do not pretend fear, Hag! Do not hope to charge strength from my ignorance. *Show* me the way." My voice echoed long over the barren earth.

The Bog Hag relaxed and raised herself from the dirt. "True answer," she muttered. "Day of birth; I am bound to point the path. So, I will show you—show you, little thing. You must follow me."

She leaped forward, all bones and joints, and danced toward the hut. She turned her head once to look back at me. "Follow, little thing! You've not much time." And she cackled and jumped for the door.

I followed her, to the single door, which she pushed open, then into the darkness. There was no window in this hovel. The boards were flimsy and gaping; little of the gray light showed through. And though it smelled of the smoke I'd sought, there was no fireplace, no fire.

"You enter," muttered the Bog Hag. "But you do not belong."

"I told you that I do not stay. Where is the path?"

I could hear her toothless smile widening. "This is the path, little thing," she hissed softly. "You are on it."

"Where?"

My blunder to show that momentary uncertainty; her grin nearly split her face. "Do you not see?" And then with her cackle, "Of course you do not see—"

"It is my right to know—" I stopped, realizing already it didn't hold the same power.

"NO!" she shouted in my ear. "It is *only* your right to be pointed the way. It is all that you asked."

"You play with me, Hag!" I cried. But then the memory came in one crushing blow: Twig warning me to be specific. *The Hag was right. The Hag was right* was the sickening realization. I should have asked her to open the path.

"Hah! I've pointed you! I've done my bound." She leaned into me. A wave of rotting leaves fell around my shoulders. But they were her fingers, playing—drawing back strands of my hair. I slapped her off, but her fingers hovered.

"Your glorious hair I will keep," she crooned. "'Twill dress me fine."

And I gritted back, trying to stay commanding, "You'll not have it, Hag. You'll have nothing from me!"

"Not true, little thing! Not true. You are trapped here. You cannot see, so you cannot move. I'll have every piece of you."

"Open the path," I hissed.

"Hah! That does not come for free."

"Then what do you want?"

"Something you cannot give."

"Name it!"

She crowed again. "What matters a name? You are lost, Birthday Guardian. You shall stand here until you waste away."

I turned immediately to leave, but she was right. No longer was there any door. We merely stood in this dark place, no way in, no way out. I reeled back to her, desperate. "Open the path! Tell me what you want!"

"Why?" She preened. "You cannot deliver it—"

"Tell me! I demand it!" I stabbed my hand into my pack, the moonstone the largest thing to grab. "Here! A great gift for a Guardian! I will give you this!"

"Hah!" the Bog Hag screeched, and slapped my hand away. "The treasure is beyond you, little thing. A drop beyond your grasp."

There was a change in her voice at that, something beyond the triumph of besting me. Something that became loss, rage, and despair. "And you do not tell me what it is!" I shouted at her. I stuffed the moonstone back in the pack and dug for something else—anything else.

"Never! I keep you instead!"

"Then I'll learn without permission!" I yelled in return, and caught up her arm in my hand before she could jump back.

She screeched, she clawed at me, but she could not break my grip. I remembered the sensation of pulling Gharain from the rifting earth—my arm was as vinelike here; I would not let go. She leaped and tugged, but I was the stronger. Desperate determination; it was my only chance. And then I felt her energy come through my hand and I saw what she wanted:

A thousand souls swirling in an ever-tightening spiral. Plant and animal—a branch, a body, all draining into that spiral—smaller, tighter, until the souls were funneled out in one tiny teardrop. A single tear of blood.

She shrieked and squirmed, even as I released her arm. And I said to her in grim triumph, "I have your treasure. Open the path."

"Give it to me!" she screamed. "Give me! I bring it home!"

I pulled open my pack, and ground my hand in once more to clench the tiny gem that Twig had bequeathed. I cried, "Open the path!"

"Let me see it!" she begged. "Let me but see it!"

"Open it first!"

"I swear it! I will open the path for you!"

I held up the little thing between my fingers. There was no light, but it gleamed anyway: a precious jewel—a thousand souls squeezed into one blood-red tear.

"Mine!" the Bog Hag whispered. Then she screeched, "Mine!" And even as she cried, a wall of the hovel shimmered and dissolved, revealing a rocky outcrop in the lonely wild of the Myr Mountains. Immediately, the eerie pull of the mountain caught at my body. I felt the drag toward its hard face.

"There," she screamed. "There you are! Give me the tear!"

"This is the way?" I hissed.

"I am sworn. Give me!"

"Take it!" And I threw the teardrop high in the air, heard her spring to catch it, and I stepped far out.

"Thank you, Twig," I whispered as the bog faded with the Hag's victorious last shriek.

# 21

MY BREATH STEAMED, then dissipated in the thin air. I watched the vapor leave where I could not, the windswept face of the mountain rigid against my cheek as I hugged it for safety. For a time I let breath waft away, and then slowly eased around to center myself on the narrow ledge—its width only half my height—to face out with my back pressed to the wall, to look far away and imagine I saw a green splash of color that would be the realm of Castle Tarnec.

I dared not look down.

My hand went behind me to the rough granite, which shot straight up through the clouds. Gray rock, gray sky, gray clouds; the sun simply dissolved against the stone. So cold it was—achingly so.

Cautiously, I slid my pack from my shoulders and opened it to pull out Gharain's tunic. I'd not been able to give it to him.

I threw it over my head and tugged it close, inhaling its still-warm scent of late summer—as when leaves have reached their peak, sun-drenched until they can hold no more. I breathed in his richness until I too felt drenched in him.

Fortified, but only briefly so. I looked around once more. I was on a thin break of stone. No seeming way up, certainly no way down. Where was the supposed path? I shuffled to one end of the precipice and felt the wall end behind me, cornering to nothing. I retreated and tried the other side. The wall dropped away there as well; I was confined to this tiny edge. A hint of panic crept in—maybe the Bog Hag *had* cast a spell, sent me to the mountains but with no direction to move. How long could I survive pinned as I was on this barren surface? To mock me, the wind whipped sideways across the face of the mountain and spiraled as it hit my little ledge. A push, a pull—a tease of movement to prove I was fixed to this spot before it whisked away, leaving the bleak cold. I sat down and laid my head on my knees, and wished for something I could not have.

The strange sensations I'd felt when I'd confronted the mountains on Rune's back not so many days before were creeping in again. What had Gharain said? That I could be made to feel things others did not, a way for the Breeders to find us—this emptying of any feeling, this drag of body to stone, the eerie whirring in my ears. . . .

The eerie whirring in my ears.

Swifts! They'd have to be near. Heart pounding, I craned my head, searching the gray sky for specks of black. Perhaps this was home to them: circling these mountains in endless flight with no ability to land. I shuddered. Though I might die by Gharain's hand, there was nothing I'd foreseen that implied I could not be badly burned by a swift strike first. Viewed from Tarnec, I would be but a tiny glint of mica in the forbidding rock. . . .

These were bad thoughts; they made my body limp. I wondered at my challenge of the Bog Hag—that I'd felt momentarily powerful in my impulse to grab her and learn her desire—for here I now sat, fixed, cold, and alone. Maybe I'd thwarted my own destiny, ripped away the end of my own story. Maybe I'd lost the chance to reclaim the crystal orb. The whirring in my ears was growing. I'd soon be able to see the first swift.

Foolish, foolish girl.

I leaned back to put my head against the stone, moving the pack to do so, and I watched my hand, almost on its own, reach in and pull out the little ally token Twig had made me. Stone, cloth, and leaf—of the Earth, of love. My fingers curled hard around the little thing, mindlessly exploring the separate shapes and textures. I squeezed it tightly and then briefly pressed it to my lips.

*Fear is what happens when you think you don't know what to do. . . .*

Out of nowhere the words flowed into my mind. I smiled a little and then grew stern. They were true, those words—too true. I was afraid.

*Think!* I charged myself. *Think! Why stay so helpless on the ledge? Climb, descend; leap if you must. . . . Do something!*

*You do not climb over the Myr Mountains; you go through them.*

Another murmur of things once spoken. And then in that moment I heard too the words of the hare I'd rescued from Gharain.

*Dark entry to the world . . . the last stand on the windswept face. Go left—stay true.*

I laughed out loud. Wisdom from allies remembered and shared, buoying me up in a moment of despair. *You are not alone,* the king's words reminded, and Twig's as well. Indeed, I was not. My ally token was speaking—the voices rang through me as clearly as if the speakers stood at my side.

There had to be an opening into the mountain. Standing up quickly, nearly losing my footing, I turned once more to the wall of rock and craned my head to search its face. An opening, somewhere. I scanned the façade, looking high and wide, slipping fingers into every crevice. I could see no entry.

That left below. Crouching sideways, gripping the sharp rim, and dipping my head down, I gingerly peered over the edge.

The drop was awesome. It was good that the mountain's energy pulled so, for the sheer view from its plummeting sides could have drawn me over the precipice. But there—to my right—I could see a dark gap. That was it: an opening into the mountain, wide enough for a person to pass through. But more than the relief I felt at its discovery was the shock at its distance. It was too far. I could not hang over the edge; I could not slide down the sheer face. There was nothing to hold me. There was nothing to catch me.

I pulled up, panting, working through all the futile possibilities of stretching, falling, and jumping in such a way as to reach impossible entry—ludicrous ideas all of them. Then I derided each acrobatic exaggeration of my unremarkable strength.

Niggling hysteria was dancing at the edges of my brain. "Now what?" I shouted out loud at my token. *Stay true,* the hare's words whispered once more. *Stay true.*

The tokens. They'd opened the way to the mountains this far. Two I'd not yet used. I opened my pack, returning the ally token and digging deep for the others. The moonstone I left alone and drew out instead the three lark feathers. Another time, another life, it seemed, when I'd found these three wisps. The cottage, the garden, the field, Grandmama, Evie, and Rileg—all so far away as to be almost unfamiliar. And neither was I the naïve recluse who'd taken the feathers from stone and bush and bird. Translucent quills, a brush of brown—

The whirring hit a shrill pitch. Gasping, I looked up. There were specks in the sky now, four, then five, growing larger by the moment. That horrid buzz pierced into my head, thrilled down my arms. I had to move.

Feather to wing—it made sense. I would fly with this token. I stroked the three feathers along my arms, against my hair. And I waited while nothing happened. I kissed them; I swept them across the pack, on stone. Nothing.

There came the swifts' first shrieks; my body shook at the sound. "Please!" I shouted at the feathers. "Show me!" Was it a tug I felt on my arm? I didn't know; I was already standing, shouldering my pack, gripping the lark feathers. "Please!" I waved them above my head. Nothing. I was rock-bound.

The swifts were close now. Enormous, ugly black bodies—talons, beaks, and haunting human eyes. For a moment I froze in horror as two of them dove straight at me with ripping cries, before throwing myself heavily to the floor of the ledge. I huddled there, waiting for the explosion, but there was none. Rolling over, I peeked up. The swifts had indeed brushed the mountain, but this pitiless mass was of their ilk—they did not explode. With skull-shattering cries, they circled and prepared another dive.

No pebbles to be thrown, no impediment there to prevent them from burning me on the ledge. Naught that I could do, except the thing I didn't want to do—no choice but the one escape.

Their screams ringing my ears, I spread flat on the narrow precipice, gripped my feathers, and waited. Waited until they were nearly upon me, and at the last moment shoved myself off the ledge.

There is nothing slow about falling.

In a heartbeat I saw the opening to the mountain fly by—up and away. Gone. My hand holding the tiny quills flung up above my head. Maybe I hoped they would spread wide and break the speed of my fall. They did not. And for a stunned moment I thought, *This cannot be possible.* But then I was simply falling, gaining speed—jagged edges of gray rock streaking by. The only comfort was that I fell faster than the swifts could fly. It was over—it had to be over.

I opened my hand and let go the feathers.

It is strange how beauty remains long in the memory. Released, the feathers did not disappear, but stayed with me, growing, changing form to become whole larks—birds of flight, soaring flecks of golden brown against the sky, like the shimmering flecks in Gharain's eyes. Their wings stretched wide in a gentle curve, feathered edges sweeping through the cold air. Free. Exultant.

The flecks grew larger. The larks were swooping, streaming fast straight for me. Small though they were, they reached for sleeve and legging—talons catching hold with delicate strength. And then we were up, winging straight up the side of the mountain, with no less speed than my fall. I was rising, high above the glorious earth, gasping, crying, laughing with the joy of rescue and of flight. And in but a moment, the three larks lightly dropped me inside the dark entry to the Myr Mountains and raced away.

Sometime later I sat up. I was not afraid. I could no longer be afraid. I stood, adjusted my pack, walked into the black, into the strange, heavy pull of the rock, and closed my eyes.

# 22

THE COLD DEEPENED.

Unused, empty passage. The darkness was tangible. It oozed through my body, surrounding and invading. I felt ancient air running over my palms, heard the soft whisper of my footstep on the solid ground. I smelled the rock, and the icy moisture. I smelled the remains of Troth.

Yet there: a faint pulse—a tiny throb. The sound washed in and out for a moment, soft and slow and steady. I felt it then, tingling inside, the Life amulet—the crystal orb. Foreign as it was, I knew it as well as my own heartbeat. It was here; I was close.

I opened my eyes, pulled open my pack, drew out Twig's moonstone, and clenched it aloft in my fist. It fizzed and burst into light, illuminating a passageway tunneling straight into black—one of a thousand to choose from, for in the gleam, the Myr Mountains were honeycombed with openings. *Go left. Stay true* came the hare's whisper. I smiled, though; the orb's throb was loud enough without her guiding words. I chose my route, into the heart of the mountains.

The dark swallowed all traces of my steps but for the tiny halo of light. I walked quickly and silently, tugging against the forceful pull of the mountains, which wished to hold me down. Though grit-strewn, the path was evenly carved—trampled flat, I imagined, by the scrabbling weight of innumerable Troths. I did not look above. Winding through, veering left at forks, sensing the tiny pulse grow stronger until it throbbed in my own breast, matching the pace of my heart. Long passages, working inward ever deeper—a moment, even, when I was reminded of Castle Tarnec's long hallways, and missed the beautiful tapestries that lined its walls. . . .

I was forced to an abrupt stop.

Bars. My hand moved instinctively to push the barrier away, but froze again as I caught the sound of something beyond the pulse of the amulet, something so achingly gorgeous that I sank to my knees to listen.

The melodious voice from my dream echoed through the cavernous tomb, lofty and lyrical. Erema was speaking. I wanted to touch the words as they glided past, so temptingly sweet, but they drifted just out of reach, not meant for me. And then, with a sudden chill, I heard another's response that evoked a yearning far more real, far deeper than anything Erema's throat could spin—a shout of desperation that took my breath away.

"Gharain!" I jumped up, reaching for the barrier to shake it loose, moonstone falling, my fingers nearly grasping, but then snatched my hands back to my chest with a sharp yelp. The bars were of hukon—thick, crossed saplings of the evil stuff, knobbed with stubs of branches that looked to be sharpened so they stuck out like ghisane thorns. Fiery hot, acidic, and negating—preventing me. Furious, I grabbed the moonstone, passing the light overhead and around, searching for a way past this hideous barricade. The roof of this cavern was high above, bars disappearing into dimness—a solid mass, with no way to climb, for the rippled walls were chipped smooth. I threw myself belly down and felt around the base of the bars. They were solidly, impossibly merged with the stone—a trick of magic, a manipulation of vision, I didn't know. And yet, this ridiculous barrier in the middle of nowhere was clearly meant to thwart, teasingly so, just as the tantalizing voices compelled me to find a way through.

I took off Gharain's tunic then, wrapped it thickly around my hands, and tentatively touched the bars. His clothing helped—I could grip the strips of black wood between its thorny weapons; I could shake the bars in my fists with little burn. But I might as well have been shaking iron. Top, bottom, sides—there was no give to the barrier. Over and over I tested each joint, each binding; I kicked at its base until I growled in frustration and impatience, and finally threw Gharain's tunic away from me so hard it skidded sideways and hit the passage wall.

A tiny spark flared at the impact. I stared dumbly for a

moment until memory of Twig's words flared too—his voice loosed from the ally token: *There are things that can help you in the midst of misfortune.*

I raced to the shirt, hands feeling over the gritty floor, looking for what had made the spark. My fingers closed on it: a little stone—a pebble, really—that the shirt had flung against the rock. I scooted over to the moonstone and held the small thing in its glow. It was grayish—not unlike the barren stone that Twig had used for Arnon, but without its silvery cast. And then I laughed and turned back to the bars. I was holding a cinder stone. *'Twould start a fire* came Twig's echo.

Hukon burns very fast, I learned. After two strikes of the little stone, a lick of orange flame whisked up one bar, spread across the horizontal rungs, and shot up the next vertical stake. Up, down, across—in a moment the entire barricade and surrounding rock glowed blue-white. Black sap bubbled down to the floor, spreading a thick, filthy puddle to which I gave wide berth. Pungent filth it was: a choking, cloying poison. I slung my pack on my shoulder, grabbed Gharain's shirt and pressed it to my face, stood back, and waited for the cage to crumble into ash. "You cannot prevent," I murmured fiercely in triumph. And then, picking up the moonstone for light, I ran.

Somewhere past the reek of the hukon, I stuffed Gharain's tunic in my pack and held only the moonstone. The path now led wide and straight, seemingly with no end. Hollow and empty and cold, working deeper into the mountains. I slowed, for oppression built—the weight of the mountains sinking me with each step. But so too did the pulse of the Life amulet. Throbbing, steady, a heartbeat's pace, ever encouraging me forward. *You cannot prevent. . . .*

The first snuffle came from above.

I assured myself that the passage's ceiling was very high, that the Troth could be far away. Then a grunt, a soft snarl. More than one now, but I insisted this was to be expected—these were their mountains. It was only after the swish of many feet along my track that I could no longer hope they'd not yet seen me. Even if I held no light, their eyes were made for this dark. Soon after, I knew they were following me. Soon after that, I was surrounded.

My breath quickened, but I was not afraid. These were foot soldiers of the Breeders, I reminded myself. Erema would need me; I could not yet be their sport. Besides, Gharain was to be the instrument of my death, not Troth. It was that hideous thought that kept me calm as I continued on, calm at the sounds of clawed fingers scratching on the rock, calm against the snorts and growls that echoed along the tunnel of stone—

Opaque eyes gleamed suddenly in the dark, hundreds of pairs peering over slabs of rock: on ledges high above, behind me, ahead around corners—dots reflecting the moonstone's light that could be seen as clearly far away as they could close by. My steps hastened; so did the skittering of clawed feet and hands. The eyes doubled in number, tripled, quadrupled, closing in. I was running now, as best I could, heavy as I felt, and then the Troths were so close I could feel their stinking breath on my skin. I bit teeth into lip, pushing forward, willing myself to stay ahead. One beast reared itself suddenly in the circle of my light, and I yelped. In a wild move I struck out, losing the moonstone, and caught its arm; it made an awful scream and rolled away.

I tore down the passage, gasping for breath. I burned them; they would not attack.

And yet, I could not outrun them. Sheer numbers of the creatures herded me in a direction I might have gone anyway, for the throb of the Life amulet was now vibrating my skin, pulling me toward it. Down the passage in the pitch dark, I didn't need the moonstone's light; I ran by my senses and by the steady push of the Troths from behind, closing in.

And there, far away, appeared a new light—something luminous and isolated, suspended in the dark, bobbing slightly before disappearing. I remembered my vision then, of the crystal orb revealing itself, only to be choked by strands of hukon. And I cried out, thinking I could somehow warn it. Then I stopped short, crashed to my knees—for I'd burst into a room, a blue-tinged, oppressive, and dank room hewn into the very heart of the Myr Mountains. I hunched there, panting, watching the bluish light waver and brighten and reveal I was at a dead end. And I was not alone.

Erema.

She stood quite still—her figure tall and lush. The orb, caught as it was by the poisoned netting at her breast, illuminated her face and blackened her already black, staring eyes. She scanned first her horde of foot soldiers, searching through the creatures beyond my collapsed figure, and then her gaze drew down and focused on me.

In her exquisite voice she said, "There you are."

My dream, come to life. Erema smiled as if she knew, and it might have been one of the earth rifts that opened behind her smile—a void, a nothingness as black as her stare, yawning deep behind the beautiful lips and glistening teeth. The mouth gaped, saying, "Look what I have."

I could not wake from this. I was surrounded by the slimy, death-reeking Troths and gaping Breeder, entombed in these dark mountains. I stood up slowly, turning a full circle, hands wide in defense. And I said, plain and true, "Return the crystal orb."

I heard her laugh, musical and delicious. I spun around again. The Troths shuffled back. And then I laughed too, to show I was not afraid of this army of beasts. "Do you see? They cannot hurt me. Give me the orb."

"Try, little Lark. Try and take it," she coaxed.

I stepped toward her, still fearless. I'd come this far, I'd survived this much; here was but one Breeder to confront. The shuffling and scratching of the Troths gathering in and blocking the exit did not make me flinch.

With a simple shift of cloth, the orb's light was doused once more behind Erema's cloak. She leaned close, so that I felt the void within her drawing me. "The orb is mine," she sang, and stepped back.

But I reached anyway, unafraid, as if I could simply take it, as if she would have to relinquish the amulet because its

Guardian demanded. Unafraid too of the Troths stirring behind me, restless.

It was only when I felt the violent shock of pain exploding inside that I screamed in utter terror.

Hukon. They'd punctured my shoulder with a spear of hukon.

## 23

WRETCHED, SCALDING WOUND!

I curled into a ball and tried to rock away the searing pain. I retched until my body broke into sweat colder than the air. I slammed my shoulder onto the slab floor, where I writhed until, sore and spent, I lay crumpled in some exhausted stupor, wishing for anything but this torture.

And then, but for the orb, silence. I rolled onto my back—the cold of the stone the only thing to cut the agony in my body—and forced my eyes open, letting dim blue light filter in.

There was a swish of fabric, footsteps, a growing intensity of the Life amulet's pulse, and Erema loomed over me. The orb gleamed, ensnared in its web of hukon. It was so close, and yet I could not think to lift my hand.

Erema said with what seemed sweet pity, "Lark, you look so ill. The hukon burns the life from you."

It was too hard to speak. I stared instead at the orb. It should have been radiant with light, but black streaks slashed the glowing surface in the same crude shape I remembered branded on Ruber Minwl's hand. Even as I watched, another lash scored its surface—the net was alive. Yet these were not the creeping tendrils of vine as in Dark Wood; this was hukon, the black willow: striking blows across the light, ever looking for a way in, for a way to destroy it.

"Lovely, isn't it?" Erema said, following my gaze. She put her hand up as if to cup the orb. "So pretty how it glows: sun-filled earth colors, like you. Imagine how it would help your pain if you clasped it in your hands."

"You have what does not belong to you," I groaned.

"I know! It was so easy to take!" She laughed at me, and her laughter grated, lilting as it was. "And now look at you, the little, timid thing! Thinking you deserve this. That you are worthy of this."

"I am its Guardian." I was hoarse.

She leaned over me with that smile. "Come get it, then."

And I did. Or tried to. I think I made a futile swipe with my arm—fingers reaching to grasp at nothing, crying out in misery from the acidic burn of hukon.

"Tut, Lark, you are too weak a thing. Try again."

But I was looking at her hand, which did not touch the amulet. "You cannot hold it," I whispered, remembering.

That seemed to make her pause, slight as it was. Then she laughed again, the sound discordant. "But you can. 'Twill soothe your ill, you know. Come, Lark, take the crystal orb. Both hands."

Perhaps it would be this easy, if I simply used both hands. My fingers trembled, lifting from the cold stone floor.

"Come now, Lark, take it. Don't you wish your pain away? Let the amulet be your balm."

Hands lifting—one, then both. "Grasp it tightly, now, Lark," came her soft whisper. "Do not mind the net. You will be whole again."

And then the king's words drifted in my head: *They will attempt to trick you into destroying your amulet. . . .* My hands fell back to my sides. "No."

Her voice was still soft. "Must I make you try harder?"

"Then I will fight you."

At that Erema leaned in and snarled. She sounded like a Troth. But her threat came low and seductive: "You might think you've learned power. But it is nothing to mine." And with an infinitely graceful gesture, she pushed two fingers against my left shoulder and I screamed in agony before she let go.

"Are you finished with pain yet, foolish little Guardian? Know that it can be made better." She was very close to me, her breath like flowers. "Would you like to know instead how you *could* feel?"

And she was no longer Erema but Gharain, over me as I first had seen him in a dream—his glorious smile, the chestnut curls skimming his temples—oh, it burned to see him safe and so close before me, his sage-green eyes lit from within. "I am what you want," she whispered, but it was Gharain's voice, low and rich, stirring the pit of my stomach, making my heart ache with need. "Come, place your hands on my heart and feel my love."

I groaned. I knew it was not real, and yet it was too real. Gharain was tangible there before me, safe and unharmed, inviting me to kiss him, to touch him. I couldn't think clearly.

"Be with me," he whispered. "There is no other." His hands were reaching for mine to draw them to his heart.

I shook my head, blabbering, delirious—mad with desire, mad with pain. "Say it, then, first. Promise me Evie will not part us—"

"Evie?"

The spell was broken. Gharain was no longer there. Erema was bending over me, a quizzical smile parting those lips, opening the void behind, and I snapped at her, angry that I'd lost sight of Gharain. She ignored me, curious at the other name. "Evie?"

She'd not known of my cousin. I gasped, "No!"

But Erema had stopped smiling. "Who is she, Guardian? Part of your line?"

"No!"

Her hand reached and squeezed my shoulder, and I shrieked. "Tell me," she said. "Tell me." Her fingers tightened.

I'd let the haze of pain take me before I gave in. I gritted my teeth—groaning, sobbing at the torture, biting my tongue until it bled. I'd not let the Breeders find Evie.

But Erema suddenly released my shoulder. Panting, I opened my eyes onto her grinning face, now garishly cast in the blue light. I remembered the grin—the one that hung over my vision with poor Ruber Minwl's hand, the one of such malevolence that shot cold horror through my spine.

"Indeed," she hissed from that grotesque mouth. "You think you can bear pain? You have the Sight: look and feel what true pain is!"

Her smile yawned wide, and I could see right into her void, right into the blackness. She cried out something in a brutal voice. The hair pricked on the back of my neck, and I screamed as before me a wall of flame erupted, throwing myself back from the heat before I could say to myself, *This is the vision, the vision. . . . This is what you warned to the Riders. . . .*

A tent, charred black, fell in tatters before my feet, and what had been a pretty ribbon went flaring up in a puff of smoke. The village square, market day in Merith. The booths were ablaze.

A voice was screaming for Grandmama, for Evie. My voice. I was louder than the cries I heard around me, and I ran haphazardly through flames, screaming for my family, for Quin, for Krem Poss and Dame Keren. Figures stumbled in the smoke, but I could not see who they were. I ran toward the silhouettes, dodging shreds of burning fabric and collapsing framework. A Troth leaped from out of nowhere, nearly colliding with me, a tangle of slug-textured limbs made even more grotesque by their bloodied state. I lashed out, but my hand went through him. I was a ghost in the midst of turmoil. I was not there.

With a thunderous rumble of hooves, the Riders pounded past, first in single file, then breaking form to sweep through the square, leaping the flames with swords drawn. The Troths were howling now, deafeningly. The smoke was stinging, blurring my vision. There were other sounds: sword against Troth, Troth upon villager, the shrill neighing of the horses tearing straight into my soul.

For a moment the smoke cleared—a whim of the wind, perhaps. The square was laid bare and burning before my gaze, a chaos of debris beneath the fighting bodies of beast and man and horse. Black was everywhere; blood was everywhere. There—Taran's steed reared to avoid a Troth who went with jaws open for his legs. And there—Cargh had swept his sword across the neck of a Troth. I shut my eyes.

And yet I could not shut out the scene, for this was a vision; the violence poured in through each of my senses. Sight, sound, smell, taste, and even touch pressed upon me the heat and dirt and sticky blood. I gagged and choked and reeled from one direction to another, but I could not escape my Sight.

I tripped, face-first onto the filthy cobbled square, avoiding something—no, some*one* who'd been struck. I rolled to sit up, to look, and choked, "Raif!" Raif.

He lay faceup, mouth working to catch any kind of breath. An impossible task—he could not fill his lungs, for there was a gash torn from throat to chest.

"Raif!" I screamed it this time. And then I gasped, for his desperate eyes focused on me. Saw me.

"Lark." He struggled horribly for air, but his gaze stayed steady.

Raif was dying. He was dying—that was why he could see me.

"Lie still. Let me help!" I pushed my hands to his chest to staunch his wound, then raged to see the blood rush through my ethereal fingers. Utterly helpless, I'd be forced to let him bleed to death as others were too mired in battle to notice, and my voice was nothing more to them than the wind.

"Raif . . ."

He knew. He needed no consoling. But he was glad for my presence, glad he was not alone. He worked at something like a smile, gasping, "You are like sunshine on a summer day. You are brilliant."

"No, don't speak—!"

"Thank you for your friendship. For your bravery."

"Raif, stop. Please! Stop."

"Evie." His eyes flicked to look, the blood seeping faster as he strained. "Evie."

I was weeping, for his voice was bleak with regret. I could not bear this grief. And I said it, anything to make him live: "She loves you, Raif; she *loves* you. Please, please hold on!" I could swear his face lit at those words. "Evie will come. She will!"

"Tell her love cannot die." Then he said, barely, "Look." His eyes slid downward and mine followed. His hand in the dirt opened and a little object fell out. I leaned down to peer at the thing. It was a Merith man's ring, the thin braid of leather.

I looked up at Raif. "Your grandfather's."

"I got it back." He would have said it proudly. I think I heard him say it. But it no longer mattered. Raif's wound ceased flowing and his eyes closed.

"Raif!" My hands were in his blood, useless, and yet I kneeled there shouting at him. Shouting. Shouting. A blast of hot air rushed by from the fire, and his lashes flickered, and I thought, *He stays!* I screamed aloud for anyone to help; I screamed until my throat was wrecked—but the din of the battle was louder; the flames were louder. I sobbed with fury and helplessness, and then I looked up through grimy, miserable tears and saw her running.

Evie.

She was dirt-streaked and bloodied, but she was whole. She was beautiful. Her silver-blond hair was nearly transparent in the smoke, flying back like a cape as she ran. I croaked, "Evie, stay back," but she was not looking at me. She'd never heard me. It was Raif she was running for, her face terrible in its dread. The breath went out of her body in one thin exhale, and too late, the Healer sank at his side, her hair spilling into the dirt and blood about her.

And from some great distance, I heard Erema make a little crow of delight, for I had exposed my cousin. "So there she is. Now you shall feel true pain, Guardian. Watch."

Erema called out things unintelligible and frightening. And from behind the flames, a Troth reared its ugly head, breaking through smoke and fire, its milky stare fixing on Evie. I shrieked for my cousin, but she did not look up.

"Take your amulet, Guardian," Erema cried to me. "Take it with both hands and squeeze hard. Crush it here within its net and I will save your friend."

I had no voice left; screams would go unheard anyway.

"She will be torn asunder," came Erema's hideous threat. "Crush the orb or you will watch her sacrifice."

It was what I could not do. It was unbearable. The Troth was loping toward Evie, her back open and vulnerable as she covered Raif. I threw my head back and screamed anyway, again for help. Another Troth slithered by. People's footsteps stampeded past; others screamed too. But no one saw. And I was nothing—

"Sacrifice, Guardian. They will all be sacrificed."

—Nothing, until I heard the pounding of a horse's hooves. Through swollen eyes I saw the huge and powerful shape of Rune wheeling in the distance.

"Rune! Help! Help me!"

Rune reared back, bloody hooves lashing up, neighing from a depth impossible to ignore. A clarion, a warning. And Evie lifted her head, stunned to see the Troth springing at her with claws and teeth spread wide—her mouth barely parted in surprise.

Rune was too far away. I whimpered, "No," but the Troth, at the height of his leap, was suddenly gone, sword-stabbed and flung by Laurent galloping between beast and prey. Evie never flinched; she simply looked at the Rider as he reined and turned, a barest moment of acknowledgment—

I was back on the cold stone of the Myr Mountains, huddled and shivering after the scorching heat of the market square, eyes unable to adjust to the sudden darkness. But I was laughing too, in hysterical relief. "You heard me, Rune, you heard me!"

"You dare," Erema whispered. After the roar of battle I could barely hear her words, but I felt the ugly anger beneath them.

I didn't care. Rune's cry had saved Evie, and that was all that could matter. I curled into a tighter ball, laughter fading to gasps, trying to squeeze out the wretchedness of the vision. I'd never felt so sick. It was not only the vision that made me ill; the poison was spreading. I groaned and rolled on my back and wiped the cold sweat from my damp cheeks. And then I heaved over and retched, for in the blue dimness I saw Raif's blood staining my hands—a remaining vision or impossibly real.

"You dare," Erema repeated. "You dare manipulate."

And then somehow, ridiculously, I was incensed. Raif, Gharain, the amulet; I could not give up. I would not give up. I struggled to sit upright, the room so close, I could barely breathe. I forced out, "You are but threats and fury as empty as whatever is within you. You cannot kill me; you need me for the amulet. And Rune will save the others."

She shrieked at me then, and there was nothing pretty

left in her. "Look!" she screamed. "Look at me! Look at what you've done! Look at what you need!" And she wavered from one image to another to break me and to tempt me: she was Gharain, she was Evie, she was Ruber Minwl, she was the king, she was Raif. Each one called to me in voices that stirred or crushed, yet those I could force myself to ignore, realizing too that Erema was only repeating in image what she'd learned I'd been exposed to. The Breeders might read my energy, but they could not create from it.

I was on my knees now, my wrists wobbling as I pushed to straighten, to stall, to work it out in my sickened brain—how I could take the amulet. "Give me the orb, Erema," I gasped. "You cannot kill me."

"That," she hissed, "is where you are mistaken. Destroy the orb or I will destroy you."

My ally token; I needed words of help. My fingers scraped along the floor, reaching for the pack where it had fallen away somehow.

Her laughter bellowed, vulgar. She reared up, seeming to fill the space, stamped a foot that shuddered the mountain, and with lyrical sweetness cried out, "Rider!"

And from beneath her, the stone broke and opened. Gharain rose as he had in my dream, torso gleaming naked and wet with cold sweat and damp of the mountain. He stood there blankly, his long sword glittering in the blue light, passion emptied from his most expressive face.

"Gharain!" This could not be; it was too soon. My death dream made real, but too soon—this ending was too soon.

"He won't hear you, Lark. I've claimed him." Erema reached her hand and slid it over his shoulder, leaning in from behind to press a kiss against the curve at his neck. "Do you see?" Then she smiled, her vile mouth against his skin. "But I can give him back. Break the orb and you can be with him. Look, Lark. He waits for you."

"You ask me to choose?" I rasped.

"*You* choose?" Her voice was ever musical in its taunt. "Nay, the choice is mine. You are here because of me. You will destroy the amulet because I wish it, or you will die because I demand it. Either way I win."

"I will not give you what you want," I mumbled.

"No?" Erema laughed back, "But you already have, Lark. You are here."

This was the world upside down and meaningless. It was all for naught—I'd journeyed far and achieved nothing. *Too soon!* I mouthed to no one. My hand fell listlessly from the pack— nothing. It was simply my time to die.

And Erema was speaking in her lovely voice, gaily saying what I already knew she'd say: "Now, Gharain, finish what you began. Finish what you meant to do."

My time to die. I looked up at my Complement. I'd do this the Merith way, with dignity.

Gharain raised his sharp sword over his head, arms stretch-ing long, muscles flexing across his chest. In that suspended moment I saw him in the too brief days we'd shared: I saw his glorious smile, his beautiful face, felt the connection radiating through his vibrant touch. *Stay true,* I heard the hare's whisper.

*Stay true.* I remembered Nayla's words, remembered repeating them to Gharain under the oak in Dark Wood: *It is what we give to the Earth that allows her to provide. . . .* And I remembered Gharain murmuring, *What, Lark? What do I give to you? Say it. . . .*

*Complete the circle.* I would finish what he'd begun; I would admit out loud what I could not before: my truth. I smiled up at Gharain—his blank gaze glittered, for my own eyes were filled with tears. And I repeated clearly, despite the hoarseness in my throat, the same words he'd offered to me, returning freely what I'd claimed from him: "I love you."

Erema growled. And beneath that growl, Gharain murmured, "Trust yourself."

The sword came slicing down.

# 24

A THOUSAND LARKS soared in flight, pulling the colors of the Earth with them on their wings and returning to her their cascading song. Four of us stood high on a peak watching them: Evie, the ragged waif, the girl with red-gold hair, and I. A bounty spread out below us—a sweep of color and texture: grays and browns of rock and soil, brilliant greens and ochers of grass and tree, the vibrant blues of lake and stream, and fruit and flower sparking the landscape with splashes of scarlet and plum. A nestling of valley within the arms of encircling hills, the depth of a lake against the soaring reach of mountain . . .

*Awaken!* The word shuddered on the breeze. One by one the three other girls lifted arms to sky and soared up, to be lost among the larks. And for a moment I alone remained.

*This is what I give to you, Guardian,* came the whisper. *This is what I give.* I was filled with the richness of it all—it poured into my body, radiated outward; it strengthened my bones and charged my blood.

I lifted my arms like the others, exuberant. I was rooted; I flew high. I was power. I was home.

And the voice of the rowan tree echoed through my entire being:

*Bring light into dark.*

Erema's growl contorted into a howl and then a roar. It was the first thing I heard, the first thing that made me realize I was still alive, still in the middle of the Myr Mountains.

And then it was cold, and my body roiled with the hukon poison.

I was very alive.

Gharain stood above me, breath heaving as if he'd forged through battle. My gaze slid down to where the point of his sword had gouged the rock beneath my tumbled legs. He'd struck straight through me. I looked up. His eyes were no longer so blank.

He forced something of a smile. "The sword . . . is not for you."

*No weapons for you.* I lay there, still stunned that I was breathing, stunned that I could be alive, but comprehending the Rider Laurent's words fully for the first time—weapons forged from the Earth could not be used by the Guardian of Life, but neither could they be used against her. The metal had sliced through as if I had not even been there.

Erema's roar became a shriek as terrible as the swifts'

screams, making the stone tremble. Gharain's expression turned fierce, his eyes leaving mine at last, and with his own roar of anger, he wheeled on Erema, shouting, "You do not claim me!" Like a blur, his sword went winging sideways, catching the Breeder full across the front.

He did not kill her; maybe he knew he could not, or maybe he understood this was a revenge far more powerful. The sword sliced across, cleaving the hukon from its prize. A strike through its roots and the crystal orb sprang from Erema's chest like a gasp. We watched the amulet fling against the hewn ceiling: Erema's shriek gurgling in thwarted fury; I cringed, thinking it would shatter—but it was a silly thought, for the orb rolled safely to one side, brighter now that it was free from its bonds. I groaned, reaching for it—

Erema lunged at Gharain—pushed, threw, I never knew. Gharain was simply launched against the wall, slamming into it with a sickening thud. I screamed his name, I watched him crumple to the hard floor, and I rolled back to face Erema— she was moving toward me, toward the orb; she was pulling strands of hukon from her breast, braiding it. She lashed out at me with it like a whip, throwing me back, keeping me from my amulet.

"Mine!" she screamed. And lashed with the hukon again.

I jerked away hard against the cavern wall, her threats ringing off the stone, into me, then wormed my way forward again, sobbing that Erema already stood over the orb, blocking it, weaving a new web from the lengths of hukon she pulled from her own body. I saw my palms pushing on the rough floor, thinking inanely of my ability to calm the Earth through my hands. . . .

*Power of hand renders dark into light.* The verse from my fate rushed through me, so similar to the rowan tree's whisper: *Bring light into dark.* Twig's voice called over: *Understand a moonstone's power within the hands of a Guardian.*

But I'd lost the moonstone long back. It was probably cold and dark now, only a simple blue gem that—

A simple blue . . . *Power of hand* . . . I pushed myself from the floor with a wrenching groan, stumbling to stand upright—leaning into the walls and beginning to laugh as I did so, for I felt already the little buzzing beneath my palms as I pressed against the blue-tinged rock.

Erema's head jerked up at my noise, glaring at me. "What do you do?" she hissed.

Her hands held the net she'd created, complete, ready to capture the little orb that gleamed in the corner. But my hands had bested hers, for the cave was already shimmering. I pushed palm against wall, against ceiling, against anyplace I could reach, sparking the stone, raging at her through pain and joy. "What do I do, Breeder? I bring light into dark."

And the boundary of moonstones caught my energy and mirrored it back, and the hall burst into dazzling radiance.

Moonstones. These caves were carved from them; maybe the whole mountain was carved from them. Everywhere I pressed, light exploded, until there was such brilliance I had to squint against the glare. They were rougher; they'd not the precise clarity of the palm-sized oval that Twig had cut for me.

But however this cave was hewn, facets had been created, and they pulled a Guardian's energy and reflected it.

"You . . . clever . . . girl . . ." The words hissed out of Erema as she stood stunned. Then, with venomous and turbulent violence, she began hurling her net with shrieks of need, of wrath, looking to sweep the amulet back within its folds. But the room was too brilliant now; she could not see where to throw. And if hukon burned me, then this light burned Erema. Suddenly she was no longer the image of the beautiful lady; she was whatever desire looks like when it contorts to fury—something huge and dark, of glaring eye and gnashing ferocity. And yet that was neither she, for as soon as that monstrosity appeared, it was gone, spiraling in the room like a whirlwind and exploding with a wail and a shriek. As if it turned her inside out, the bleakness within her unleashed. She was vapor, and then she was nothing. Her cloak fell to the floor in a puddle.

She'd been consumed by Chaos.

There was no time to consider her ruin. The whirlwind shuddered through the tiny room, shattering the moonstones, my eardrums. It tossed me to the floor even as the floor cracked and lurched upward, and I threw myself sideways toward Gharain, wrapping my arms around his still form, rolling us both to avoid being crushed or stabbed by shards of ceiling.

We had to move. We had to leave. I let go of Gharain, twisting up to look for the orb. It shone still, steady and true and unharmed by all the bits of rock cascading like rain from the ceiling, wedged in that corner between floor and wall. I crawled my way to it, ducking my head, dodging pieces of moonstone as they hit the floor, their light fizzing out in streaks. And then at last, my hand wrapped around the little sphere and I pulled it to me, holding it the way I once held its image when I first learned of the forces and Balance.

The crystal orb, amulet of Life. Its pulse throbbed with a tiny burn in my palms, but it did not hurt, and for a brief moment the feel of the glowing thing alleviated the sickness of poison and gave pause to the heaving cave.

*The four who alone may carry them*, I heard the king say to me of the amulets, *who alone may hold them in their grasp, and who alone can return them to their rightful place in Tarnec.*

The crystal shimmered with the threading of gold and green. There were filigrees of blue as well I could see, now that it was close to me. The elements of Life—Fire of gold, Earth of green, Water of blue, encased by the crystal to represent Air— all of them at once in this founding piece: simple and exquisite, solid and delicate, ancient and alive. Everything in the palms of my hands. And in my hands the orb glowed with renewed strength, though my own body groaned from the poison.

The ground shifted again, and I fell back against the wall. I pressed the orb briefly to my cheek and then scrabbled for my pack, wrapping the orb in Gharain's tunic, tucking it in snugly beside the ally token, and shouldered the bag. Panting, I crawled back to Gharain.

He had not moved. Not dead, *not* dead, I knew, for I could feel his energy passing through my touch. I put my lips to his brow, gritting out, "I will help you," though in all honesty I'd not thought how I could do so. With its sheer drop, we could not go out the way I'd entered the mountain. I'd have to find another route.

Erema's cloak. I reached for it, tumbling against Gharain as the floor shook violently. I refused any fear that it might be a magic cloak, for I had no other way of carrying Gharain. I spread the wide fabric and rolled and pushed him into its center. He was impossibly heavy. I might have wondered at the amulet, why it could not endow me with some mystical strength, but I'd seen how the hukon had trapped it. The orb could not expel the hukon poison from my body any more than it could break from its bonds. Everything has its weakness.

I forced myself up, gathered folds of cloth to drag Gharain from the narrow room. The silky sheen of Erema's cloak ran smoothly on the rough floor, but it was barely enough. I panted, I strained, I twisted the fabric in my grip until my hands were chafed raw, any progress achingly slow. The more effort I made, the deeper the poison burned.

Into the large passage at last, and straight into the midst of Troths. I lashed out at their nearness, watched them jump back in fear. But they crowded me, suffocating my breath and body with their filthy stench, their violent energy. Their clawlike fingers hovered, wanting but afraid to touch. I reeked of hukon; I was both familiar and terrifying to them. I ducked my head and bore down, screaming through gritted teeth as if noise could help me forward. The Troths clung to the cloak, petting it, snuffing it, dragging us slower with their added weight. The passage heaved and threw us all sideways—I fell against two Troths and they rolled away, singed and screeching. I could not do this alone. I had no idea where to go.

I screamed at the creatures, "Let us out of here! Show me the way!"

A hundred opaque eyes stared at me. Then the cloak was gripped and pulled from my fingers, drawn so that I was behind suddenly, stumbling after it. The creatures scurried through the dark, through the collapsing tunnels. I forced a run, barely, following the trail by sense more than sight. Along one passage, then another—the scrape of padded feet, the snorts and grunts and vile, vile smell . . . I clung to my pack, pushed through the pain, and scrambled after the Troths.

And then all at once I crashed into the beasts, paused and huddled at the side of a tunnel, at a dark opening. I shrieked, "Where's Gharain—?" for the cloak was empty in their claws. But with one great move, they swept the cloak behind me, forcing me forward through the gap. I was released like a slingshot.

My scream cut short when I hit the ground hard, rolling, tumbling downward. An incline, steep and bumpy, an endless slide. Senses no longer mattered; time no longer mattered. I rolled and skidded, groaning from pain. And when I slammed hard into Gharain at the bottom, I turned into his side and braced there, wracked with agony at the poison closing in— the abuses of the mountain clenching every bone, every muscle into a taut fist of pain. I dragged my arm over Gharain, searching for his right hand. It was futile, almost silly, this attempt to charge my strength with his, his with mine.

"Help us, Gharain!" I mumbled, clawing my tunic away

from my neck, rolling to push his hand against my bared shoulder—my mark to his mark. "Rider . . ."

It wasn't working. The hukon had been stabbed there; maybe it had erased our connection. I screamed at him, crushing his limp hand into my skin. He couldn't be dead, I swore at everything around us. He couldn't be dead.

No. There—a tiny thread of energy pulsed. I gripped his fingers harder. *The give-and-take of energy, the Balance, allowing life to . . .* Hand to hand, I wrapped the length of my body against his. "Thrive," I whispered, knowing he could not hear the word.

Sometime later I felt Gharain's renewed warmth; I felt his breath, faint but steady. I wrenched myself to a sitting position, and then managed, somehow, to stand. A breeze was coming through the passage—the dark tingeing to something more like gray. We were nearly out of this tomb.

"We're there, Gharain," I gasped, and reached down with exhausted limbs to catch his wrists and tug him forward, crying, "I'm sorry," as I scraped him across the stone flooring.

It was but a few lengths and we were outside in the early dawn, at the base of the Myr Mountains. There was grass, scrubby though it might be, grass and warmer air. I wept with the pleasure of being free and sank back down next to my Complement, nesting the pack between us, putting my arms around him with face to the sky. I'd no strength to do more.

Thought lingered and drifted. For a while I felt not much beyond two things: I'd found the amulet, and Gharain was alive. Beyond that was the poison, spreading, creeping, dulling my senses, and killing my body. But I could breathe still, labored as it might be, and I took the breaths with as much depth as I could.

Clean air, fresh scent—the ground close to my ears humming in harmony, sun sliding higher, light warming over my body. And I was lying next to my heart's desire.

I smiled then, for my own little victory. I'd championed against my last dream. I would go out in the arms of Gharain, holding pure the memory of his love for me—never have to exchange that love for friendship, never have to witness him give that love to someone else. It was a sweet way to die.

The earth was drumming. A thudding that shivered the dirt and stone and made the sparse grass shimmer. And then I heard the hooves, pounding across the land, swift and powerful. I forced myself to look—

I was wrong. It would not end my way.

Rune. The white horse was there—soft nose against my cheek, folding low so that I might drag Gharain across his wide back and fall over him myself. I hesitated, though, curled tightly around my desire to keep this moment close—as I had the very first time Gharain appeared in my dreams. That point of recognition, where dying turned to rescue, was stabbing through me more huge and sharp and unbearable than any poison. For with it came the recognition that I wasn't ready to let Gharain go. So help me, I would never be ready.

And yet, my wants had never been part of this journey; if so, I'd never have embarked on it. And the journey was not done. I had to finish; I had a task to fulfill. I slowly uncurled, let go my hope. Sacrifice—I'd not expected it to take this shape.

"Carry us to Merith," I murmured, and Rune reared up, patient as I tugged Gharain into some haphazard position. I pulled off my pack and knotted it around Rune's neck like a collar where it would stay safe.

Gharain's head fell against my shoulder. He mumbled something unintelligible and let his arm fall around me.

*To Merith.* I closed my eyes.

"Evie will heal you," I whispered. "She's beautiful, and wise. You will love her so."

I meant to say *All will be well,* but I couldn't.

## 25

MAGIC IS A wonderful thing. It can transform a creature, protect a village, empower an ordinary soul. It can transport a white horse with his riders swifter than a wish. It can take away pain. Sometimes.

We'd leaped the distance to Merith unaware. Amid the burned rubble of the market square, Gharain had been gently lifted from Rune's back, as had I. We were brought to Grandmama's cottage, which had barely missed the battle's wrath; the herb shed and field, like many in the village, were burned flat. The Healers went to work, mending bone and muscle and drawing the poison from my blood. These were no easy tasks, skilled as Grandmama and Evie were. A day and a night and a day and several more were anxious vigils over our broken bodies. But there is magic too in the hands of Healers, and with knowledge and patience it may be applied for the best outcome. And so it was with us.

But no magic, no matter how expert, can heal a broken heart. True, it can be masked or it can be diverted; heartbreak might even be forgotten using magic—but it is never healed. That sort of healing only the person can do for herself.

I do not know how to heal.

There were no dreams while I recovered. Time ceased for a while, I think. I was told later that it took far longer to be cleansed from the stab of one hukon tip than the repair of all the abuses to Gharain's body. But that is the vileness of hukon— the poison turns blood black; a victim's body must be drained of the filth, leaving her to a long, unconscious recovery. And the wound is permanent, the victim vulnerable. Hukon leaves its taint forever.

I wonder too if there was a part of me that did not wish to wake, to witness the one dream that was yet to become reality. But, inevitably, and rather simply, the light crept into my chamber window one morning and my eyes opened. I saw my room for the first time in what seemed ages, and drew in a deep breath of the familiar scents. I pushed at the sheets that were tucked around me, struggling, for they seemed tucked too tightly, before realizing it was I who was ridiculously weak.

It came back to me then, my dream, and I knew I was here at last. I could wish that I'd been wrong, I could wish that I had died instead of this, but I could not change what I'd seen, and—by that very reason of having seen—so given my gift to

Evie: to choose her love. I'd promised, and a promise is never broken.

I lay there for a time, thinking up these wishes to make it less agonizing. But there was nothing to be done, and so I tugged the sheets back and forced myself to stand on the floor and walk to the window, where the glorious sun was spreading over the fields and lawn, and a lark was shooting from the grass to arc like a spray of water against the sky. And I smiled at that, before turning my gaze to the garden path where Gharain and Evie were walking so closely together. He was whole again, beautiful and strong—so much time had passed. Time spent with Evie.

I would be happy for them; I would, I insisted. But there my smile faded—they had paused, their arms brushing, and my heart was tearing in two. I could not prevent its rupture any more than I could prevent Gharain's arms going around Evie and her returning the embrace. And heartbreak leaves no ability for one to stand straight. I slipped to the floor, or rather, more likely crashed, for my dream had ended there, and I did not know that Grandmama and Rileg would come stumping and scampering up the stairs after hearing me fall.

Rileg! He snuffed at my face, he licked my hand, he panted and slobbered all over me until I opened my eyes and put my arms out to hug him, which I did with all the enthusiasm I could muster. Grandmama stood patiently by the door while I wept and laughed into Rileg's fur, happy at least for this wonderful lame companion, whom I'd missed.

Rileg finally plunked down on the floor by my side, and I

pushed myself up to a sitting position and looked at Grandmama. Her face had not changed, though it felt like years since I'd seen her. She had that look on her face. The knowing one.

"And here you are," she said.

"I'm glad to be home." My long-unused voice was hoarse. *Home.* I wasn't certain it felt so anymore.

Grandmama nodded. And then she added, "Bravely done, Lark." It was as simple as that, our welcome. But then, Grandmama was a Healer. She expressed little through emotion and much through her touch.

"Tell me of Merith?"

"Few villagers were lost, though each brings its own sadness. The square and cottages we will rebuild. Fields and gardens will regrow. We have you to thank, Lark, for sending the Riders in time to save most."

"It was not," I said, shrugging a little, "what I expected."

"Things never are."

And then I asked, "Is it safe?"

Grandmama knew I meant the amulet. She inclined her head, and I felt a small relief. "It is safe, whatever it is. Your pack is still on your horse. He would not allow anyone to touch it."

*Though no one could have tried.* I asked another question: "The Riders?"

"They have returned to their realm, all but the one. They knew you and your friend were healing; they would not stay beyond that." She added, to stray the topic, "The horses, you know, caused a great stir once the battle was done. The village youths lined up to have a chance at currying their coats."

But I did not hear such inconsequential words. *All but the one,* she'd said of the Riders. My *friend.* I knew it, of course. Still, it hurt.

She moved into the room and helped me get to my feet. I felt her hands on mine—warm and worn, capable always of making me feel better. And yet my throat was choked.

"Will you go downstairs?" Grandmama asked me.

"I think I'd rather stay here for a bit." I moved a little shakily to sit in the single chair in the room. I could feel the sun through the window there without being able to see anything but sky.

She nodded again, accepting what I wanted. "They've been waiting to see you," she added, moving to the door. "Evie and the Rider."

"I know." I mustered the pleasantry: "'Twill be so good to see Evie."

I couldn't help my voice. It made Grandmama pause. "Lark," she said a little roughly, for her own voice was hoarse. "We cannot stop things from changing. Heartbreak will be borne. You must trust that."

*Trust.* How often I'd heard the word. I must have made a noise, or a movement, for Grandmama came back to me. She laid her hand on my head, and for a moment I rested my face against her apron front. She smelled of honey and lavender. I would cry if I breathed.

"Lark—"

But I took her words and forced them out this time. "All will be well, Grandmama." I gave her a brilliant smile.

I did go downstairs sometime after Grandmama left, holding hard to the handrail and careful not to trip over Rileg, who could not be more thrilled to escort my every step. Dreading or not, I'd wrestled with myself long enough. Gharain and Evie would be on the garden paths still, hidden somewhere in all the beauty. I had to find them, hear their happy news, and go on.

Go on. *How does one go on?* I wondered. I looked at the garden I stood in. These were the cutting beds, the ones closest to the cottage, in full bloom now, so deep into summer. They were for pleasure's sake, for delighting the eye with winsome color—mallows, lilies, maribels, and glenn. These were blossoms that I would pause at every morning to place a finger on—to touch their loveliness for memory. I'd have to find that loveliness again, for there was none today.

And then Gharain was there, coming toward me at a run, his face alight with that smile, and I froze.

"Lark!"

It was a barely drawn breath, his word, his shout of gladness to see me awake and standing. I shook myself, blinked stupid tears away, and focused on choosing stems for the kitchen vase.

"Lark, you are up at last! I saw you at the door." He'd reached me, arms out. "I waited—"

I broke in without looking, taking a step away so his hands fell back to his sides. "You've healed well, racing toward me as you did. I'm glad."

There was a pause. Gharain said somewhat curiously, "I was

broken and you brought me out of there. How you did it . . ." He took a breath, and I think he looked away for a moment. "You saved me again."

I nodded. I would shrug this off; I would look matter-of-fact. "Always, Gharain." There. That was simply said.

"Both times you pulled me . . . from out of the earth." Now his voice changed, and I knew what would come: the words would soften and deepen and he would thank me, and I could not bear that. I moved a little down the path and inspected the garden borders.

"Lark."

It made me angry that I could not yet return his gaze. This was silly. I was young, able. I'd brought back the Life amulet; I could claim much satisfaction. And I was in the gardens of my beloved cottage, in my beloved Merith . . . even if it had not the same feeling.

Gharain followed me. "You pulled us both out of the mountain, Lark, and your wound was far more serious."

I shrugged it off. "Obviously, then, not so serious. You see that I am well."

"The hukon—"

"The hukon will be in me always. 'Tis a simple fact."

"Hardly simple. But you will do better in Tarnec." Gharain said it with certainty. "You will be safe there."

I shook my head. "I am home, Gharain."

That seemed to throw him, soft as I'd said it. "You will not return to Tarnec?"

"No." It was cruel of him to ask such a thing. I reached to

snap a mallow from her stem, but then I didn't want it. My hand dropped, useless.

"Why?" His voice hardened. "Look at me, Lark."

"No. I am choosing flowers for the kitchen vase." I forced myself to grab the mallow again.

"Fine." He nearly bit the words: "We shall pick your flowers, and then you will look at me and tell me why you won't go back—"

"Go back!" I said it as lightly as possible. "To be sure, 'tis unnecessary; I've done my task. Rune will carry the orb safely from here." I added ungraciously, "You'll be well accompanied."

Gharain turned and paced away, holding tight to some emotion. He came back, saying "Then here, Lark, take some pink things and some blue," tearing a few random stalks and pushing them at my hands. "Don't let them fall like that. Here, here are some others."

"Stop."

"Why?" He was not angry, but I could see his hand shaking slightly. Or maybe that was because there were tears brimming and everything was shimmering. He was grabbing fistfuls of stems now, piling them in my arms.

"Stop, Gharain. Please. I do not want anything to put in the vase, I—"

"Why?"

I could not hold back the tears. "Because there is no pleasure in these any longer!" And then I could neither hold back the words: "Because you fill all my senses and leave no space for anything else."

"Lark—"

It came out on a sob. "All of this made me happy once. This—the flowers, the herbs. I should look forward to weeding the gardens, even pulling the ghisane, but I don't. It feels gray and sad now, and—and I hate that! I *hate* that you've ruined this for me." I threw my armful of flowers on the path and turned and walked away. I'd never exploded so in this dear cottage. My voice was all wrong for this place. *I* was wrong for this place.

"Lark. Lark! You leave us like this?"

*Us.* Again. I forced myself to walk back to him, to look up at him through the silly tears and clenched teeth, and grit out, "I am sorry. Trust me that I am happy for you. I *truly* am."

"Happy for me? What are you speaking of?"

"Do you have to make it worse by forcing me to say it? I *told* you of Evie; I knew it long, *long* before this morning. The dream's been made real now; the choice is done, and—and even if I behave this foolishly, trust that I am all right. I *will* be all right." I paused for breath. "There. 'Tis out now, finished. You've no need to tell me anything yourself."

"Your dream? You saw us?"

Stupid tears! "Yes! Only now I am doing everything that I promised myself I would not!" And I ran off, forgetting that I'd no energy to run.

Gharain was behind me before I stumbled, his hands on my waist pulling me close, and I think we both cried out at the shock. We went down on the ground, I within Gharain's arms and worse for that.

"Don't!" I was savage. "Don't! It's not fair."

"Not fair!" he growled at me. "Don't struggle so!"

"It's not fair to Evie—" Nor me.

"What has this to do with Evie? What do I care if Evie sees us?"

"Stop it!"

"Evie knows, Lark!"

"You told her?" I pushed at him. "Why? She need not know! Gharain, what we shared—it was only for that moment. She's suffered already; she does not need—"

"She knows, Lark, I said. She's very happy for us!"

That shocked me into silence.

He said fiercely, "Why would she not be happy? She loves you."

"You don't make sense!"

"I don't make sense? Or for some mad reason do you not want to hear this? I told Evie what I felt for you, I told her I would take you back with me to Tarnec, and she was happy!"

I was sobbing now. "It can't be helped. The Sight *chose* you for her. And your arms were around her. You leaned to kiss her, and you were so full of joy."

"I *leaned* to whisper in her ear that I love you!" He was furious. "Is this what you meant? You saw us embrace in a dream, and you thought I was to be with Evie?"

I suspected later that Gharain would have shaken me if I had not been recovering from the hukon. "I told you: you can misinterpret what you see! You, Lark! Bearer of the Sight!" He said this through clenched teeth and was not gentle as he held me. "I love you. How can you think anything less?"

"And what of Evie? I cannot hurt her! You are to be her love."

"Me? Why are you so committed to being so *blind*? You cannot make my choice. And Evie does not love me; she loves someone else." His voice changed and sobered. "Loved. She loved someone else."

I wept against his arm, long, shuddering sobs that gathered up the past days and threw them out of me with each heaving breath. I wept for Merith, for the queen, for the foxes and Twig and the long-witnessing rowan tree. I wept for the loss of the amulets, and then I wept for Raif and for Evie. Gharain waited through it all, never letting go, until the sadness was emptied and what remained was the exquisite knowledge that this young man held me—that he might hold me forever. This man. This Rider. My Complement. And when I finally raised my head, sobbing laughter now rather than tears, he looked at me with that beautifully curving smile and said, "Did I not tell you that our connection ran deeper than a single touch?" And he brushed the wet from my cheek with the lightest sweep of his thumb.

"You did." I nodded and kissed him with a desire that held no more regret.

I found Evie trimming haricots in the kitchen. One look took my breath; I had to sit down. Her eyes, her lips, her skin, her hair were all as lovely as I remembered. She even smiled with great joy when I entered the room. And yet, she was a pale memory of her own beauty. If love had filled me whole, the loss of it had drained her.

I reached across the table, and she gave me her hands. Usually hers warmed mine, but it was no longer so. And for the first time I could sense Evie from touch, as if she were no longer too close to me to read her. Something had changed—if no less love between us, then a separation. We watched one another for a time without speaking.

"Raif," I finally murmured, and she nodded.

"I'm so sorry, Evie. I tried—I couldn't help him."

She kept her eyes on me. "The battle?"

"I was there in a vision, and—and he saw me."

Her fingers tightened on mine. And there was a flicker of envy for that—that I had shared his last moment. She spoke it slowly, admitting it as if some terrible secret: "I never told him."

Her pain was excruciating. I felt its stab in my own heart. I squeezed her cold hands, saying impulsively, "But I did, Evie. I told Raif you loved him. I thought it would keep him alive if he believed. I didn't care truth or not, he needed to hear. . . . I want to believe it comforted him. . . ." I watched her a bit helplessly. "It was not right for me to say, that I spoke for you, but I was—"

"Lark, stop. It *was* right. You chose for me." There was a long pause. Evie's lip curved ever so faintly in relief. "Do you remember? I asked you to choose the one I would love, as my birthday gift."

Of course I remembered; it was just unexpected. I thought I'd chosen Gharain, but it was our birthday when I'd found

Raif in my terrible vision. And it was Raif whom I told of Evie's love.

"I said you would know because you have the Sight. I said you would choose well." Evie's eyes were dry, but, soft as it was, her voice broke. "You chose well, Lark. You chose well."

I tried to smile for her. "Raif's last words, Evie. They were meant for you. He said, *Love cannot die*."

"I know," she said.

Love can be that simple. Evie shared her heart with few words, and with just as few words and no tears, she suffered its loss. It hurt to look at her. Grandmama had not been speaking of me when she said that heartbreak would be borne, but I was not at all certain that Evie could bear it. Or maybe it was I who could not bear so uneven an ending for my dearest friend.

Haunted, but no less perceptive, Evie turned her frank gaze on me. "Let me see you, Lark." After a while she said, "You've changed."

I took a breath. "Evie, if I could begin to tell you—"

She shook her head. "You don't need to. You shine. It's glorious." Another moment and then she murmured, "I imagine Tarnec to be very beautiful."

"Yes," I said. "But so is this."

Her eyes dropped briefly, and then she looked up, away. "This cottage, this village were a most special place to grow, weren't they." She wasn't asking for response; she wasn't even asking a question. I shivered a little that she spoke of our home in past tense.

There was a wistfulness in her tone: "Love, purpose, challenge . . . all of those things to open your heart and mind." And then she feigned a smile. "Look, Lark, Rileg paws at the door. He wants you. We will talk later."

She was slowly releasing her hands from mine, and I gripped them to make her stay. "Evie."

She shook her head. "What a journey this must have been for you, Lark." She gave a last squeeze to my fingers. "Everyone should make such a one."

Evie was gone the next morning. She left her goodbyes in a scattering of marjorie and willow on the kitchen table as an offering of happiness and love to all. She took some provisions, she took her turquoise cloak, and she took some small bottles of herbs; which ones they were I would not have known, but Grandmama did, for I saw her later frowning at the empty spaces on the shelf. Grandmama seemed little surprised at Evie's departure, though it must have made her heart heavy to lose her. And I? I'd not even been able to tell Evie of our shared marks, of what it could mean.

I cried. I might have cried longer, but a message dove came winging down to our porch and waited patiently for me to dry my eyes and untie the tiny roll of parchment that was on her leg. The ribbon was the brilliant rose color of Tarnec. It was the color of the flag I'd brought to Bren Clearing.

I gave the note to Gharain, watching his face darken as he read it.

"The king will not recover," he announced heavily. "I must

go back now." He pulled me close for a moment and then said, almost hesitantly, his jaw against the top of my head, "Lark . . . the amulet."

"He must see it," I murmured back. "He must know it is safe returned."

Grandmama filled a satchel with food. We invited, but she would not come with us. Merith needed its Healer. It needed a third elder as well, for sadly Sir Jarett was one who'd not survived the Troths' attack, and Grandmama had taken his place with the eldest villagers. She hugged me very hard and said that it was not to be our last embrace. "Evie will return someday, and so shall you. In the meantime, we must each follow our paths."

I walked through our cottage, letting my fingertips sketch over all of the things that made it home. I walked through the gardens and fields; I charged the ghisane not to overrun our land, though I strongly doubted it would heed me. And I said goodbye to neighbors and friends. They had no knowledge of my true journey; I'd been lanced by hukon, they knew, and understood my healing would be better protected wherever it was we headed. No one spoke of Castle Tarnec, and I would not tell of its secrets. I was merely going back with Gharain, the Rider, to live somewhere in the hills of Tarnec—the beginning of those territories that would remain unknown. But Dame Keren bowed to me when I went to bid her goodbye, and when I looked surprised at that, she simply fixed me with her bright gaze and smiled.

Quin knew my story, because I told it to him, and he'd not reveal my confidences. He put down his reed flute then, and claimed he would be a Rider. I grinned and said what of his sweetheart Nance, and what of the silly, smitten Cath, and did not our village need his music more than the hills needed a sword?

"'Tis not the sword I want, Lark. 'Tis a horse."

Foolish as it was, I offered, "And if I can send you one horse?"

Quin looked at me with a stern shake of his head. "But you cannot, should not, do that. Think of the imbalance it would create in Merith."

Balance—ever precarious. I made Quin promise that he would not attempt to enter the realm of Tarnec without first unfurling a flag from the rowan tree. And then I picked him a sprig of fern and said it was my offer of friendship and it would protect him. *Not from Cath, though,* I'd said with a wink.

And so, not two hours past the dove's arrival, I set out with Gharain on horseback to Castle Tarnec. We rode side by side. The Life amulet stayed tied around Rune's neck, swinging gently in the pack, for I would need both arms to hold Rileg when he tired.

After all, it was a distance to travel and he had only three legs.

# 26

BY HORSEBACK, MY original journey was halved. Even the rift the Breeders had opened between the Niler marshes and the Cullan foothills was bridged and offered no delay—we rode across the new timbers that spanned the crevasse, still oozing tree sap, while I held my breath and imagined the endless depth beneath us.

And it seemed in short time we were climbing the narrow trail to Castle Tarnec, four Riders having come to meet and lead us up. I greeted them happily and by name now: Laurent, Taran, Evaen, and Wilh. They were glad to see us.

Laurent asked after Evie, nodding when I told him of her departure and thanked him for saving her life. "I imagine she is missed," he said evenly.

And then there were all the others to welcome me home. *Home.* Had I said it? I stood in the bedchamber where I'd spent but one full night, breathing in the scent of bell roses cascading outside the window. Home. Rileg curled up contentedly on the deep-piled carpet, and I sat on the great bed, closed my eyes, and breathed. This was not the moss and brown earth and milk soap scents of my cottage, and yet it smelled pure and sweet, and good.

"My lady?" Nayla was at the door. "The king is asking for you."

I got up immediately, shouldering my pack with the crystal orb undisturbed inside, and left my chamber. But Nayla stopped me. "Not that way."

And she led me away from the Great Hall, to a set of stairs that opened deep into the rock upon which the castle sat, and down many steps until she finally paused and said from there I must continue alone. And I did until the steps ended, opening onto a wide octagon of smoothed stone lit by single tapers ensconced on each of the eight facets. A large font stood in the center, the only furnishing. Cool, a little musty . . . I stood in the keep of Balance, where the amulets rested. Except, not now.

"You did well, young Lark. I thought you would."

The king was there, waiting. I walked quickly to him, bowing hand to heart, glad to see him, yet also sad. This was but a wan figure of the king. He was upright, but strongly supported by a stout wooden cane topped with a knob of crystal. I thought suddenly of Twig—how he'd faded from sight. The king looked to do that at any moment.

I'd forgotten he could read my thoughts. "Ahh, the gnome." The king smiled. "He was gathered at your request."

"I could not have claimed the amulet without his help."

"Then you were wise to have asked." The king shifted his weakened stance. I heard the deep weariness beneath his words. "And now you have brought the Life amulet home. May we see it?"

I opened my pack. *It.* The crystal orb. I'd rescued it, carried it, ready now as I stood there before the king to return it to its home.

My hand closed around the amulet, scooping it in one palm and drawing it close one last time. "It seems brighter here," I said, marveling at the little thing glowing in my palm.

The king made a small nod. "Yes. But not as bright as it will be."

He was right, of course. The orb pulsed with lovely warmth, and yet within the crystal, only the green threads gave off light.

"You must place it now," he said. I followed his slow steps to the font. The bowl was wide and shallow on its tall pedestal, crafted from woods, stones, and metals—varied colors and textures all twisted and carved and shaped into a spiral of support for four unique holders.

"The small slash in the stone will hold our blade of Light," the king said, pointing. "The nest of pearls is there for Death's shell. The stone of Dark will be set inside the iron ring, and the center is for the orb."

The special places for the Dark, Light, and Death amulets were points of a triangle surrounding the spot for the crystal orb: a simple bed of moss. I looked up at the king. His eyes crinkled.

"Go on," he said.

With two hands I placed the orb gently on the moss. So simple. I heard the faint intake of breath—my own and the king's—and then the whole room seemed to sigh with relief. It was a settling of the floor, of the space—firmer suddenly. Grounded.

"Ahh. Well done." The king sighed, and I looked at him sharply. He was bent further, hunched over his cane as a final support before falling.

I moved to him. "Let me assist you back to your chambers."

"Lark." He wheezed a chuckle. "You do not imagine I can climb those stairs."

"Then let me run for help. The Riders—"

"No. My time is over." He looked at me shaking my head, refusing his refusal. "It is all right, Lark. I am glad of this."

"But why can we not heal you?" I begged.

He sighed, but it was not a sorry sigh. "Lark, regardless of effort, a Complement cannot survive long after the loss of his Guardian."

My hand was on his arm. "You were Complement to the queen? The queen was a Guardian?"

"She was," the king said, pushing himself to stand taller. "Life Guardian."

My hand fell away. "I cannot be queen."

"My dear, you already are." He nodded at my stunned stare. "Hear this, young Lark, and understand it well, for time is short. You, Guardian of our Life amulet, with the mark of Balance, you are now the rightful ruler of Tarnec. It is no easy demand.

It is your charge to see that the other amulets are restored, and that the natural world is returned to Balance. In this you *must* succeed."

I turned then and moved a little apart. I did not deny his words, but I needed a moment to let them sink in. To my side the orb pulsed its steady light. I had done that. I had brought the amulet home. Whatever uncertainties and fears had thrilled through, determined to wreck me, I endured. I'd brought it home.

I shifted, then stared, startled, because I saw there were other items in the room. A narrow bench had been hidden by the size of the font; four books were placed side by side upon it. For all the intricate crafting of the amulets' font, this was quite spare in comparison, almost too simple.

The king knew my thought. "This keep was never intended for them."

"These are the Guardians' books," I said, "which hold their destinies. Is this how we find the others?"

"Guardians awaken when crisis demands," he reminded me. "They don't know it yet, of course, but they are ready to be wakened, just as you were. The books are not necessary, but they do hasten discovery. And since they were loaned to us for this purpose, we should not ignore the opportunity. Read only the first page, the single verse that begins each book. It will hold the clues for your search. Aid the Guardians as you can."

I walked over to the bench. The books lay so simply, so harmlessly on their makeshift shelf. There was my book, with the orb etched on it. The covers of the other three books were also etched: a shell, a stone, and a small, slightly curved blade. The books were beautifully made—the gilding on the edges, the smooth leather bindings—and yet they were not ornate; there was no fanfare to these lives, or the fates held within. And what were those fates? I wondered. How did they merge and intertwine with mine? Would the amulets each be returned and Balance restored? And if I opened to any page, would it speak of beauty or horror?

"It is not for you to read ahead, Lark," the king whispered solemnly to quench my curiosity. "Leave them the freedom of choice. That is the honor of Balance."

And what would be their choice when faced with the magnitude of the task—would they believe they could do it any more than I had? Poignance. Hope. That much I could feel from the books. Beyond that . . . "I have seen them, these Guardians," I murmured. "They are young. We are all so very young."

The king smiled. "Worry will not help them. Trust yourself."

I laughed a little. "That was what Twig said."

"A wise gnome, I'd say."

My eyes widened. "You sent him," I whispered. "You helped me through. The moonstone, the ally token, the things you meant to give to me—"

His smile broadened, though he shook his head. "The rowan tree is our friend. She helped me help you. Lark, remember Twig's words: *Your truth will be your greatest aid.* The ally token was your truth. The voices you heard were carried within your own memory. You trusted yourself."

I said, almost breathless, "The ruby drop that Twig gave me, that the Bog Hag wanted, which allowed me to step through to the Myr Mountains. Was it the Bog Hag's tear?"

"A tear, but not hers. The last red drop of our queen's blood, before the hukon turned it black." The reverence was plain in his voice. "Our Guardian of Life is the essence of all things of this Earth. Her blood is every being's blood. We must preserve a single pure drop to return to the rightful harbor so that souls will not be left in Chaos. Life returns to Death, Lark. Ever Balance."

"You hadn't intended to give it to me."

His eyes crinkled. "It was my charge to return the drop, but since you took, shall we say, a shortcut to the Myr Mountains, I thought you might need such an offering to help you through. The Hag will carry it home."

The Bog Hag. I'd crossed through one of Death's realms to reach the Myr Mountains.

The king was murmuring, "The last pure drop of your blood was saved as well."

"How—how do you know that my blood was still pure? I was in the mountains forever, it felt; how is it possible it was not completely tainted?"

"Because you would be dead." The king looked at me very calmly. "Lady Lark, the queen was of great age; she had not your youthful strength."

I asked what I'd always wondered: "Did she know?"

He made a faint smile. "Remember that we willingly make our sacrifices."

"But then she *let* Erema steal the amulets!"

"Unless the amulets are destroyed, war will ever wage between Balance and Chaos, for even Balance must be balanced," he reminded me. "And yet Tarnec was breached so easily this time—perhaps the queen understood that a new era of Guardians was necessary, that the Keepers of Tarnec as well must strengthen to their task." He waited a moment before saying, "The Life Guardian keeps watch long after the other Guardians have passed on. She knew a strong successor would be needed. She trusted you."

And now it was his time. The king was fading before me. My hands reached out reflexively to draw him back, to shake him into solid form, but he pulled away from me a little with a heavy step, leaning hard on his cane. My voice went shrill: "That is made of hukon!"

The king turned his head to me with a wry grimace. "Balance is necessary, even when it seems a burden." He raised a gnarled finger to point at me. "You carry yours within."

I could feel the scar as he said it. The hukon stab would never be healed.

He looked up then, this king—eyes closing and a beautiful smile making his face glow. "Complement," I heard. He was going to her.

"My love, my Life . . . ," he said very softly, and faded from sight. The hukon stick fell sharply to the ground, the crystal bursting into a thousand shards of flame and burning the evil wood to ash before I'd had time to catch my breath.

Done. I was Tarnec's queen.

It was dark when I reached the top of the stairs. The hour was very late, for I passed no one in the corridor. I walked back to my chamber, pushing open the heavy door with a heavy heart, glad then when I saw Rileg, the fire in the hearth, and some tea keeping warm nearby. I scratched Rileg's ears, took up my cup, and sat for a while watching it, waiting for the liquid to shiver, to prove I trembled at the challenges ahead, the way I'd crumpled, shivering on the cobblestones that day in Merith. But I did not tremble.

Nayla had left me a sprig of minion next to the teapot, a faint scent of honey and mint. And then I noticed something else on the tray. I gathered them with the minion, got up, and turned to the door to the garden.

He was in the pool; I knew he would be. The water made the lightest rippling sound from his swim. I walked along the footpath. The candlelight in the windows glowed golden, but the stones were silvery under starlight. And then Gharain was rising from the water, pushing his streaming hair back with his hands.

He took a deep breath. "The king . . ."

I shook my head. And then I ran to him, and he reached for me over the stone edge of the pool and clasped me in his warm, wet arms as I kneeled on the stone to claim his embrace, whispering, "I am sorry."

"It is all right," he murmured. "I knew this would be. We all knew it."

I pressed my forehead against his chest. "I feel I should weep for him, but I'm not sad. He was happy to be with his Guardian again. His queen."

Gharain drew away from me then, but only slightly—enough to look into my eyes and brush my now-damp hair back from my shoulder. And then he smiled his beautiful smile and said, "*My* queen." And he kissed me.

That brought the tears up, but only a little, only from joy. Gharain kissed my mouth, my cheek, my jaw, and my neck, letting his fingers trail over my collarbone to my shoulder blade, where he turned me slightly so he could press his lips against the small black point hovering just above my birthmark. A mark of light and of dark burned into one flesh.

"I wish I could take this scar from you," he whispered against my skin.

"It is mine to bear." I reached for his face, to draw him back to my gaze. "We each make our sacrifices." And I laughed a little that I'd said that. Tarnec had its influence.

He nodded. And then, perhaps in response, he said, "Laurent left earlier this evening. He's gone to find your cousin."

"Evie . . . *Laurent*? Why?"

"Maybe he's just making sure that no Breeder finds her first."

Our birthmark. A bond seeking. A Complement to be determined. "Gharain! I never told her of it: of our marks, what I'd learned in Tarnec, the amulets, none of it! I never had the chance—I never thought she'd be gone. Oh, what sort of queen am I that I've left it all undone?" I leaned my head into his shoulder. "I am . . ." And I laughed a little. "To say that I am awed by what has happened is to simplify all feelings."

Gharain kissed the top of my head. "You are strong, love. And you are not alone."

It made me remember what I still held in my fist. I opened my hand to show Gharain. "Look what Nayla left for me."

The objects were small and my palm was shadowed, but there was a glitter from them nonetheless. Gharain's finger brushed the minion flower first, briefly, murmuring, "The most powerful of healing herbs. That is for you." But then he touched the two rings, which lay as sparkling circles against my skin, and said, "You understand what these are." Gharain raised his eyes to catch mine as I shook my head. "They are gifts. Gifts from the Earth—precious metal mined from her stores, passed from Life Guardian to Life Guardian. Look closely."

He cupped his hand beneath mine and raised it so we could both look at the delicate things. They glittered, catching the starlight, and warming from our completed touch. Crafted from strands, seemingly of a spider's thread—strands of brilliant gold and copper, woven in an intricate, webbed design, no wider than a blade of grass and almost as thin.

"It's beautiful," I whispered.

"It is a sign of the Keepers and their allies," Gharain whispered back.

The weaving design—like what the young men of Merith made from leather. Allies, all. I took the smaller of the rings and slid it onto my finger. It was warm—like a blade of heat that ran from my finger and into my whole body. Simple and whole.

I held the other ring out to Gharain. "Rule with me."

He smiled, and after a moment lifted my hand, pressed a kiss by the remaining ring, and closed my fist over it. "I will. But Tarnec needs its queen first."

And then he released me and glided to the other side of the pool, where he walked up the steps, grinning—because he knew I watched him—and pulled on his leggings and shirt.

"Come," he called out. "The dawn is nearly here. Let us watch it together."

And so we passed once more through the quiet halls, our bare feet silent on the paving, and stepped out onto the back terrace, which circled Castle Tarnec to where the cliff dropped away. We faced northward first, to see the Myr Mountains still dark as night. Then we turned, walking to where we could look east at the sun piercing its first rays over the hills of Tarnec, watching the new light flood over the pale canyons and green valleys. We gazed south—where Merith nested at the foot of Dark Wood, and the Cullan foothills and Niler marshes carved out their empty and crowded spaces. And last we turned west, to see the wealth of the land behind Castle Tarnec—grass and tree, stone, field, and cottage refreshed in the morning light. A pale moon was just setting beyond the rise of woods. I wondered which direction Evie had chosen.

And then the morning was waking the birds—their songs were pealing through the air, and my eye was caught by something shooting up from the ground to catch the first light.

"Look!" I cried. "Look, there, how the lark rises against the dawn!"

Gharain turned to me; I could sense him watching me, his beautiful smile curving his mouth.

"I see her," he said.

# ACKNOWLEDGMENTS

IT IS TRUE that this story was born in the field behind my house, where beauty and magic grow faster than I might try to mow them back. But that this story became a book is due to the collective life breathed into it, and so I owe heartfelt thanks . . .

To my agent, Jenny Bent, who took a seed and coaxed forth a bud, and to my editor, Diane Landolf, who nurtured that bud into blossom. That you both believed so wholeheartedly in this story leaves me speechless.

To my friends in my writers group, the dynamic trio of authors—Tatiana Boncompagni, Melanie Murray Downing, and Lauren Lipton—who so carefully critiqued the way-too-many installments with keen eyes, warm hearts, and good humor.

To those who paused in their own creative pursuits to go beyond the call of friendship, sisterhood, and spousal duty by accepting armloads of pages with enthusiasm and offering incredible support along the way: John Gahl, Lisa Worth Huber, Lisa Klein, Jacklyn Maddux, Kathy Waugh, and Jonathan Stern. And those who lent their artistic talents: Deborah Chabrian, Ed Martinez, and Melanie Kleid.

To my family at large—my mother, Diana; my father (in memoriam), Hillary; my sister, Kathy; and my brother, Lawrence, who shared the growing up in a house where creative expression was a given.

And to my family at home—Jonathan, Christopher, and Jeremy—who all graciously accepted my setting up camp on the most prominent chair in the house because it is my favorite place to write. I love you.

Turn the page for a sneak peek at the next book

in the GUARDIANS OF TARNEC series

Available now!

1

SUMMER'S WANE

"YOU HAVE NO fear of death."

The woman lay wide-eyed on the ground gasping this at me—gargling, really, for her throat was torn open, her voice shredded. She'd not last two breaths beyond those words; 'twas sad she had to waste them on me. But there was no one familiar left with whom to share meaningful last speeches of love or regret, nor anything that might ease her mind. Just the stranger who held her hand.

I smiled and soothed as I'd done through the final moments of all the dying, kneeling next to her on the hardened earth while she struggled, our fingers linked. I said softly, as if we'd continue this conversation, as if we took afternoon tea and commented on the dearth of rain, "There is nothing to fear."

The woman looked to challenge, but then her eyes drifted from mine and stilled. I kept my hand on hers for a moment longer, slumped back with a sigh. And then all that moved was the smoke.

Smoke. It filtered through the dull green of the trees, carrying the stink of burning things. We were a distance from the ruined village, but the gray wisps slipped through, swirled and surrounded, blinding the eye and polluting the soul. My soul.

"Mistress! Mistress Healer!"

I'd been called that since I first entered Bern, since I dropped my satchel in what remained of their growing fields and kneeled to assist those sprawled among the charred stalks. That I no longer cared about the title made no difference. One is born with one's gifts.

"Mistress! Here, *please*!" The brown-bearded man was crouched by some little tumble of clothing. He'd been zigzagging about the field ahead of me, avoiding bits of lingering flame, yelling and pointing at anyone who still breathed. How he'd spied survivors through the choking fog, had found the few among so many, I didn't know.

I shut the staring eyes of the woman, crossed her arms over her heart, then scrambled up and ran to the man, shoving up my sleeves once more. I forgot my satchel, hastened back for it. The satchel had been light in weight when I abandoned my own village of Merith; it was even lighter now. I'd taken only herbs— minion, yew, and heliotrope—hardly intending they'd serve anyone but me. Now I was nearly out. Three of five villages I'd passed through had been ravaged, the wounded begging to be tended back to life or eased into death. It was a trail of destruction, of pure savagery, witless and cruel. I'd never seen such except in my little town, never imagined that the vicious Troths would attack any defenseless community other than mine. But this time the creatures had run beyond Merith, burning and slaughtering for no fathomable reason. As a Healer I'd seen my share of violence from accident or misfortune; I had no aversion to it. But this was different. This was violence for pleasure.

"Here! Here." The brown-bearded man clawed at my skirt, pulling me down next to him at the side of a small boy—limp but seemingly unharmed.

"Is he the last?" I asked. I kept my voice light and calm to stave off Brown-beard's mounting anguish. He'd been far too eager in his assistance searching through these fields. Now there were the first trembles in his hands and face. Despair, catching up.

The man nodded awkwardly at my question, eyes darting about. He'd given me his name somewhere in the frenzy of tending: *Rafinn*. I had not used it. "So many dead." He fidgeted. "So many."

I touched the back of my hand to the boy's temple. "He might live, this one, if we are quick."

"As if that is good news."

True. Only seven villagers remained, by my count. This was hardly a triumph.

The man's voice dropped to a pathetic quiver. "Why did they come?"

"I don't know," I answered honestly, peeking under the boy's eyelids. The whites were still pure.

"But you are from Merith," Brown-beard muttered. "I heard you say it. I know the story of your village. The beasts came out of the Myr Mountains, attacking you fifty years back, then fifteen years back—"

"Thirteen," I corrected.

"And then midsummer. *Three* attacks." He said it roughly, as if he were jealous of our plight. "Merith survived the Troths *three* times."

"They only killed those of childbearing age before." I opened the boy's mouth to check his tongue, that his throat was clear. "And this time . . ." My voice hitched. "This time . . ."

This time we'd had warning. That was how we'd survived. My cousin Lark had come back from our field not three months past carrying a severed hand. Lark had the Sight—a rare gift that included the ability to sense people's histories—and she'd told us how the hand belonged to the kind old tailor, Ruber Minwl, how he'd been killed by the Troths and how the beasts had once again turned their vicious gaze to our town. We'd had ten days of warning to ponder, to worry. Ten days to hope.

Lark was the one who sought help for our defenseless village—bound to the task for which she should never have been chosen. She was Merith's most timid member, had never ventured beyond its rose-hedged borders. Yet somehow she pushed herself north into the hills, found and persuaded the Riders (the twelve of legendary might) to come and protect us. Eleven of them charged into Merith with horse and sword just as the Troths attacked, saving us from the worst. Lark returned afterward with the twelfth Rider in tow, both gravely wounded. And then it was our turn to save—Grandmama and me healing the two of them to the best of our abilities. Shy, beloved Lark, my almost-sister, my dearest friend, had rescued our home.

It seemed a good story. But neither did I attempt it for Brown-beard, nor was he interested in hearing it. "*This* time? This time is different!" He shuddered. "They've gone beyond your Merith; they've gone beyond child bearers! Look around. They killed everyone they could!"

"You must think what to do now." I changed the subject firmly, wiping my palms on my cloak. "Rebuild. Regrow. You'll need shelter from this sun at least. You'll need to find clean water." I dug into the dusty satchel for the vials of herbs, spilling them on the ground in front of me. I selected one and pulled its stopper. Minion. The most healing of any plant we knew.

"No purpose to rebuilding." The man was whimpering. "No purpose. We are lost. Drought, death, savagery—there is nothing more to suffer. There is nothing to save!"

"Here." I took Brown-beard's hand and sprinkled some of the dried bits into his ash-smeared palm. There was no water; we'd use his spit. 'Twould give him something purposeful to do. "Chew those, counting to ten. *Slowly.* Do not swallow any." He obliged, eyeing the little bottles. I pushed the minion under the satchel, out of sight.

I lifted the boy's shirt from the front—pale little belly, pale chest, unmarred. Very gently, I rolled him to one side, my fingers instantly sticky with blood. I tore away the shirt. There, by his left shoulder blade, was a jagged rip of skin. A Troth's claw had snagged him—a single claw thankfully, or he'd not have a shoulder blade . . . or a back. I'd seen close-up the brutal results of a Troth's hard swipe. The boy had not been the target of those slug-skinned creatures; he'd just been in the way.

"Spit into your palm," I told Brown-beard, lifting the boy's arm and draping it over his head. I wiped away the blood and dirt and pointed at the soft underarm. "Spread it here. Make a thin coating, cover all."

Brown-beard was sweating now, a cold sweat in the aftermath of shock, a bad sign. "Focus," I urged. "Focus." His hands shook as he smeared the mess onto the boy's skin, and then I had to pull those hands away as the man seemed to forget he'd finished.

I tucked the boy's arm down, then cradled his cheek against his palm and brushed the hair from his brow. It was feather-soft, and for just a moment I lingered, combing back the fine curls, thinking this must be what it was like to tuck a child in to sleep, to watch him sweetly dream.

Yearning pierced through, sharp as any needle; I swallowed it down . . . away. 'Twas quick—only a breath, a moment to steel myself. Then smoke wafted over and I looked at Brown-beard. "Clean your hands," I told him, pointing at the blackened grass.

He did not hear me. His hands lay limp on his knees, the corners of his mouth twitching with words that didn't come. I ripped tufts of the grass and did it for him, scrubbing the herb from his palms; he didn't flinch.

"Do not falter now," I warned. And I clutched his shoulder, willing my own energy to seep in and erase the stupor. "You are whole. You can help."

He turned his head and looked at me strangely, this man with the too-close name, Rafinn. The smoke fingered between us, the last hisses of flame like an ugly, mocking whisper: *Ruin and death, ruin and death, all gone, all gone, all gone.* I let my gaze slip, scanned the charred field we crouched in. The other survivors had long stumbled off, and I did not like that I was suddenly alone with the one whose name was too painful to use, who had the stare of one who needed to confess. "Listen to me," I gritted, turning back abruptly. I gave his shoulder another shake and squeezed harder. "*Listen.* You are all right. 'Twill be all right."

"All right . . . ," Brown-beard echoed. "All right . . ." My grip was stirring something at last, my energy igniting his. Guilt burst open, a whisper running to a shriek: "I am whole because I *didn't* help!" he blurted out. "I am whole because I was afraid! I ran. I let my village burn . . . and I ran! Do you hear me? I *ran*."

The man broke down in wrenching sobs. I held still, half sorry for him, half revolted. I should have liked to pull my hand from his shoulder, let him bear his shame alone. I should have liked to run far from this seeping darkness and nurse my own grief. But that was not what Healers did. He ran. I could not.

I waited until his breath calmed, then released my grip and brushed his misery from my palms. "What was before makes no difference," I said. "You are helping now. Look."

The boy lay soft and still in his lullaby pose, but the wound was bubbling along its jagged edge. "There is poison in the claws of the Troth," I said low. "The minion is pushing it out." I took the warm little hand and pressed it within my own to speed the process. As we watched, purple-black blood dripped from the wound and was replaced by a bright, clean red. It quickly scabbed over.

"Do they all react like that?" The man gulped.

"Different poisons respond to different herbs." I glanced up at the ash-dead fields and added, "Some poisons do not respond at all." Hukon, of course, was the vilest poison; nothing could completely cure it.

I wondered if anything could cure fear.

He looked sideways at me, then touched where I'd gripped his shoulder. "You—you hold much ability for one so young." There was a hint of awe in his voice now, like the dead woman's. "I thought Healers were of great age."

"I am seventeen nigh two months." That seemed substantial enough. What I'd witnessed in those months had aged me greatly, and I was done with it all anyway.

Once more I took the boy's arm and raised it, wiped the smear of minion off with a clean patch on my cloak. My cloak was turquoise—or had been before I left Merith. The minion went black against the brilliant blue. "This child is small. The medicine cannot be kept there too long or he would not wake again," I explained. "Things that heal will themselves become poison if used unwisely. And they are not for *you*."

I said the last bit severely because the man had cast his eye on the vials of heliotrope and yew that lay in the dirt. There was a new eagerness in those furtive glances. He might have recognized one of them, known either of those plants wrongly used could put out his fear forever. 'Twas like that, healing and death. They were always near one another.

I slipped the vials back in my satchel along with the minion and slung the thing over my shoulder to keep them safe. *Safe*—I'd never thought like that before. In Merith, my home, my past, we'd never barred a door; we'd never argued in anger; we'd never even feared Dark Wood at our doorstep. Now in this blackened, empty field, I felt the first prickings of danger. Not from the bloody ravaging of Troths, but from what remained in their wake.

Another feeling to push away, sweep under the mat of rigid focus. I was sick of being stoic. Still, I turned to Brown-beard with no expression to betray me. "Let the child's eyes open on their own," I instructed. "Find something to feed him, to feed all of you. A broth is best. You'll have to make a fire. You'll have to find water, a pot. Put whatever food you can scavenge to steep. Do you understand?"

He nodded, shivering. I pushed myself from the ground.

"You are leaving?"

I nodded back. I was late enough for my own destiny.

"But you cannot leave! Not yet!" He shouted it, jumping up. "You must help us finish what we started. We—we do not know what to do. You can help."

*No.* I closed my eyes. *Let me be done. Let me finally be done.*

But Brown-beard turned me to him, all nervous and eager

again, and easily forgetting the boy that lay at his feet. "You *must* help," he insisted. "This way." And he set off at a skittish pace.

"Wait!" I called. "Take the child!" Brown-beard returned and impatiently scooped the boy in his arms as I bade him take care. 'Twould have been better to let the boy heal where he lay, but he'd have been forgotten. I wasn't even certain the man would do anything more than dump the poor little thing on some cold cobblestone. I had to follow.

I shook off the burr of disappointment, crunched over smoldering stalks and blackened leaves to the closest body for something to cover the boy. The old man there no longer needed his coat, so I slid it gently from his shoulders. I took as well the apron from the corpse of a woman.

"This way," Brown-beard said as I neared. He led me back toward the ruin of Bern, where we laid the boy in the market square by the well, pillowing the apron under his head and draping the jacket. "This way," Brown-beard repeated, edgy and hushed, and continued. I followed, blurring the footprints he left in the ash.

It was near the last cottage, a long garden shed at the very end of the village, one of the few structures not destroyed. Five remaining villagers mingled there, hobbled and restless, away from its shut door.

"What is it?" I asked. "Is another hurt?" I was at the door lifting the latch before Brown-beard yelped, "No!" He grabbed my wrist, yanking me back. "Not one of us! A—" He could barely name it: "A Troth."

In perfect response, a howl curdled from the shed. The crowd gasped and stumbled closer together. Even I reeled a little at the suddenness of the revelation, the threat. *Troth*.

"Wounded," someone whispered.

"The first beast to arrive. Tamel managed to stick it with a hammer before he was killed," said another. "It ran in there. Then the rest attacked. . . ."

That was two days past, from what I'd learned. I straightened. "Has no one opened the door?" I asked. "Has no one looked? Where was the creature wounded?"

They shook their heads at my questions, and I shook my head back at them, upset. "You cannot leave the Troth like this."

"We thought it would die—"

"Except it hasn't!" someone broke in. "And what if it's mended—"

"'Twill burst through the door and kill us all!"

"'Twill have its *revenge*!"

Their words scrambled over one another in fearful spurts. Six adults—four men, two women—and the little boy asleep in the market square. Seven left. A sad straggle of survivors. The Troth keened, rattling the shed, and panic shivered through those standing, fevered their stares.

"You could cast a spell to keep it inside, to keep the door bolted hard, couldn't you?" the youngest man there begged.

"She's a Healer, fool!" A second man knocked his shoulder angrily.

"A Healer, nonetheless! They weave spells!"

"A Healer is no wizard!" I exclaimed.

"But she has knowledge of *herb*," Brown-beard announced to a chorus of gasps. He turned to me, echoing my own warning with jittery enthusiasm: "You carry things that poison, no? That thing must be parched or starving. If we mashed your herbs, smeared it on some meat—"

A woman shrieked, "Meat! When we starve?"

"There are dead things all around us," Brown-beard hissed back. "Take your pick."

The angry man would have none of it. "Too easy after what they've done! As painful a death as we can make for that thing!" He turned. "*You*, Mistress Healer, have you something in your bag for that?"

Someone giggled wildly in agreement, saying "If poison contorts even a little, we can pull the tools from the shed and finish it!"

"Finish *slowly*!"

"*Our* revenge . . ."

*It. Thing.* The opportunity to pay back suffering with suffering. "The herbs are not for that," I bit out over the ugly chatter. "You cannot ask me to take a life." Defense, yes, but not cruelty.

"It's a *beast*," one woman muttered.

"No more than any of us," I muttered back, repulsed. I'd had enough of violence. I pushed past the closest man by the door and grabbed the latch. "I will finish this my way."

No one stopped me this time; instead, they ran back a distance and fell into a huddle. They cried to me, a mix of fearful voices: "Do not let it out!" " 'Twill kill us!" "Tear you in pieces!" "You'll be raven pickings!"

"I do not fear any Troth," I called back. I opened the door and shut it hard behind me with grim relief. Better to face a wild brutality than a reasoned one.

The interior was dusk-dark. The windows were patches of gray from the smoke. A tumble of rakes, hoes, and shovels clotted the planked floor like jackstraws; wheelbarrows and carts were tossed upside down—the Troth had crashed into everything in a fury of pain. I could smell the leaked blood, hear his sharp panting, but I could not see him.

I kept my hand on the latch and whispered to test: "Where do you hide?"

A low growl emitted from the back shadows. Then nothing. I waited, learning by that eerie silence what I needed to know—'twas a warning only; the Troth could not attack. I let go of breath and latch, began climbing over the mess with as little noise as possible. Halfway, the stench of blood and beast stopped me cold. I swallowed, hitched a little to the left, and peered into the dimness, watching shadow resolve into form.

"There you are," I murmured.

The Troth was horribly wounded, his left arm half ripped from the shoulder, the blood smearing him more black than red. Two days he'd lasted like that, an impressive feat. But it left him more dangerous—he'd die soon enough, but not before becoming even more ferocious in a final gasp of agony. The

Troth would explode out of the garden shed just as the villagers feared and take them down. And he *would* take them down. Even one-armed, the Troth could take us all.

I studied him, wondering how a physique no greater in size could hold more strength than any human. The goblin-hunched frame; the mottled, spongy skin; the strings of hair and dagger teeth; the slits for a nose. And those eyes—they were meant for the dark. They caught the gray light in sudden gleams and flashes. It made me vulnerable that the Troth could see better and kill with a single blow. But I held my ground, held my gaze, wanting to see this foreign creature up close and wanting to *know*—as if somehow in the dim light and mess of blood I might recognize this Troth as the one who killed the young man I loved. And if I might recognize, then . . .

The end of the story I did not tell Brown-beard: that the Riders had saved Merith from the worst. Almost.

It was not two months since I saw the Troths leaping from Dark Wood, through the gardens and growing fields, through barn and cottage, thudding over the pretty paths that led straight to our village square. But then the Riders stormed in and . . .

And compared to Bern we'd been spared.

There was one slaughter, though, that stood out as breathtakingly cruel. A young man lay with his chest ripped open in the middle of Merith's market square. Raif—*my* Raif. A Troth had slain my love, whole claw.

Perhaps this Troth.

We eyed each other. The Troth was cornered; I was exposed. An unfavorable standoff, truly. For him.

In that moment, in that space of wonder and possibility, I was invincible—a strength not from knowledge of cures or fearlessness, but from rage. I had a culprit to take it out on, finally, a way to release the screams I never screamed. My blood was heating, surging through veins, flushing cheeks, quickening heart—expanding until I dominated the shed and could crush this puny creature without a flicker of movement, and in silence.

The Troth sensed it. He remained wary; those luminous disks fixed on me. I returned his stare with arrows of ice-cold fury and a fierce smile.

"I would leave you like this," I hissed. A minute ago I'd shunned such viciousness in the frightened villagers beyond the door. Now I wished and whispered a similar curse—a glorious, livid, and far too brief curse: "I want you to suffer. I *want* you to hurt."

His gaze stayed fixed. The Troth didn't understand me . . . or maybe he did. For though I might pretend I'd entered the shed with dark intent and hurl hate-filled words, Healers could not act out of malice. I could not harm, nor prolong agony. I could not even leave this creature to those villagers outside.

I could not avenge Raif's death.

Still, rage illuminated, awed me, even—pure and fleeting like a shooting star. And then it was done. Smile gone, I settled to the task of ending his suffering quickly. My eyes roamed the room for something to use. There—a scythe. Sickle-shaped, with a sharp tip, honed blade, and sturdy wood handle. It hung on the back wall. Behind the Troth.

*Healer's task . . .* I eased forward; the Troth shifted. I stepped over a rake, and he growled—a little game of dare, with me unafraid and he so very wary—ever closer until we were face to face, my cloak almost brushing his feet. I wondered that he neither attacked nor ran—wondered if he was truly too exhausted from pain and loss of blood. But the Troth stayed hunkered against the wall, snorts of breath flexing those ugly little slits, leaving me to stretch over him for the tool. The rank breath and the stench of his grisly wound mixed in overwhelming foulness. I swallowed against it, then slowly reached my hand above his string-haired scalp. Those orbs slid up, tracked my move—

"Mistress Healer!" Cries came pounding through the shed, shocking both of us. "Mistress Healer! What happens?"

With a hideous shriek, the Troth sprang and I lunged for the scythe. Then his claws were gripping my throat and it was I who was pinned to the wall, dangling, my fingers scrabbling for the sickle blade. And still the villagers shouted for me, their terror whipping frenzy. "Hush!" I tried to yell. There was barely a voice, barely air.